The
AMERICAN
WIFE'S
SECRET

BOOKS BY CHRYSTYNA LUCYK-BERGER

Chrystyna Lucyk-Berger

The

AMERICAN WIFE'S SECRET

bookouture

Published by Bookouture in 2023

An imprint of Storyfire Ltd.
Carmelite House
50 Victoria Embankment
London EC4Y 0DZ

www.bookouture.com

ISBN: 978-1-83790-431-0
eBook ISBN: 978-1-83790-430-3

PART ONE

SEPTEMBER–NOVEMBER 1943

Istanbul, Turkey

1

SEPTEMBER 1943

Kitty was holding the 9mm pistol in her hand.

As the wind off the Bosphorus Strait picked up, she laid the gun on the patio table and yanked off the red wig. The reflection staring back at her in the French doors revealed a fraught woman. She had found Edgar. Had worried herself sick over him. But he was alive, standing right before her. He *and* Khan.

"Damn it!" She swiped at her eyes. Black, wet streaks of mascara smeared the top of her index finger. "And damn both of you!"

Khan and Edgar began talking to her in soothing voices, as one would to a lunatic. Or someone dangerous. Their shadows were reaching for her. But Kitty dodged them—her friend and her husband—and stormed into the villa.

Khan, *her* old friend, *her* former partner, was somehow linked up with Edgar now? Edgar *found* Khan? *Edgar* brought him to Istanbul? While *she'd* hoped and prayed for *months* to find Edgar alive? She'd spent months of worrying and grieving, before she realized she had to come here, to the Sunrise Villa. Now these two were involved in some new conspiracy!

"Kitty?" Edgar shouted.

She was dashing up the staircase, two steps at a time. She shot into the bedroom and slammed the door.

"Can we talk, please?" he pleaded from the other side.

"Shut up! Both of you, just *shut up!*" But she knew Khan had not followed.

Kitty hurled herself into the Turkish bathroom and leaned on the marble countertop, panting. Edgar stepped inside. She ignored him and popped out the green contacts, staring at herself. Who *was* she? The blond hair she'd cut short to fit the wig was in disarray. She grabbed a hairbrush and yanked it through her curls. The blue eyes—her real color—were blood-shot and tired. Her makeup was streaked, and she threw cold water onto her face just as she heard Edgar's voice edging closer.

"Darling? I know it's a shock. I know you've been distraught."

She whisked the fluffy white towel off the rack and rubbed her face, then tossed it into the sink. She walked by her husband without looking at him.

He kept talking. "Do you know how much I wanted to reach you? How I tried over couriers and contacts to drop hints—"

"Ha!" She whirled around at the wardrobe. In her hand, she clutched a fresh blouse. "I *got* your hints. I'm here, aren't I?" She snapped the blouse in her fist. "You just disappeared. Why? Why didn't you just let me know that you were all right? That you were *alive?*"

Edgar dropped his hands to his sides in exasperation. "Because I was not all right, Kitty. I was not all right."

She narrowed her eyes. "Why?"

"There was an accident."

She was not convinced and jabbed the blouse towards him. "What kind of accident?"

"An attempt on my superior's life in Paris. I was with him. Kitty, I suspected that my superior was not the target."

She dropped her hands to her side, speechless.

"I told you, my handler at MI6 and I were not getting along. The suspects were apprehended and executed while I was in the hospital and I never got to ask questions. Afterwards, I quietly returned to Germany and ducked low for a while. I had an offer to return to the Foreign Ministry, as a hero, so to speak, a survivor of an attack by the French resistance."

Kitty's shoulders sank. "Why didn't you... Why didn't you get a message to me right after?"

Edgar swallowed. "I didn't know whose side you were on."

"What?" Her throat grew tight with anger again. "How could you—?"

"If MI6 had ordered you to eliminate me, would you have?"

"How can you even *ask* me that?"

Edgar tilted his head, like the curve of a question mark. Kitty stared at him. She didn't have an answer.

"All right," he said softly. "Take your time."

He left her. Kitty sank onto the mattress, the blouse limp in her hand. Would she have? If the Brits had ordered her to, would she have assassinated her husband?

Edgar. The man she'd fallen deeply in love with. And not just once. He was her best friend. The man whose thoughts she had once been able to read, and who could read hers. A long time ago, anyway.

MI6 knew she'd never have been able to carry out orders to eliminate him. Wasn't that why they had thrown her out of intelligence? A lot of good that did them. She had joined the Americans, become a trainer for the fledgling Office of Strategic Services. And then, the OSS spy chief in Bern, Allen Dulles, had given her the chance to set things straight with Edgar.

Dulles needed an insider, a German source of intelligence, after all.

By the time she strode into the dining room, Edgar and Khan were talking in low tones over dark glistening olives, white Turkish cheese, and tightly rolled grape leaves stuffed with rice.

"You can stop whispering about me," Kitty snapped.

Khan rose, one hand smoothing down his tie, the other already beckoning her in for his customary kisses on the cheeks. She went to Edgar next, and let him peck her cheek as well. He pulled out a chair for her at the table.

"Are you going to be all right?" he whispered as she sat down.

"Don't patronize me," Kitty muttered. She glared at Khan. "So, who's going to spill the beans here?"

The men shared a look. Khan placed an elbow on the table. He had gotten re-dressed after his swim, was immaculate in his silk shirt, the cufflinks—white gold, not silver—and the shiny suit. His gray eyes were focusing steadily on her.

"I want to start," he said. "It was I who went looking for Pim."

Kitty glanced at her husband. "Of course," she muttered. "You didn't know all this time that Pim was Edgar's code name, did you?"

Khan frowned and smiled at once. "Pim was the one who communicated with me when we were in the resistance. But it was Edgar who had come to the Vienna Woods cottage. He pretended to find us. Helped us to clear out the cellar."

"Except for the last of the ink and ration coupons," Kitty reminded them.

"There wasn't enough time," Khan said. "You're right. That was sloppy. After Big Charlie and I tried to flee to Prague—"

"Big Charlie?" Kitty stiffened. "Where is he?"

Khan dropped his arm beneath the table. "Big Charlie was detained by German border patrols right away."

Kitty gasped. Big Charlie had been desperate to keep a low profile in Vienna, which was nearly impossible. An Olympic wrestling champion, he was hugely popular and easily recognizable. And everyone knew he was Jewish.

Her voice was weak. "What happened to him?"

Neither man answered at first but Khan hung his head.

"He's in Mauthausen," he finally said.

Kitty went cold. Intelligence had been gathering reports for over a year on all the concentration camps in Nazi-occupied territories. Mauthausen was one such located between Vienna and Linz.

"Edgar? Did you know?" she demanded.

"I just learned of it myself."

Khan's mouth was taut. "I haven't heard anything from or about him since. I'm on the run myself. His family, Kitty—his sister, his parents—they are all gone. The Nazis emptied out Leopoldsdorf."

She leaned back in her chair. "Is there anything you can do?" she cried softly.

Edgar shook his head.

"He made me run," Khan said, his voice thick with grief. "Big Charlie made me run."

Kitty reached for him across the table. "You were the best friend he ever had. So I know you would never betray him."

She did not look at Edgar when she asked the next question. "How *did* you two find each other?"

The men looked at one another again before Edgar quietly asked, "Do you remember the priest who married us?"

"Father Maier," she said. "At the Gersthof parish."

"Khan got word to the right people," Edgar started.

"I stayed low in Prague for a while," Khan interrupted. "But someone from the O5 resistance got word to me about another clandestine cell. I got across the border again and was looking for a little guidance."

"Father Maier knows some of those O5 members," Edgar added.

"When he heard I was looking for Pim, he put me in touch with Franz Josef Messner," Khan said.

Kitty gaped. "Dr. Messner? I remember him." She looked at Edgar. "When you were working for the Department of Economics, he was the one whose coffee shop we always visited near the Stephansdom."

"That's right," Edgar said. "He's also the general director of Semperit, the American-Austrian rubber manufactory."

Kitty's eyebrows shot up. "Semperit."

"It is now the second largest rubber manufactory in the Reich," Khan added.

"Wait," she said. "Messner is a Nazi then?"

Edgar and Khan looked at one another before Edgar said, "Messner has a convincing pro-Nazi *reputation*."

Kitty narrowed her eyes. "Like you." She then addressed Khan. "And? What about you?"

Khan retrieved something out of his shirt pocket and slid a business card over the table. She picked it up.

"You're the general manager of Semperit Istanbul? But how?"

"That's where this story really starts," Edgar said. He brushed a hand over his short brown hair, the waves tamed by the close cut. "While Khan was trying to resurrect the O5, or what was left of it, Franz Messner and Father Maier were already involved in clandestine work against the regime. Messner, as you can imagine, has immense access to strategic intelligence. As a matter of fact, the information about Peenemünde came from them."

Kitty frowned. "I thought that intelligence came from you, Edgar."

But Khan raised his hand. "It was a concerted effort. It came from Messner, I couriered it to Berlin, and Edgar got it to the right hands in Switzerland. That's how I learned about nearly everything. Including that you are... Well, Kitty." He opened his hands, his eyes bright with cautious admiration.

Kitty put together the pieces now. "Edgar's not getting through to MI6—his handler thinks he's a liability—so Edgar sends someone to the Americans in Bern. To Allen Dulles. In the meantime, Dulles hears about me and how I've been nagging the OSS to establish intelligence sources directly within the Reich. Then he gets a whole lot of intelligence dropped into his lap, and needs to know whether it's viable. And here I am."

Edgar rested his chin in his hand. His dimples were deeper than ever before, and she realized how much older he looked. Worn down.

She faced Khan. "You two say you want to deliver the war to the Allies. That you need my help. So what is it that I am supposed to help you with?"

Khan smiled at Edgar, reached for the bowl of glistening olives and popped one into his mouth. "This is where you come in."

"Messner and Maier have built up a network of spies," Edgar started quietly. "It's not small stuff. They have influential members from Austrian industries, including politicians and policemen. Doctors. People who are vehemently against the regime, and prepared to bring it down. They need help though. We've got an idea, but we need you to be well prepared to take on a role within the company. You're going to work with Khan, and get to know Semperit from the inside out."

Frowning, Kitty tapped the table with her fingers. "I'm assigned to a new handler here. I have orders to stay in Istanbul and revisit my haunts, the ones from my time with the Brits. At least for a little while."

Edgar glanced at Khan. "That's perfect."

"What is the plan then?" she asked both men.

Khan deferred to Edgar.

Her husband took her hand in his. "We're going to make sure that German productivity falls in the water. We must mortally wound Germany where it hurts the most, in its war industry. Manufacturing, production, the infrastructure. Those are the Achilles heel. We need to slash it and make sure the Nazi regime never gets back up."

Kitty pulled her hand away. It was an ambitious idea, but with Edgar's touch, her anger and her months of concern, her suspicions, all returned. "How long have we got?"

"For what?" Edgar tilted his head.

"You said we were here to stop time for a while. To rest."

"Two weeks. I've got two weeks of holiday time."

"Is that right?"

"It is."

Kitty glanced over at Khan. Her voice was laced with bitterness. "And who am *I* going to be now?"

"To me? You're always Kitty Larsson," Khan said.

Edgar laid a hand on her forearm. "For the interim. We'll need a new identity for you in either case."

"For the interim..." she murmured. *Always* Kitty Larsson. That wasn't true. Her handler now only knew her as Dahlia.

Where would the OSS send her next? Back into France? Budapest? Semperit headquarters in America? But what would she do from there? Either way, everything would change once more. And she and Edgar would part ways again. His return to Berlin meant continuing his work with the German Foreign Office and funneling the Reich's secrets to America's OSS. Meanwhile, Kitty was to try on new roles until one fit their purposes. *Again.*

She pushed her plate away, blinking back sudden tears.

"Darling?" Edgar's expression pooled with concern.

"Don't," she snapped. She took in a deep breath and smiled wanly at Khan.

"What is it?" Edgar asked.

But Kitty shook her head and forked a stuffed grape leaf. "We don't discuss these things in polite company, *darling*. Let's eat." She dropped the *dolmades* on her husband's plate and pursed her mouth before stabbing a second for herself.

Besides, I've got two weeks to settle scores with you.

2

OCTOBER 1943

Istanbul

Two weeks later, Kitty was standing up to her ankles in the cold, shallow water of the Bosphorus. She studied Istanbul's skyline across the strait, the water lapping at her feet.

The silhouette was formed of purple and blue domes, square buildings and towering minarets. Interrupted by the calls of seagulls, the melody of the muezzin's final coda was replaced by the cooing of mourning doves. Shivering, she turned away from the water and looked at Sunrise Villa above her.

The white stucco walls were brightening in the rising sun. The sheer curtains in the second-floor master bedroom hung limp. Behind them, Kitty pictured Edgar as she had left him a few moments before, half-covered in the cornflower blue sheets, the soles of his feet exposed, and still asleep.

Leaving the room had been no easy feat. Edgar usually awoke at the slightest noise, automatically on the defensive. But this morning, she had managed to slide out of bed without stirring him. She had needed this time alone with her thoughts.

Her jaw tense with anticipation, she stepped out of the water, and put on the Turkish *babouche* slippers before climbing the path through the dark olive grove. On the terrace, she remembered the scene from weeks earlier.

She'd come to terms with all that had happened. Or not come to terms with them, as it turned out. She was instead overwhelmed by the decisions and circumstances that had led her to this villa and the fact that everything between Edgar and her had changed. *She* had changed.

Edgar had, possibly long ago, reconciled himself to this way of life. His love for Austria was deep and he had plans for after the war. He was certain that the Allies would win, and was doing everything to make sure they did.

He'd tried. God love him. He'd tried to rekindle their romance, their previous intimacy. But War was a jealous mistress, and she would not be ignored. Their work for her consumed the little time Kitty and Edgar had together, and Kitty resigned herself to stop competing for her husband's attentions.

She took off the leather *babouche* and carried them to the front door before padding barefoot up the marble stairs. She'd left the bedroom door open, the multicolored mosaics in blues, pinks, and oranges gaining brightness together with the sunlight. Indifferent to Kitty's mood, their cheerfulness mocked her.

Edgar had rolled over onto his side since she'd left, his back to her now. It was a miracle that he had slept on. Stacked near the door were her husband's bags, packed and ready to go.

She feared for him; she always feared for him. Until seeing him—alive and well in Istanbul—she'd had no idea how much those fears had cost her. They had not dissipated in these past two weeks, either. Instead, her worries had hardened and calcified. And they had transformed into resentment. That gave her the courage to do what she had to do now.

When Edgar's breathing changed, she prepared for him. She kept telling herself it didn't matter. She was uncertain whether it did, but the proverbial elephant in the room had to be addressed.

Edgar stirred, went suddenly still then quickly rolled over. He aimed the pistol at her. Kitty did not flinch. He groaned and dropped the gun next to him before rubbing his face.

"Sorry," he muttered. He beckoned her to him. "How late is it?"

She remained leaned up against the doorjamb.

Edgar untangled his legs from the sheets and checked the watch on the table next to the bed. "I was dead to the world. Have you been up long? I have an hour before I have to leave."

"Who was she?"

Edgar blinked. "Who? She?"

Kitty wrapped her arms around herself. She wanted an answer. No more games.

"When I was in Paris in November, last year," she said impatiently. "I told you I'd gotten into trouble. I needed new identity papers. Everyone else I knew had scattered. The Gestapo infiltrated the British circuits in Paris, in Lyon, in Marseilles. Maybe I did what I shouldn't have. I found the forger."

"Kitty, that is unacceptable." Wide awake, Edgar swung his legs from the bed, propping himself on both hands. "You were with the SOE at that time. Not MI6. That contact was established by and for MI6. I trusted you!"

"I was desperate! I was stuck in Paris, Edgar. The Gestapo was closing in."

"Desperate? Or *selfish*? Looking for me?" He pinched his nose, his tone irritated. "I wasn't in Paris in November."

"No?"

"I already told you. I'd left by then. I went underground—"

"Nobody could track you down," she argued. "Not even MI6."

He dropped his hand and sighed. "I knew the Brits were suspicious, might have already thought I'd defected—"

"I thought you were Dr. Max. That you would deliver the forgeries."

"Me? Dr. Max?"

"Instead this woman... Who was she? Who was Marguerite?"

Edgar's eyebrows arched. "*Marguerite*."

"The emergency forgeries, Edgar. It was Marguerite who showed up and told me Dr. Max—so you—didn't ever want to hear from me again."

"Kitty, Marguerite—"

"Don't you dare go cliché on me," she warned. "Don't you dare say she was nobody. Nothing. She meant nothing..."

Edgar sagged in half, shaking his head slowly before lifting it again. "All right. I won't use clichés. But if you already believe you know, then why are you asking?"

"I deserve to hear it from you."

"From me? Good. Then, yes. Once."

It hurt. Kitty had expected it and still it hurt. Badly. "Did you love her? Did you sleep with her?"

"Usually the questions are the other way around, Kitty. Yes, I slept with her once. No, I did not love her. Are you telling me that in all these months—*years*—apart, during all the flirting you conducted to extract intelligence, you have never been with someone else?"

Kitty flung her arms to the side. "No, Edgar. I have not."

His face fell. "Darling. *Liebling*. What can I do...? I'm so sorry."

There was nothing he could do. Marguerite was really only a distraction, a detour from what Kitty had already decided for herself. Infidelity was not the reason.

"We are divorced on paper. And it's going to remain that way officially, after the war." Her voice broke and she swore to herself. "You do what you must, Edgar. But you want to return to Austria, to help rebuild it. I know you're ambitious. God!" She slapped her sides. "I can't. I can't go back there. I will do whatever the OSS wants me to do but we... you and I... we're never going to find our way back to each other. Not after this."

Edgar's head fell back for a second before he gaped at her. "Kitty, you can't let this... I thought we've settled things. You're bringing Paris up now? What's changed? Why now?" He glanced at the clock on the nightstand.

She ducked for the safety of the doorway again. "You're not listening! It's not about her! Everything has changed. Everything, Edgar. When this war is over, there is no way back. No way. We are not the same people and never will be. Hell, Edgar, I don't even know who I am anymore! What am I supposed to *be* right now? We sleep with *guns* beneath our pillows!"

He stood up, was looking for his clothes. She followed him with her eyes as he whipped up the trousers from the floor and slid into them. "This is just great, Kitty. Just great. I have to return to the bloody wasp's nest, and you—"

"I didn't see it coming either," she said quietly. This was beginning to remind her of those horrible fights they'd once had in Vienna. War's sisters—Politics and Ambition—were wedging them further apart.

He faced her, his shirt half on. He began saying something, but Kitty held up a hand.

"I don't want to know about you any longer." Her voice was flat, steely. "I don't want to know what it is you're doing. Where you are. You once said we are in this work alone. I want to be free of you so that I can do my job. And you're free to do yours."

He huffed a laugh, looked at her as if waiting for the punch-line. When she did not change her expression he released a sad sound and yanked the shirt down over his midriff. "This is beautiful, Kitty. *Im Ernst?* You aren't serious."

His green-blue eyes were hot with anger. He marched past her into the bathroom and turned on the faucet but not before peering out. "You know, I've been meaning to tell you that I'm concerned. You don't sleep, and you get these headaches."

She glanced at the bags. "Your taxi will be coming soon. Khan is expecting me. When I come back, you'll be on your way to Germany."

"We're not done yet," he said, his voice muffled behind the towel. "We're going to talk about this."

Kitty sighed as he disappeared behind the door. She should wait. Go kiss him. One last time. But if she did, if she cracked the door open again, then she was afraid of relenting.

"Goodbye, Edgar."

He was calling her name as she was going down the stairs. He was at the top of the landing when she slid into her shoes, grabbed her purse, and left the house. He was tossing words at her like they meant nothing, and they landed flat, shattered at her feet, crashed against the slammed door.

Outside the compound of the Sunset Villa, Kitty hurried down the road, sobbing the first several yards, then furiously wiping the tears away. She pulled herself together and walked on.

This was what she needed. Focus. Distance. Peace. She might actually be able to do the job she had to do now without losing her mind. And in the last two weeks, she'd realized how much she had lost. Either way, there was no way back to the kind of life she'd once built—dreamed of building—with Edgar.

Too much had happened.

This damned war!

3

NOVEMBER 1943

The sediments of war had lodged into Turkey's neutral territory. As Kitty wound through Istanbul's Grand Bazaar, beneath golden chandeliers, her heels clicking on the tiled floors, she was audience to a concert of languages, which beyond English, Arabic and German, included all the languages of the war's displaced. Half the visitors here belonged to families taking refuge in a neutral country. But that very neutrality also drew another category of people. They were usually alone and watching, even when they did not appear to be.

As she walked, she saw the spies and emissaries of Istanbul, the backstage players in the world's war. Each of them was looking for something to sell, each of them was prepared to sell their secrets to the highest bidder, and more often than not, they received payment for the same information from multiple buyers. And with Italy recently having switched sides to fight with the Allies, these hidden figures were forced to realign themselves with new partners and old adversaries.

Like on a chessboard, Kitty spotted likely pawns positioned around the bazaar: the "bishop" lingering at a coffee bar; a "rook" with a Fedora perched on his head had a blank expression as he read a newspaper. The "queen" wearing a fur stole and red lipstick checked her image in the window of a spice shop. Each figure was here to sway and steer the war's course, and Kitty Larsson had a hand on one of those very rudders. Her other hand was never far from her OSS 9mm pistol.

She stopped at a green door between a stand selling a variety of teas and a shop riddled with ornamental tin and copper wares. It was several weeks after Edgar had returned to Berlin. He'd written her a lengthy note despite the way she'd left him. *Because* of the way she'd left him. Besides an outpouring of regrets, he'd made a special request *"based on a bad feeling."*

Edgar rarely worded concerns on intuition. He was too pragmatic for that. So, Kitty felt compelled to follow up and, after weeks of observations, was distressed with what she had found.

Discreetly, she looked about and knocked on the green door. It cracked open and she slipped inside, the din of the market muffled behind her.

She greeted the Turkish man standing before her. "Hello, Tarık."

"Dahlia hanim," he replied politely. Dahlia was her code name in Istanbul now.

As her eyes adjusted to the darker room, the earthy scents of leather and wool clashed with the sweet aromas of cardamom and cloves. Tarık, a very principled father of three, was wearing his signature embroidered gold and white kaftan and led her somberly, like an altar boy, into the dimly lit room in the back. It reeked of cigarette smoke. Beneath the lamp and behind a worn desk, was the large Hungarian Kitty was meeting. At the sight of her, he licked his teeth and made a sucking sound. His eyes flicked over her from head to toe.

Kitty took a seat across from him. "Hello, Gedeon."

His grin was slow. "Pleasant greetings to you, Dahlia."

She waited as Tarık poured them chai in curved glasses. Someone was hammering in the room next door. There was a bright plate of honey-dripped baklava cut into perfect squares. A trail of sticky, greasy pastry crumbs, from the rim to Gedeon's side of the desk, told all. The ashtray to his right cradled three crushed butts.

"*Teşekkür ederim*," she thanked Tarık.

"*Hanımım*." He bowed a little before leaving, closing the door softly behind him.

She faced Gedeon. He was in his fifties, with meaty lips and a sagging jowl, which at once gave him a wise-guy and hang-dog countenance. He had a perpetually damp brow that he dabbed at with a stained burgundy handkerchief.

Allen Dulles had told her that proper agent recruitment began and ended with persuasion, just as tight operational security began and ended with the recruiter's ability to assess the psychology of a candidate. Was he or she trustworthy? Were they resilient? Did they have access to the kind of information that made all the risks worthwhile? And most of all, what were the candidate's motivations to become a spy?

There were plenty of prospects who had access to state secrets and many people Kitty had met over the years had expressed their desire to do damage to the Nazi regime. But if that prospect could not handle the strain, could not keep their mouth shut until appropriate, or was only a notorious gossip who wanted to feel important, then he or she was no prospect at all. She had learned—albeit the hard way—the need to keep her ego in check. But Gedeon was a conundrum and something about him made her suspect he came from a long line of hood-winkers.

As a sub-source and not a recruiter, Kitty could do little about it. As a matter of fact, Gedeon had not been recruited at all. According to Leonard, who was both their handler and the OSS Istanbul chief, Gedeon appeared in Turkey by chance, and the two had already had a history together. Which was why, for Kitty, the whole thing stank, like this room, of hidden agendas.

But when Kitty went to Leonard about a potential disaster waiting to happen, he had sent Gedeon to chase down her lead. She was about to find out whether the Hungarian was worth his weight. Literally.

Eyes narrowed, Gedeon slid a gray envelope over the greasy crumbs on the table but did not remove his thick fingers right away. Kitty kept her eyes on the onyx and gold ring on his right hand.

Sighing, he lifted the envelope, opened it, and placed a half dozen black-and-white photos onto the desk between them. He then wiped his brow.

"Do you see the one in the slick suit?" Gedeon asked in his thick accent.

Kitty leaned in and peered at the top image. It was Cicero, the Albanian agent spying for the Brits. She knew *of* him. "Maybe," she said.

Gedeon removed a photo from the pile and handed it to her. "I snapped this outside the British consulate. The man in the next photo, the one in the tweed jacket..."

Kitty pressed a hand beneath her ribs. It was Masterson. Edgar's former handler. The man she'd been trailing all this time.

Masterson might have been the link to my falling-out with MI6, Edgar had written.

In the photo, Masterson was receiving a briefcase from Cicero, or possibly the other way around. That alone was not suspicious as they both worked for the British. Supposedly. She looked up at Gedeon, expectant.

"The story just starts to get interesting," he said, "Just before Slick-Suit delivers this to the Tweed... Well, look at the next two snaps."

Kitty slid the next photo on top. Cicero was at a restaurant with another man. They were in a circular booth leaning toward one another. There was a pool of light beneath a lamp on the table. The other man had a hand on the Albanian's outer shoulder as if he were propping him up, but the bend of their heads was a posture of two men colluding. The second man's face was hidden in the darkness but the briefcase was beneath the table.

Kitty looked up, and pointed to him. "Who is the phantom?"

"Georg Meindl."

She knew that name, but from where?

"The general director of Steyr-Daimler-Puch," Gedeon answered for her.

Kitty went cold. "The largest steel manufacturer in—"

"In the Reich."

"They're in Linz," Kitty remembered.

Gedeon smacked his mouth with satisfaction. "The Tweed, who I know is British, the German industrialist and..." Gedeon nodded at her. "The Albanian playing British spy. All together."

"My God," Kitty mumbled. She studied the next photos more closely.

Gedeon's eyebrows moved upwards before he stuck a thick finger into his mouth and fished around. He extracted it long enough to pronounce his question. "Have you heard about Organization Todt?"

"Yes, it's the Reich's plan to expand concentration camps into production facilities." She looked up. "The Nazis are building secret factories and manufactories."

"Specifically," Gedeon said, his tongue sliding over his teeth, "Albert Speer's plan. The Ministry of Armaments and Warfare has been sending regular envoys to Turkey because they can't get the resources and materials they need with all the sanctions and embargoes against them."

Kitty kept her gaze steady, but her mind was steaming full speed ahead, thinking about Albert Speer. Speer was Hitler's favorite architect. He had grand visions for Germany's future cities. Huge and modern metropolises made of stone. Stone that came from the Reich's many quarries. But when Speer took over as minister of Armaments and Warfare, and Germany faced unprecedented military losses, he directed all his energy into producing the equipment the German military needed to win the war. And used slave labor as their human resource.

"The German industrialists come to Turkey to negotiate terms," Gedeon said before slurping his *chai*. "Terms, and conditions. A lot of money to be made. Look, I know this Tweed. You and I both know he's called Masterson. The other one is Cicero."

Kitty looked blankly at him.

Gedeon raised his chin. "Isn't Masterson well connected to some of Great Britain's industrialists? Some of whom hang around a lot in Istanbul?"

"Damn it," she muttered. That would certainly give Masterson the motive. It could very well be that Cicero and Masterson were playing both sides of the coin now. If war was a mistress, then racketeering was the byproduct of a business-man's affair with her.

"Let's give them the benefit of the doubt for a second," Kitty suggested.

Gedeon sighed impatiently but gestured for her to continue. "I like you, so I listen."

"What if Masterson and Cicero are negotiating a way for Steyr-Daimler-Puch to give *them* information? What if Meindl here is disenchanted with the Führer and is now selling the Allies intelligence?"

The Hungarian shrugged and pawed the photos back into the envelope. "Because Masterson's family has connections to an industrialist in Cologne where Masterson's brother also attended university. That's why I don't buy your theory. It's more plausible that Masterson is looking to finagle business around blockades. Won't surprise me if he's only a single cog in a very large wheel."

"One rotten egg doesn't mean everyone's involved. We need proof."

"One rotten egg stinks up everything. And proof? What more do you need?" Gedeon shrugged once more. "Besides, Leonard says shoot first, ask questions later."

Leonard! She'd had enough time to make her assessment of the businessman-cum-principle agent. But maybe he was proving her wrong. Masterson and Cicero appeared to be indeed consorting with the enemy. Masterson knew Edgar. Masterson knew of Kitty. And that was more dangerous than anything Kitty could think of. It was the reason she had stopped tailing him and had asked Leonard for help.

Kitty sat slowly back, her head squeezing tight with pain. "Leonard wants me to do it?"

The Hungarian finally found what he was looking for in his mouth and wiped his finger on his trousers.

"No. He is giving me the honors."

"Meindl?" she asked flatly.

Gedeon shook his head. "Just the two supposedly on our team."

The Hungarian would angle Cicero and Masterson out of the stream of intelligence. *Shoot first. Ask questions later.* The Brits would make a big stink of it.

Kitty stood, a mixture of regret and relief clenching her gut. She left without shaking Gedeon's hand.

Tarık ushered her to the front entrance once more. Back in the busy bazaar, she noticed the woman in the fur stole and red lipstick—the "queen"—pulling away from a man in a gray suit, and quickly exiting through the portico ahead.

Another transaction; another gust of wind for the enemy's or an ally's sails, another ripple in the river of war. And Kitty was caught in that current.

NOVEMBER 1943

Later that day, Kitty arrived at Semperit Istanbul in the eastern district of Bakırköy. The rubber company had a number of branches all over Europe and partners on several other continents but the location in Turkey was a pivotal oasis in a world at war.

Before entering the building, Kitty spotted Khan in the window above, black hair slicked back, his arms crossed, as if he'd been impatiently waiting for her. He was wearing one of his immaculate suits and jewel-toned silk shirts. Today's was ruby red, the collar open.

Khan acknowledged her arrival with a curt nod. By his manner, she braced herself for more bad news, and wondered whether something had happened with Messner's and Maier's spy ring in Vienna.

She dropped her head, and stepped into the busy building. After greeting the receptionist, she took the stairs to the top floor. Khan stood in the center of a wool rug, stirring his glass of tea. He dispensed another lump of sugar before striding over to greet her. As he embraced her, his reedy frame pressed lightly against her, she caught the scent of anise.

The Kazakhstani was exotic in every manner. His face was smooth and nut brown. His almond-shaped eyes were gray, set off by the red shirt. Most of all, Khan was sharp. He was street smart and charming, a real diplomat in negotiations but the kind of person few people trusted themselves to say no to. When his guard was down, Khan was also one of the wittiest and most gracious people Kitty knew. From the first moment he'd danced with her in Vienna at Achmed Beh's nightclub, his multi-layered persona, his charisma had fascinated her. They'd become fast friends, and if she had not already been wholly devoted to Edgar, she was certain they would have become fast lovers. But not all desires had to be physically satiated. It was their shared secrets that developed a special intimacy and an ironclad trust between them.

Khan held her hands as he kissed her cheeks. "Coffee?"

She nodded and they went to the narrow room adjacent, where he lit a single gas burner and placed a copper *cezve* on top. When it began to bubble, she rubbed a slice of lemon peel on the rim of her cup, which Khan kept in a porcelain dish, then watched him pour the thick mocha in a graceful stream.

Back in the office, Khan gestured to a seat. Kitty set her cup down on a low, square table before smoothing the skirt of her navy-blue dress and sinking into the leather chair.

Khan raised his tea glass, his eyes creased in teasing. "And? Did the Hungarian treat you to a slew of compliments?"

Kitty clicked her tongue with impatience. "It's not good," she said and raised an eyebrow.

Khan steepled his hands beneath his chin. "I'm sorry. I'm really sorry to hear that."

She drank her coffee.

"You're worried about Rover," Khan said.

She flinched at Edgar's current code name. The bottom of her stomach dropped anytime she thought about those last moments at the Sunrise Villa. All those months she'd been in a lurch between escaping France and finally reuniting with Edgar in Turkey had been nothing less than traumatizing. After leaving him like she had, she'd expected to feel a vacuum, an emptiness that she would have to learn to embrace. Instead, she was irrevocably connected to her husband. It was not emptiness she carried, but the jagged pieces of their relationship, like a box of shattered knickknacks, everywhere she went. Edgar still rattled inside her.

Kitty picked up her coffee and stirred it. "When you and I joined the resistance, we did so of our own accord. We volunteered to put our lives at risk. We were in charge."

Khan pointed his steepled hands at her. "We were *never* in charge. You know that. We fumbled about like a couple of teenagers in love with the idea. But we were not in charge until you pulled Pim into it... before either of us knew Pim was Edgar anyway."

Kitty sighed. "Well, it *felt* like we were in charge. Now, it's not only my job, I'm trapped in a system made up of lies and politics, and so many secrets. So many *lies*." She swallowed, chastising herself for complaining. What had she expected? To never be held accountable? Her actions now were going to get two men killed. And that was just in the last couple of hours.

Khan was mercifully silent and patient as Kitty wrestled with herself. The Gestapo had a file on her. MI6 had a file on her. SOE had a file on her. The OSS now controlled her. If she veered off track, any of those entities might have a reason to take a closer look at her and assess their risks. Eliminate her if they decided the risks were too high. She had no choice but to stick to the protocol. It would have to be Leonard. The OSS had decided Leonard was their man in Istanbul, so Leonard it would have to be.

"When I met you," Khan interrupted her conclusions. "All you wanted was for people to recognize you for your strengths. You were so driven, and very optimistic about changing the world. But you weren't really going to pander to that stifling Viennese society."

"That is very true!" Kitty laughed drily. She raised her coffee cup.

"You didn't change the world, Kitty. It changed you. Yet, you do have a say about who you are going to be. What you are going to be. What did you expect would happen when you first saw me, here in Istanbul? Saw Rover? That it was over? Mission accomplished?"

"I have no idea. Maybe. Maybe I'd hoped my experience as a..." She lowered her voice. "As a spy would get easier? Because it isn't. That I would get used to it? Well, I haven't. Is what we're doing still necessary?"

"Very much," Khan broke in.

"Very much," Kitty murmured in agreement. She shuddered at the memory of Kristallnacht. "We've lost some of our dearest friends. Our gang. Judith. Artur."

"Big Charlie."

Kitty released an involuntary whimper. "I miss Big Charlie."

She knew how inhumane the camps were. She'd had access to the reports from prisoners who'd escaped, who'd pleaded with the Allies to bomb Auschwitz. Now the Allies suspected there were dozens of Auschwitzes, Mauthausen included. And with Operation Todt, those inmates were being subjected to the sub camps as slave labor.

"We are doing this for them," Khan said. "For the injustice and brutality of their deaths."

Kitty sniffed. How did Khan think she otherwise put her life in the way of danger every day?

"At least we know that Oskar is all right."

"Yes, Oskar is all right," she said. He was in England, working with the British military.

"Let's get to work."

Khan meant to focus on Cassia and the business now.

Kitty stood up, took his tea glass and bussed the dishes back into the kitchenette. She had spent the last few weeks learning everything about Semperit. The company used to produce bicycle tires and automobile tires. Since Brazil's siding with the Allies, the company was no longer able to receive rubber from South America. So, Semperit had begun experimenting with synthetic rubber and then, like hundreds of other Austrian and German companies, veered toward producing materials and goods for the war industry. Besides tires, Semperit now made rubber military boats and rubber boots for the Wehrmacht; tank rollers and gas masks. It proved to be a lucrative business.

The project Semperit was looking to land soon would gain them entry to IG Farben, a German pharmaceutical and chemical conglomerate. Like Semperit, they had a production facility near Auschwitz, where the notorious concentration camp in Poland was located.

The project involved producing rubber tiles that would sheath German U-boats, making them into stealthy war machines. Kitty was scheduled to go to Budapest and meet with Franz Messner, the general director, as well as another member of the spy ring, Dr. Gina Böhm, the production manager in Budapest. Kitty was to head up there, retrieve a case full of intel that Messner and his group had been collecting, including production figures, maps of facilities they toured, and technical drawings. From those documents, she would help Leonard produce the analyses required for the OSS.

Kitty returned to Khan's desk. He was leaning on the back of his chair. "I want to talk about what we have to do next. The OSS has assigned a code name to Herr Messner's and Father Maier's spy ring. They are calling it Cassia. I think it's time you meet Leonard and we get Cassia an official memorandum, a contract of sorts."

"Interesting. What does that bring us?"

"Financing, for one."

"What about your doubts?"

"About Leonard? I admit, I have reservations." Gedeon's work should have dispelled the rest of her uncertainties, but something continued to niggle. "So, when am I to go to Budapest?"

Khan eyed her gravely. "I'm afraid Budapest has been postponed."

So that was what she'd caught a whiff of before she'd come upstairs. Kitty put her hands on her hips. "Why?"

"You're being summoned to Bern."

"Summoned? To Bern?" This was it then. Whatever the OSS had been planning, it was time for her to be integrated into that operation. "When?"

"You're to book passage as soon as you can."

Kitty shrugged. "Women and war. You can't live with them, and yet you can't live without them."

She picked up her purse, fished out her hairbrush, and unscrewed the handle. Khan went to a locked cabinet, then opened the false back and retrieved the microfilm the two of them had prepared over the last few weeks. It contained a jackpot of intelligence Khan had collected from his business dealings in Istanbul. She should take it to Leonard but, now that she was going to Bern, she'd take it directly to the spy chief there.

She reached for the tight roll from Khan, but he did not let go. "You know, Kitty, it has been nothing but a pleasure working with you, again. I'll be here. Waiting on the other side when this war is over. And we're going to drink lion's milk together, and look out onto the strait from our favorite cafe, again. In peacetime."

She also regretted that she would be leaving him. "You know I feel the same."

He inserted the film into the handle of the brush.

"I'm going to make sure Cassia is made official," she said when she dropped it back into her purse.

"A contract?"

She nodded. "Leonard complains that Cassia is more committee than action, but resistance costs money and needs resources. To be honest, I don't think he sees past the money he can make at this business. I'll talk to Bern, too, but you will need a principal agent you can go to here."

Khan peered at her. "What you're telling me is Leonard is not all that altruistic."

"Leonard is keen on growing his network as big as he can," Kitty said. "That's the bit I find most dangerous about him. And most irresponsible."

Khan winced. "Most? There's more?"

"I think those are the two biggest things."

"Big is not good. Big means too many moving parts. If there's one thing we learned in the early days, it's that big is not good."

"No, it's not," she agreed, and repeated what Allen Dulles had said about Leonard before she'd come to Istanbul. "Trouble is, Leonard's so well connected that if you wanted to know what color nail polish Hitler's secretary wears, he would find out, straight from the source. Look, with the analyses Istanbul's been supplying—thanks to Cassia, of course—the OSS is not going to tell Leonard how to run things. But please be careful. We can still channel information through Bern if you feel in the least bit insecure..."

"But we need him? We need Leonard?"

Kitty nodded. "Believe me, I've been trying to figure out a way around him." Him and Gedeon, but Gedeon had just proven he might have been as good as Leonard had touted him to be. "There is also Cairo, if you need a quick escape. Or Bern. I trust Dulles in Bern."

Khan sighed. "Can you set up a meet with Leonard for me?"

Kitty put a hand on his wrist. "I will. It's going to be you, though, who can likely gain his respect. Make him understand how sincere Cassia is. I've tried, but to Leonard, I'm only a woman with ears."

"Good ears, at that." Khan clicked his tongue. "We could use that money you mentioned."

"And a radio."

He raised an index finger, his eyes widening. "And a radio." He suddenly pulled open a drawer. "Semperit has a vast catalog of production numbers and call letters, Kitty."

Kitty's spirits suddenly lifted. "A code. We could create a code."

"It's like old times." Khan smiled. "Remember the postcards in Vienna?"

"You bet I do," Kitty said. She and Khan had communicated over the back of postcards at the flower shop across the road from her penthouse. It had been their first code with one another and, because of that, had contained a lot of guesswork.

There was a tingling in her gut. Excitement. A good feeling. And a thought. "We're not only going to assure Leonard gets Cassia the resources it needs, you'll not only get him more strategic intelligence, but make sure that the members of Cassia are protected after the war. Father Maier. Dr. Messner. You. All of you."

Khan gazed at her, his brow furrowed. "And you."

And *me*, Kitty thought. What was awaiting her in Bern?

PART TWO

DECEMBER 1943–JANUARY 1944

Bern, Switzerland

5

DECEMBER 1943

Though Christmas was in four weeks, Bern was dressed up for the holidays already. Kitty arrived in Switzerland to find snow piled up along the streets and sidewalks. She'd gotten used to Istanbul's milder weather and, despite the three layers she was wearing, she was shivering with cold.

At the Zytglogge, Kitty stood still for a moment and viewed the Christmas market stalls. Six years earlier, she'd been at the Vienna Christmas market with Sam, her youngest brother. It had been just weeks before her wedding.

At the memory of what her worries had been about back then, Kitty scoffed. Edgars' parents and their arrogance had revealed blatant anti-Semitism. Kitty had had no idea how her problems were about to get exponentially worse just months later.

She went to the nearest stall where a woman sold glass ornaments. A translucent one with hand-painted swirls and Edelweiss could be for Millie. A bright red one with lace would work for Allen Dulles. She was, after all, grateful to him for the leg-up in the OSS. Kitty fingered a dark green one with *Weihnachten 1943* written on it but decided against it. There was no reason to have a souvenir of this year. It had been one filled with horror and sadness, some successes, yes, but mostly the year had fractured her heart into pieces like the thin layer of ice that lay splintered in the cracks of the cobblestones. She paid for the two gifts and continued on to the Bellevue.

The doorman wore the hotel's livery beneath his winter coat and moved aside to allow a stream of laughing guests out. Sandbags were piled up along the foundations. This close to the French and German borders, Bern was prepared for possible stray shelling, or even targeted bombs.

A Christmas carol piped through the speakers in the lounge where the hotel staff were stringing up colored lights. Kitty checked in, accepted the keys and followed the bellhop to the elevator.

"Hello, Kitty."

She spun around at the sound of the familiar voice. "Millie!"

Millie Quentin was dressed in a gray fox coat and matching hat. Her bright green eyes were warm, and her cheeks were pink from the cold. Kitty embraced her old friend, and asked the bellhop to take her bags upstairs.

Millie pulled her back into the front lobby and informed the bellhop they would come up later. "How was your trip?"

"Far too long. It took me *days* to get here."

"I bet," Millie peeled off her gloves.

Her eyes were lively as always but the war had worked its way into Kitty's friend's features, too. When they'd first met in Vienna, as giddy, idealistic young women, looking to break through as foreign officers, neither had imagined they would be working for America's first intelligence agency. And during a world war.

"Do you want a drink?" Millie asked.

"I'd rather not," Kitty said. "If anything, I need a strong coffee. How about you come upstairs with me?"

Millie offered to order a pot of coffee and sandwiches to the room first, then joined Kitty in the crowded elevator.

When they reached the fourth-floor room, both women set to the task of checking for bugs. The hotel was the first address for dignitaries and diplomats, and it was wise to check as a precaution. They found nothing, and Kitty pulled shut the blue and green drapes before switching on a lamp. The room was essentially the same as the one she'd had been in some five months earlier, though the furnishings were arranged in mirrored image.

Kitty set her case onto a stool and turned to her friend. "When is Mr. Dulles expecting me?"

"This evening. Six o'clock. Come hungry, as he's offering dinner. But use the back entrance." Millie pulled off her hat and ran her fingers through her dark hair. She checked herself in the mirror before removing a tube of lipstick from her purse.

With a fresh layer of her signature bright pink, Millie grinned at Kitty from the mirror. "I'll be at Pickwick's with some others from the office, tonight. You should join us for drinks."

"Are you and Mr. Dulles still...?" Millie's affair with the spy chief had really surprised Kitty.

Her friend winced before facing her. "Yes. And no. Bob knows. And he refuses to give me a divorce. He'd rather tolerate it instead."

"How very modern of him," Kitty observed.

Millie popped the tube of lipstick back into her handbag, her mouth taut. "I'm also not the only one, you know?"

Kitty raised an eyebrow. "You mean having an affair...?"

"With Allen. No."

"Really?" Kitty did not mean to draw the word out with such disbelief.

"Allen is, well, very magnetic. Quite a number of other

women have fallen under his spell... or he under theirs." Millie shrugged dismissively, but Kitty could see her friend was hurt.

Allen Dulles was charming, sure, and he had charisma, but Kitty could not understand Millie's sexual attraction to the older man.

She leaned back, scrutinizing Kitty. "What happened in Istanbul? With, you know, reunions and all that?"

Kitty shook her head, the sadness that was Edgar weighing on her instantly. "It was... hard."

"OK," Millie dragged the word out. She took a seat in the high-backed chair and clicked on the lamp next to it.

"I had no idea how worn out I was, Millie. When he finally appeared in Istanbul, and he was all right, I wanted to kill him." Kitty laughed abruptly to counter the ache. "Anyway, I told him it's over. For real this time. It's gotten too... We're not the same people."

Millie stood up, came over, and put a hand on Kitty's shoulder. "None of us are. That's kind of the point of growing. Besides, marriage is the pits, with or without a war. Don't give up yet."

As Millie sat down on the bed, Kitty saw that dangerous sparkle in her friend's eye.

"What about you?" Millie cocked an eyebrow, and dropped her New Yorker volume. "In all these years, you've never been with another man?"

"No," Kitty cried hoarsely. "Not me. But—"

"But?" Millie snapped at the word like bait.

Kitty frowned and rose. She looked in the mirror but her attention was on Millie. "Oh, I don't know..."

"What don't you know? Ah! You mean Rover had an affair. Is that why you're calling it quits?"

At the mention of it, Kitty took in a sharp breath and shrugged, that same humiliated shrug her friend had made just moments before.

"I'm sorry. It's a shame. Such a shame," Millie tutted. She went to the dresser and leaned against it. "You know what Bob says?" She laughed airily. "He says he understands me. He believes that war, the dangers, the intrigue, it brings our survival instincts to the forefront. Gets the blood boiling. After every narrow escape, he says, or every win, we feel the insane need to mate."

"Mate?" Kitty snorted. "Is that what you and Mr. Dulles call it?"

But she had flashes of the passionate love she and Edgar had made, the kind of passion that came with the knowledge that it might be the very last time. And it was not as if she had not been attracted to other men. There had been Khan, for example. Now, *Khan* was magnetic.

"Well, that's what it is," Millie said matter-of-factly. "Animalistic sex. What else do we get all hot and bothered for? It's our instinct to produce life if we think we're about to be extinguished."

Kitty winced. "Good Lord, Millie! Are you pregnant or something?"

Millie laughed, waving a dismissive hand. "Have you and Rover never talked about having children?"

Kitty flopped into the armchair. "No, not really."

"We were very young then," Millie said. "And three months later, the Anschluss... well, the rest is history."

"So, can you give me a hint as to why I'm here?" Kitty asked, desperate to steer the discussion away from Edgar, affairs, and history.

"Nope, that's work-related, and I'm here to make you think of anything other than that."

Kitty gazed at her questioningly.

"How is your family?"

"My family? You really are challenging me today, Millie. My family is... well, they may as well be on another planet."

"Sorry!" Her friend put up a hand. "I'm just trying to get you to relax."

Kitty rolled her eyes. "I don't know, to be honest. My dad retired from the senate, so I imagine he's at home driving Maman crazy. I talked to him very briefly before I left for Istanbul. He said he felt guilty for not sticking with Roosevelt through this war but he's done in. And I know how he feels. I'm worn down to the bone myself, Millie."

"Exactly!" Millie cried. "That's one of the reasons you're here."

"Because Mr. Dulles thinks I'm *tired*?" Kitty crackled with sarcasm.

"Work again. What about your brothers? Sam? Nils?"

Kitty's heart melted at the mention of them. "Sam is in Africa. He was wounded while evacuating soldiers."

Millie's eyes popped wide. "Is he all right?"

Kitty nodded. "As far as I know, he's recovering in Morocco. And Nils is in London, as you well know." She was relieved when a knock sounded at the door. "My interrogation is over now, right?"

Millie answered it, returning with a tray of coffee and sandwiches. She was also grasping the neck of a champagne bottle.

"I didn't order that."

"I know," Millie chided. "I did." She waved the bottle a little before tearing off the foil and popping the cork. She poured two glasses, handing Kitty the first one. "Try to let your hair down, Kitty."

Kitty was trying hard to ignore the dull throb in her left temple, but accepted the glass anyway. "What is this all about, Millie? You're making me more suspicious than relaxed."

"Just one and then I'll leave you to it," Millie promised. "But not before you hear what I have to say to you."

Kitty braced herself, clinking glasses with her, and waited.

Millie held hers in the air after she drank. "Whatever you do in the next few weeks that you are here—"

"Weeks?" Kitty was astonished.

"Yes. Weeks. You are to have Christmas dinner with my husband and me, and you are to go to the Christmas market, and drink *Glühwein*, and have some fun. Go ice skating. No, better yet, we'll go skiing. Yes, we'll go skiing. Friends have a chalet we could use. We want you to have some fun while you are here."

"We?"

"Yes. The whole office."

The whole OSS? Whatever was coming, it was going to be huge. Kitty took a big gulp of the champagne and held her breath.

"I'm afraid it's an order, Kitty. An order, do you hear?"

Kitty shook her head. "Do I look like someone who remembers how to have fun? Skiing, Millie? Really?"

"You were an incredible amount of fun, Kitty. The whole gang was an incredible amount of fun..." Millie took a long drink.

"Millie, do you know that Big Charlie was captured and sent to Mauthausen?"

"Yes," Millie breathed. Her mouth was taut again. "Do you know how he is? Does Khan?"

"We assume the worst."

Millie took a deep breath. She pointed her glass at Kitty, trying on a smile but her tone was flat. "Skiing. You love skiing."

The very idea of doing something so carefree made Kitty feel anxious. "I don't know."

"Mellow out for a little while. Ride the surf instead of battling every wave for a few weeks."

Kitty looked curiously at her friend, grimacing more from the pain in her head than at what Millie had said. "That's awfully Californian of you," she half-joked.

Millie shrugged. "Maybe. But I just spent a week in Portugal."

"With Dulles?"

"No," Millie chided. "With my husband, silly."

Kitty did laugh at that, and was surprised by the easiness of it.

Millie left her, as promised, after her glass of champagne and a sandwich. As soon as she locked the door behind her, Kitty fell onto the bed and stared at the ceiling. How was she supposed to go skiing when her brother would be sent back to the front anytime now? When Edgar was in Berlin, at great risk of being discovered? When traitors like Masterson were everywhere? When a group of Viennese were risking their lives each day to bring the Allies information from the Reich's regime?

She had no right to have any fun. Those days were over and anyone who did not understand that had no idea—whatsoever—about what her life had turned into. She was in so deep now, she could not get out.

It was safer to stay in the eye of the storm; safer to have no time to think about anything else but the job.

6

DECEMBER 1943

Allen Dulles' apartment was located on the ground floor at Herrengasse 23. It was a late seventeenth-century building, with the south side facing the Aare River. The main entrance, however, faced the road, where the streetlights were all off. The reason behind this was due to the interesting visitors the spy chief received at his home, meaning there was always the chance someone was watching.

Kitty walked past the building, glancing at the plaque that read, *Allen W. Dulles, Special Assistant to the American Minister*. She had had a laugh with Millie about the ambiguity of that title.

Just as she was about to turn into the courtyard where she could enter through the back gate, Kitty felt something behind her. She whirled around. Something dashed from the bush. She clamped a hand over her mouth, stifling a shriek as a cat bounded across the road. The animal was not what made her jump, though.

She spun away from the gate and swiftly walked around the corner. Ahead of her, a dead end. Her pulse fired rapidly, and her knees were jelly as she backtracked, hurried across the street and returned to Herrengasse, nearly fifteen minutes later, now approaching from the other end of the road.

She was at the American consulate building, some yards away from Allen Dulles' apartment. There was only one light in an apartment across from her, and then a blackout curtain extinguished it. There was nothing else. Only silence, save for the light snow that fell around her. Yet, she could not shake the feeling that eyes were on her.

She aimed for number 23 again, and let herself through the back gate, her nerves frayed.

Jacques, Allen Dulles' butler, opened the door on the first knock. "Madame? Is everything all right?"

"Fine," Kitty lied. "I nearly slept through the night. Sorry."

He led her to the study she'd been in the first time she'd visited Dulles. She made a beeline to the window and peeked out from behind the curtain.

"Something amiss, madame?" Jacques inquired again.

Kitty dropped the curtain closed and shook her head.

"Mr. Dulles will be with you momentarily," Jacques assured.

She looked around the room. A cheerful fire crackled in the fireplace. The portrait of Dulles' wife—whom Kitty had learned was named Clover—hung above the mantel. She wondered whether Clover approved and consented to Dulles' extra-marital affairs, just as Bob Quentin accepted Millie's, however many they were.

Dulles suddenly strode in with that briar pipe of his, exuding the air of an intellectual and pleasant professor. His silver hair was combed back and he wore a tailored suit. Behind rimless glasses, his eyes were friendly but piercing, constantly analyzing. Beneath all that was the vitality and *joie de vivre* that likely drew women to him. Mostly, it was hard not to miss how much he loved this job.

Despite not respecting the choices he made in his private

life, Kitty owed him a lot. He was the one who had put enough faith in her and sent her to Istanbul to search for Edgar. He helped prove her husband wasn't a defector like the Brits had accused Edgar of being.

"Kitty, it's very good to see you." He shook her hand warmly and led her to a comfortable armchair. A plaid blanket was draped over the arm, and she shifted it onto her lap before retrieving the photos out of her purse. She put the envelope she'd brought with her on the edge of the coffee table.

"I can never seem to stay warm anymore," she explained as Dulles eyed the blanket. "It's been like this since my first escape from France."

He lowered himself into an armchair across from her. "Did Millie talk to you? I really feel a bit of normal life would do you good. Refresh you. Re-energize you. Give you the strength you need for what I'm about to ask of you."

Kitty stiffened. "What are you going to ask of me?"

He pointed the pipe at her. "That you take some time off. I need you ready, with stamina and energy. I need you sharp."

"Do I really look that bad? I just had over two months in Istanbul."

"Hardly relaxing, I imagine, after the experiences you suffered, the terrible shock. And then having to orientate yourself with Cassia." He squinted at her. "I am serious about this. Take the time off for real this time. You need a breather. Maybe it will help you if I tell you that your troubles in Istanbul have been settled."

Kitty looked up from her lap. "Both of them?"

He nodded.

Masterson and Cicero had been eliminated.

Dulles pointed at the envelope. "Are those the originals?"

She nodded and slid the packet of Gedeon's photos across the coffee table. Dulles took it, laid his pipe off to the side and opened it.

"That's Georg Meindl you'll see in there," Kitty said.

Dulles inhaled deeply as he rifled through the black-and-whites. "From Steyr-Daimler-Puch."

"It's the largest steelworks in Linz," Kitty added.

He tucked the images back in and wrapped the envelope closed. "I'll let OSS HQ and MI6 know first thing. They'll want me to get these for the agency's records."

Kitty bit her lip. Dulles rose and took the envelope to the sideboard where he kept all OSS secrets locked up.

"Listen, we have a few minutes before the rest of my dinner guests arrive," he tossed over his shoulder. "And I imagine you want to know why I've asked you to come to Bern."

"As a matter of fact, I do." She chuckled nervously. "I feel like I'm being punished, either that or sent to the corner for something I did wrong."

Dulles took time to light his pipe, but the quavering grin made her wary. She could sense his excitement, like a child about to open his first Christmas present.

"First, you should enjoy a good dollop of satisfaction. I got a cable from your old friend Colonel Thomas Kendrick. It took us five months to sift through a treasure trove of information from Rover."

At the mention of Edgar's code name, Kitty's heart sprang.

"Kendrick admitted that their agency is awfully sorry about having doubted our reports from Rover. He begrudgingly added that Rover is probably the most successful source the Allies have ever had."

Kitty ran a hand over her mouth and breathed deeply. "That's good. That's very good."

Edgar's intelligence from the German Foreign Office had to have been like finding the gold at the end of the rainbow.

"We've disseminated information throughout our networks now, and Washington is finally giving us a nod to infiltrate Fortress Germany."

She sat back, eyes wide. She'd been trying to convince the Allies for a long time to do exactly this.

Dulles sat down closer to her, his grin conspiratorial now. "Kitty, to send in operatives we need to organize a strong network within the Austrian resistance. I know they are spread out. We want to start with Vienna, though."

"You can trust Cassia to help you there."

"Yes, of course, they will be involved."

"As a matter of fact, I wanted to suggest to you that you convince Leonard to have them sign a memorandum."

Dulles' head bobbed in agreement. "We're in the process."

"They need finances."

"A radio."

"Yes," Kitty said. "How else will they know how and where to receive your agents?"

"How will *you* know when and where, you mean."

Kitty took in a sharp breath. "Me?"

Dulles inclined his head. "The way it looks right now, the Soviet Army has a good chance at pushing the Germans west. They'll likely reach Austria and eastern Germany before we do. Which means, there will be serious discussions about how those territories will be controlled. We need our men on the ground to remind them we're Allies. And we need power to hold over them. That means intelligence. A jump ahead."

Vienna was full of spies. Including Soviet spies.

"Or at least we need sources in the know," Kitty said and leaned forward. "This sounds like there's a lot more to this plan though."

"Of course." Dulles stuck his pipe in his mouth and puffed, his gaze steady on her. His tobacco was some type of spicy blend.

"And what about the U.S.? Great Britain? Where will they push from?" she prodded.

Dulles smiled behind the pipe. "I'm not going to lie to you, but you know Eisenhower is working on that. I'm getting rather excited about it, but of course I can't say what. I do know this: you know the teams you trained in England?"

"You mean the three-man operative teams?"

"Exactly. They're headed to where they are meant to head. And things are in motion. I guarantee you that, Kitty. My guess is that we don't have more than a year of this. And even if it is a year, then only a few months more. Sixteen, seventeen?" He beamed at her. "That's why I want you to rest. You need to be ready for the big push."

Kitty winced at the sharp stab to her left temple. "To hell with a vacation, sir. What is it that you want me to do?"

He removed the pipe, went to the fireplace and faced her again. "It's called Operation Redbird. You'll head up the resistance activities in Vienna. I want you to go back in."

Kitty clutched the blanket. "Vienna? I can't go back there... Sir, Vienna is like a small town. Someone will most certainly recognize me."

There was a soft knock at the door. Dulles had that eager grin on his face again as he strode over. "Perfect timing. Your Christmas present is here."

Kitty slowly rose from the armchair. Jacques appeared first, but behind him there was another man. She immediately recognized his gait. Her heart flipped somersaults in her chest.

Edgar was in Bern.

DECEMBER 1943

Edgar!

His name was on her lips, but a second man was with him. Shaken, Kitty forced herself to go to Franz Josef Messner first and offer her hand.

"Good evening, Dr. Messner."

Messner, the Austrian who had served her coffee in his café in Stephansplatz, trying to urge her it was better without whipped cream. He had pale blue eyes that lit up when they'd talked about his extended trips to Brazil. They were dull now. His smile was wan. He had aged rapidly in the last six years, the last of his yellow-blond patches, white as fresh snow. And when Kitty thought back on Cassia's reports, she could understand why.

"Dr. Messner, I thought you were headed to Budapest."

Messner smiled and put his hands on both her shoulders. "But you are here, in Bern."

Before she could ask what he meant, he moved on to shake Dulles' hand. That left Kitty alone with Edgar. The mix of guilt and tenderness in his expression made her drop her eyes. Her face was hot. Her heart thumped hard against her ribs.

Their embrace was awkward.

"When did you arrive?" Her voice trembled.

"The day before yesterday."

She turned slightly to Dulles and muttered, "So."

Edgar's left hand was on her lower back as he greeted Dulles next.

As they exchanged pleasantries, heat radiated from Edgar's palm. She could not help it; her body was in control and ignoring her effort to stay cool.

"The foreign minister appreciates my trips to Switzerland," Edgar joked. "He asked me to return with Brazilian cigars."

"We'll take care of that," Dulles promised. "Make sure everything looks legitimate."

He directed Edgar and Kitty to the sitting area in front of the fireplace and Kitty stepped away from Edgar's touch but his scent lingered. Behind them, Jacques closed the doors but when Edgar took the sofa, and Messner took her seat, the only space left was next to Edgar. As a fifth wheel, she hovered awkwardly between the furniture.

"Anything else to report?" Dulles asked Edgar, oblivious to Kitty's displacement.

Edgar's gaze landed on her only briefly before returning to Dulles. "Our train was strafed by a British airplane."

Kitty steadied herself on the back of Messner's armchair.

Dulles reached over and patted Edgar's arm. "Nothing serious, I hope?"

"We would not otherwise be here," Messner said.

Edgar beckoned to Kitty and she finally sat on the opposite end of the two-seater.

The whole orchestrated meeting was embarrassing. A single glance from Dulles revealed he knew what she had decided about her marriage. Edgar had probably related the whole discussion to him. Conflicted, she stopped paying attention to what the men were saying until Messner suddenly reached out and grasped the sofa's armrest.

"Frau Dr. Ragatz?"

Kitty stared at him. Nobody had called her that in years. "I'm sorry... I'm just so surprised that you are... both here." She took in another breath and looked at each of the men. "I have introduced Khan to Leonard, but if Cassia is to become official with the OSS, Leonard has some stipulations."

"Go on," Dulles said.

Edgar twisted toward her in anticipation. "Yes, go on."

She faced Messner. "Leonard wants to meet you personally, first," Kitty warned the Austrian industrialist.

Dulles assured her he would arrange it. "Cassia and the O5 will get what they need. We need you strong, Dr. Messner. We need you active."

"It's not..." Kitty started. She still harbored doubts about the OSS operations in Istanbul. "I'm just wondering whether Cairo wouldn't be a better choice. At least for the interim. Of course, Khan will continue working with Leonard, but..."

Edgar's presence distracted her. She wanted to be with him. Alone. To reprimand him for orchestrating the meeting. To thank him for caring enough about her that he'd come to Switzerland personally. To confess her misgivings to him alone.

"Kitty?" Edgar asked. "Why Cairo?"

Maybe she was making too much of it. "Because... well..." She looked at him pointedly. "Of what's just happened there."

Edgar's expression darkened.

Dulles cleared his throat. "All right. Then Cairo. Is that all right with you, Dr. Messner?"

Messner opened his hands. "Whatever you feel is best."

Kitty relaxed a little. Dulles turned his attention to her.

"Maybe it's best if we continue all of this over food. You must be starving." Dulles rose and Kitty followed him, Messner and Edgar into the dining room.

Dinner consisted of filets of lamb, mashed potato and nut puree, a red beet salad and figs, washed down with a fine claret.

"Here's the plan," Dulles said over the main course. "Messner will return to Austria and issue an invitation to work at Semperit's headquarters in Vienna."

Kitty was slowly shaking her head and pointedly looked at all three men in turn. "The Gestapo has a *file* on me. If I go to Vienna and they discover who I really am, I will blow Edgar's entire cover."

"We've thought about that," Edgar said. "But you've worked undercover, and have proven to be very good at it. Besides..." He shared a furtive glance with Dulles. "I'm likely going to disappear again."

Kitty's heart lurched. "Like... like you did in France?"

There was an uncomfortable silence before Dulles spoke patiently. "Our goal is to work with all the Allied forces—all of them, Kitty, even the Soviet Union—and finish this war. That's what Edgar is doing, it's what Cassia is doing. The faster we push this to the finish line, the more lives we can save."

"In the process,"—Edgar opened his hands toward Messner —"we're looking to protect Austria's economic interests."

Kitty's stomach tightened. *Indeed.* That sharp pain in her left temple stabbed her so hard she bent over her empty plate.

"Hey! Are you all right?" Edgar whispered near her. "Your head?"

She waved him off. "I'm fine."

Dulles shifted, lightly tapping his plate with his knife. "We need Rover for a different operation. Which makes way for you, Kitty."

She blinked, still not convinced, yet she had to hear them out. "Under what pretense am I going back to Vienna?"

"We're moving you from secret intelligence to special operations."

"Again?" she asked wryly. "I was just getting comfortable."

"We need you on the inside, Kitty. You're going to combine the efforts of what's left of the O5 with Cassia. Messner is, as you well know, a key player in the industrial elite. You'll be our middleman—sorry, woman. You'll be collecting and disseminating intelligence from Cassia. You'll also be communicating with our own OSS agents once they are on the ground. There is also Khan's idea to organize the remaining O5 members to conduct sabotage."

"Whoa," Kitty breathed. "OK. What about you, Edgar?"

He closed his eyes and shook his head. "For the next few months, I will be above ground. But then..."

She deflated. Then he'd disappear again. "What will my cover be in Vienna?"

Dulles indicated Franz Messner with the tip of his knife. "You'll be the general director's personal assistant at Semperit."

"Something I've been proven to be good at, too," Kitty muttered glibly.

"You'll have access to all the departments that we need you in. From research and development to logistics."

Unconvinced, she pleaded with Edgar. "You must certainly realize that if I am ever questioned by the Gestapo, and they link me to Messner, to you, to your family, that you will *all* be in danger, right?"

"Messner will take care of you," Edgar said calmly. "I plan to be deep below the surface before you are well entrenched. And Kitty?" Edgar glanced over at Dulles.

"We'll get you out of there," Dulles said assuredly. "As soon as OSS ops are on the ground and set, we'll extract you, Kitty. Two, three months at the very most. Both of you."

"Even if the war is ongoing?" she asked incredulously.

Edgar grasped her hand. "As soon as possible. You and I, we're making the way. But we don't have to do more than that."

Dulles nodded at her. "No sense in increasing your risks."

"And what about you?" Kitty asked Dr. Messner.

He wiped his mouth and replaced his napkin before answering. "I'm in for the duration, Frau Doktor."

Kitty studied Edgar. She had no control over this. None. They expected her to simply accept the mission. Two, three months. At most. What had she learned about the SOE's time recently? Agents had survived an average of only a few weeks in Nazi-occupied territory?

"Edgar and Messner will set this all up, Kitty," Dulles said. "Before he returns to Berlin."

"When are you returning?" she asked.

"In two days," Edgar said. "But I could be back for the Christmas break and stay until the sixth of January." His voice trailed off and he bent to her. "If you want me to. We could celebrate our wedding anniversary."

Kitty ducked her head and lay down her cutlery. "I don't know..." she muttered.

"We have a lot to talk about," Edgar addressed the table.

"And you'll have that opportunity," Dulles said.

"I can't go in as an American," Kitty said quickly. "That would be suicide."

"Why not as a French national?" Dulles asked.

"Semperit also has a branch in France," Messner offered. "And the United States."

"Millie and a couple from my team will help with the cover story," Dulles added.

"Take the time off, first," Edgar said.

"But we'll get started on our end," Dulles assured. "And we will build your cover story as close to your real identity as possible."

Kitty frowned. "Why?"

"It's a stressful situation. You can't remember the number of a bus you never took, Kitty."

She hesitated. He did not trust her. She was giving too much of her anxiety away.

Or worse, this mission was even more dangerous than she'd anticipated.

After dinner, Messner made his excuses but, before he could leave, Kitty pulled him to the side.

"How do you *really* feel about all of this? About me coming to you in Vienna?"

Messner smiled tightly. "I know that we are not as familiar with one another as we should be for such an assignment. But I assure you that Cassia otherwise takes every precaution when recruiting. Edgar is someone I know very well, and trust. He brought me Khan. Once again, your husband delivered. Now he has reassured me—and not only he, Frau Doktor, but Khan, and Mr. Dulles have as well—that you have capabilities, and the experience, we need. I am confident that Cassia will benefit from your assistance."

Kitty relented. "If I have your confidence..."

"You do. There will be so many things to discuss, Frau Doktor." He put a hand on her shoulder. "Do as Mr. Dulles suggests. Remember what we are fighting for. I'll see you soon." He offered her a firm handshake. "Merry Christmas."

Kitty then rejoined Dulles and Edgar in the study and Jacques prepared snifters of cognac. She warmed her hands on hers, her jaw tense. Her headache, in the meantime, was dull but had spread to both sides of her head. She rubbed the base of her neck.

Dulles settled into the armchair opposite her, Edgar on the sofa. This time, she kept her distance from him, wary about what they would reveal to her next.

"I have an offer," Dulles began. "I've readied a guest suite for you. You can make yourselves at home here, in Herrengasse. Kitty, I'll have someone fetch your things from the Bellevue if you'd like. I think both of you could use a few days alone together."

Kitty frowned. If she accepted the offer to stay, she would be admitting she was waffling about the declaration she made in Istanbul.

"You mean you want Edgar to have the time to persuade me to go to Vienna."

"Save the rash decisions for when you're out in the field," Edgar said gently.

Kitty shot him a look. They could still read each other's minds.

"Right now, I need to have you two working together," Dulles broke in. "And enjoying yourselves. We are living in strange times. Dangerous times. But for the next few days—over the holidays—just make this about the two of you."

Edgar shifted in the seat next to hers, eyebrow raised.

"All right," Kitty muttered.

Dulles rose, drained his cognac and nodded at them. "Then I'll let you two get to it. When you're ready, Jacques will show you to the suite. Good night."

When the chief left, Kitty turned to Edgar. "I only agreed so that he would finally leave us alone."

"I think we have plenty to discuss," Edgar said. He placed the snifter of cognac on the table and moved closer to her armchair. "I know you're nervous about Vienna, but I have thought long and hard about this. We need you and we'll make sure you're ready. You can trust me."

"You know what I've learned, if anything?" Kitty said, resting her head in her hand. "Hard-won trust evaporates the moment you are caught in a lie."

"Ah, that's it, is it?"

"Edgar," Kitty checked whether the study door was shut. "I don't think I've been given any other choice than to give you a second chance."

"I'm going to earn your trust, Kitty. I promise you."

"We'll see."

8

DECEMBER 1943

The suite Dulles had arranged for Kitty and Edgar was decorated much like the rest of the Herrengasse apartment, with rich textiles of reds, hunter greens and dark blues. The tiled oven radiated heat. A round table held a lamp whose base was made of deer antlers.

Kitty maintained her distance from Edgar as she took in the enormous space. She did not know how to feel about the two bedrooms located on opposite ends of the expansive sitting room. She told herself she should be relieved about that.

In a nook was a desk with a black typewriter and stationery items. A small kitchenette allowed for a quick coffee, refreshments and included a fully stocked bar. The decadence alone felt edacious.

Before leaving them, Jacques announced that her suitcase and personal items would be brought from the Bellevue. "I've asked Mrs. Quentin to fetch them. We reached her at Pickwick's. I thought you might prefer it that way."

Kitty was sorry for having to interrupt Millie's evening, but Jacques was right. It was better to have Millie, rather than some stranger, collecting her belongings. She thanked him.

After Jacques left, she turned to Edgar. She could not quite keep the flippant tone out of her voice.

"So, what's the reason that you're really here?"

"It's not enough that my boss wants Brazilian cigars?"

Kitty put her hands on her hips.

He stopped smiling. "I brought more cables and documents. About another two hundred."

Kitty whistled softly. "Dulles said it took the office nearly five months to disseminate the last bundle you gave them."

Edgar indicated the round table. She took a seat but kept a chair between them.

"I have some distressing information," he said, now very earnest. "It's to be included in my reports to Dulles and some of it comes directly from Messner. But I wanted to tell you personally."

Kitty was on high alert now. "I'm listening."

Edgar took her hand. She allowed him to cradle it.

"Do you remember the suspicions we had about the Reich developing a new chemical weapon?"

Kitty nodded. "That put us on the trail of Zyklon-B."

"Yes. I've been—as you *Amis* say—connecting the dots for some time now. And then I got a report that blew the whole thing open. Wide open. Zyklon-B is used in pesticides in Germany. It's a nerve gas. Odorless. Colorless. And deadly. But we were wrong, Kitty. It's not being produced for the military."

The first time Kitty had met with the OSS, she had warned them that Zyklon-B was probably being produced at the concentration camps, but for what exactly, nobody had been quite sure. Half a year had passed since that discussion.

Edgar's eyes turned a dull green. "Soon after the minister got that report, Messner called me in Berlin. He was returning from meetings at his plant in Monowitz."

"Near Auschwitz, right?"

"Correct. As is IG Farben."

Kitty tilted her head and frowned. IG Farben was the largest chemical conglomerate in Germany.

Edgar continued. "Messner refused to tell me anything on the phone. He asked me to come down to Vienna. Kitty, I'm going to tell you what he told me."

She held his look. A shadow passed over his face.

"OK," she said warily.

"Auschwitz is a... a death camp."

"A *death* camp?"

"That's what Messner called it. The Nazis are using Zyklon-B as a gas to exterminate..." He swallowed and his jaw twitched. "The sick, the weak, the old. And essentially all Jewish inmates."

Kitty clenched her hand in his. "How? How are they... A gas? Death camp... What are you suggesting, Edgar?"

"An eyewitness watched the guards lead a huge group of women and children into a building with showers." Edgar's voice was deep. "Then they sealed the rooms off. It was filled with people. Messner says the witness claims it was packed."

Edgar released her hand.

"Tell me," she said.

"When the camp guards opened the doors, all of those people... They were on the ground. Women and children huddled together. They... they died like that. They were all killed."

Kitty made an involuntary noise. *Big Charlie!*

He continued, speaking slowly, as if getting the words out was like walking over cut glass. "This eyewitness was forced to pull the corpses apart; women pried from their babies. Women pried from the embrace of other women—then they did the same with a group of men. Sick men. Weak men. It was the Zyklon-B that killed them, Kitty."

She covered her face and sobbed. Her head fought the picture Edgar had painted. He was talking about murder on a massive scale! She stood up, unsteady, and Edgar reached for her, but she brushed by him. Her gut clenched and she wrapped her arms around herself.

"The Polish officer I helped escape to England," she said, her voice sounding far off. "He told me that in Auschwitz the SS had made many inmates build new structures. They were showers, he'd said. Showers, Edgar. And he didn't think it made sense." She faced her husband. His face was pale. "How did Franz Messner find out? Who told him this?"

"When Messner was in Monowitz, a Semperit foreman told him this. He had heard it from a group of inmates. They had learned about it from a man who was on a crew to remove the corpses. The same foreman also overheard an SS guard *brag* about it."

She clutched her throat. "Is this the only eyewitness report we know of? Is it not hearsay? An embellishment?"

Edgar bent his head. "A similar incident was reported by someone who escaped a camp in Treblinka."

"So Auschwitz is not the... Not the only camp? Edgar! How many?"

He was shaking his head, and rubbed his mouth. "The Red Army sent a reconnaissance plane over Treblinka after the eyewitness report was published. The recon team found nothing there."

Kitty's head swam as Edgar reached down and opened his briefcase. "How many?" she asked, choking.

He withdrew a sheet of paper and placed it before her. She could not look at it.

"There was nothing in Treblinka," Edgar repeated, "and I'm suggesting that the Nazis dismantled the camp to get rid of evidence. But if you look at the numbers on these reports, death camps would explain where these transports were heading and why so many people have not been accounted for."

"Death camps," Kitty said, stressing the plural.

She finally looked down at the sheet, chills sliding down her spine. It was a mimeograph, a very neatly typed report. A list of deportations from September and October 1943. From Belgium, from France, from Holland, from Poland, and on and on. The Third Reich's seals approving the fastidious attention to detail. Every transport. The exact head count. Where each train took the seized Jews and dissidents. They recorded everything. The Nazi regime was a narcissistic psychopath, requiring acknowledgment and proof of its deeds.

When Kitty calculated the number of those transported in just those two months alone, the sum was over ten thousand Jews. Tens of thousands of souls rounded up, often in the dead of night—she had witnessed the SA's and SS's brutality in Vienna herself—terrorized and transported to places like Dachau. Ravensbrück. Bergen-Belsen. Treblinka.

Auschwitz.

Mauthausen.

"My God!" Kitty had to lean against the table, dizzy with the weight of grief. She felt sick. The paper drifted to the floor.

"Kitty?" Edgar reached for her but she moved away, sending him a warning look.

"Reconnaissance planes also took photos over Auschwitz and the outlying camps," she croaked. She wiped her face. "I told you, I saw the photos in Bern. There were large smokestacks on the buildings. My Polish informant said they were going day and night."

Edgar stood, his head bent.

Kitty tried to fight back against the growing nausea. "Donovan didn't believe it. MI6 didn't believe it. Not even Dulles wanted to hear it when we examined the photos. But those smokestacks... that means—"

"No." Edgar looked up. "Zyklon-B is colorless. Odorless and colorless. This escapee from Treblinka reported mass graves, but the ground water got contaminated, and then... The Nazis found a different solution." Edgar said. "The smoke is likely from cremation. How else do you get..."

Kitty gaped. "*Solution*. Do you remember what you called it when we were in France? When you got word about that conference in, what? January, nearly two years ago? *The final solution*. Now we know what that *solution* is. How...? How many?"

"We don't know."

Thousands, Bonaparte had said. *Tens of thousands*. If that one transport record was any indication—just one record for two months—then it was hundreds of thousands. Could it be millions?

"This is genocide," Kitty said faintly. "We can't turn away from this, Edgar."

It was not the first time she was accusing the Nazi regime of it. She swayed on her feet. Edgar took two steps to her and grabbed her.

"Kitty, you're so tired. I see you. I'm worried about you."

She sank into the nearest chair, folded in on herself, the tears sliding into her hands. "We can't turn away, I can't... I *can't* turn away! Someone has to do *something*. *Now!*"

She had experienced futility when working at the U.S. consulate in Vienna. How the governments refused to help the Jews escape the Nazi pogroms. Hitler's tyranny. Now, here they were. Witnesses—*knowing*—that these prisoners were being murdered and their bodies burned to ash.

"I've lost so many of my friends already!" she wept.

Edgar was on his knees before her, kissing her hands, her knees, stroking her arm. "I know, my darling. I know. I never talk about it, but I have as well. Many people. Good people. But these camps are far from the front lines. There is nothing we can do right now except wait until the Allied forces reach them."

An old fury—one she was certain would be a part of her

forever now—shook her. Edgar was right. Any action now would bring few results, would save few people. Their allies would announce policies and make decrees aimed to punish the Nazis but they'd argue that there was nothing—positively nothing—other than words, sanctions, or embargoes that they could impose—to help the inmates of these death camps *right now*. They had to win the war. Move the front lines to the heart of Germany. To Berlin. And crush the Nazi Reich once and for all.

"We're going to win this war, Kitty," Edgar said. "We *have* to win this."

"And when we do?" Her voice was high-pitched. She was crying helplessly now. She felt guilty for turning this on herself, and their future. "What? We just go on living like it never happened? How, Edgar? Damn it! Tell me how we would ever be able to look one another in the face again! If Big Charlie...!"

She sprang up. He tried to catch her but she escaped into the nearest bedroom. The very last person who could comfort her was the man who had just stolen her last hope.

It was the next morning when Kitty emerged from the bedroom. Edgar was still in his suit from the night before. A pile of papers and notepads were scattered around him. He looked up as she entered the room, and smiled tiredly.

"Coffee?"

Kitty accepted. She too had slept in her clothes. The window was open. She shivered. "What time is it?"

"Six thirty. Almost."

Edgar handed her the cup, then went to his suitcase. He removed a heavy wool cardigan and draped it over her shoulders. She slipped her arms inside and gratefully wrapped it around herself, inhaling the scent of him on the collar.

"What are you working on?" She nodded at the table.

"I'm writing a detailed report. About... Well, about what we talked about. I didn't want to wake you by using the typewriter."

Kitty perched on the edge of the sofa and Edgar poured himself another cup before joining her. They sat close to one another, but did not touch.

"Edgar, about me going to Vienna. You do understand that this would put you at a massive risk if I am captured and identified? And it could also cost me my life."

"Yes."

"So, why won't the OSS put someone else in?"

Edgar winced. "I volunteered to go. I know the industries well enough. But Dulles informed me that OSS headquarters claim I'm not the kind of asset they want to have."

"Why on earth not?" She faced him.

"I'm Austrian. Either way, not a local yokel."

Kitty slumped, placing the cup and saucer onto the table. "Just like with MI6," she muttered angrily. "Like me, what do *you* have to do to prove yourself?"

"I miss Kendrick," Edgar said morosely.

Kitty leaned back. "Me, too. Those days seem so much more..." She shook her head. It was stupid. What she wanted to say was stupid.

Edgar beckoned for her. His eyes were bloodshot. She came and he gently pulled her to him, then reached for her coffee and handed it to her.

"After me, you were the next best candidate."

She let herself relax against him, submitting to the logic. Edgar's chin rested atop her head. Kitty sighed. It felt so good to feel him against her, and she was filled with regret. Regret that she had spent the night alone. He'd come to Switzerland, she realized, because of Masterson. To assure her that he was all right. She regretted lashing out at him. Of being disappointed in him. This man, who risked his life every day, trying to do what was right in a world gone dark and hopeless. Tears began to roll down her face again.

Edgar soothed her, stroking her hair. It was as it had once been. They did not need to speak. He understood.

"You know what I want?" he whispered, close to her ear. "I want to take a walk with you, in the sun, somewhere warm. I want to just be with you. Doing nothing but holding your hand. Choosing you. We should have done more of that in Istanbul. It's just—"

But now she shook with quiet sobs. He was not helping. "When?" she choked through the sadness. "When should we do something like that? When will we wake up to absolutely no upheaval?"

"Kitty, I'm so sorry. For everything. For *everything*." He sighed deeply against her. "Do you remember how Nils never wanted me to get involved with you?"

She released an abrupt laugh. She had nearly forgotten that. "He sent you packing in Tokyo. I was so livid!"

"We could finally celebrate our wedding anniversary. Here, in Bern. And we could ring in a new year, together. One where we'll help the Allies bring this damned war to an end."

"And then...?"

"And then..."

She turned into him and buried her head into his shoulder. He stroked her back.

"I'll go to Vienna," she said.

He kissed her head. "I knew you would."

9

JANUARY 1944

Edgar returned for the holidays as promised. They celebrated New Year's Eve and their wedding anniversary for the first time together in years. They went skiing. They ate cheese fondue. Kitty met Bob Quentin for the first time, and yes, he was a dullard but also very kind and generous, and he adored Millie.

Right after New Year's Eve, Kitty began meeting with the OSS team responsible for developing her new persona. First, Millie took her to a stylist, who streaked Kitty's hair with a dye to make her blond hair look darker. Next, the OSS magicians created a new birthmark below her right ear and hid the one that was below her right elbow.

She'd been feeling awful as well. Her stomach often ached. At times, the headaches woke her. Her sleep was further riddled by nightmares—vivid and violent dreams that felt all too real. And the anxiety never let up.

"This is normal," Millie assured her.

What the hell was normal about any of this? Nothing! What had she hoped to become? A foreign service officer. Helping people with their visas. After falling head over heels for Edgar, she enjoyed the privileges of a diplomat's wife, relishing her cocktails and conversations, scandals and secrets. Now, here she was, preparing to return to the city where she had lost that life.

Edgar was on the opposite end of the sofa, working through his own pile of documents. She looked up from her file, which contained the first sketches of the new person in the making, and stared out the window. Snow was falling.

As this "new person," she was to build up the O5 into a more organized resistance like the French maquis. Meanwhile, Cassia's mission would be to provide sketches, production figures, factory locations and building plans. Anyone involved in building tanks, aircraft, land vehicles—any war equipment— for the Wehrmacht were targets. Except in Austria. Austria was to be spared as much as possible, because the idea was to make Austria a neutral self-sustaining country at the end of the war.

It was also clear that Edgar wholly sided with the idea. He had plans, and those plans meant returning to Vienna after the war. For the first time in all these years, Kitty only wanted to go home, back to St. Paul. Take refuge at the Larsson mansion, and drink real coffee under the red maple with her father, and have stupid spats with her mother. If even for a little while.

But Minnesota was a world away, and she had agreed to help prepare the way for OSS operatives in Vienna.

The day before, over lunch and gin rickeys, she and Dulles had discussed logistics.

"I'll need a radio," she'd told him firmly.

He rubbed his hands together. "You'll get one. Over Istanbul."

"And money."

"You'll carry that yourself."

Her eyebrows shot up. "Through a lot of checkpoints."

Dulles had half-smiled. "We can't just simply post a hundred thousand Reichsmarks to you in Vienna."

She had reached for her gin cocktail and taken a big gulp.

Now she was watching Edgar sort his papers into piles.

"There is something I need you to be prepared for," he said without looking up.

She set aside her file. "Sounds ominous..."

"It's about my parents and the house in the Cottage District."

Kitty frowned. "Go on."

"It's been converted into a convalescent home, and as far as I heard from Dr. Messner, it's an important hub for Cassia."

Kitty's eyes bulged. She knew that Josef Ragatz had been posted as prefect somewhere south of Prague and that Dorothea was with him there. "How did *that* happen?"

"Dorothea Ragatz's charity work."

"I don't believe it!" Kitty tried to imagine her mother-in-law handing over the keys to her prized villa out of the goodness of her heart. It didn't add up. "What is she getting in return?"

Edgar smiled ruefully. "A commemorative plaque from Hitler."

"A-ha!" Kitty pointed at him. "*Now* I understand."

"And a stipend. Leaving the house empty was not an option for the Reich. I can imagine why with the Soviets pushing our army back. Which is also the reason that Margit has nowhere to go."

"Wait. Margit?" Kitty stared at him.

"She's returning to Vienna from Linz."

Kitty shook her head violently. "No, no, no. Your spoiled socialite sister?"

Edgar put a palm up. "You were the first to scold me for saying that about her."

"I was joking," Kitty said. "She doesn't... Christ! She doesn't know about you? Us? *Me?*"

"No. Not unless you want her to, that is."

"Why would I want her to?" she asked, astounded.

"Because you need recruits, and she might be able to help."

"With what?" Kitty demanded. "Doesn't she believe you're a Nazi?"

Edgar dropped his head, put a fistful of papers into his briefcase.

"Edgar? Does she *not* believe you are a Nazi?"

"She knows me better than that. She knows I'm doing this to bide my time."

"But...?"

"I trust her. I spent time with her in Linz."

"In Linz?"

"I didn't tell you because I knew you would overreact—"

"Pardon me?" Kitty shouted.

Edgar tipped his head, a satisfied grin on his face. Kitty jumped off the sofa and threw her hands up, but stared him into further explanation.

"I didn't tell you, but it was with her that I stayed when I disappeared off the map. After Paris, she took care of me for a while."

"You hid with your sister in Upper Austria? And she knew you were hiding?"

"She knew something was wrong. She never talked about it to me, but she kind of saved me in the end. She bought me time."

Kitty began pacing. "So, she's moved back to Vienna. And she's at the Vienna Woods cottage? She had no place to go but she's at the cottage?"

"No. I'm letting her stay at the penthouse in Rennweg."

Kitty spun to face him. "The penthouse?"

"There is a child."

Kitty spluttered. "What? When?"

"A boy. He's five." Edgar looked pained. "Jerzy's."

Their Polish butler's, he meant. Margit's long-time lover.

"My mother sent her away to Linz, supposedly—or had us

all believe—to take care of our aunt. I didn't know. Nobody told me anything until I was in Linz."

Kitty lowered herself on the back of the sofa. "Wow. Well, this is a bombshell."

"His name is Andreas."

"And Jerzy?"

Edgar blinked up at the ceiling and shook his head. "No word since he returned to Warsaw. Margit believes he was executed with the rest of the home guards."

Kitty dropped her head in her hands. She stared into the darkness of her palms before spreading her fingers open and looking at Edgar. His aquamarine eyes were steady. He was solidly convinced about Margit. "And that qualifies her to be privy to our secrets?"

"It gives her the motivation to want to bring down this regime, yes. But I haven't decided anything. If I do, I will let Messner know."

Kitty giggled, because if she didn't laugh, she'd cry. "You're hilarious. Margit. Sure. Why not? OK. She's at Rennweg. What does it matter? Kitty Ragatz doesn't exist any longer, what the hell do I have to say about it?"

He rubbed his face and gazed at her. "Don't be like that."

"Be like *what*?"

He frowned and clicked his tongue. She watched him go to the desk, to another stack of documents, which he carefully put into his briefcase. She stood up and stepped behind him, grasped his arms and drew him close to her.

"Edgar, my decision in Istanbul... It has nothing to do with loving or not loving you. Because I do love you. So much that sometimes I don't think I can function."

He leaned against her, and his chest expanded before he let out a long breath. "I only have one question," he said to the window. "Do you trust me?"

She hesitated. He gently pulled away and stepped off to the side.

"It's not about you," she repeated and leaned on the table.

He slowly turned to face her. His eyes bore so much pain. So much regret. "Are you referring to Marguerite? Because it really meant nothing."

"Do you know how much I hate that you said that right now?" She pushed herself upright. "It's not about her either, damn it! Can you honestly imagine ever living a normal life after all that we have been through? Waking up on Saturdays and going to the market, buying flowers, having friends over for dinner? Oh, and let's not forget your ambition to be Austria's next prime minister or whatever it is that's churning in your head. Like nothing happened? The moment the Nazis marched into Austria, our lives as we knew them were over."

Edgar said nothing.

"Who are we now? Look at us. What have we become, Edgar?"

"I've never—ever—wanted anyone else—nothing else—like I've wanted you," Edgar said in a low voice. "Do you not think that my nerves are at the end of their line? That I'm not looking over my shoulder every few minutes? That I sleep well at night? I swear to you, Kitty, there have only been two things in bed with me since Paris. Either you or a gun. Every night."

"Me, too. But I never took on a Marguerite."

His smile was derisive. "For someone who used to fall in love every few days..."

One wide step, and she was close enough. She reached out to slap him but he caught her hand, and held it fast.

"I fell in love with *you!*" she cried earnestly. "All those other times I was learning what love was. And, most importantly, what it was not. But I wanted *you!*"

Edgar blinked, let her go and spread his arms out. "Well,

here I am. This is me. All of me. My mistakes, my failures, my desires, my ambitions, this is it."

Kitty groaned. She remembered how he'd said something similar to her at the Vienna Cottage. When he'd asked her to be sure about him. She had said yes to him then. She had promised him that she would always say yes.

She blinked away the tears. He came to her and put his arms around her.

"I was going to slap you," she muttered feebly against his chest.

"Yes. But you didn't."

"I could have. Had I meant it."

He chuckled against her.

Kitty sniffed and cleaned her face. "I have to go to Millie. She's put together a team to create my new persona."

"Not so fast." Edgar reached for her again and stroked her hair. "Kitty, we both have new bones. But our hearts are the same. You'll see that again. You'll see the light. You'll *be* the light, again. I promise."

She looked up at him, her heart breaking. *He* used to be her beacon. That smile. That easy gait. He had lit up at the sight of her and she'd always been drawn to him. A moth to the flame.

Now, both of them were overshadowed by grief, by dark secrets.

In the middle of the guest suite in Herrengasse on the morning of January 5th, Millie set up the full-length mirror, her expression full of anticipation as Kitty examined herself.

This was not Kitty's first transformation. She'd been the vivacious socialite, Elizabeth Hennessy, a red-headed Boston widow, while in Istanbul and in France. Then, when helping to build the French resistance networks for the British SOE, she'd been chiseled into Yvette Archambeau, the mousy French assistant to an art gallery owner—and Kitty's aunt.

Now Kitty was dressed in a plain blouse, a pencil skirt, wool stockings and dark, flat shoes. Besides the darker shade of blond, she would depend on colored contacts to hide her real self. Her eyes went from blue to hazel when she inserted them. She would also wear dark-framed glasses, similar to what her persona as Yvette Archambeau had once worn. They gave her a studious appearance, which was appropriate because the vivacious, fun-loving Kitty Larsson had been beaten out of her. She'd been in prison, witnessed murders, detained and questioned by Gestapo, and run for her life. She'd lost people she loved, could not tell her parents what she was doing, and loved a man she did not believe she had a future with. And whom she could not let go.

"Fräulein Katrin Handel," Millie said as Kitty stepped back. "Your story is not all that dissimilar from your own, and common enough that it should raise no suspicions."

"I'm listening." Kitty buttoned up the blouse.

"A French mother," Millie began listing. "A Swiss German father. You spent a good deal of time in France. Lyon."

"Paris," Kitty interjected. "I know it like the back of my hand."

"Fine. Paris, then." Millie carried the mirror to the far wall and propped it against it, then went to the desk and picked up the steno pad. Kitty watched her, Millie jotting something down before continuing the story, and noted how the powder blue skirt accentuated her friend's curves. Millie was polished, and a stick of dynamite in comparison to the drab and buttoned-up Katrin Handel.

Kitty undid the top two buttons of her collar.

"You worked in Zürich at the Semperit offices," Millie continued. "Franz Messner was on one of his trips, invited you to work at the headquarters in Vienna. Your translation capabilities will help the Reich with their business partners in France."

Kitty began to say she didn't know Zürich well enough when Edgar strode into the suite with Allen Dulles. They both halted when Kitty faced them.

"Wow," Edgar said. His assessment traveled from head to toe. "*Es ist gut.*"

Dulles also seemed to think "it was good." He walked around her at a distance, stopped, crossed his arms, and beamed at Millie before saying to Kitty, "A pleasure to meet you, Miss Handel."

But Edgar narrowed his eyes. "She needs a good reason for the American accent, if it should come up."

Millie snapped her fingers and grasped the steno pad again. "Your father had a job with Semperit in America but, when you were a little girl, your parents divorced and you moved to Paris with your mother at the age of...?"

"Sixteen," Kitty said. "I spent a year in France in summer for the first time at sixteen. Under duress..." She halted.

Edgar's eyes locked on hers.

"Under duress," Kitty continued and turned to Millie, "I'll connect that to my first overseas trip."

Edgar rested his chin on his hand as the other two reviewed all the details of her fake parents, her fake studies, her fake credentials—which were not *so* fake—and her whole fake background.

Kitty turned to Edgar, silently pleading with him, but then he walked over to the others and was arguing with Millie about some insidious detail she would have to adapt and Kitty would have to adopt.

"I'm right here," Kitty muttered. "Here in this room."

Everyone turned to her.

She waved her hand over them. "You three are like Dr.

Frankenstein, but I'm living and breathing already, and I want to determine the part I play."

"I let you have Paris," Millie admonished.

"And I was never in Zürich long enough to know the city," Kitty argued.

"Then you'll go there," Dulles declared. "You'll learn it before we send you to Vienna."

"Do that, darling," Edgar said. "Go to Zürich."

Dulles made a sucking sound and beamed at Millie. "Then it's settled. Edgar has a train to catch first thing tomorrow. Mrs. Quentin, I assume you won't say no to lunch, today?"

Millie flushed and began following him out. Before she passed Kitty though, she linked an arm around her waist and pulled her in. "Don't be sore. We're going to work this all out so that it suits you, all right? I'll see you tomorrow."

When they were gone, Kitty turned to Edgar. "And here we are again. Having to say goodbye."

"At least we have time for a proper one."

"And then?"

"You'll go through the usual rigmarole, learning your story backwards and forwards, getting your instructions until they are ready to send you in."

She removed the glasses then popped out the contacts into his waiting palm. He put them into the container, then turned to her and straightened the collar of her blouse and buttoned it all up. His eyes roved over her face, like a soft caress.

"It's almost over, Kitty. I promise you."

She turned to the mirror and ran her fingers through her hair. Not her color. Not her length. "Then what? I just grow my hair back to my shade of blond again and go back to being... me?"

Gently, Edgar led her to the window, and opened the curtain. Below, the Aare River glistened, its banks crusted with snow. The Bernese Alps were bright white in the sunlight.

"We can build a new life. Not an old life, Kitty. A new one."

So much had been said between them in these weeks. There was no room for jokes. No room left to say anything but the truth. They had lived an intensive time—fitting in a year's worth of moments into days. Because beyond that brilliant scene, beyond the door of the suite where she had just begun to feel comfortable, even cocooned, was the violent world of war she would soon be entering.

Head first.

PART THREE

MARCH – MAY 1944

Vienna, Austria

10

MARCH 1944

With one hundred thousand Reichsmarks sewn into the linings of her skirt, her blouse, and her blazer, as well as tucked between two pairs of wool stockings and the heel of her shoes, Kitty was heading for Vienna. Allied air forces had scrambled behind enemy lines and released their bombs on the Reich's infrastructures and industries. In their wake, they'd left destruction, havoc, and added to the toll of civilian casualties.

This recent news explained the somber mood among the passengers on Kitty's train. After the week-long bombardment by Allied air forces, the locals wore expressions manifested by the wreckage of their city. Hard and unfriendly mouths. Eyes half-closed in suffering and grief or blazing with angry disappointment, even defiance.

In early spring, the warmer weather seared the dingy skin of winter and exposed Vienna's façades. The tree branches—still bare—clawed toward a cold sun. There was no new growth. Even the birds looked lean and hungry, flitting and scolding over waste among the patches of melting snow. Which was why, when she disembarked, Kitty was astounded to discover a map of the city where the boundaries had burst and oozed onto the flat countryside. Nearby, job listings hung for the factories and businesses in those expanded districts. It was ironic that, while the Nazis had unleashed devastation upon London and Paris, Vienna appeared to be flourishing under the very regime the Allies were trying to topple.

Kitty did not trust her eyes, however. Like everything the Germans propagated, she suspected this was the Third Reich's effort to showcase a healthy economy, a virile military.

There was, however, one sober reality. Along one wall of the train station hung rows of photos, while wreaths and flowers were propped up against the foundation. Kitty walked over and scanned the hundreds of photos of men of all ages in military uniforms. Handwritten beneath their names were the pleas of their loved ones:

Missing in Action!
Eastern Front! Netherlands! France! North Africa!
Have you seen my brother?
My father? My son?

Kitty turned away. This was the true face of war, all these lost men.

To reach the 18th district—the Cottage District—Kitty caught a bus, resistant about returning to the neighborhood her in-laws, the Ragatzes, had lived in. Her dark blond hair was pinned back beneath her hat. She wore glasses over her hazel eyes. At each checkpoint on the train and now in Vienna, she meekly presented her documents, head bent low. She was Katrin Handel now, had developed a persona for her. This was going to be her biggest role yet.

Among her documents was the letter of invitation from Semperit and her work permit. She received very few remarks. This was more unnerving than assuring, for as she traveled through the city, she had the sensation people stepped aside to let her in so that they could scrutinize her more closely. Not only the thick groups of Wehrmacht or police, but even the dog walker or the butcher cleaning his window threw her suspicious glares. It was as if they were making way for her in order to close in on her.

There was something else. The parks—where she and Edgar had picnicked in the summer and early fall of their courtship, where they had walked the gardens or kicked around a football—were now guarded by flak towers, the heavy anti-aircraft guns pointed to a cold and relentless winter sky.

Kitty's bus stuttered to a stop at Türkenschanz, a vast park on the very edge of the Cottage District.

She wound her way through it and exited onto Hasenauerstrasse and looked for house number 61. In the distance, poking above the bare branches of the treetops, was the red church spire of the Gersthof. She and Edgar had gotten married there. She pictured the mild-mannered and calm Father Heinrich Maier. He'd been in his early thirties when she'd met him. Some had referred to him as a friend, others a counselor, a psychiatrist even. Edgar also held the priest in high regard, and found him to be the ideal spymaster.

"He won't invite the fox into the hen house," Edgar had assured her. "Maier is a natural with people. He reads them quickly and accurately. He understands people, their weaknesses, as well as their strengths. He knows how to bring them together. He'll do all he has to in order to protect Cassia, trust me."

Messner had confirmed all this as well over that first dinner in Bern, explaining how he and the priest had become good friends.

"I was interested in Buddhism," Messner had explained. "And discovered that Father Maier is very knowledgeable about world religions. I would have to say that was how we unified against the Nazis."

Personally, Kitty remembered Father Maier as warm, with dark, twinkling eyes and an energy that was enviable. He was a powerhouse. She'd had the sensation that he could see right through her and, when she and Edgar were preparing for their wedding ceremony, he'd taken their hands in his and just held them, eyes closed, and meditative. Afterwards, he'd gazed at Edgar, then at Kitty and smiled.

"Good," he'd said. "Very good."

That was all. But those three words implied so much. Back then, it had given her a deep feeling of peace.

Now, the recollection of that moment broke her heart.

Kitty reached the Messners' villa. It was understated in comparison to the Ragatzes'. Modest and compact, the house was painted a soft shade of blue accented by white latticed shutters. Surrounding the villa was a large garden. The entrance faced the road and the slope leading down to Türkenschanz Park.

It was Messner's wife, Franka, who greeted Kitty in the foyer. Kitty had only met her a few times over Edgar's work events, and Franka was warm and polite as usual, but she referred to Kitty by her operative name.

"Fräulein Handel, please, do come in. Franz Josef is on his way home from the office and should be here very soon."

She reached for the heavy suitcase, but Kitty needed to retrieve the Reichsmarks hidden in her clothing. "Would it be possible to freshen up first?"

Franka showed her to the washroom, where Kitty shut the door and carefully tugged the lining of her skirt and blazer loose. She removed the single layers of bills, then did the same with the money in her wool stockings before transferring the cash into a linen pouch. After slipping into a fresh dress and tidying up, she found Messner's wife waiting in the parlor. The money that she'd hidden in her purse Kitty would hand over to Messner personally.

"Would you like some Linzertorte and refreshment?" Franka asked when Kitty entered the room.

Kitty accepted and went to the windows overlooking Türkenschanz until Franka placed a plate on the table next to the sofa.

"Are those Sorgenthal?" Kitty asked, pointing at the plate.

"They are." Franka smiled patiently.

"And what lovely furniture you have. Did you furnish everything yourself?"

Franka looked amused, but what should Kitty say? *So, do you know who I really am, or have you forgotten? And if you know, how's the life of a spy treating you?*

"I've just had the sofas and chairs refurbished," Franka said. "This rose chintz was dear, but it goes so well with the cherry-wood. *Meine Liebe*," she stressed. "We're all friends here."

"I'm sorry." Kitty let out a deep breath.

"My husband should have told you." Franka smiled.

Messner strode into the room just then. "There you are, Fräulein Handel. You've made it." He nodded brusquely at Franka and lowered his voice. "We've all agreed to call you nothing else. How are you?"

"It's been quite a journey," Kitty admitted.

"Did you have any troubles?" He placed a hand on his wife's shoulder before taking a seat at the other end of the sofa.

Kitty shook her head. "Except for the number of times my heart stopped beating, no."

"That's a relief then."

Franka poured him an ersatz coffee and Kitty, famished, gladly accepted a second slice of torte.

"I'd like for you to settle in," Messner continued. "We found you an apartment near the church. Franka has made sure it is comfortable. The building is used by some of the students who attend the university here. I think you will find it more than adequate."

"Thank you."

Franka shared a knowing look with her husband and excused herself. "Lunch is in twenty minutes. And Fräulein Handel, you're invited to join us."

Kitty settled into her seat after she left, and passed Messner the linen bag with the Reichsmarks.

"To pay forgers and bribes, buy equipment," she said after telling him the sum. "Whatever is necessary."

Messner tilted his head. "I signed the memorandum last month. In Cairo, like you suggested. The OSS and Cassia are now bound by agreement. Now we need the radio."

"It's my next priority," Kitty assured him. "We must coordinate how to get that over the border."

"Khan told me that Leonard is supposed to handle it out of Istanbul," Messner said. "Budapest is the safest route."

"Please," Kitty began. "I'd like to go over my tasks with you and confirm that your expectations are aligned with what the OSS has requested of me."

"Of course. You'll be drawing maps of the production facilities I visit, collecting correspondences and cables from other businesses I have dealings with. We'll be sending these via couriers and coded cables to Prague and to Khan in Istanbul until we have our own radio. In the meantime, you'll be in touch with Khan's people in the O5."

"And assess whether the O5 stragglers are prepared to commit acts of sabotage," Kitty said.

Messner folded his arms and leaned back on the sofa. "With our information, you will help them decide what sorts of operations they can or should take on."

"Understood," Kitty said.

The OSS had her on two operations, as well. Operation Redbird was the first phase, Operation Dupont was the second. In the first, Dulles wanted Kitty to regain the trust of the O5 stragglers she and Khan and Edgar had worked with after the Anschluss. There were not many left, but she was to continue recruiting candidates, some in the very factories where the Wehrmacht weapons were being manufactured.

At the same time, Kitty would also look for assets that would make up her local reception committee to help integrate their OSS team. Eventually, she wanted a network that would help cast a wider net to other areas of Austria. Messner knew of a large network of Tyroleans prepared to help the Allies as soon as they set foot on their soil, too.

She listed for Messner what she would need: a radio operator, hiding places and safe houses, equipment for the American agents, forgers for identity cards, ration cards, clothing, food, good landing zones for the parachutists, and a secure escape line.

When that was all set, she would give the all-clear for Operation Dupont, which entailed parachuting in three-man teams made up of OSS agents. Those men—she assumed they were all men like those she'd trained in Great Britain—would then infiltrate themselves into the city to assist the O5 and continue collecting strategic intelligence.

"It is a lot of work," Messner said.

Kitty agreed. "Smoke must be coming out of my ears." Her tasks were not dissimilar to her work as an SOE agent in France, with one difference. She'd been in the non-occupied zone there. She had since learned that the SOE agents who had landed in Nazi-occupied France had survived an average of only a few weeks. She guessed her odds were not that different in Austria if she did not practice extreme caution.

"It's going to be painstaking work," Kitty said. "Slow-moving. The only way for me to do this without arousing suspicion—"

"Without being caught right away," Messner interrupted. "That's the only way. If you can make yourself seen without raising suspicions, you will do well."

"I was going to say that I'll be spending an awful lot of time doing nothing for the operations until I feel invisible."

Messner peered at her. "I believe patience is good practice, but my dear, I do not know whether you realize how very many lives are depending on our expediency. There is plenty you can be doing right away."

He checked his watch and threw a look over his shoulder. He then leaned forward. "I regret to inform you that the first thing you will report to your *office*, Fräulein Handel, is that one of Cassia's members has been arrested by the Gestapo."

Chills ran down Kitty's back. Shakily, she balanced her coffee cup on her knee. "Who?"

"His name is Dr. Caldonazzi. He's an outlier in Cassia, but he is now in the Liesl."

"The Liesl? What is that?"

"It's the prison on the Elisabeth-Promenade. Named after the former empress."

Kitty let out a slow breath. "The prison. That's right. I remember now."

"Father Maier and I don't have many dealings with Caldonazzi directly, but he was taken in for questioning in January. Only now—it's been nearly six weeks—are we discovering that he's been detained all this time."

"Does this change anything for me?" Kitty asked with concern.

"On the contrary," Messner said. "We're going to rely on you more than ever."

"Do you fear this Dr. Caldonazzi will talk?" she whispered.

"There is always that chance. But he does not know me

personally, or of my involvement in Cassia. Father Maier never introduced us like that. It will not slow our activities. As you see, there is a greater urgency to implement our plans."

"What was this doctor's role?"

"Debilitating soldiers."

"I'm not sure I understand..."

"Dr. Caldonazzi was available to those men who did not want to join the Wehrmacht or the Waffen-SS. He helped them avoid conscription or redeployment. Father Maier sent the boys to him."

"How?"

"In many ways. By making them sick, for example."

Kitty's eyes widened, but she couldn't deny that it was clever.

"Thank goodness, Dr. Caldonazzi was not apprehended for that. People reported that he was carrying anti-Nazi flyers. Not as bad as the intention to commit treason. However, the fact that the authorities took so long to press charges, leads me to believe that the police might suspect other clandestine activities. But Cassia cannot simply stop operating."

Kitty bit the inside of her lip and realized her leg was bouncing. She stilled it.

"I want you to go to the convalescent home," Messner said.

"At the Ragatzes' villa?" Kitty asked.

"Exactly. There is a Dr. Wyhnal there. He is the chief surgeon. He will be expecting you. He's taken over what Caldonazzi has left behind. He'll have a package you need to take to the building where your apartment is."

"Does he know about me?"

Messner nodded. "He knows to expect someone."

"And Father Maier?"

Messner narrowed his eyes. "No. In this business we work alone."

How often had she heard that before?

"When you establish your own team, I want to know nothing about them. None of us do. These recruits are your decision. You are accountable. But we need you to help at the convalescent home. It's a good cover, too. You'll have a nurse's uniform and everything."

"When should I go to Dr. Wyhnal?"

"You'll have lunch with us, of course. Afterwards, there is no time to waste." Messner leaned forward, palming a swath of white hair from his forehead. "One more thing. You said you need a radio operator. There is a young man in your building. His name is Giovanni Ricci."

"He's Italian?"

"His grandparents are. His father owns a restaurant in Nussdorf and has a small vineyard, which may result in some special dispensations. Giovanni might be worth talking to."

"You called him a young man. Why isn't he on the front?" Kitty asked.

Messner wagged his head. "Dr. Wyhnal has seen to it that he is not up to muster."

Kitty rose with him. "So, Dr. Caldonazzi does not work alone. And why do you think Giovanni Ricci would agree to work for us? For me?"

"Because Father Maier brought him to my attention. He believes he could do more than just courier messages. Much more. Like operate a radio, for example. This is naturally your decision if you recruit him, but so far, he's made a reliable impression."

Kitty smiled a little. It was excellent, really.

"Dr. Wyhnal will give you a package to hand to him today. That will take care of first introductions. Herr Ricci is reasonably cautious, however. Not a bad thing in this line of work."

Messner rose and Kitty followed but, at the door to the dining room, he stopped and turned to her.

"We will be working very closely at the office, and I will be doing everything I can to protect you from scrutiny. To outsiders, you'll be leading a very boring life, Fräulein Handel. However, should anything happen to me, I want you to convince Franka to go to the Brazilians. We are naturalized citizens. I trust her implicitly. She is the one who, after all, got me into this business in the first place."

Kitty wondered whether into rubber or espionage. Perhaps both?

"Duly noted," she replied.

As she took her place at the dining table, she fervently hoped that nothing would happen to him. It was abundantly clear that Franz Josef Messner and Father Heinrich Maier were the cornerstones of Cassia. If they were ever apprehended, the entire spy ring would be in jeopardy of sinking into obscurity. And she, with it.

11

MARCH 1944

Messner only lived a few minutes' walk from the Ragatzes' house. On her way, Kitty was flooded by the cold memories of meeting Edgar's stiff and arrogant parents. She did not miss them and could not imagine how Josef and Dorothea were getting on in the little Bohemian town Josef now governed. Or, rather, how the locals were getting on with Edgar's parents.

Kitty took a left onto the main boulevard, then another side street. She passed by a villa with a rounded tower and another with intricate plasterwork around the windows. Balconies jutted out over front terraces and ample yards. People had parceled the properties with the idea of making space for large gardens rather than living one on top of the other as in the city center.

Before reaching the wrought-iron gate of Edgar's parents' house, Kitty saw a bearded man in a wheelchair sitting on the veranda. He was missing his right leg at the knee. His head was tilted toward the weak sun. A cigarette dangled from his hand. He had a dark green wool blanket spread over his lap. Two orderlies were also smoking in the garden. They nodded Kitty's way as she came through the gate.

"I'm looking for Dr. Wyhnal," she announced.

One of the men pointed with his cigarette. "Inside."

In the foyer, where Dorothea Ragatz's butler used to meet Kitty and take her coat, several veteran soldiers were sitting and playing cards together. One of them pointed her to Josef Ragatz's study. There was a small plaque off to the side of the door: *Dr. M. Wyhnal.*

It was a strange feeling to be back in Edgar's parents' home. The elephant tusks were standing upright, but now in a corner next to each other. The vase from Manchuria, which Dorothea had received from her brother and always used to hold flowers, stood forlorn and empty on the floor.

A very thin woman with frizzy red hair and a grim-set mouth looked up from the desk at the end of the room.

"Dr. Wyhnal?"

She frowned. "Certainly not. Who are you?"

"Sorry." Kitty approached with her hand outstretched. "I'm Fräulein Katrin Handel. Dr. Messner sent me. I believe Dr. Wyhnal is expecting me."

The woman shook her head and when a man in a white coat walked in, her expression was one of bewilderment as she indicated Kitty.

"Corporal," the woman began. "This woman is looking for you."

The doctor looked older than Messner, and had pale, sad eyes on a lean face. But he was curious as Kitty quickly introduced herself.

"Dr. Messner told me to expect you," he said and moved to the desk, where the woman held a stack of papers for him to sign. He spoke quietly to her, asking whether one of the soldiers was truly ready to be discharged. The woman nodded, and Kitty noted something conspiratorial in their manner.

"Prepare the surgery for me when everyone else has gone to the canteen. Bring the private in, then," Dr. Wyhnal said.

"Yes, Herr Doktor." The woman walked out, hardly glancing in Kitty's direction.

Kitty was alone with him.

"Should I address you as doctor?" she asked. "Or corporal?"

He studied her a moment before moving to his desk and taking a seat. "Doctor is fine. I was with the Wehrmacht Medical Corps before the war broke out. I had just finished studying medicine in Graz."

There were books on infections and pathology in the bookshelf. There was also a plaque on his physician's license with a Nazi stamp. "Are you a member of the party, Dr. Wyhnal?"

His eyes flicked up at the shelf. "It was required."

Kitty nodded slowly. And then he said it.

"I was in Paris when Hitler marched into Poland."

"Paris. Yes."

"I believe Dr. Messner told me you are French, Fräulein Handel?" He indicated the chair across from his desk and they both sat down.

"My mother is," Kitty explained. "I lived in Paris and studied languages."

"I see. A good talent to have, if I may say so."

"I did some medical translations." It was Messner who had prompted her to say this if Kitty felt comfortable with Dr. Wyhnal. "A friend of mine works as a doctor in America." *Katrin's* story did not include siblings, but she was referring to her brother Sam.

"What is his specialty?"

"Toxins and pathology," Kitty lied.

Dr. Wyhnal nodded and his entire countenance shifted. He shut the office door first, withdrew a key ring and went to a cabinet which he unlocked. He withdrew a paper bag with a prescription clipped to it.

"Put this into your dress or coat pocket. This is for your

neighbor at the apartment building where you will be living. His name is Giovanni Ricci."

That was the same man Messner had suggested for her radio operator. She tucked the package into her coat.

"What's the prescription?" she asked.

"It's a light antibiotic. We'll get you a uniform and armband," Dr. Wyhnal continued. "You'll come in as a volunteer and courier prescriptions for me. Come on Mondays after work."

The woman from earlier suddenly reappeared in the room. "The surgery is ready."

"Frau Jovanovic," Dr. Wyhnal introduced. "This is Fräulein Handel. She'll be volunteering here on Mondays."

Frau Jovanovic narrowed her eyes and gave Kitty a reluctant smile. "Fine."

Dr. Wyhnal studied Kitty once more. "Is everything clear?"

Kitty said it was.

After she left the house and the yard, she turned back toward the Gersthof parish. Messner had withdrawn with Kitty into his study after lunch and explained that the Cassia network was not only made up of business people and physicians, but that they had a number of politicians, active soldiers and deserters from the Wehrmacht, and even police officers.

"One common method to debilitate the enemy is to make key figures sick," he'd expanded. "To hinder a particular policeman or politician from showing up for work, they have access to fever inducers. It could buy an asset some time with a matter."

Kitty learned that the medicines most commonly associated with causing fever included penicillin, quinidine, and phenytoin. But there was also a clandestine group who funneled conscripted men to these doctors. Giovanni Ricci had been one of those men.

Kitty had listened as Messner explained that there were ways to inject bacterial cultures into wounds to cause sickness.

"It's tricky," Messner had told her. "If not carefully administered, it could cause septicemia or gangrene. But it's better than dying as cannon fodder for a man they do not want to follow. It may not seem like it, but there are a great many of us working against Hitler and the Nazi regime. We want nothing more than to see justice. These scum have permanently scarred our country in the eyes of the world."

Her apartment building was just down the road from the church. It was painted yellow with a dark russet base and had a very different feel to the rest of the Cottage District.

At the curb, she had to step carefully as the sewage was backed up. Beer bottles littered the small square between the iron gate and the building. There was a sad looking park across the narrow road, with a single bench occupied by an old man wearing the worn Austrian Army jacket from the Great War. It was stripped of any badges, emblems or medals he might have once carried.

On the door outside, she read the small handwritten labels for all the residents. It was a mixture of German, Hungarian, and Slovak names. On the buzzer next to her apartment— rented under Messner—Kitty read RICCI.

She climbed the stairs to the third floor, her bag heavier for the long day of traveling and all the impressions she had collected along the way. She dropped her things in the hallway near her new place and crossed the hall to Herr Ricci's apartment.

After knocking, a young man appeared in the doorway. He was wearing a gray-green cardigan with a dark blue scarf around his neck. His left foot was wrapped up in a bandage and he leaned on a crutch.

Kitty found him immediately striking, utterly different. His dark brown, shoulder-length hair was combed off his forehead, and tucked behind his ears. His nose was a little pinched, and his eyebrows were unruly. He had light brown eyes that landed unabashedly on Kitty's face, taking her in with interest. Those eyes, she thought, were *working*.

A poet's eyes.

"*Ja?*" He drew out the word.

"I'm Fräulein Handel," Kitty said, irritated that she was flushing under his keen scrutiny. "I'm your new neighbor. I was at the convalescent home and Dr. Wyhnal asked me to bring this to you."

She presented the bag of medicine.

His eyebrows twitched upwards, but his gaze did not release her. Finally, he took it, then turned around, hopping inside on his good leg. Over his shoulder, he called, "Would you like to come in?"

She followed him, and watched him hobble to a couch where several books were lying open on the cushions and on the coffee table, face down.

"What happened to your ankle?" Her eyes darted about the room.

His eyes narrowed. "Injury."

"Are the pills to help?"

"The swelling, yes." He tossed the packet onto the table. "Who are you again?"

"Katrin Handel."

"That part I understood," he said. "But what are you doing here, in Vienna?"

"I'm Dr. Messner's secretary at Semperit AG."

"Uh-huh."

It was a small apartment with a narrow kitchenette off the main room and another room she guessed to be the bedroom. She'd passed the toilet on the way into the sitting room. On a table between the kitchenette and sofa was a typewriter. Other than the table and two chairs, there was a music stand in the corner. Behind that was a beautiful cello.

"Are you a music student?"

"A passion of mine. Just a hobby. I studied electrical engineering. I'm an interrupted student."

"Interrupted student?"

"I was studying engineering at the university. Until, that is, I was called up for a military fitness examination."

"And your name?"

His eyes narrowed at her, but he slowly reached across and offered his hand. "I think you already know." He jutted his chin to the bag where the prescription was attached. "Giovanni Ricci."

"Nice to meet you, Giovanni Ricci," Kitty said.

His hand was slightly damp, and he released her grip quickly. There was a dull thump from the room adjacent and Kitty turned to it. A gray cat with slitted yellow-green eyes snaked over to Giovanni.

"Who's this?" Kitty bent down to pet it as it passed between them.

"Sirko. He belonged to... Well, he was left behind." Giovanni's jaw clenched before he added, "I promised I would take care of him. We only have each other now."

Kitty frowned and straightened. "I'm sorry."

"For what exactly?" he asked coolly.

Kitty indicated the cat, who wound around Giovanni's good leg and meowed.

"We like each other. Nothing to be sorry for." He lifted the medicine packet and patted it against his thigh. "So...?"

"I should go," Kitty said. "It was nice meeting you both."

When Giovanni began to hobble forward, she told him she would show herself out.

"Fräulein Handel," he called after her.

She peeked back in from the narrow hallway.

"The nearest air raid shelter is in the church basement."

"Thank you." She gazed at him for a brief moment. He was striking, even handsome in a... *poetic* way. And young. Maybe in his early twenties. Five, maybe six years younger than her. With a start, she realized that was the age she was when she first became involved with the O5.

She raised her hand and left. It was time to discover her own apartment, right across the hall from her new neighbor.

And it was time to unpack the OSS kit secreted in her suitcase.

The OSS 9mm. The brush with the compartment in its handle. A pen where she could squirrel away microfiche. During her training with the OSS, she'd also taken a cigarette case that exploded. The L-pills. With those, her death would be quick and certain.

Like Giovanni's apartment, hers was tiny. She assessed the sparse furnishings. A bed. A table. Two chairs. No sofa, but an armchair and a side table. There were fresh linens and she guessed Franka must have brought them over. Towels. A little bit of food. She had ration cards from Messner. There was an entire Linzertorte in the cool box. That was definitely Franka. A cake could perhaps help her to tease more information out of Giovanni later. As Messner had suggested, it might take a while for the "interrupted student" to warm to her.

She shut the curtains—green with red roses embroidered at the edges—and fell onto the bed, unbuttoning her dress. She took one of the blankets and pulled it on top of herself. Sleep was instant.

It was dark in the apartment when she suddenly sat up. She did not know what had awoken her. Beneath the pillow, she felt for the pistol.

"Hello?"

She was alone. She rose and went to the door. A muffled meow came from the other side. She cracked it open and Giovanni's cat—*Sirko?*—darted in. Kitty turned on a lamp on the side table and squinted back at the gray tom.

"What are you doing here?"

There were muffled noises in the hall—the sound of people living: cooking, talking, a baby crying—but when she padded over, Giovanni's door was firmly shut.

"Did he lock you out?" she asked the cat again.

Sirko meowed, long and drawn-out.

She knocked. There was no movement.

"Herr Ricci?" she called softly. She did not want to draw the attention of any other neighbors. She rapped again. There was a heavy thud followed by a low groan.

Heart thundering, Kitty tried the handle. The door yielded. The cat dashed inside. Kitty paused for a second. If the animal felt threatened, it wouldn't do that, she told herself.

There was a small pool of light in the main room. Giovanni was lying on the floor, between the sofa and the coffee table topped with books.

"Herr Ricci?" Kitty stepped carefully inside. "Are you all right?"

He groaned again. Kitty quickly checked the kitchenette. The bedroom. It wasn't even really a room but more like a walk-in closet. The bed was in disarray. He was alone. She dropped to his side.

"Herr Ricci? What's happened?"

He was gripping his leg and his face was awash with sweat. When she tested it, his skin was on fire. He had to have gotten the wrong medication.

"My ankle. It hurts so much," he complained.

Remembering Messner's warning about bacterial cultures,

she undid the bandage, except there was no wound. But the ankle was tremendously swollen and hot.

"I'll get Dr. Wyhnal."

She helped Giovanni back onto the sofa, hurried into the kitchenette and poured water over a cloth that she pressed to his head. "I'll be right back."

The cat was crouched in the corner near the cello, its green-yellow eyes unblinking and accusing as she left.

Twenty minutes later, Kitty returned with the doctor, who'd been working in his study. As soon as she locked the door behind them, she asked what had happened to Giovanni's leg.

"Herr Ricci was Dr. Caldonazzi's patient," the doctor said. "When he received his draft notice to the Wehrmacht he came to us for help."

Kitty glanced at the young man. Giovanni was lying on his side on the narrow sofa. "Bacterial cultures?"

"No, it had to be more permanent," the doctor said. "I injected his ankle joint with turpentine."

Kitty recoiled, covering her mouth.

The doctor's shoulders dropped heavily. "The military just waits until the men are better. He begged me to do this. It started to wear off so I gave him a second dose a few days ago. He'll sleep off the infection, though."

"Do you do this often?" Kitty whispered.

Dr. Wyhnal nodded into his chest. "More than I care to say. It's against my Hippocratic oath, I know. But when I weigh it against sending them straight into Hitler's meat grinder..."

Kitty nodded, blinking back her shock.

As Dr. Wyhnal tended to Giovanni, she rose to pet the cat who had, in the meantime, jumped onto the table. There was a small sheet in the typewriter and Kitty read the first line in passing and froze.

She quickly rolled it out of the carriage and called to Dr. Wyhnal. "Is Herr Ricci...?" She brought it to him. "If any of the authorities came knocking," she whispered.

The doctor peered at it. "Can you please get rid of it? Destroy it." He glanced at Giovanni, who was deep asleep after a dose of morphine. "I sometimes think he's willing to die for this, that he is just waiting for it. Maybe inviting it."

"That would make him a high-risk candidate for any clandestine activities," Kitty muttered.

Dr. Wyhnal took the paper out of her hand. "Giovanni was engaged. Rachel was her name. A very pretty young woman, a singer. But... she was Jewish. Her religion was one of the reasons that Giovanni's parents told him to find his own way. He decided to pursue music instead of engineering. And the woman."

"What happened to this Rachel?" She dreaded the answer.

Dr. Wyhnal's eyes closed and he shook his head.

Kitty hugged herself and glanced at the cat, who arched his back in greeting. Had Sirko been Rachel's? That had to be it.

"Giovanni lost his mother soon after. He needs guidance." Dr. Wyhnal patted her hand. "Maybe you're the one to give it to him. But I can tell you, he is ripe for recruitment. He wants to do more."

Kitty nodded. She would tread carefully, however. Giovanni Ricci's motivation was highly emotional, highly personal. It could be good. It could be very bad.

She looked down at the sheet he'd typed up, translating from the German. Even the tone and style was a plea.

Eastern campaign has cost Hitler 1.5 million men. Why should thousands more sacrifice themselves? We must free ourselves from this tyranny. Unite for a common goal: the destruction of Hitler, the greatest, most accursed criminal of all time!

She crumpled the note in her hand. She would burn it in the kitchenette. The doctor was about to take his leave and called to Kitty.

"Will you stay with him for a little while?"

"Of course." She saw him to the door. "Is he going to be permanently injured?"

Dr. Wyhnal rubbed his forehead with the back of his hand, his black doctor bag cradled beneath his other arm. "Herr Ricci knew the risk. But he told me he can still play the cello with a limp."

12

MARCH 1944

Weeks later, as Kitty was getting ready for work, the music on her *Volksempfänger* was interrupted by a broadcast.

She stopped brushing her hair and turned up the volume. The calendar on the wall read Monday, March 20th.

"The German Army has entered Budapest and has fully occupied Hungary!" The voice on the radio proclaimed.

She groaned and flung the brush onto her bed. How was she going to pick up the radio in Budapest now?

"So much for a fast end to the war," she chided her reflection.

Kitty dressed quickly, seething over the excited news announcer's details—the propaganda—and peeked out the window of her sitting room. It faced the park, which was empty save for Wilhelm, the old veteran who spent nearly every day inhabiting his bench. He was sitting there already, binoculars hung around his neck, his cap tilted on his head. Several beer bottles were scattered at his feet and his head sunk into his chest. People were going to work in the half-gray morning. Some of them called the old man "Willi."

Kitty took an apple out of the bowl of two she had left,

considered the second one and took it as well. She sliced a piece from the rest of her bread and wrapped the food in brown paper.

On her way out, she passed Giovanni's apartment and knocked softly on the door. Over the last few weeks, they had developed a careful friendship. He was guarded—rightfully so, Kitty thought—and she was unnerved by him. It would take her a while to figure out Giovanni Ricci. Once she did, she would know whether to recruit him and divulge her role in Vienna to him, or leave him to Caldonazzi and Wyhnal.

The fact that she had found the words in his typewriter was the main reason she was cautious. He was devastated that she had found it, grateful that she had burned it. He'd admitted that, in his feverish state, he'd made a terrible mistake.

"I was emotional," he'd said. "I've been thinking... too many thoughts."

She leaned an ear to the door and rapped one more time. He did not hobble over. Only Sirko acknowledged her with a single, tenuous meow from behind the door. Not wanting to disturb, she left the building.

Across the road, Kitty placed the two apples and bread next to Wilhelm. He did not stir from his dozing but she realized the risk of someone stealing the food from him was rather great, so she nudged him awake.

He snorted and blinked up at her in surprise.

"*Bitte. Nehmen Sie es.*" Please. Take it.

He grabbed the packet. "*Danke.*"

Kitty smiled and headed to the streetcar stop, and picked up a paper on the way. Outside the window, the city brightened as sunlight filtered through the gray clouds. Instead of reading the news, she watched the people lean with the streetcar as it took a curve. Everyone avoided looking at one another, as if ignoring the very existence of others.

One night, when she'd brought Giovanni some medicine

and soup, he had given her a warning. "In this city, neighbor suspects neighbor. One careless word, and the secret police will hear of it. It is difficult to do anything—go to a music club, attend a reading, meet friends—without someone suspecting you of subversive activities."

In other words, undermining the regime, taking part in clandestine activities, was more difficult—and dangerous—than ever. She almost missed the stupid brutes that made up the SA. They had run things on the streets in the beginning. The *Sturmabteilung* were easy to spot, thugs disguised as enforcers of the law. But now, the regime was very well organized and collaborators and secret police were harder to spot.

It was therefore important that she create a routine for public appearance. Go to work. Come home. Attend church. Visit the convalescent home as a volunteer on Mondays. All so that, while she couriered for Cassia, and recruited new assets, and searched for safe houses, no outsider would suspect her of being anything other than a humble, low-key secretary and translator. Not even Wilhelm in the park, who she hoped was eating the last of her apples.

The next time she peeked out the window of the streetcar, she realized they were passing through Alsergrund. She slouched beneath that stone of grief around her neck. This was the neighborhood of her old "gang," the people with whom she had bonded instantly. Judith and Artur had been murdered. Big Charlie was gone. Oskar and Khan were the only ones who had escaped somewhat intact. And she had fled. Except she was back. Right in the wolf's lair.

Kitty lightly placed a hand on the window of the train as they passed into the next district. The rustling of paper behind her. A man muttering to someone in a flat tone.

"Looks as if we just regained what we'd lost after the Great War. Hungary is now part of the Reich again."

Edgar, Kitty thought with despair. *You promised me this*

war was almost over. You lied.

The Semperit headquarters were on the corner of Wipplingerstrasse, a six-story stone building with a bayed structure, paned windows, and dormers jutting from the mansard roof. Kitty entered the foyer, where a receptionist greeted her, then took the stairs. Most of the departments worked in offices behind closed doors, and the hallways at this time were often empty.

Her workspace was adjacent to Messner's, attached by a door from the inside. Messner was at a meeting with the board of directors as he was every Monday at eight, which meant he came into the office very early.

As she removed her coat, Kitty glanced at the pile of files on her desk. On the top was a folder for a new employee with Messner's quick note attached: *new employment contract.*

Head of Research and Development was on the label. Kitty opened it and was surprised to see a woman's picture on the curriculum vitae atop the contract. *Frau Dr. Stella Beck, PhD in Chemistry.*

Kitty examined the woman's black-and-white photo in the file. She had high cheekbones and a short, broad nose. Her stare penetrated right through Kitty. In the photo, it was not clear what her hair color was, but it was chin-length, straight and thin. She had a widow's peak, too.

Reading the woman's contract, Kitty was taken aback by the pay. Just over half of what Dr. Getzner had earned before he was conscripted. And then Kitty stiffened as she read the woman's *curriculum vitae.* Leader of the Deutsche Mädels in Cologne, Germany. Nazi party member. Graduate of the University of Leipzig in physical chemistry. Another degree in physics.

This woman was not only overqualified for the job, she was

a professional Nazi!

What had Messner been thinking when he had agreed to hire her?

Kitty had the chance to ask him when he came in a half hour later. She followed him into his office with Frau Dr. Beck's file.

"You have a lot of Jewish employees scattered among our branches," Kitty whispered. "*Three* of whom are in R&D."

"Not in Vienna," Messner said brusquely. He sat down at his desk, palms flat on his table. "I had no choice. There were not a lot of qualified people here to replace Dr. Getzner. Besides, she was forced on us by someone on the board, who got the recommendation from someone in the German Ministry of Armaments and Warfare."

"All the more reason to say no," Kitty stressed softly.

Messner's head rocked on his shoulders before he rested on her. "Fräulein Handel, do you know the difference between the philosophies of *Sein* and *Schein*? One's perception of a condition versus something as it really is? My *Schein* is that the Nazis are convinced I am one of them. It would do you well to keep your enemies close. I want you to welcome Frau Dr. Beck warmly."

Kitty balked. "Me?"

"Yes, you. Make friends. As a matter of fact, as my right-hand woman, so to speak, I expect you to supervise and observe not only our meetings, but also my personnel. You're my watchdog. It's time you are not only perceived as an indispensable arm of my management team, but embody it."

Kitty's head was racing with questions, but Messner was already waving her off.

"We both have a lot of work to do. Consider yourself the one-woman welcoming committee. Take her out to lunch. Get to know her."

Kitty rolled her eyes as she left the office. When was she

going to learn to keep her mouth shut?

Frau Dr. Beck was in Dr. Getzner's old office. Kitty knocked softly at the open door and looked in. The woman was hanging something on the wall and when she turned, Kitty could see it was the University of Leipzig diploma. Stella Beck was tall. Taller than Kitty, in heels at any rate. Her hair was bright blond —dyed—and pinned back from her face. But those intense eyes from the photo were an unusual light amber color, like a cat's.

"*Grüß Gott*," Kitty greeted, and strode in to introduce herself.

Dr. Beck took her hand in a hard grip, her assessment of Kitty, direct, unapologetic. Her instant disapproval vanished beneath a saccharine smile. "*Guten Tag*. You are Dr. Messner's assistant."

"Yes. I brought the copy for your records." Kitty handed her the employment contract, and took note of Dr. Beck's dark, plaid skirt and blazer. "I wanted to welcome you to Semperit."

"Thank you."

A gray coat hung on a rack near the window, a plaid scarf in red and blue was draped beneath the collar. Kitty glanced at the photos lined up on the desk, face up. Frau Dr. Beck with a group of teenaged girls in Deutsche Mädels uniform, receiving some sort of medal. She was wearing a wool blazer, buttoned all the way to the neck. The next one was of Stella Beck in a hat, a frilly blouse and pencil skirt—also plaid—standing with a man in a German military uniform.

"Is this your husband?" Kitty asked her.

"Günter. Yes."

"Which front?"

The woman smiled thinly. "Commander of the First Panzer Division. Currently in the Soviet Union."

"You must be very proud," Kitty tried. She knew the

Wehrmacht was being mercilessly driven back west but, by way of the German news, the Reich was winning.

"We are all proud, are we not?" Stella Beck picked up another photo, this time with Günter in civilian clothing and herself in front of a large house and garden. She was wearing a high-collared blouse with lace, her arm was linked with Günter's. Three children were around them, two boys in Lederhosen and a girl in a Dirndl. Kitty recognized the girl; she was also in the photo with the Deutsche Mädels, two long braids draped on either side over her shoulders.

"You have a lovely family," Kitty said.

"Thank you. And you? Where is your husband? Children?"

Caught off guard, Kitty stammered. "I am still unmarried."

The woman scrutinized her. "What are you waiting for?"

"I'm... I'm not from here."

"Yes, I can tell by your accent. *Trotzdem...*" Regardless.

"I was engaged once," Kitty said half-truthfully. "But... well. There's a war, isn't there?"

The woman looked her up and down. "I'm sorry to hear that. Austrian?"

"French," Kitty said.

"I see." Stella Beck seemed to consider what she could say next. "As you say, there is a war."

"When did you arrive in Vienna?"

"A few weeks ago," the woman replied.

"Same as me. So then the city is new to us both."

"Hardly," Dr. Beck scoffed. "I've been in Vienna many times. Many times."

Kitty forced a friendly tone. "I wanted to invite you to lunch. There's a really nice place around the corner from here. Would twelve suit you?"

The woman revealed a row of straight teeth for only a second. "I do have a lot of work to do. Maybe another time."

Keep her close. Kitty pointed to the document on the desk.

"At some point you will have to eat. It says so in your contract. The Herr Direktor insists that all employees take an hour for lunch. And it's your first day."

Stella Beck relented if that was what was meant by the falling shoulders. "I'll meet you in the lobby."

Kitty smiled, forcing it all the way up to her eyes. "Good, I look forward to it."

She calculated the score of her first attempt. One for Cassia. Zero for the Nazi.

Lunch was complicated. Kitty realized the woman was stiff, formal and would not warm easily, if at all. Not even as they were finishing their first course had Frau Dr. Beck offered to drop the formal *Sie* and change to *du*. She continued calling Kitty Fräulein Handel although Kitty had offered to address one another by their first names.

Kitty was prepared for this after the first impressions Frau Dr. Beck had made, and after their course of soup, she turned to the tactic of showing interest in the woman's work. The way to prying open a door was by showing appreciation. Kitty had learned that a long time before from her father.

"Have you been brought up to speed on the company's projects?" Kitty asked.

Stella was maneuvering a piece of aspic onto her fork. "I was here last week to meet with the project head."

"I know Dr. Messner is impressed with your skills and expertise," Kitty said. "What do you think about the synthetic rubber Semperit is experimenting with?"

Stella lifted her chin and folded her hands, keeping them on the table.

"Between us," Kitty added, "I think we have a real chance of developing something that will give the German Navy the advantage."

"What do you know about that?"

"I helped fill out the tender we made to IG Farben," Kitty said. "I saw the drawings, and they are very impressive. But are our materials going to measure up?"

Dr. Beck shook her head. "That is not the correct question. My job is to make sure they do. That is why I am here."

"But according to some of our latest tests—I mean, Dr. Getzner's reports were relatively adamant—Semperit could find a way to export substances from the east, like from the Kazakh SSR, via a back door, that is."

"Nonsense," Dr. Beck snapped. "We have everything we need right here in the Reich."

"We do?"

"Of course! Let me tell you how..."

By the time their main course arrived, the German woman was opening up like a clam in a pot of hot water.

Later, even as Kitty paid the bill, Stella continued her chemistry lecture, finding obvious pleasure in setting Kitty's limited knowledge straight.

"Chemical agents are used to turn the individual polymers into polymer chains," Stella was saying. "This forms a rubber substance. In a process called vulcanization, the rubber substance is processed into a rubber product. Vulcanization works by converting polymers into more durable material by adding accelerators such as sulfur."

"So these rubber pieces for the German U-boats," Kitty began.

"Rubber pieces?" Stella frowned and dropped her voice, leaning over the dark wood table. "They are anechoic tiles, or Alberich tiles."

Kitty also whispered, her tone conspiratorial. "And now Semperit must produce them synthetically?"

"Correct, but only the coating."

"Only the coating?" Kitty motioned for the maître d'.

Frau Dr. Beck folded her arms, scrutinizing Kitty. "*Natür-lich*. We can get by with a more economical product beneath the coating."

More economical, Kitty wondered. She meant cheaper. Cheaper meant room for defects. That certainly was not what Dr. Beck meant to happen, but Kitty—and Messner—did.

"Have you shared your findings with the Herr Direktor?" Kitty asked, then thanked the maître d' for her coat.

Stella absently stood up and let him drape hers over her shoulder. He had to stand on tiptoe to do so. "That's how I got the job, Fräulein Handel. There is a product which is a non-polar, high molecular weight polyisobutylene homopolymer with low-temperature elasticity manufactured by our partners."

"I see..." Kitty said. They drifted toward the door.

"The coating is made up of sheets approximately one meter square and four millimeters thick, with rows of holes in two sizes with various sizes in diameter."

Kitty recalled what Khan had said about those holes. "So that sound used by Allied anti-submarine detection equipment can be broken up. But what I didn't understand is why the holes were different sizes?"

"Different holes for different frequencies, you see." She peered down her nose at Kitty, and Kitty felt a little thrill. Stella was beginning to see Kitty in a different light.

The maître d' held the door open for them, but Stella continued without paying him any mind.

"The holes in the tiles help to break up the sound waves and return a fuzzy echo to the ASDIC operator instead of the sharp ping that would give away the presence of the U-boat," Stella explained. "However, this works differently at different depths due to the size of the holes changing in relation to the wavelength of the active ASDIC 'pings'." She looked around, as if realizing just then that they were standing outside. She flicked her wristwatch around. "Now, I could go on about this. But look at the time."

Kitty agreed they should get back.

When they reached the R&D department's floor, Stella hesitated before jutting her hand out. Kitty shook it just as firmly.

"Fräulein Handel, thank you very much for lunch. Before you go, may I ask you a question?"

Kitty took in a breath, put on a pleasant smile, as if she'd been waiting for this opportunity all day long. "Please, Frau Dr. Beck. Go ahead."

"Will you be involved in *all* the projects?"

"I believe so. Dr. Messner relies on me to be well informed."

Stella appeared to be debating with herself before she finally said, "Then, perhaps you should come to my office at some point tomorrow and I will show you the details of what we discussed today. If you are to translate these for our French-speaking partners in Geneva, it might do you some good to learn all the terms properly."

Kitty smiled graciously. "I would appreciate that."

She headed up the stairs. At Messner's office, Kitty peeked her head in. He was at his desk writing something but glanced up.

"And?"

"No ping-ping," Kitty reported.

He frowned and brushed the hair away from his forehead. "How's that?"

"I was a stealthy submarine, Herr Direktor. She never saw me coming."

He pursed his lips and looked thoughtful before waving his pen at her. "Good, see if you can submarine that radio from Budapest next."

Kitty groaned but flashed him a salute as she did.

"I'm on it."

13

LATE APRIL 1944

A few days after the Easter celebrations, Messner returned from Switzerland, pulled Kitty aside and said, "Rover delivered a truckload of Easter eggs to the office."

Kitty stepped away from him, astounded. "Again?"

Messner winked. "The headquarters are busier than ever."

She did not miss the double entendre. Not only would the OSS be analyzing Edgar's recent delivery of intelligence, but Berlin had to be scrambling in its recovery from current setbacks on all fronts. Edgar must have been bathing in the cables and wires, the frantic messages and hurried decrees pouring into the German Foreign Office. How he was delivering those documents to Dulles, she did not know, but she could imagine it was a hairy adventure each time he made his way to Bern.

"How does he look?" she asked with concern.

Messner's head swayed on his neck, his mouth pursed before he answered. "Tired. Lonely. Also very exhilarated and determined. He asked me to give you something."

He opened his briefcase and presented her with an envelope. Her pulse surged as she took it. A postcard was inside, a depiction of Bern, cherry trees and apple trees lined up along the slopes of the Aare River. On the back, *I went for a walk today in the sun. I thought only of you. I carry you everywhere I go.*

The pang of loneliness was sudden and intense. "Thank you," Kitty murmured.

"There was one more thing Rover wanted me to pass on to you."

Kitty frowned.

"He says someone will be waiting to meet you in church one Sunday. He wants you to know that she is in earnest. He trusts her implicitly and wants you to seriously consider her."

Her first thought was Margit. "Did he say who?"

Messner shook his head. "That was the message. I'm afraid I don't know more than that." He peered at her. "Rover delivered. Now it's your turn."

She knew what Messner meant. In the month since she had arrived, Kitty had managed to draw together some of the former O5 members and recruit three more. She had also made a decision about Giovanni and approached him about working with her. It had been the right decision. He was more than keen, and brought ideas and a promising network of potential recruits. But he had left soon afterwards to treat his ankle. It had caused him severe troubles again, and Dr. Wyhnal sent him to a sanitarium for recovery. Giovanni was to return that very evening. She was anxious to see him, anxious—she told herself—to build up the foundation for Operation Dupont.

"And this," Messner said.

She turned to him. He was holding the folder from their meeting with the airplane manufacturer Heinkel, with whom they'd met before Easter.

"I'll get on these," she promised.

Kitty was to deliver a summary of the information about Heinkel's airplane prototypes. Messner had received an order for the wheels. In his meetings with them, he'd run through the production figures. In addition, he'd managed to pilfer copies of the wheel sketches and ball bearings from Steyr-Daimler-Puch in Linz.

"You can start on that Heinkel map," Messner said in a low tone.

"Right away, Herr Direktor."

Based on their visit there, Kitty was to draft a map of the compound. She noted where the guards were, how many of them, the entrances, and where she'd seen Wehrmacht trucks bringing in what might have been more POWs to work at the factory.

She would leave the map in the dead letter box she had located in Türkenschanz Park. On a small hill stood the Paulinenwarte, a rounded lookout tower. Its facade was made of red brick. A spiral staircase led to the top where Kitty had found two loose bricks which, when removed, could easily hide small notes or even a small package. This was where she regularly left materials and instructions for her O5 courier, whom she only knew as "Peter". They included messages to be shared in propaganda leaflets, and instructions on hits to production lines, and transport lines. The map of Heinkel would help an O5 team to smuggle in food, supplies, and medicine to the POWs who were forced laborers there.

She finished the map, rolled it up around the cigar tube she would leave at the tower, placed the shell of a second cigar tube over it, and tapped it closed. She had limited personal contact with the members of O5 now. However, she had met with a group about four weeks after arriving in Vienna and rallied them to continue finding new recruits, new safe houses and to set up an escape route—one through Yugoslavia and into Italy— while promising them funds and American support as soon as her agents landed. Together, she assured them, they would finally gain momentum against the regime.

The O5 got to work and on Easter Sunday they blew up a small railroad section outside of Vienna. Sixteen plane engines, on their way to Heinkel's assembly hall, were destroyed. The Nazis retaliated immediately and the SS arrested and tortured the locals and rail workers alike until they captured a man whose confession they accepted and whom the SS then summarily executed.

Kitty knew, however, that the explosives had been set by a woman. A young schoolteacher with bright eyes, a round face, and fiery courage had been in the group she'd met with. The woman's husband had been a quiet man, who'd said little while his wife was the first to volunteer for the explosives team. It was the woman's husband the Nazis had arrested. Kitty could not imagine the discussions, the pain, the fear, the sheer panic that had led to his incarceration, and his death.

She did not *want* to imagine it.

That evening, after Kitty returned from her routine walk through Türkenschanz, the knock on the door from Giovanni finally came.

Her heart skipped several beats as she opened the door. Sirko darted inside and went straight to Kitty's bed. He sprang up and placed his paws on the windowsill, his gray tail twitching. Giovanni limped in, dressed in a white linen shirt and dark trousers. He had a bag slung over his shoulder. Smiling, he indicated the cat.

"Looks like he was eager for that view. Thank you for taking care of him."

"We got on very well while you were away," she said. She went to Sirko and stroked him. The cat's eyes were roving over the park, widening with each movement outside.

"How are you doing?" she asked Giovanni.

He lifted his left leg a little. "Fine. It's better. I built up strength in the ankle, and get around much easier and with less pain."

"That's very good news." She put a hand on his arm, an automatic reaction, and he looked down at it before putting his hand over hers.

"Thank you, again, for taking care of Sirko," he said.

She slipped her hand from beneath, her chest warm. "Of course it's no problem. I can't offer you anything, I'm afraid. I don't even have any ersatz left."

"Did you give that to Willi, too?"

Kitty reddened more.

Giovanni slipped the bag's strap over his head, and placed it on her table. "Over Easter, I was with my family in Nussdorf," he said. "My aunt packed a lot of food."

He removed a braided bread, the smell of egg and milk and raisin filled the air. Then he pulled out six hardboiled colored eggs. A hunk of salami. And a bottle of red wine.

Kitty stared at the feast, her mouth watering at the scents and sight of it all. She pulled two round wooden cutting boards out of the drying rack above the sink, fetched two knives out of the drawer and the shaker of salt. Giovanni had already wiped the two drinking glasses and now snatched the bag again.

"I almost forgot." He fished out a small chunk of fresh horseradish that he then began shaving onto the cutting boards. Kitty took a seat and sliced thin circles of salami.

"How is your family?" she asked.

Giovanni wiped a hand beneath his eye, blinking from the horseradish fumes. "Very well." He grinned at her and tilted his head. "Contrite."

"How's that?"

"My father has asked me to return to Nussdorf. He said he was wrong to be angry with me about wanting to pursue music. Now he wants me to consider taking over the family business."

"The restaurant?"

He nodded. Though she wanted to, she did not ask about the girl, Rachel. Kitty did not want to ruin the festive mood.

Giovanni took his place at the table and yanked off a piece of the braided bread. He presented it to her. She put the chunk to her nose, grinning at him.

Giovanni smiled and lifted his chin, then pulled the cork from the wine bottle, pouring them both a glass. "I also met with some friends."

Kitty had been savoring a strand of the egg-bread, but now she stopped chewing. He was holding the wine glass to her. They toasted.

She tapped the shell of the egg against the wooden board and began peeling. "So, these friends of yours...?" she began.

Giovanni picked up an egg, too. "Stefan and Gustav. We knew each other as kids. Old friends. They are the kind of people you can steal horses with."

Kitty swallowed the egg and took a sip of wine. "And this Gustav, this Stefan, are willing to help?"

Giovanni nodded, those eyes working on her again. He tucked his hair behind his ears. "There are also two women in Wiener Neustadt who are prepared to hide your people."

Neustadt was in the south of Vienna. She was mulling it over when Giovanni added, "They are both related to Gustav's family. His sister-in-law and her aunt."

Kitty smiled broadly, covering her mouth as she swallowed. Messner had been right to direct her to him. "Giovanni, I need a radio operator. When we get the radio, I will need to find a good place to hide it. And maybe even in three different places. Good ones."

Giovanni brushed eggshell off his board. "My father's house has a large attic with bedrooms we used for live-in help before the war. There's one room that has a hiding spot. I used to play there with Gustav and Stefan when we were children. We can move some furniture in front of it and stash the radio there."

"I'm not sure..." Kitty said slowly. "Nussdorf would be difficult for me to explain. I can maybe get there once a week, but when things get going, I will want contact twice a week. I think Dr. Wyhnal might be helpful. What about using the convalescent home as a base?"

Giovanni appeared to be considering it. "Sure."

"I'll need you to learn Morse code inside and out, and our encryptions. I can operate a radio. I can teach you to do it properly, but I really need to make sure that I am available for all the other things I have to do."

Giovanni tore into a piece of salami, nodding. "Here is the bonus. Stefan knows someone who worked for the DWF, the Wehrmacht division responsible for detecting and confiscating radios. The information he was able to get over a couple of beers is gold, Katrin."

The way he said her first name was so informal, it was intimate. This was it. They were co-conspirators. Partners. She felt heat rising up the back of her neck.

"What did he find out?" she asked, busying herself with a second egg.

"There are three ways that the DWF relies on detecting signals. Snoopy neighbors being top, poorly hidden outdoor antennas are next, and the lower-powered oscillator inside the radios. They give away too much."

"Those are needed for the radio to work properly," Kitty said, removing the last of the shell.

"Part of solving a problem is understanding where the weakness is," Giovanni said. "The oscillators work like a transmitter, which the DWF can pick up in their vehicles. But if we keep the radio moving. Take it apart and assemble it in other places on a regular basis..."

"We only transmit for a certain amount of time and on certain days," Kitty reminded him. "But, yes, it could work. So,

I'll ask Dr. Wyhnal, but where else could we use as a hiding spot?"

"One part in my room? One in yours?"

Kitty caught her bottom lip between her teeth and considered for a moment. "Wait! The cellar! There's the old coal chute."

"Very good. It's perfect." His eyes were working on her again, and the heat now reached her face.

"Good," she nodded. "I'll meet your friends and see how that develops."

"Also..." His eyes flashed. "I've drawn up a list of students I know who are on our side. Students and professors. People I believe would at least be able to help put together equipment, clothing, food. Maybe safe houses?"

Kitty smiled. "Weapons, too."

Giovanni's eyes narrowed and he suddenly wrapped his hand around hers. He brought it to his mouth and kissed it. Her insides lurched with an unbidden pleasure. Then he released her hand as quickly as he had taken it.

Giovanni looked down at his wooden board and popped a piece of salami into his mouth and chewed. She quickly picked up her glass of wine and slowly released a breath she hadn't realized she was holding.

The following Sunday, she set off for the Gersthof church, a few minutes' walk away. The facade was exposed red brick. Four clock faces adorned each side of the spire, which was sheathed in copper. Inside, the stone-paved floor held two rows of wood slat pews. Father Maier was hurrying behind the altar in a black cassock, his dark hair oiled and combed back.

Kitty had watched him play soccer with the kids in the park the day before, joking with them and the parents. They called him "Hansdampf"—Hans Steam—for all his energy. He'd even sat on the bench with Willi and talked with the old man for a very long time.

As she took her seat, Kitty was struck by how familiar the church was, although the only time she'd spent here was just before and on the day of her wedding. She also realized, as she peered around, that she might have been the most dangerous person in the parish. She knew all about Father Maier. About Franz Messner, about Franka. About Giovanni and Dr. Wyhnal. About this ring of spies now called Cassia.

And now someone Edgar wanted her to meet was coming to find her. She looked around the church as subtly as possible, but there was no sign. No signal. No familiar face. *No Margit.*

After the Lord's prayer, Kitty lined up for Communion, but did not look Father Maier in the eye. He did not know of her existence as Katrin Handel. Could not. Instead of returning to her pew, she made her way down the side aisle when she suddenly halted near the back.

Margit, blond waves carefully coifed, that familiar nose and blue eyes, was watching her near the back of the church.

Edgar's sister's eyes widened and she quickly snatched up her purse. Kitty strode out before Margit could reach her. She expected to hear the big wooden door slam shut behind her.

Instead, it was Edgar's sister calling after her in a hushed, urgent tone. "Wait! Fräulein Handel? Excuse me, *please!*"

Margit knew her operative name?

Bewildered, Kitty stopped in her tracks and slowly turned around, her head reeling. Why had Edgar done this? Why had he told Margit about her?

Margit hurried across the paved square. She was thinner. Like everyone these days. Lingering near the entrance was a little boy with sandy brown hair. He was wearing Lederhosen and wool knee-socks.

Edgar's sister stopped, and licked her lips before coming

closer. "Rover wants you to know that if you need it, my door is open."

"*Rover* wants me to know..."

Margit looked down. "*I* want you to know."

"Is that your son?" Kitty asked, nodding to the boy. "Jerzy's?"

Margit's face flushed. "Andreas is my cousin. My aunt is now a ward of the hospital in Linz. He has nobody else."

Kitty stared at her. Had Edgar not told her about the boy, she'd believe this story. But the boy had Jerzy's broad forehead, the bright blue eyes. His dimples, however, were just like Edgar's, a Ragatz trait.

"I'm sorry," Kitty said. "I'm just... Why are you...?"

"Will you come to the penthouse? I'm living there now."

Kitty bit her lip. Her home—with Edgar—in Vienna was in the third district. The sprawling penthouse on Rennweg was spacious. She hadn't been back since late 1939, never saw it again after being released from the Gestapo headquarters at Hotel Metropole.

"I can't."

Margit deflated. "I had hoped I could be of... I don't know... help?"

"Is that what he told you? That I am supposed to... *let you help*?" Kitty's voice was hoarse with fury.

"He said you would make a final decision."

"How generous," she hissed. This was simply a terrible situation. Motivation! Time and again, she had analyzed a potential candidate's motivation. Loneliness, repentance or something of the sort, was not a good reason to take someone on. What had Edgar been thinking?

Kitty glanced at the boy again, then took Margit's hand and squeezed it hard. With finality.

"Goodbye, Margit. And good luck."

14

MAY 1944

The air raid sirens ripped through the air at the first light of dawn.

Kitty flung herself out of bed, pistol in hand, and pulled back the curtains. The park was empty. Not even Willi was out there. Through the canopy of tree leaves, the pale blue sky was clear—a perfect day for another bombing raid.

She was dressed in a flash, her rucksack containing the things she would need most: her documents, the pistol hidden at the bottom in the lining, some provisions, a canteen of water. Giovanni was in the hallway, waiting for her, a leather draw-string bag slung over his shoulder.

"Are you all right?" she asked.

"I'm fine," Giovanni answered.

"I didn't mean *you*." She pointed at the bag.

Sirko's head poked out, his eyes slanted in a grumpy expression. Giovanni laughed drily and took Kitty's arm, pushing her forward. Outside, people were already streaming toward the Gersthof. There was relative calm; people were used to the raids already.

Kitty hurried with Giovanni and the cat across the park,

then lined up in the church square. At first glance, she did not recognize anyone, except for Father Maier, the curator of spies, who was directing people to the cellar.

A small white dog barked wildly behind an iron gate across the courtyard. Kitty stopped. *Macke!* The dog looked almost like Judith's, and for a heartbeat, she wondered what had ever happened to him, or Bella, the woman whom Kitty had entrusted the dog to.

A woman hurried out of the house just then, scolding two children to hurry up—a little girl, and a teenaged boy—and shouted at the Maltese to shut up. The boy protectively scooped the dog into his arms, the mother rolling her eyes.

Opening the gate to them, Kitty offered the little girl her hand. "I'll help you," she said to the harried mother and followed the woman and the boy to the church.

In the stairwell to the cellar, Giovanni was pressed up against the wall, waiting for her. Sirko, his eyes two slits, hissed. The stream of refuge seekers followed the stone steps into the arched basement corridors below. Benches were lined up along the wall and people squeezed onto them, children in their mothers' laps, or on the cold ground with a quickly snatched toy. Here one learned about a child's most prized possession.

The little boy and his dog found a spot up against the next arch, and he sank to the ground, holding the dog tightly against him.

The cellar air was musty, the scent of beeswax candles fighting against the primal stink of fear. As she maneuvered through the press of people, she caught sight of Willi, huddled in his ragged coat.

Further in, Kitty found a group of older women, their faces drawn in resigned suffering. Children huddled around their mothers and a cluster of older men. One little boy was urinating against the wall, quietly sobbing as his mother scolded him. Another youngster's eyes were wide with fright. As Kitty moved along, a mother pulled her sleepy daughter close so Kitty could get by. Someone muttered a curse at the Allied forces.

"Katrin!" Giovanni called ahead of her. "Over here! I found a spot."

Three older women moved over to make some room. Kitty sat down next to Giovanni as he settled Sirko onto his lap. At the sight of Kitty, the tomcat meowed pitifully.

She stroked his head. "Poor Sirko. You're so humiliated."

Giovanni also reached out to pet the cat. His hand stroked Kitty's instead.

It was not clammy this time. It was warm, and dry. But the electric current it sent through her went straight to her chest, and Kitty went rigid with surprise.

She dropped her hand into her lap.

"Are you all right?" Giovanni now scratched Sirko's ears, his eyes watching her.

She could only nod.

"Cat got your tongue?" He chuckled.

"No." She was suddenly conscious of where his body was pressed up against hers: his upper arm, his shoulder, his hip, his thigh. There was no space on the bench to move away from him.

Kitty eased herself off the bench.

Giovanni's gaze followed her. "Your face is flushed. Can I get you some water?"

"I'm fine," Kitty insisted. "I'll be right back." She moved down the cellar, pretended to be interested in the mother with the two children, and asked the boy if she could pet his white, shaking dog.

"Fipsi," the boy said when Kitty asked its name.

She smiled, but was distracted by the effect Giovanni's touch had had on her. She glanced down the corridor. Giovanni was talking to a man across from him. Kitty wondered whether he had felt the current between them, too.

Not much time passed before people began guessing what the Allies were targeting this time. Father Maier was making his way through the press of people. She followed him back to her bench, where the priest stopped and addressed Giovanni by name.

He peered at Kitty then. "I have seen you in church. I wanted to introduce myself the other week, but you left in quite a hurry."

"I'm sorry. I should have... I had things to do." She offered her hand. "Fräulein Handel. Katrin."

"Sunday is a day of rest," Father Maier said, shaking it. He reached over and patted Sirko next, who closed his eyes with a conflicted demeanor of suspicion and pleasure. "Herr Ricci, for Sirko's protection, you should pray to St. Gertrude."

Kitty flinched. Gertrude Larsson was her Christian name, the name she'd used when she'd introduced herself to Father Maier when Edgar first brought her to the church. She held her breath, not daring to react in any way.

Giovanni looked puzzled. "St. Gertrude?"

Father Maier's eyes took in Kitty, a gesture of conspiracy or to politely include her in the conversation, she could not tell. "St. Gertrude is the patron saint of cats."

"Is that so?" Giovanni asked. He looked at Kitty. "Did you know that?"

She shook her head. She really hadn't, and she was now speechless for a whole different reason. Giovanni had no idea who she was, but Father Maier?

The priest lightly touched her shoulder. "How delightful, no? We discover something new every day. Or *someone* new. Welcome to the neighborhood, Fräulein Handel. If you need anything, you know where to find me." He grinned and stretched his hands over him to indicate the cellar.

He then stepped over to the other side and was immediately in conversation with the next group of people.

Giovanni rose, holding Sirko against him. "I know it's a tight squeeze. Please, sit."

Kitty shook her head. She was too distracted. Instead she stood next to Giovanni against the exposed brick wall. Father Maier's comment about St. Gertrude was not casual conversation, not a coincidence. Either he knew from Messner, or he recognized her, and if *he* recognized her, then what would happen if she ever met the Gestapo chief in an interrogation room?

When Father Maier turned back, a group of children had gathered around him, begging for him to play some game Kitty did not know. He smiled at them, his hand touching their heads but stopped in front of Kitty.

He started to say something but suddenly, there were tremors. The earth shuddered beneath Kitty's feet. Father Maier held protective arms out around the group of children and made a joke about God's rollercoaster. Another rumble of thunder rolled beneath them. Everyone shifted, as if expecting the hard-packed earth to open up and swallow them.

Giovanni grasped her hand. Instead of shock, she felt something else. Warmth. Comfort. She wanted this and yet she did not dare look at him.

Then there was a different sound. Not rolling thunder, but rapid, stuttered explosions.

"The anti-aircraft guns," Giovanni muttered. His head was near hers, and she trembled.

"There's an oil refinery in Floridsdorf!" a man called out knowingly.

Some accepted his explanation.

"The damned Allies," someone cried.

A few feet down the tunnel, Willi suddenly croaked, "Damn Hitler to hell!" He pushed himself off his bench and shook a fist. "Damn your Führer!"

The corridor went quiet. Kitty slipped her hand out of

Giovanni's and looked about, interested in the reaction. Father Maier, his eyes steady on hers, smiled slowly. Despite the seriousness of the situation, an absurd need to laugh bubbled within her.

And then she had to. Kitty laughed into her hand but tears sprang to her eyes. She stared at Giovanni. She was not laughing about the Hitler comment. She was laughing at how she missed the feel of her hand in his.

Unsmiling, Giovanni stood before her and drew her to him, one arm around her shoulder in solidarity, in comfort. In protection. Kitty's body began dissolving beneath his touch. This time, when she looked at him, she knew that he felt it, too.

Before she could pull away, the older man cried out again, "It was Floridsdorf! Probably the oil refinery."

The people muttered among themselves, secure in the growing knowledge that the bombs had at least not hit their neighborhood.

To Kitty's relief, Giovanni moved away to help a woman with a screaming baby.

Father Maier suddenly stood before Kitty. "Do not worry, Fräulein Handel." He tapped his nose. "Only God knows. Only *God* knows."

And he moved on down the line, echoing the all-clear signal that was coming from voices in the stairwell above. The people began herding each other upwards, to the sun.

Giovanni, securing Sirko back onto his shoulder, flashed her a crooked smile. "Only God knows what?"

Kitty shook her head and shrugged, confounded by the effect Giovanni had had on her, and confused by the multiple meanings she could read into Father Maier's one phrase.

Only God knows.

. . .

Even though she was arriving an hour late to work, when Kitty stepped into the building of the Semperit headquarters, it was ghostly quiet.

Not even the receptionist was at her desk. Police sirens and firefighting sirens seeped through the doors and windows. One of the Semperit board members came through the front entrance. On the way up the stairs, he quickly told Kitty that the air raid had not only hit—indeed—the oil refinery in Floridsdorf but also several factories in the new industrial sectors to the south.

"Any of ours?" Kitty worried.

He shook his head solemnly, and without apology disappeared up the stairs.

She was just reaching the second floor when she caught sight of a familiar plaid skirt and the bony ankles of Frau Dr. Beck. She was holding a stack of files against her, one eyebrow cocked as Kitty reached the landing.

"You missed the meeting," she complained.

"Meeting?" Then it dawned on Kitty. "The Alberich tiles. Your report to the board. That was today."

"Yes, it was today."

"I wasn't the only one." She mentioned the board member who'd dashed ahead of her. "I was caught in the air raid."

"That was in Floridsdorf," Stella said flatly. "We're in the first district."

"All right." Kitty said sharply. The woman who'd been to Vienna many, many, many times obviously had no idea that the Cottage District was near enough to Floridsdorf to warrant an air raid warning.

She was about to move past her but Stella blocked the way.

"Because of those air raids, by the way," the woman said tersely, "the meeting with our partners has been moved to Budapest. Dr. Messner wants the production of the rubber tiles to also be moved to Budapest. I have set everything up here for absolutely nothing."

She stared at Kitty. What did the woman want her to do? Convince Messner to *not* move production to Budapest? Or just whine about it?

"Thank you," Kitty said. "I'll go see Dr. Messner about it."

"I offered to go along." Stella was plaintive as she finally stepped off to the side. "But the Herr Direktor apparently believes you are more qualified to join him on the trip."

Kitty finally got around her. "I'm sure that the Herr Direktor has his reasons."

Messner was in the office, looking out the window, the telephone pressed to his ear. He turned at Kitty's knock and, when she entered, finished the call quickly, waving for her to shut the office door. He then propped himself on two fists against his desk.

"Franka rang me," he said.

"I'm sorry I wasn't here," she said.

"My wife said you were in the church."

Kitty balked. She hadn't even noticed Franka there. There had been so many people in the cellar. What had Franka seen, though? Kitty's face grew warm at the thought of Giovanni and his touches.

But Messner broke into her thoughts and asked her to take a seat. "I received a cable yesterday," he said and looked at her as if she should know what he meant. "From Dogwood."

Leonard! Kitty went ramrod straight. Her handler in Istanbul had finally come through! "The radio?"

Messner nodded. "In Budapest. Today's air raid gave me a good reason to move the meeting and get Frau Dr. Beck's hands off this project."

"That's why," Kitty muttered. "I met her on my way in. She feels she should be the one who goes with you..."

"You now know why she cannot." He lowered his voice. "Budapest's best developers are..."

Jews.

"So, what are the instructions?" Kitty whispered.

"Frau Dr. Böhm will take over the production of the tiles there."

Kitty recalled the name of the woman who ran the Budapest plant. "And sabotage the glue mixture?" she whispered.

Messner nodded, and Kitty caught a regretful gleam in the Herr Direktor's eye. He was proud of turning the company around after he'd taken over Semperit. Now he was purposely creating defects in Semperit products. But they were finally getting the radio. The only outstanding task was to vet the forger, and then she would have everything she needed to complete Operation Redbird. She could let the OSS know they were ready to receive agents into Austria. And she could get out. She was going on eight weeks since she'd arrived. And feeling lucky—perhaps too lucky.

"When do we leave?" she asked.

"Friday. We'll take the early train in and return on the late afternoon train back. Is that all right with you?"

"Of course."

"There is one more thing," Messner said. "Semperit has been asked to prepare a tender for Steyr-Daimler-Puch out of Linz. The call came from Georg Meindl directly."

Kitty's eyes widened, and she recalled the Austrian that had met with Masterson and Cicero in Istanbul. "For what?"

"Aircraft wheels and ball bearing seals."

Kitty nearly laughed. "You got them, didn't you? You got them to give us the tender?"

Messner winked. "I'll need you to work with Frau Dr. Beck on the technical details, please. Supervise the final process."

"She is not going to be happy to see me," Kitty said tersely. "She already feels undermined."

"Then make sure she feels important again." Messner waved a pen at her. "And I look forward to some interesting dinners with Herr Meindl."

Kitty nodded. "Right. I'll distract her. I'll be ready for this Friday morning, too."

She would have to meet with Giovanni that night to coordinate how she would pass the radio on to him. He would then have to deliver it to Dr. Wyhnal and take the other two parts to the hiding places in their building.

The thought of seeing him again made her head reel as she shut her office door.

"Get a hold of yourself," she muttered, then brushed her hands briskly over her hips, as if to free herself of the memory of how his body had felt against hers.

15

MAY 1944

It was drizzling when Kitty and Messner arrived in Budapest. The company car waited for them outside the station. Kitty stepped onto the sideboards to avoid the puddle and made room for Messner on the back bench. She set the brown leather satchel containing Stella Beck's prototypes between them.

The driver soon swished through Budapest's rainy streets past baroque and neoclassical buildings and boarded-up shops.

Kitty eyed the familiar graffiti on the buildings. The Nazi enthusiasts had gone to work, leaving their mark.

One nation! One blood! One Führer! All Jews out!

"It won't be long," Messner mumbled next to her. "Hungarians will get their marching orders next."

Kitty looked down at her lap and said drily, "And the administration will round up Jews yesterday."

Messner grunted and shifted in the seat, then turned to the rain-spattered window.

They did not speak as the automobile inched through the streets. Kitty noted that Budapest was crawling with Wehrmacht. The reason they were moving so slowly was soon clear. A tank rolled by, its turret turning lazily as if trying to get its bearings. There was a checkpoint set up along the street. Next, came a convoy of trucks filled with soldiers bouncing in the back, hunched against the wet weather.

Kitty glanced knowingly at Messner and he shrugged. She looked back out. She was here to pick up the radio and then head back to Vienna with their dangerous cargo. Khan had sent a coded message to inform them he was prepared to deliver the radio himself, but Messner had refused to let him come up now that Abwehr agents were stringently patrolling Budapest.

Juniper will be delivering, was Khan's coded response.

Juniper was Gedeon.

Kitty was not surprised—and also not overly pleased—that it was the big Hungarian she would be meeting. Khan's instructions were for Kitty to meet Gedeon near the Great Market Hall, at a café, where he would transfer the equipment to her.

When the car pulled up to the Semperit offices, the driver opened the door for her and Kitty followed him to the entrance beneath the umbrella, then waited for Messner. A dark-haired woman in a red blazer met them in the foyer. She was shorter than Kitty with black hair rolled and pinned back. She had large gray eyes, exuded intelligence and a brusque manner. Kitty guessed her to be in her early forties.

After warmly greeting Messner, the woman turned to Kitty and said in a thick Hungarian accent, "Frau Dr. Gina Böhm. Pleased to meet you. Welcome to Semperit Budapest."

"Thank you. I'm Katrin Handel, Dr. Messner's assistant."

Gina ushered the two of them up a broad concrete staircase. The walls were painted in a pale mint green. At the end of the hallway, a door stood open, revealing a long, dark table. The conference room.

Several men in gray and brown suits mingled just outside. Kitty's shoe suddenly snagged on something and she stumbled.

The block heel she had wiggled loose earlier for this very scenario twisted off.

Gina assessed the situation quickly before bending down and whispering to Kitty with concern. "Do you have another pair of shoes with you?"

"I don't," Kitty said irritably. "We're not staying the night."

Messner turned and faced them, annoyance spreading across his face. "We're going to be late."

Kitty looked pleadingly at Gina. "I could quickly go to a market. Unless shoes are rationed here?"

"No, the market is a good idea," Gina said. "Or I can have my secretary go out for them."

Messner waved at Kitty dismissively. "Go, Fräulein Handel, and return right away. Frau Dr. Böhm, would you be so kind and send your secretary in for my purposes?"

"Of course, Herr Direktor."

Gina looked up at Kitty. "The driver. He can take you to the Great Market Hall. It's not far away."

Kitty feigned embarrassment and promised to be back as soon as she could, then handed the leather satchel of prototypes to her. "Please. Would you see that these are set up for the meeting?"

She found the driver smoking outside. He agreed to take her and she left him on the outskirts of the Great Hall. She found the shoe shop Messner had told her she would find, went inside and bought a new pair at an outrageous price. She then headed into the main hall, where the voices of hawkers and buyers collided in the high roof above.

Outside, Kitty scanned the area across the road, and recognized the small park Messner had told her she would find. The gray-blue Danube was like a steel slab beyond. Café Habsburg was near the entrance to the park. Kitty spotted Gedeon right away, a cigarette between his fingers, his other hand busy mopping his brow. But there was no sign of any case or container that might hold the radio.

The terrace was covered, and customers were lounging in the seats with blankets over their laps in the chilly, spring air. Gedeon was at the table in the middle row at the end of the terrace. The table behind his had a *reserved* card. Kitty removed it, placed it on the next table and took a seat, her back to the big Hungarian's.

"Juniper," she muttered stiffly. "How are you?"

"Delighted to see you, Dahlia."

The waiter came, frowned at the reserved card she'd moved, and looked down his nose at her.

"Coffee," she said. "Black. Please."

She waited until he'd gone before muttering to Gedeon behind her. "I thought I was supposed to pick something up."

"There's been a change of plans."

She did not like changes in plans. At all.

"Your napkin," Gedeon mumbled.

Kitty lifted the corner of her napkin. Underneath was a small key on a metal ring. She pocketed it quickly. There was also a slip of paper with numbers and letters printed on it. She slipped that into her pocket as well.

"What's the ticket?"

"Claim check," Gedeon said. "Herr Szergey. *Szergey*. Got that?"

"Yes."

"He's at the baggage inspection at the train station. The case will have all the necessary custom stamps and seals for you to carry it onto the train to Vienna. The key is for the case."

She heard a wet sucking sound. He was poking around in his mouth again.

"I thought it would be easier that way," he said. A cup clanged against its saucer. "There are guards and police patrolling nearly every street corner and having great fun stopping anyone for any reason at all."

"Is this Szergey to be trusted?"

"Do you want the thing, or not?" Gedeon grumbled. "Or did you want to carry it across town and past a dozen checkpoints?"

The waiter returned with the ersatz coffee and Kitty dropped coins into his hand.

Her mind was ticking away the possibilities of everything that could go wrong. But Cassia really needed that radio.

"A thank you would be nice," Gedeon muttered.

"Thank you," Kitty said noncommittally. She blew on her coffee, took a gulp and scowled.

"Don't drink the coffee," Gedeon said.

She looked over her shoulder. The Hungarian tossed his napkin on top of the table. He was wearing the gold and black onyx ring. When he pushed back his chair, he nearly crashed into her. Gedeon turned his head, his gold tooth gleaming. "It's real crap, the coffee."

He smacked his mouth again, held her gaze and nodded. With a satisfied grunt, he added, "Very good to see you again. You be careful now. Good luck. You'll need it."

He stood up, lit a cigarette, dropped the match into the ashtray on his table and left.

With the claim check and the key in her coat pocket, Kitty also made her escape. She just managed to watch him cross the road to the Great Market Hall.

Good luck to you, too, Gedeon.

Kitty returned to the market, stepped back into the shoe shop, left it again, dove into a side alley, and waited around corners to see if anyone was following her. When she was certain it was safe, she backtracked to the waiting driver and car and instructed him to return her to the Semperit office. She checked the rearview mirror several times but was confident they were not being followed.

Upon her return, Kitty waited in the hallway until there was a lull in the meeting. Quietly, she took her seat and waited for Messner's cues. One glance from him and she let him know with a nod that she had at least made contact. But whether the radio was at the station—whether this Herr Szergey was there—whether she would actually get her hands on the case containing Cassia's most prized possession...

That was a question left unanswered for the next several hours.

On both sides of the conference table, Frau Dr. Beck's miniature submarine prototypes were being handled by the production managers. Kitty smirked to herself. Stella would be delighted about how these men—all Jews—were both admiring and criticizing her work.

The meeting ended promptly at half past two, at which point Messner strode over to her.

Kitty told him she did not have the radio. That they would have to pick it up at the train station.

Messner's blue eyes flashed dangerously. "How do you feel about this?"

Kitty shrugged. "Unsure..."

"Do we have any choice but to try?" he asked with quiet resignation.

Kitty said no, and made way for two men who were looking to speak to Messner. She went to Gina and requested one of the model submarines to return to Vienna, which Kitty promptly stuffed into the leather satchel where she also stored her broken shoes. Gina then handed her two metal pots of glue.

"Take these to your R&D in Vienna. I am sure they will find they are perfectly all right." Gina winked at her.

The adhesives. Stella would find nothing wrong with them. But Gina would see to it that plenty went wrong when those submarines got underwater.

Messner and Kitty left the building right after, and took the car back to the main train station.

"Maybe it's better this way," Messner said quietly as they entered the station. "At least we didn't have to carry the case across town."

That had been Gedeon's excuse, too. Kitty turned to him, took a breath, and then said it. "I think we should take the later train."

Messner's head tilted left then right. "Are you sure? What about your...?"

He was referring to Giovanni, who—having convinced his father to let him borrow the restaurant's Volkswagen—would be waiting for her and the case, which they would smuggle to the convalescent home.

"I think we should take the later train," she said again, with more conviction this time.

"All right. We'll take the later train."

The driver returned them to the train station as planned, but Messner—the claim ticket now in his possession—split away from her once inside. Kitty backtracked to the entrance and then crossed the road, where she ordered a bowl of soup at a little pub. When she had paid, she went back inside the station.

Kitty found the baggage claim easily. As Messner had requested, she approached the claims desk first. From the corner of her eye, she saw her boss in the waiting area, reading a paper, or so it appeared.

She pretended to read a poster on the wall next to the claims desk. When an older freckled man with curly red hair beneath his cap appeared, Kitty squinted at his name tag. *Szergey.*

She turned and walked away, passing behind Messner. "That's him."

Messner turned the page, folded the paper and stood up.

She stopped at a souvenir shop and rifled through the postcards in a rack while watching Messner stride over to the baggage inspection desk. He had to wait for Herr Szergey to serve two other people before it was his turn. Messner slipped him the claim number. Szergey looked down at it. Kitty's heart lurched in her chest, but the red-headed man turned around, and disappeared.

Kitty scanned the station for any suspicious people hurrying toward Messner. Instead, Szergey returned with a light brown case. A normal-looking suitcase. Even from where she was standing, she could see the seals and the paperwork attached to the handle and over the lid. Her pulse thrummed at the base of her throat.

Messner grasped the handle, turned around and carried the case to the platform. Scanning for anyone who might be rushing toward him, Kitty was relieved when nothing happened. She rejoined him, the brown leather satchel in her hand, just as their train steamed in.

The platform was busy. This was the last train to Vienna and would bring them back to the city shortly before curfew. They stood next to one another and Kitty glanced down at the case between them. It was sealed. Stamped by the controller's approval. Leonard and Gedeon had made this all work.

Their train came to a halt, steam rising all around them. Kitty and Messner made room for the passengers to disembark. They were just about to climb into the carriage, when Kitty saw a flash of gray and black plaid. Descending from the carriage next to theirs was Frau Dr. Stella Beck.

The woman mirrored Kitty's own surprise.

"What a coincidence," Stella said distractedly. "I thought you two would be on your way back to Vienna by now."

Messner was frowning sternly but his face was pale. "Frau Doktor?"

Stella straightened her hat. "Günter has leave this weekend. We're meeting in Budapest." She gazed at Messner with those amber cat eyes. "It was one of the reasons I wanted to go to Budapest with you."

"To meet your husband," Messner said slowly.

Stella adjusted her purse over her forearm. "You can't blame a woman for trying to get the expenses partially paid."

Her eyes darted to the bag Messner clutched, then to Kitty's satchel. She bared those straight white teeth. "How was the meeting? It went late, I see. Looks like you have a lot of work for me."

"Good, fine," Kitty blurted. "Herr Direktor, we need to get on board."

Stella eyed the light brown case once more. "Enjoy your weekend."

Messner finally got a full sentence out. "See you on Monday, Dr. Beck. Enjoy your weekend, too."

She flipped her hand in the Nazi salute. "Heil Hitler!"

Messner hurriedly returned the salute and boarded the train.

Kitty got into the carriage, and studied the platform. But Stella had disappeared.

Messner's frown deepened. "What a coincidence," he muttered again.

Kitty shook her head, searching for a sign of Stella through the window once more. "I don't believe in coincidences," she muttered back. *Not like this, anyway*.

"Her husband," Messner huffed. Then very quietly, he said, "You must miss yours..."

Kitty was startled by the remark. "How do you mean?"

He tipped his head a little. "He's a very good man. I've

known him a long time. A very long time. I was very happy for him when he met you."

Kitty flushed at the remark, then looked out the window again. Wouldn't Stella's husband have met her at the station after so long a while?

She returned her attention to Messner and whispered, "I need to get a message to Dogwood."

He frowned, his eyes flitting to the case above her head. The question was clear. *Why go over Leonard in Istanbul?*

But she shook her head. It might take days—weeks even—before she could get the radio running now. "The old way. Have Dogwood look up the husband."

Messner's brow furrowed ever deeper. "Frau Dr. Beck's—?"

"Günter. First Panzer Division." Kitty took in a deep breath before she said, "Better safe than sorry."

And the radio was not going to Giovanni as she had planned. She needed a backup. She returned to her old mantra from the SOE days. *Just in case.*

16

MAY 1944

"There's a change in our plans," Kitty muttered to Messner. He was holding out her coat for her. Outside the carriage window, the platform materialized as the train pulled into Vienna's central station. She'd had enough time to think things through.

"*Another* change?" Messner blocked the carriage door.

"You'll just have to trust me. Take the satchel."

But her boss did not budge. "I want to know—"

"Please," Kitty stressed. "I have a bad feeling, and I haven't been able to shake it off. Frau Dr. Beck showing up in Budapest might spell trouble."

Messner mulled this over as passengers bumped through the narrow corridor to the exit doors. He finally took the satchel from her and moved out of the carriage before descending onto the platform. Kitty picked up the case. She might as well have been carrying a ticking time bomb.

The first thing she saw was that Giovanni was positioned just as she had instructed. He was wearing a trilby, the rim shadowing his face. They were hours late and he had waited. Her chest constricted. He was near the doors leading to the station. He pushed back the trilby on his head, his anticipation crackling in the air.

Messner strode with her, shoulder-to-shoulder, her leather satchel tightly in his grasp. At the last moment, Kitty veered right, and Messner followed her through the station. She risked one glance at Giovanni and saw his confusion, but he turned away. On the opposite end, he also walked toward the exits that led to the main thoroughfare. They were well guarded by patrols.

"Leave me now," Kitty muttered to Messner. "If anything happens, please let Rover know."

"No," he said. "Let me go first."

There was no time to argue. From the corner of her eye, she saw Giovanni waiting. A guard beckoned him, and Giovanni withdrew his documents.

Messner stepped up to the checkpoint where Wehrmacht and police were checking identity papers and searching baggage. Kitty lingered near the seating area and pretended to adjust her shoe buckle. Messner placed the brown satchel onto the table.

Messner has plenty of reasons to be traveling outside the Reich.

Then there are even more reasons to check him more thoroughly.

The Wehrmacht guard read Messner's documents. A policeman then asked Messner to open the satchel.

Kitty's heart raced. The official rummaged through the bag, looked up at Messner, and waved for him to close it.

There was no escape. If they made her crack the seal on the case, she was done for. Her entire trip to Vienna would come to an end. She buttoned up her coat, her fingers shaking. She pressed the bottom of her ribcage, took in a couple of deep breaths and withdrew her documents from her purse.

Then, clutching the handle of the radio case, Kitty

approached a table at the middle of the entrance, and placed it flat onto the table. She turned it to the inspector, handle first, her expression blank.

Kitty presented her forged documents, then her stamped documents from the customs clerk in Budapest. Her heart thudded in her ears. She forced herself to breathe regularly and to keep calm.

The official was in his fifties, with a furrowed brow and gray eyes. He glanced at her identity papers, then at the bag, checked the seals and the tag on the handle. She dropped her eyes to the floor and pushed her glasses up her nose.

"What's inside?"

Kitty did not answer. Instead, she handed him the official order from the Reich for the Alberich tiles. He flipped through the sheets, then clicked a salute to her.

"Heil Hitler!"

Kitty raised her hand, and passed by him.

On the other side, she received her identity booklet back and the case.

Kitty grasped the handle and strode out onto the street, the back of her knees tingling, threatening to fail her. Wehrmacht and police officials were only the gatekeepers. Behind them lingered the Gestapo or the Abwehr. One signal from the former and the latter—the secret police or the counterintelligence unit—would be on her tail. She wondered whether she should have said something instead of remaining mute.

Her heart lurched at the sight of Giovanni at the newspaper stand. She shook her head ever so subtly, and strode past him to the tram station. He had to understand now that he was not to receive the radio.

When the next tram passed her by, she ducked away and slipped through the back streets. Her heart was galloping and she was breathless. Secret police or Giovanni could not be following where she had to go now because the only other place she could think of—the only other place close enough—was the penthouse in Rennweg. If Margit was obliging.

Kitty waited until a fiacre passed by, the horse clopping along at a lazy gait. Then she crossed the road and walked down Rennweg to her old home.

She came to a halt as she reached the park. Two enormous flak towers, anti-aircraft guns jutting out, were now positioned on either end of the green. Kitty shook her head. They were awful. Godawful ugly. She crossed the street and met the doorman in the lobby. He buzzed up to Margit, then led Kitty to the elevator.

Edgar's sister was dressed for bed. Her hair was wrapped in curls, and she pulled a robe tight around her. It was Kitty's old robe. She stared at it and Margit hesitated.

"Katrin. Katrin Handel," Kitty reminded her.

Margit stepped away from the door. "Come in." She eyed the case, and Kitty jerked her head toward the sitting room.

"May I?"

"Of course." Margit moved aside.

Before Kitty could slip into the other room, a ball of energy bounded down the hallway. "Tante Margit. Where are you going? You were reading me a story."

At the sight of Kitty, the boy came to a halt. In his hands were toy soldiers.

"You remember my cousin," Margit said. Her face was contorted by the silent plea.

"Of course," Kitty smiled uncertainly. The child did not even know that Margit was his mother. "Hello, Andreas."

"Pleasure to meet you," he said solemnly, his dimples wavering uncertainly. She stroked the sandy brown hair. He had to be about four years old.

He eyed the case. "Are you staying with us?"

She shook her head. "No. I just—"

"Fräulein Handel is on her way home." Margit was quicker. "She's just stopped by to visit. And you, *mein Junge*, were on your way to bed."

The boy groaned and melted against the console, but eventually parted, saying a polite good night to Kitty.

"I'll be right back," Margit said. She took up his hand and accompanied him to the furthest bedroom.

With Andreas and Margit gone, Kitty carried the radio case into the sitting room. Everything was essentially the same. There were a few photos of her and Edgar, but most of them were gone, including the collage of photos in the study. This was how it was now: their marriage had vanished from the surface.

Back in the sitting room, she found that the furniture was the same. Kitty remembered Edgar in the armchair the day she'd returned from the Vienna Woods and he'd thought she'd left him. That was the night she'd discovered Margit was having an affair with their butler.

With a heavy heart, Kitty also recalled the many fights she and Edgar had had in this room. The stony silences and unspoken accusations. When she put the case onto the coffee table, she pictured the way she'd cradled her husband's head on the floor after he'd voted for the Anschluss. The broken glass, the pain... The cracks and faults of their marriage appeared very fast after the Nazis took control of the country.

How they had managed to hang on to the pieces for so long was nothing short of a miracle. But in the end that was all they had. Pieces. Sharp, painful pieces. The war had done that to them, and they were doing their best with what they had left. But some days it did not seem enough. The war was winning— not the Allies, not the Nazis—the *war*. And it was the war that had thrust her at Giovanni Ricci. She could not figure out how or why, but her attraction to him was undeniable.

The guilt weighed on her and Kitty leaned against the back of the sofa.

With resignation, she wondered whether this was how it had been for Edgar and that woman from Paris. With disgust, Kitty recalled Millie's claim about the need to mate in the face of danger. Maybe that was all it had been?

Margit appeared again and Kitty straightened.

"I apologize about Andreas," Edgar's sister said hurriedly.

"Heavens, no. There's nothing to apologize for. I should apologize to you for barging in like this." She paused. "He's sweet. But... why *Tante*? Surely, you must tell him the truth."

Margit slumped against the sideboard. "It was my mother. She sent me to Linz, to my aunt."

"The one with the fits," Kitty said.

"It was my mother," Margit said again. "She invented the entire story. How my aunt's fits led someone to take advantage of her at the sanatorium. How I'd gone up there to care for her. How my aunt was no longer able to take care of herself"— Margit scoffed—"That part was true. And so, I would be returning with my cousin in tow. My four-year-old cousin."

Kitty was suddenly struck by it all. Margit's motivation to help ran deep. It was pure. It was viable. And completely relatable. Dorothea Ragatz had done to Margit what MI6, the SOE and the OSS had done to Kitty time and again: tried to recreate her, reshape her. Make her lie. And here they were. Recreated. Reshaped. And lying.

It was also the second time Kitty was struck by the changes in Margit. It wasn't only the lines in her face, the faded color of her hair, the sharper cheekbones. These were the physical signs of Margit's disappointments and heartbreak, her grief. Kitty also recognized the shift Edgar's sister had made in her convictions. She wore an air of defiance. And it was strong enough that Edgar had decided to trust her with their secret.

Margit folded her arms and jutted her chin toward the case. "What is that?"

Kitty steeled herself. "I need you to keep this safe for a little while for me."

Margit pointed at it. "If you want me to hide it, I have a right to know what it is."

"It's a radio."

At least she believed it was. Margit made a noise and waved for her to open it.

Kitty fished out the key Gedeon had provided her. She broke the seal and cracked open the case. There was clothing inside. Women's. An array of things including toiletries. Kitty's heart dropped. Had they been fooled? Had they the wrong case? But at the lining, Kitty found the latch which revealed the hidden compartment. And the radio. A one-man transmitter-receiver, light, compact and durable. There were three parts: the power supply, the transmitter and the receiver.

Margit made a noise next to her as Kitty sighed, relieved to find that all the parts were there. They would need an antenna. She could get an antenna, or Giovanni could fashion one.

She gazed at Margit then, unsure what to expect.

"You can trust me, Katrin," Margit said measuredly. "I'll put it away. Edgar told me where I could hide... these sorts of things. And you, if need be."

Kitty balked. "Me?"

Margit shrugged and wrapped her arms around herself. "How long should I keep it?"

"I'm not going to put you into any danger. I need a little time. Give me three or five days at the most."

Margit nodded.

Kitty packed up the case, and handed it to her. With too many questions surrounding Stella Beck's appearance in Budapest, Giovanni would have to arrange hiding places in Nussdorf after all.

. . .

Just before curfew, Kitty was back at her apartment in the Cottage District. She stood in the hallway listening to Giovanni playing the cello behind the door. But the music was not what was stopping her. She did not know how to proceed with the man behind that door, with her confusing feelings for him.

Down the corridor, a woman suddenly stepped out of her apartment. Kitty jumped. The neighbor held a baby pressed against her in one arm, threw Kitty a suspicious glance, then set a pot down in the hallway.

Kitty turned and rapped at Giovanni's apartment.

The music stopped. At the sound of his uneven footsteps, her chest tightened.

Giovanni peered at her through a narrow crack. Sirko darted out into the hallway when he opened the door wider, stopped, turned around and wound around her ankles.

She picked the cat up and slipped inside.

"You came," Giovanni said. "You heard the music."

"The music? No. I was coming to you anyway," she said. "What were you playing?"

"Handel. As in Katrin Handel."

Kitty laughed abruptly. "I'm sorry. I—"

"What happened? What did you do?" Before she could answer, he stepped behind her to slip off her coat. "You worried me."

She shivered beneath the soft breath at her neck.

"I had a bad feeling," she said measuredly. She escaped into the sitting room.

"They opened Dr. Messner's bag. I nearly thought you'd both been caught! Should I be worried?"

Kitty faced him and shook her head. He gazed at her expectantly.

"If you say so," he said. Quickly, Giovanni leaned the cello in its place and cleared away the music stand. "Did you *get* it?"

She took up a position between the sofa and the dining table. "The radio is somewhere safe for now." At least she believed so. "I need a little time to make sure that nobody suspects anything, that we're not being followed."

"What makes you think you are?" Giovanni asked.

"I have my reasons."

He stepped around the furniture and in front of her. His concern was plain. His eyes were working again. When he reached for her, she turned away and put the dining table between them.

"I have some news of my own," he said. "My father told me that some big shot in the Nussdorf administration has reserved a *Stammtisch* for his Nazi friends at the restaurant. A table for regular visits on Tuesday nights."

Kitty took in a deep breath. "And? Will you?"

"I think it's perfect. Don't you? And with my father's invitation to take more on at the restaurant? I could listen in."

She cupped her hands over her mouth and nodded. "Yes... That could work. Giovanni, I think we do need to take the radio to Nussdorf. Can we do that? Can you arrange that?"

Giovanni smiled slyly, and went to her. He reached above her head and brushed her hair back.

She withdrew but he put a hand on her arm. Again, her limbs and middle tingled with anticipation.

"I need more than a hiding spot," she stressed. "I need at least three different places where we can operate from. This Gustav—"

"And Stefan," Giovanni reminded her.

"Why aren't they on the front?" She glanced at his ankle. "Not all of you got shots of turpentine into your joints, surely."

Giovanni sniffed. "Stefan was on the front, and lost three fingers on his right hand for it. His father suffered a stroke shortly after. Stefan returned to Nussdorf to take care of his father. And Gustav, he took over his father's farm. It's the way he's avoiding getting conscripted."

Kitty narrowed her eyes. "And they'll accept a woman giving them orders?"

"They will *love* you." Giovanni laughed, shook his head then tucked the hair behind his ears.

She recognized that flash in his eye. How many times had she seen that flash in a man's eye?

He dropped his voice and moved close to her again. "None of us support this regime, and if those two have the opportunity to do something against the Nazis, they will be the first to drop down and kiss your feet. After me, that is."

Kitty backed away and around the furniture. "All right," she finally said. Her face was hot. "When? When should we go there?"

"My parents close the restaurant on Sundays and Wednesdays. We can go this Sunday."

Again, he moved to her. Close now. He had not shaven. He looked down at her hands and took them in his. Slowly he pulled her to him. Now his forehead rested on hers. Kitty held her breath.

"Katrin..."

"No. You shouldn't."

Giovanni withdrew from her. He spun toward the tiny kitchen. "Wine? I have a bottle of red from the restaurant. I was going to heat up some soup. You should stay. Eat."

Kitty took her purse from the table, draped the coat over her arm. "Sunday then. We'll do it then? Go to Nussdorf, that is," she called to his back.

Giovanni returned with the wine and two glasses in hand. He frowned at her then the coat, the purse, and took in a breath.

"Sunday is the best day," he finally said. "My father visits my aunt and uncle for lunch on Sundays. Italians. Lunch lasts all afternoon." He shifted on his feet, seemed to have gathered his courage. "Stay."

Sirko rubbed against Kitty. She picked him up, held him against her for a moment before letting him go. "I can't, Giovanni."

"Are you sure, Katrin?"

She nodded. "Have a good night. Be careful."

She hurried to the hall. In the mirror in her apartment, she caught the reflection of how her skin had flushed. She bit her lip and rolled her eyes heavenwards.

If he had kissed her, she would have liked it so much she would never have left him that night.

17

MAY 1944

On Sunday morning, Kitty was back at the penthouse in Rennweg. With very few words, Margit let her in, removed the case from hiding and handed it over to Kitty. It was repacked with Kitty's old clothing, which she'd left behind in the apartment some six years earlier.

Kitty stepped out onto the narrow balcony, satisfied at the sight of the potted red geraniums.

"Keep guard," Kitty told her. "If you feel you are being followed, I want you to put the pot to the left of the balcony. Do you understand? Your left when you're looking out on the street. Not when I'm looking up."

Margit nodded.

"Give me a couple of days. I'll make my way back here and check."

"And what if I am being watched? What if I am being followed?" Margit's blue eyes were wide but her tone was measured.

"I'll figure that out if the time comes."

"Edgar?"

"No." Kitty put a hand up. "He's not involved this time. Not at all."

Margit pursed her lips, and nodded. "*Klar.* I understand."

Again, Kitty had to admire her sister-in-law. She suddenly understood Edgar's motivation. Margit had nobody left. Nobody. Kitty pecked her cheek and grasped her shoulders.

"I promise you, if all goes well, I will be the only one who knows you are on our side. All right? *Nobody* else in my circuit will know that."

"All right."

Kitty smiled at her sadly. "You're my safe house."

Margit's eyes watered and she kissed Kitty's cheeks again, then pressed the button to call the elevator.

Kitty took the bus to Nussdorf and followed Giovanni's instructions to his father's restaurant.

It was a yellow house on a rise, the vineyard and fields behind it rolled all the way to the blue horizon. There was a wooden fence around a small flowerbed that, besides peonies, and roses, and lavender, contained a spiral of fresh herbs. The restaurant was also a small operating farm and was therefore allowed to sustain the family and the restaurant. Though she could not see it from where she stood, Giovanni had told her that they had a vegetable garden, chickens, a cow and a sow.

As promised, the restaurant was closed. And the house—save for Giovanni—empty. He held out a large oval loaf of rye bread.

"I hollowed this out as you asked me to."

Kitty checked it. It would hide the power supply box just fine.

On pins and needles, Kitty followed him up the stairs to the attic, forcing herself to focus on what she had to do now, and not the tension sizzling between them. Together and with few words, they set up the three rectangular parts of the radio in the rounded tower. Kitty plugged the power cord into the adapter, and set the spare parts kit off to the side, containing extra fuses and tubes.

She instructed Giovanni to switch to 220V first, then turn on the radio. It worked. Together, they strung up the wire antenna, and when Giovanni wrapped it over a picture frame, Kitty stopped. It was a photo of two families. Giovanni was small, standing next to a man and woman in dark clothing. There was also a small girl.

"Who's this?"

Giovanni glanced at it, and she recognized pain on his face. "That was Rachel and her family."

Kitty peered at Rachel more closely.

"She's the reason I wanted to pursue music." Giovanni sighed deeply. "She had the most beautiful voice."

Kitty turned to him. "What happened to her?"

"Nineteen forty-two happened to her."

Kitty shook her head sadly. "I lost friends, too."

Giovanni looked up, surprised. "In France?"

Yes, in France, too, Kitty thought. But she nodded and looked at Rachel again. The girl was beautiful. Long, dark, wavy hair, a steady gaze, her head tilted invitingly.

"They were taken away," he said. "Rachel and her parents."

"I'm sorry," Kitty said quietly. "I should have known. I don't know why I felt compelled to ask."

He gently took her arms, brushed his hands to hers, and grasped them. "And you?"

"Friends that were killed. By the Gestapo. By the SA. Murdered. So many scattered. Or turned."

He frowned, and took in a sharp breath. "They betrayed you?"

Kitty looked up, trying to focus, but his body was pressed up against hers. Her middle was magnetized to his. She felt his gaze on her. She could not even look at him, because if she did, she would no longer be in control. He brushed her hair away from her ear and stroked his fingers along her jawline.

"You remind me of her, you know?"

Kitty shook her head and took a step away. "No. I'm not her."

But he took her hand in his again, squeezed it. "Katrin, look at me."

She didn't at first. He repeated it.

"You fight with yourself like she did. Rachel's will always won, like yours does. I know you can't tell me everything about yourself. But I am not confused. You aren't her. I know that."

Kitty lurched from him, trying to still her breathing. "We have to finish up here," she said, but her voice was strained.

He returned to the radio and switched the receiver on. She worked the dials until the bulb was working properly, lighting up with each of her dashes and dots of the Morse code.

"I think you're ready," she said.

But Giovanni was looking at her with that intense gaze again. "I loved her deeply. But I am not confused."

Kitty flushed and glanced at that photo. "I'm so sorry... Do you know where she is?"

He shook his head.

"Is she... alive?"

He shrugged. "I don't know. They took her family, first. She volunteered... Katrin, she gave herself up. I was going to hide her."

"Oh, Giovanni!" Kitty whispered hoarsely. "Where? Where were you going to hide her in that apartment?"

"At the church."

Kitty took in a deep breath and released it. "Of course... That's how it started, didn't it? That's how Father Maier got you involved, isn't it?"

He nodded and she caressed his cheek, but he pulled away and wiped a hand over his face.

"We need to set the bandwidth," he said, returning to work.

Kitty watched him a moment, then nodded and set to fiddling with the frequency and dial settings. She switched to transmission and Giovanni put on the headphones.

Within moments, Giovanni was using her codes to transmit her first message since she'd arrived in Vienna. Both of them were instantly absorbed by their task.

News could travel on the OSS radios as far as one thousand miles. Bern was some six hundred miles away. Istanbul over nine hundred, which was why they would transmit to Bern.

Kitty checked her watch. They had a time window of ten minutes left to send and receive messages. She provided Bern with the code names of her assets. In keeping with the botanical code name of the spy ring, everyone was assigned a flower or a bush.

"Don't jog the receiver when they respond," she reminded him. She bit her nails as they waited.

In the meantime, Kitty pulled the map of Nussdorf to her.

"We're going to have to move the radio on a regular basis," she said. "Show me where Gustav and Stefan are."

Giovanni scooted over to her. His arm brushed up against hers as he pointed out his friends' properties and the two places where the women were prepared to offer a safe house for OSS agents.

"On Gustav's property, there's a shed on the hill here. We could keep the radio in there," he said. His eyes, however, betrayed that he was thinking of something else entirely. Her.

Kitty looked away and back at the map. "Is he trustworthy?"

"Very." He said it as if it disappointed him.

"I don't have time to vet him. I need to know."

"I'm telling you, he's trustworthy." His gaze remained intense when she looked up. Those poet eyes. He wanted to talk to her about what he was feeling. About Rachel. About them.

She pulled away. "OK, but remember, there are no second chances, Giovanni. You tell all of them that. You hear? No second chances. They get paid for each agent that drops in but only if my men move on to safety."

The radio suddenly came to life, the high-pitched frequencies signaling a message was coming through. Giovanni slid the headset back on, then scribbled on the sheet next to him. Kitty was decoding as he wrote. When he was finished writing it down, she completed interpreting the message.

Welcome to the world. Operation Dupont is on standby.

Inform us when you have your base. Your schedule is confirmed.

"Send confirmation of receipt," she ordered.

Giovanni switched back to transmission and they quickly dismantled the radio. They pulled apart the three pieces, hid the transmitter in a cubby within one of the walls, and together pushed a heavy dresser in front of it. Giovanni managed to stick the power supply into the loaf of bread, and wrapped the receiver around his front. He would be wearing a light coat with it hidden beneath.

They left the room, Kitty carrying the light brown case containing only her personal possessions. At the garden gate, they quickly parted ways, but not before Giovanni stroked her hand in passing.

She pulled away, holding it against herself, and did not allow herself to turn around. If she did, he would think that her feelings ran deeper than they did.

Near the train station, Kitty found a street vendor selling pickled vegetables. She bought a jar of cucumbers and found a quiet spot where she could eat. Giovanni had given her a bit of bread and some cheese, and she filled the hole in her stomach.

About an hour later, she wandered up the road toward the sprawling fields and hiked to the shed that Giovanni had pointed out to her on the map. Instead of five people waiting for her, there were only three: Giovanni and the two men.

Kitty braced herself. "Where are the women?" She was referring to the two who were supposed to offer safe houses for her OSS agents in Neustadt.

One of the men kicked the dirt with his foot before stretching a hand to Kitty, his eyes still on the ground. He was short, medium build. He had big hands for his size and brown hair that was so dirty, that the front stood up on its own.

"I'm Gustav," he said quietly. The farmer. "And this is Stefan."

Kitty turned her attention to the second man. He was ginger-blond with a long nose and light eyes. He had a mustache and beard. She reached to shake his hand, but he awkwardly offered his left one while mumbling an apology. And then she remembered. The three fingers on his right hand were missing, which he hid with a clenched fist.

She then looked questioningly over at Giovanni.

"The women want you to know that they are prepared to do everything that needs to be done, but they don't like crowds," Stefan told her.

Giovanni cleared his throat and shyly raised his hand. "I think that's my fault."

Kitty frowned at him. "Why?"

"You warned me about no second chances. I thought it would be better if we weren't all seen here together."

Kitty relented. "Good thinking. When can I meet them then?"

Gustav looked earnest. "Next week. Giovanni will let you know when exactly."

"Do any of you have any weapons?" she asked.

The men looked at one another sheepishly.

"Can I take that as a yes?" she prompted.

"I have two pistols," Stefan said. "From the front."

She nodded. "Gustav?"

He rubbed his chin. "Three."

"Give one to Giovanni," she said. "You keep it somewhere safe but accessible."

Giovanni rubbed his hand over his head and nodded.

Kitty then turned to the matter at hand.

"The safe houses are in Wiener Neustadt," she said. "I need fields where my men can parachute in. Somewhere near the safe houses, but not too near. Woods, where they can hide to get there."

Gustav scratched his head. "There are plenty of fields and woods near the safe houses. We'll give you the coordinates. Stefan here can do that."

Stefan nodded eagerly. "I can do that."

"If you agree," she added, "you three will be my reception committee. I need you ready to take the agents to where they need to go. Get them dressed. Provide them their documents. Make sure they get to safety and swiftly. If there is trouble, I need a backup. Where can my men store emergency items?"

"Stefan's place," Gustav and Giovanni said in unison.

"There is a hidden cellar behind the house," Stefan explained. "If we need to transmit messages, we can do so at the house."

"And the radio?" Kitty asked.

"It will also be there," Stefan said. "And here, in Gustav's shed."

"Each of you are going to have parts of the radio," Kitty said. Giovanni was already removing the loaf of bread from his rucksack and handed it to Stefan. To Gustav, he passed over the last box.

Kitty told them the agreed-upon schedule. "Giovanni will transmit and receive messages from me. I will only come if necessary, to make sure the locals don't suspect me."

"You can count on us," Stefan said.

Gustav nodded, rubbing his hand over his head. "Whatever you need."

She then turned to Giovanni. He tucked his hair behind his ears and waited in anticipation.

"Good," she said to him, tearing away from his gaze. "Thank you. Very glad to meet you, Gustav and Stefan, and very glad to have you. But I'm afraid I have a bus to catch."

She shook the men's hands again.

"I'll walk with you a ways," Giovanni said.

Kitty reluctantly agreed. He limped next to her but she did not slow down, moving a stride or two ahead as they followed the country road.

"That went well, then?" he asked behind her.

"We need to make sure that Stefan and Gustav have documents that they can use in case they need to use the escape line."

"Did you find the forger?"

"That's next. Now that we have the radio, I can focus on that. You'll need papers, too."

"A fake identity? A name?"

"Yes."

Giovanni's hand suddenly slipped into hers and he tugged her to him. Kitty stopped, staring at him and tried to remove her hand but he squeezed it harder, those eyes pleading again.

"Katrin... Whatever your name is."

"Katrin."

"All right. I don't know how to thank you. You have given my life a new purpose."

"Don't thank me. What you are about to do could cost you that life. I would never be able to forgive myself if you..."

Gently, he pulled her the three steps she needed to be against his body. His hands cupped her face, then his lips were on hers. His kiss was like fire and her body ignited, responding with a violent hunger. She moaned, an angry, primitive sound. When he pulled away, his eyes bore into her. She nodded.

He yanked her off onto the side of the road. They were out in the open, on a remote road. Giovanni jumped down. A ditch. He wanted her in a drainage ditch.

Fighting back the reasoning, Kitty scrambled to join him. Her body was humming, vibrating. The ditch was deep, the sides made of rough stone. He held her by the waist and removed her glasses, then pulled her to him. They tugged and pulled at each other's clothes in turn, kissing in between. His hands were on her skin, beneath her blouse, on her breasts. His torso was smooth and taut beneath her hands as he stretched over her body. She wrapped one leg over his hip, felt him against her and gasped. He suddenly swung her around, her back now against the wall. She grabbed the buckle of his trousers but then he fell over her, one hand covering her mouth.

"Shhhh... shhhh... shhh..." he hissed into her ear between breaths. He was watching the road.

He ducked his head, covered hers, crushing her against the rough wall. Above them the click and whirr of bicycles, and then a woman's irritated voice.

"Yes, I'm positive. I *just* saw him."

"Giovanni Ricci?" said an older man's voice.

"Of course, Giovanni Ricci. Long, dark hair. He was right here. With a girl!"

Kitty bit her lip and hid her face in Giovanni's shoulder.

"Well, he isn't here now, is he?"

The voices and the bicycles were fading away as they

headed west. How had she missed them? Where did these two people come from?

Giovanni nuzzled her neck. "It's clear now," he said and moved to kiss her, but the moment was gone. She crashed right back into herself.

Kitty squirmed out from beneath him and snatched up her glasses from the rim of the wall.

"Come with me to the restaurant," he said.

She tugged her skirt down then tucked in her blouse. As she adjusted her wool stockings, she looked up at him.

"It's more private," he insisted.

"No."

Disappointment washed over Giovanni's face. Slowly, he straightened his clothes. "I'm—"

"Don't." She crawled out of the ditch.

"Katrin, wait, I just want to—"

"There is one thing you can do," she interrupted. Her body was still tingling from his touch. What she was about to do was more for her than anything. She reached down and clasped his hand, and helped him out.

When he was standing before her, he looked repentant.

Kitty's heart was racing. "I'm not... I'm not *her*, Giovanni. I'm not Rachel."

"I *know*."

"Your father offered to have you move back to Nussdorf," she said.

Giovanni began to interrupt, but she raised a hand to stop him. "The Americans will soon be here. I need you at that *Stammtisch* listening in when the Nazi administrators gather. You remember everything they say. I'm putting you in charge to make sure everything is ready. You don't need me to send the messages to Bern. You'll report on Wednesdays what you heard on Tuesday nights."

Giovanni was shaking his head. "And you?"

"Move back home, Giovanni." She brushed through her hair with her fingertips and set the glasses back on straight. "It's an order. I have a bus to catch."

She did not wait for his response but, this time, she did turn to look behind her. Just to make sure he was not following her. He was not. Giovanni raised a hand. It was a desolate, lonely gesture.

Facing the road again, she congratulated herself bitterly. It had been a close call. A damned close call. She had *wanted* him. Even in a ditch. But to hell if she was going to let that happen.

Soon, she would help OSS agents land here and when that was done, she would be extracted from Vienna. Then she could clear her head for good, face what was ahead.

She paused on the road. It hurt. It hurt her to know that she had nearly been unable to prevent that tryst with Giovanni. Either way, she suddenly understood Edgar.

As far as she was concerned, they were now even.

On Monday after the trip to Budapest, as Franz Messner boarded the streetcar, Kitty brushed his shoulder before she sat in the seat across the aisle from him.

Messner palmed the forelock of white hair from his forehead and met her gaze, blue eyes darting to the light brown case.

She mouthed, *It's done.*

He returned his attention to the newspaper in his hand but not before Kitty caught the relief sweep over his face. As she watched the passing scenery, she, too, admitted that she was relieved. She'd checked on Margit, and found the geraniums on the right-hand side of the balcony. But it was no time to get comfortable. They were all just getting started, she reminded herself, and the clock was ticking.

Messner and she disembarked and walked together to the office, Messner holding the door open for her.

They both moved swiftly. Messner put the leather satchel onto his desk. She slammed the case next to it. They transferred the documents and files from their meeting in Budapest, the prototype and the two pots of glue from the satchel into the case, and headed out with purposeful strides.

At the R&D department, Kitty knocked on Frau Dr. Beck's door, did not wait, and walked in. Stella looked up, annoyance washing over her face. She was not alone. An engineer straightened from behind Stella's chair where he'd been peering over her shoulder.

"Good morning, Dr. Beck," Kitty said stiffly, before greeting the engineer as well. She placed the light brown case next to the woman's desk, unable to hide a satisfied smile. She'd found a way to explain it.

Stella peered curiously at the case, then at Kitty.

"Dr. Böhm's reports are there, as well as the drafts, production figures, and the Hungarian R&D's feedback. I've also returned one of the prototypes," Kitty announced. "I'll be typing up the minutes from the meeting this morning and should have them done before lunch."

She turned to go, then eyed the engineer and Stella. "How was your visit to Budapest?"

"It was fine, thank you." Stella smiled tersely. She tilted her head to the waiting engineer. "We're in the middle of test analyses."

"Let's do lunch," Kitty said brusquely. "I'll bring you the protocol and we can go from there."

Stella looked about to protest. The engineer shifted and the good Frau Doktor finally took in a deep breath before saying, "Twelve."

"Good," Kitty said. She glanced at the photo on Stella's desk. It was the one with Günter Beck and the two children in it. Until Messner cabled Khan to ask for information about Günter Beck, Kitty was going to keep a close eye on Stella.

On her way back to her office, she kicked herself for not sending a message to Bern about it right away. She would have to try again on Sunday next week. As she pushed into her office, she dreaded the idea of having to face the dejected Giovanni, but she had a job to do.

The more hounds searching for Günter Beck, the better.

PART FOUR

JUNE 6TH–13TH, 1944

Vienna, Austria

18

JUNE 6TH, 1944

On the week of the Corpus Christi holiday—which always fell on a Thursday—Messner strode in after lunch and waved for Kitty to follow him into his office.

"Tell everyone that they can have Friday off," he announced buoyantly. "An extended weekend, and it will be paid. Except for the telephone operators. There should be at least two here to take messages, just as on the weekend."

Kitty was surprised. "That's very generous. What's the occasion?"

Messner smiled broadly at her, then shook her by the shoulders gently. His bright blue eyes were alight as he whispered, "The Allies have landed in Normandy. Father Maier heard it all on the BBC wire."

Kitty cheered hoarsely, then covered her face with her hands. She had to take deep breaths to quell the giddiness.

"Successfully?" she whispered. "Any response from the Germans?"

"Hitler believes it is a feint," Messner whispered back. "There has been no coordinated response up to now. He believed it would happen at Pas-de-Calais. He told everyone it was certainly going to be at Pas-de-Calais."

Kitty shook her head, unbelieving. Pas-de-Calais was on the northern Atlantic coast.

"So, a memorandum for all," Messner said in his normal voice again. "And what will you do with your free time?" He blinked at her, looking ten years younger.

She grinned. "I think I'll be enjoying this glorious weather, Herr Direktor. Maybe plant a few flowers in my window boxes."

Messner tilted his head back in a silent laugh. He understood her reference to recruiting further assets.

The telephone on her desk buzzed. Kitty hurried to answer it.

The operator's voice came through. "I have Herr Direktor Meindl from Steyr-Daimler-Puch on the line for Herr Direktor Messner."

Kitty rose and clutched the phone to her chest. She could imagine the industrialists were jittery if they, too, had heard the news about Normandy.

"Good morning," a man's voice came through the line. She immediately pictured the blurred figure of Meindl in the photos Gedeon had snapped in Istanbul. Meindl had a deep voice, nononsense and impatient as he requested to speak with Messner.

Kitty put him through and Messner picked up on the first ring.

"Georg, what can I do for you?" his voice boomed. "Tonight? I see. Just a moment."

Kitty was ready, and bustled in with his appointment diary. She showed him that his evening was free.

"We could do dinner tonight. At eight." Messner looked at her.

She mouthed, *Nussdorf*.

Messner raised his eyebrows. "Have you ever been to the

Gasthaus Weinberg in Nussdorf? Excellent. Yes, we must go there. You'll be arriving by train? What time?" Messner listened, the phone cradled at his ear.

It was Tuesday. Kitty was gleeful. Giovanni would not only have his Nazi regulars, but Messner would have them as well, right under his nose. She almost wished she could be there herself.

"I will pick you up with the company car at the station," Messner said into the phone.

After he replaced the receiver, Messner returned his attention to Kitty.

"I'll reserve a table for two," she said.

"Four." Messner grinned. "Heinkel and Messerschmitt are also coming."

Kitty sat back, smiling. "This sounds important. Do you know what it's about?"

"It certainly is not going to be about ball bearing seals." He tapped the side of his nose and waggled his eyebrows.

"I'll go type that memorandum," Kitty said. "And make your dinner reservations."

Kitty called the restaurant, but nobody answered. She would try again later. She mentally ticked off her checklist as she rolled a fresh sheet of carbon paper into the typewriter.

Despite suggesting that she would use her time off to work, Kitty decided a weekend off would be an opportunity to rest. She had been working hard to build a base for the OSS agents. She had visited the two women and checked the safe houses. Giovanni had come through with a list of potential assets for her. They were all university students or professors that he'd had contact with. Grateful for the backup, she undertook the massive effort to meet individuals, court them, vet them and coordinate them. It was painstaking work, slow and meticulous, and she had to maintain her routine in the process.

They were all busy in keeping up those appearances on the

outside, while preparing for their clandestine activities. Giovanni, Gustav and Stefan collected and safely stored equipment, weapons, food, blankets, and clothing. Stefan got his hands on a camera to take photos for identity cards. He fashioned a darkroom in the cellar to process them. All she had to do was pick up the identity cards from the forger that evening. If all went well, she would go to Nussdorf tomorrow evening and have Giovanni give Operation Dupont the green light.

She thought of the last time she'd seen him, nearly a week before. He'd had a pained look in those brown eyes. He was taken by her. And she? No matter which way she turned, her attraction to him was real. She waited for the pang of guilt.

But it did not come.

Later, with the copies of the memorandum in hand, she went to the departments and handed them out, then hung some in the common room. As she made her way to the research and development section of the building, Kitty mulled over again the fact that she still had not received word about Günter Beck. Patience was the order of the day but she had put in a follow-up request to Bern.

She knocked on Stella's door and peeked in, waving the memorandum at her. "Good afternoon. Surprise news."

Stella was startled from hanging up her coat.

Kitty stepped inside and handed her the sheet.

"What's this?" She frowned as she read. "This Friday?"

"Yes. And it's paid."

Stella shook her head. "I have lab work to get through. Testing we're doing. I can't take a day off."

Kitty shrugged. "You can come in if you want to, I suppose."

Stella was agitated. "And the Herr Direktor?"

"He's off, I imagine," Kitty said.

"How very disappointing," Stella muttered. "I, for one, will be here."

Kitty shrugged. It was a strange thing to say but then Stella moved to the cabinets and picked up the model of the Alberich submarine.

"We're done with these. Messner has no children. My son already has one. Maybe you know someone who might want it?"

"Certainly," Kitty said, immediately thinking of Margit's Andreas.

"Take it," Stella said. "The only thing my son really wants is his father back. I imagine a lot of children are feeling like that. But who knows, maybe, for a little while yet, we can keep them distracted."

Kitty thanked her and left, mulling the sudden change in Stella. Was she wrong about Frau Dr. Beck? Had Budapest only been a coincidence? Or...? Kitty halted in the middle of the hallway.

Had Stella heard of the Allied landings, and lost heart?

The pavement radiated the late afternoon heat and birds sang their evening song. Kitty crossed the road from the university to Türkenschanz and climbed the hill to the Paulinenwarte. She was alone. She hurried up the staircase and loosened the bricks that served as her dead letter drop. She withdrew a slip of paper. On it was a scribbled sketch of a willow tree. She knew this spot.

From the lookout tower, Kitty took a moment to observe the park. There were quite a few people enjoying the early June sun. This was good. It would make a meeting easier.

Below, a woman was selling strawberries and cherries. They were dear, but when Kitty climbed down the hill, she purchased a small mixed carton. A little boy passed by and gaped at the berries so, Kitty handed him a strawberry and a cherry. His mother scowled impatiently first, then thanked Kitty before pushing ahead with a baby carriage.

She followed the curved walkway past men playing chess, a woman sitting on the bench and soaking up the late afternoon sun. An old couple was playing cards under a tree. Pigeons and turtledoves muttered in the flower beds as they stabbed at morsels and litter. Ravens watched the other birds keenly, strutting about as if they knew of better secrets.

At the pond, the willow was bright green and thick enough that someone could hide among its hanging branches. The man she was looking for was sitting on a bench near the shore. She knew him only as Peter. He had gray hair beneath his hat, and a clean-shaven face. Kitty guessed him to be in his mid or late fifties. He only met her when he had important information to share. Otherwise, they used a dead letter box, and the messages left at the tower. On occasion, a courier would meet Kitty somewhere either outside Semperit or outside her building in the park.

Peter was her bridge to the O5. It was over him that she received news, passed along information, gave instructions and ordered forgeries. She had no idea what his background was, but he gave the impression of being an educated man, perhaps someone influential, though he came and went like a shadow.

While she was several feet away, he slowly stood up. On the back of his bench was a suit jacket. He extracted a paper bag from one of the pockets, and stepped toward the water, where he began tossing breadcrumbs to the ducks and swans.

Kitty stood a little way above him, pretending to watch, and ate a berry.

"Would you like some?" she asked.

He looked at the extended carton. "No, thank you."

She nibbled a second one, relishing the fruit.

Peter then crumpled the bread bag and tucked it under his

arm as he brushed off his hands. The swans and ducks followed him as he took a few steps below her on the shore. He turned his profile to her.

She sneezed twice then opened her purse and retrieved a handkerchief.

"Allergies?" Peter asked quietly.

"Yes. To Nazis," Kitty muttered behind the handkerchief.

Peter grunted, his mouth twitching. "Seems to be contagious these days."

"We have word about this Dr. Caldonazzi," he then said. "His trial has been set for the end of the month."

Dr. Caldonazzi was the doctor Messner had told her had been arrested earlier that year.

"Did he talk?" she asked anxiously.

Peter bent down and tossed a lone breadcrumb onto the water. The ducks scolded, the swans hissed back. "We don't know."

Kitty sighed and wrapped the berries in their paper. "Anything else?"

"On him? No."

"Then on what?"

"Do you know what V-men are?"

"Paid undercover agents." She moved nearer to him. They were talking very quietly. "To infiltrate enemy organizations."

"That is correct. The Gestapo has stockpiled on them. An entire O5 group in Linz was apprehended."

Kitty slung the purse over her arm again, studying the back of Peter's head for a moment, her bottom lip caught between her teeth.

"They pay very good money," he said. "They're not only recruiting the people who are fervent Nazis, they're recruiting V-men who have a lot to lose. The Gestapo has been blackmailing them. It's much, much more dangerous."

Kitty took a few steps away from him and stared across the water. "Then they are getting desperate."

"Everyone in this country is."

A cloud passed over the sun. Peter maneuvered further down the bank, the waterfowl gliding alongside on the water. She returned to the bench, and took a seat. She placed the container of berries next to her purse, and slipped the microfilm beneath the paper.

Peter came back for his jacket. He was behind her.

"Then I need you to check on someone," she whispered. "I put in a request at my office, but have no answer. First Panzer Division, Eastern front. Günter Beck. Leipzig. Dr. Stella Beck. Chemistry. University of Leipzig. I need to know who they are."

Peter stepped around the bench, went to the water and slung the jacket over his shoulder. He took off his hat and wiped his brow. "All right."

He turned sideways again. "It's a shame how people just throw their trash about, isn't it?"

He checked his watch, picked up the carton of berries, and strode away. Kitty turned to the back of the bench. Beneath, lay the crumpled bakery bag.

"Hey!" She called half-heartedly. When Peter did not respond, she waited, then bent down and clutched the paper bag in her hand.

It was heavier than it looked. She opened her purse, watched Peter move up the slope to the street, then dropped the package inside.

She would find identity cards. And, she hoped, ration cards.

Like the ducks and swans, she still had a hole in her stomach to fill.

19

JUNE 7TH, 1944

By Wednesday afternoon, the news of the invasion in Normandy had been spun into a tale of Allied blunder.

Hitler's propaganda machine worked to reassure the *Volk* that the German military had met the enemy and was beating them back. But Kitty pictured the Allied forces not only piling up on Normandy, but forming an arrowhead, its tip directly aimed at Berlin.

Messner did not show up to the office until nearly lunchtime. He strode in with hardly a word of hello and called Kitty in. He had her lock both doors.

"I'd like you to type up my notes based on my meeting with the general directors of Steyr-Daimler-Puch, Heinkel and Messerschmitt yesterday evening. They have offered to make available a production facility in Gusen. They want Semperit to move its assembly of the rubber tires for the airplanes there, and quite possibly the ball bearing seals."

Kitty didn't have time to think, as Messner plowed on.

"I need to prepare the information I have for the board. We'll be meeting first thing Monday morning. As tomorrow and Friday are a holiday, this takes top priority."

He indicated she should step around the desk. "Could you please read these notes? And then you can ask me what you don't understand."

He handed Kitty two sheets of paper with his handwriting.

I will write the questions you need to ask below. Do not comment on anything you read here. Remain neutral.

She glanced up, and he nodded brusquely.

Dr. Wyhnal was picked up for questioning last night.

Kitty stared up at him, suddenly realizing the reason for the extra precautions he was taking. She was relieved that she had not been to the convalescent home at all since she'd received the radio.

Messner waved a hand for her to keep reading.

We don't know why. The Gestapo came in the middle of the night. Fr. Maier informed me this morning. Last night, I was meeting with Georg Meindl. The general directors from Heinkel and Messerschmitt were also with me. Giovanni was not at the restaurant.

Where was he then? He was supposed to be listening in at the table of regulars. She was supposed to go to Nussdorf that afternoon, to give the green light for Operation Dupont. She and the boys in Nussdorf were ready. The ground was ready. But now? With another Cassia member arrested? Her mind was jumbled, but she continued reading.

Meindl and the others have asked me to do two things. First, to add a production facility to Mauthausen's sub camp in Gusen.

Messner stood up, pulled out his seat. She slowly sat down and held the sheet with both hands.

Your first question. Ask me whether I need a map for the board meeting.

"Do you need me to prepare a map for the board of directors?"

Messner nodded, his eyes on her. "Yes, they should see where the production facilities are. And I've drawn up a preliminary budget. Can you read my figures?" He pointed to the next paragraph.

Over a very drunken dinner, the men complained about the conditions in Gusen. Not the conditions for the prisoners but for their foremen and supervisors.

The last fragment was underlined twice. Kitty shook her head angrily.

They have now made arrangements with Knorr to have soup delivered to the POWs to keep them fed, because these prisoners are dying in droves from malnutrition. And from brutality, executions, illnesses.

Next question: What are the numbers here? My answer will give you an idea of the number that die each day.

Kitty cleared her throat. "What are the numbers here, Herr Direktor?"

"Nearly fifty Reichsmarks a day."

That old grief—that horrid helplessness—flared in her. Fifty men died a *day*? She blinked away the tears, her thoughts immediately turning to Big Charlie. "I understand."

The men say they are investing too much money in trying to keep their skilled labor alive. Meindl and Messerschmitt especially. They complained about the brutality of the SS guards at the camp production facilities, that they are killing the inmates the companies trained to do precision work. As Meindl put it, "The SS guards have no regard for our human resources, no regard for the investments we have made in Gusen."

Next question: What are these notes here?

Kitty repeated the question, bracing herself for his answer.

"These are the numbers SDP could deliver in wheel parts and which we are supplying the tires for. If we move our production there, they will make room for our machinery there and can do all the assembly on site. Right now, they are producing rifles and other weapons."

Kitty's eyes widened, her thoughts jumping ahead. *Weapons!* They would have Semperit foremen on site, in Gusen. Access to prisoners. Access to information about what went on in these camps. Access to ways they might sabotage the very goods that were being sent to the Wehrmacht. They could even make defects that would keep planes grounded. She had questions now, but Messner interrupted her.

"I must meet with Frau Dr. Böhm tomorrow on this matter. I'll be heading to Budapest this evening. So much for my long weekend. Franka will join me, however."

He then tapped the paper for her to keep reading.

Meindl and I spoke over a bottle of wine afterwards at his hotel. That is when he made his second request and revealed a secret.

"What are the advantages for moving our production facilities to the sub camp?" Kitty read aloud.

"With the Soviets coming in from the east and the Allies—at some point—likely to land at the northern Atlantic wall..." He rolled his eyes. He was sticking to the Führer's script. "We expect heavier bombing campaigns in our industrial sectors. There is a good argument that the Allies will spare the POW camps when their own soldiers are there. And the cost efficiency, of course, is also advantageous when we do not have to transport our goods to two or three manufactories. It's all there, in *one* location."

He picked up a pencil and began scribbling on a separate sheet of paper. She read his notes further, her heart skipping beats.

Meindl shared with me that he has a grave conflict with the SS. His foremen have reported that the SS are not sending all the shipments to the Wehrmacht. Instead, they are pilfering the very weapons meant for the front! Himmler is building up his own paramilitary operation, because he expects Hitler to fail!

Kitty covered her mouth. "Oh my God," she breathed into her hands. Her next question on the script came, followed by

My answer will tell you how long Himmler has been preparing for this.

"How long do we have until the industrialists need a decision?"

"They would have liked us there *last* fall."

She frowned. Himmler had been building up his private army since... "*Last* fall?"

Messner nodded and pointed to the last paragraph at the top of the second sheet.

Meindl's second request is for me to intervene on all of their behalf regarding the SS. He wants me to meet with August Eigruber, the Gauleiter in Upper Austria.

Eigruber! The name sent a shockwave through Kitty. She recalled the steel magnate from Linz. Edgar's father's friend. August Eigruber had been at her wedding. She had been forced to dance with him. She had *laughed* about his Hitler-styled mustache with Edgar! Kitty read on in horror.

They took their complaints to him, believing that a fellow industrialist would sympathize with them. But Eigruber met them with disdain. All three general directors believe he is siding with the SS because he has great political ambitions himself. But if Semperit is in Gusen, it would change the dynamics. It's no great secret that he has a great deal of respect for me.

Kitty was numb as she read on.

You must inform your office of all of this. I plan to make contact with Istanbul from Budapest. Prepare microfilms for me of everything I give you before you leave today.

She looked up from the paper. Messner opened his left drawer, removed the large crystal ashtray and lighter he kept for visitors and nodded to her. She should do the honors.

"I have one more thing to give you," he said. He went to the window and pulled down the shades.

"That light," he said. "Is very bright."

Kitty held the first page and lit it, carefully lowering it into the ashtray where it burned off. She quickly lit the second sheet. He then set his briefcase on the table and opened it, the sheet he'd written on while she was reading was now beneath it.

From inside the briefcase, he withdrew a dinner napkin. On it, in ink, was an illustration.

Messner spoke normally. "We had a lot of wine last night, so I apologize if some of these notes are unclear. I wonder if you can make this out?"

He put the napkin down in front of her. "You'll want to reconstruct these for the board of directors."

Kitty studied the cloth napkin. *Gusen.* This was a map. The town of St. Georg was labeled in the far-left corner. The Danube river wound its path over the map. Then a square, labeled *the compound*. It contained several rectangles lined up neatly near the far end. All over the cloth, there were labels. One last rectangle at the very back was angled slightly. Arrows pointed to the individual buildings with Messner's handwriting.

SDP. Messerschmitt/Heinkel. Guard tower. Prisoner bunkers. Most brought in daily from Mauthausen. Railroad.

Railroad! A railway led *directly* into the camp! Kitty stared up at him, astonished.

"I tried to make things more clear this morning," Messner said, holding his forelock away with one hand. He straightened and gazed at Kitty, handing her the third sheet he'd been writing on.

Gusen is the only camp that has a rail line. The POWs were preparing stone from the quarries until the Ministry of War ordered a switch to the production of war goods.

Kitty quickly turned the paper and wrote in the margin. *Any weak spots?*

He pointed to the middle of the rail line and wrote beneath her note. *Conductors/SS switch here.*

"A takeover?" Kitty whispered, and looked up at him.

Messner nodded. That was the weak spot, indeed. She pictured saboteurs taking over the train, dressed in SS guard uniforms. The idea was easy. The execution, however, would be exceptionally difficult. And deadly.

Kitty folded the napkin and tucked it into her skirt pocket. She would have to microfilm it and courier it to Peter.

"I think everything is clear," she said in wonder. "I'll get on this right away."

Messner looked grave, however. He took that third sheet of paper with their notes scribbled back and forth and turned it over.

"One more thing, Fräulein Handel," he said quietly. "I want you to please type this up for the board of directors. These are my final conclusions from my meeting."

He handed it to her. She read:

When this is all over, when the worst of our secrets are uncovered and laid bare, we will never be forgiven. Our souls will be blackened for generations. We will pass by memorials for those who died unjustly, but people like me, we will be absorbed into the collective whole and our contributions overshadowed by the horrors we invited into Austria. I am an Austrian. I will automatically be viewed as complicit. History will not be kind to me. I am no hero, Frau Doktor. I don't ever want to be remembered as such. I only want to be remembered as a human being. A good Austrian who did all he could to pull the brakes.

No, she would not type this up for the members of his board. He had to share it with someone, and he had chosen her. In so doing, he'd referred to her as Edgar's wife. She knew that he meant it with only the greatest respect.

Kitty inhaled deeply, and reached across the desk. She placed her hand on his and held his gaze.

"*I* know," she whispered.

Back at her desk, Kitty wrangled with all that she had just learned.

She was going to Nussdorf that evening, and her entire message for the OSS would change. But she could not possibly radio all of the intelligence in. She had to courier parts. Split up the information. Cable Khan with some of it, who would then pass it on to Leonard in Istanbul. She would have to radio the fact that she had important details headed to the office that they would have to piece together. But whether she was going to give the green light now for Bern to go ahead with OSS operatives? That she was still unsure about.

Dr. Wyhnal had been arrested. Dr. Caldonazzi's trial was coming up. It was easy to assume that Caldonazzi had talked, had given his colleague away. But that was not always the case. Maybe Wyhnal's time and luck had simply run out.

And hers? If she wanted a chance of getting out of Vienna before it did, she had to get Operation Dupont going.

As Kitty rolled a fresh piece of carbon paper into the typewriter, Stella Beck popped her head into the room and Kitty nearly jumped out of her own skin.

"Good morning. Is the Herr Direktor in his office?"

Messner had just burned the last sheet of his missives, which meant the air would not be cleared yet. "He's busy. Is there something I can help you with?"

The woman sniffed. "I'll come by later."

"I'll fetch you when he is available."

Stella narrowed her eyes and lifted her chin. "Fine. If that is more convenient."

The woman pushed herself away from the doorjamb and disappeared. After a moment, Kitty stood, checked the hallway, and locked the door. She pulled out a hidden drawer in her desk, took out the miniature camera, spread the napkin out and photographed it in three close-up shots. She would finish up the rest later, but this was most important. She would have to go to the maintenance room in the cellar and process the photos. Copies would go to O5. Messner needed a roll to take with him to Budapest. She had a pen in which he could hide it and he could carry that in his briefcase.

Folding the napkin with the illustration of Gusen's labor camp first, she then tucked it into the drawer with the camera. Hurriedly, Kitty unlocked the door before anyone else decided to drop in. She did not need anyone wondering what was going on between the Herr Direktor and Fräulein Handel that required so much secrecy.

20

JUNE 7TH, 1944

The day flew by, and at five o'clock, Kitty nervously gathered her things. She said goodbye to Messner—so many unspoken words between them that day! She wanted to say he should be careful, and all she could say was, "Have a good trip to Budapest."

The local Nazi government tamped down any news about the Allied landings as rumor only but kept up the outrage about the RAF's continued reconnaissance flights over the city. It was as if Germany could not recall that they had started the conflict, and then stuck their head in the sand to avoid the growing truth: they were no longer set to win.

As tempting as it was to celebrate the Allied forces' progress, Kitty knew they were all far from danger. Cassia and the O5 were nowhere near finished, and they were sitting on a ticking time bomb. Those who knew the truth—the High Command, the Abwehr, down to the Gestapo and the local police—also knew their jobs were now reaching a fever pitch.

Kitty planned to go to the apartment—she thought of it as only her hideout, not a home. She had to finish photographing the intel she had, store the microfilm, have supper, and catch the bus to Nussdorf. The boys expected her at around eight o'clock. They would assemble the radio, gather news, and take the few moments they needed to send the core of Messner's intelligence. And there was Operation Dupont. It was with Messner's guidance later that day that she came to the conclusion she had to give it the green light.

"The coast will *never* be clear," he said to her, as they bent close to one another over her desk. "They all know what the risks are. You have to trust your assets that they are prepared to receive and plant your agents. You have done all you can to make the best of it."

On her way out the door, Kitty spotted the submarine prototype on the cabinet and packed it into a bag. Who knew? Maybe she would have a chance to deliver it to the building on Rennweg, and leave it there for Andreas. She hurried to the ground floor and waved goodbye to two of the salesmen as she walked out and onto the corner. She looked left and right, and then crossed the street where she would make a beeline across the green then to her stop.

Before she had gone a few feet a woman's voice called behind her.

"Fräulein? Wait, please!"

Kitty spun around at the familiar voice. *Margit!* She was wearing large octagonal-shaped sunglasses and a brimmed hat. Andreas was with her. Why was she at Semperit?

Margit had two bags with her. Andreas was clinging to her side. She had not called Kitty by her name. By any name at all, in fact.

"How can I help you?" Kitty asked cautiously.

The little boy scooted behind Margit.

"Could you please..." Margit started. "Could you please tell me the time?"

Kitty tipped her head. "It's just after five o'clock."

"We're looking for the best way to get to the train station

from here. I'm afraid this young man needed to release some energy, but we got distracted and now I'm not quite sure—"

"Where are you going?" Kitty eyed the two travel cases.

"The Vienna Woods. For the long weekend. Could you maybe show me the way?"

Kitty looked around her first but kept up the theater Margit had started. "I'm heading in the opposite direction, but there is a tram station up ahead that will get you to the main train station."

Margit smiled weakly, and told Andreas to follow her.

"What is it?" Kitty muttered after she offered to take one of the cases.

"The penthouse," Margit said under her breath. "Will be empty. I've set a pot of geraniums out—"

Kitty's step faltered. "Left or right?"

"It's not about that."

She halted at the opposite end of the park. "Then?"

Margit drew up to Kitty's side. "If they are on the right side this evening, he's waiting for you."

She stared down at Margit. *Edgar!*

Margit looked behind her. Andreas had found some rocks that he was examining. "He's arriving tonight."

"When?"

"Seven."

"Damn it," Kitty muttered. She had to get to Nussdorf by eight.

Margit gently touched her arm. "If it helps, he said it's up to you. But..."

"But?"

Margit shrugged. "That's all he said. 'But.'"

Kitty's tram was drawing up, the bell clanging for her attention. She pointed to the adjacent street. "You'll catch your streetcar there." She then gave the second case back to Margit and reached into her sack. She removed the submarine, and held it out to Andreas. "Would you like this?"

"Wow," Andreas said with wonder. He took it into both hands, turning it over. "For me?"

Kitty glanced at Margit. "Thank you. Stay safe."

She got onto the streetcar, and then bent down to watch Margit and Andreas hurry across the road. Andreas slipped his hand in Margit's, the submarine bobbing and waving in his other as they hurried to the next stop. Kitty took in a deep breath, her insides roiling like mad at the thought of Edgar waiting for her at the penthouse on Rennweg. And cursed him for his timing.

Shortly after seven, Kitty was leaning against the lamppost just across the road from the penthouse. The sky was turning a dusky blue. She'd seen no movement behind the lace curtains on the top floor. The potted geraniums were on the right side of the balcony. Three of them, like three exclamation marks.

Come!!!

As the church bells started ringing seven, Kitty gritted her teeth and crossed the street, her heart beating wildly in anticipation and fear. She was being cautious although Margit had given her no reason to believe this was a trap. *Just in case.*

In the foyer, Kitty requested the concierge to ring the penthouse.

"Herr Dr. Ragatz," he said into the phone. "Fräulein Katrin Handel is here to see you."

The man led her to the elevator, inserted the key and closed the gate behind her. It jerked and started, and Kitty, her heart pounding, stepped out on the top floor.

Edgar appeared wearing a dress shirt, the top two buttons undone, and a gray blazer. He smiled at her, his eyes melting, and with it, Kitty's resolve. She stepped out and he shut the gate with a final clang.

"Hello," he said in English.

"Hello." Her smile wavered.

They stepped into each other's embrace, their arms tightly about each other. Her heart hammering, she turned her head so that her cheek rested on his lapel and pressed her palms against his shoulders, reveling in the familiar smell and feel of him. For several moments, they stood together like that.

"I was wondering whether you would come," he finally said. "I've been on tenterhooks since I boarded my flight."

She pulled away, and brushed a hand over his face. When he made to kiss her, she did not resist. But when he became more urgent, it reminded her. It reminded her of that ditch.

Kitty pulled away, one hand pressed up against his heart. A gesture of apology. A gesture of guilt.

"I have half an hour," she said, and moved behind him, toward the sitting room. "Where did you come from?"

On the dining table, Edgar had lain out a cold supper for two, including a bottle of wine. He intended for her to stay.

"I was in Salzburg."

She frowned and turned to him. "What were you doing there?"

"Austria's Foreign Minister and Chancellor Hitler are meeting there. I was at the preliminary meeting, but because of the holiday, I made my excuses and skipped the evening."

"Don't you think you'll miss something?"

Edgar grinned wryly. "You forget that I am a most effective delegator."

Kitty smiled back. "I have not forgotten."

"But," he raised a finger. "This might entertain you. Hitler slept in yesterday and nobody in the High Command had the balls to wake him with the bad news."

"Of the Allied landings?" She was astounded. "They let him sleep through it?"

Edgar grinned and rubbed a hand over his head. "Nobody wanted to contradict the Führer. He doesn't believe this is *it*. That's what he told the foreign minister, too."

She waited, expectant.

"The Nazis will never recover what they lost on the Eastern Front last winter. The end is very near."

"That is what we hope for, no? What you all promised me..."

He nodded. "You said you only have half an hour. Where do you have to be?"

She looked at him pointedly but did not answer.

He raised his eyebrows. "I see. I'm interrupting."

"I'm sorry," Kitty said. She went to him again, kissed him. Let him hold her. The touch of him, the solidness of him beneath her hands, suddenly made her realize how desperately lonely for him she was.

"What about you?" She sighed. "Why are you here?"

Edgar eased gently away and led her to the sofa. "Because it's time."

She did not sit. "Time for what?"

"As of tomorrow, I will..." He opened his hands and rubbed his fingers up into the air before opening his hands.

Disappear. She shivered.

He sat down and pulled her down with him. In Bern he'd warned her that he would be assigned to a mission that could either be the end for the regime, or the end of Edgar.

"Must you?" she whispered. "If we're so close to an end, is it necessary to take even greater risks?"

He squeezed her hand. She had the sensation that he required an extra amount of effort to speak.

"You told me you didn't want to know anything. And I can't

tell you anything. But I need to be as far from the German Foreign Ministry as possible when it's over."

"So, you're about to do something that is going to expose you once and for all and get you killed, is that it?" She laughed drily and wiped her mouth. "I feel like we're locked on a bus, careening toward a cliff. And we've grown used to it because we've been headed that way for so long. If that bus came to a stop, if you had the chance to get off, would you?"

Edgar frowned. "I don't know what you mean."

"You can't get off," Kitty whispered hoarsely. "Because facing what's outside that bus—a normal life, *normal!*—is more terrifying than just careening off the cliff." She stabbed at her chest with her finger. "I know that feeling. I feel better when I am *in* it! When I don't have time to think."

"When you only have to function," Edgar said.

"Yes!"

He pursed his lips. "I know."

"The thought of the war ending, Edgar? That black hole in front of you when you ask yourself, what will we do then? Isn't that terrifying?"

She stared at him, and he sat back on the sofa, examining her. After a moment, he said, "I am not out to get myself killed, Kitty. I don't see a black hole. I see a very busy future of rebuilding this country. Of rebuilding a life. With you."

It was too much. The whole day was too much. She could hardly juggle all the things she had to do that very evening, much less think about what would happen after the war.

"You're giving me a headache."

Edgar clicked his tongue. "Kitty..."

She should explain herself. "When was the last time we thought about nothing when we woke up in the morning?"

"Which is why I asked you to come here, to come home, here. And it's why I'm here in Vienna."

She swept her arms around the room. "I don't have happy

memories from here, Edgar. If you plan to return, then you have to stop thinking of me in your future."

He looked down at his hands. "I'm sorry to hear that."

"This is where it all started for me," Kitty cried. "This entire nightmare."

"And you can't imagine facing it head on? Rebuilding Vienna into what you wanted it to be?"

She dropped her head.

He leaned forward and took her hand. "Then you must go." He leaned toward her, his hands caressing her face, her neck, her shoulders, as he sighed again and again, like someone mustering up the courage for the next step. "Then you must go," Edgar said. "Then go."

He stood up, taking her hand. His Adam's apple bobbed and he tipped his head to the hallway. She swiped at the tears. He meant to send her away now.

Instead, he led her to the console and opened a drawer, then scratched at the top of it. Kitty watched as he removed two photos. A headshot of Margit. One of Andreas.

"Please, do one favor for me," Edgar said. "Get them the papers they will need to leave the country. In case... in case it comes to light who I really am—what I've been doing—they need to be far from Vienna."

Kitty grabbed his arm. "Germany will fall, Edgar. Sooner or later. Must you?"

He kissed the top of her head. "This operation was partially my idea. I am going to see it through."

He stroked her face and tried to smile but he looked heart-broken. His hand was suddenly on her waist. "Stay with me tonight. Or come back when you do whatever you have to do. But come back to me. For just tonight."

She put her hand on his, the one around her waist. "This might be the last time I see you. Is that what you are saying?"

He nodded ever so slightly. "I'm not going to let them get me, Kitty."

She understood what he meant. They all had access to L-pills. To weapons.

She shook her head and rubbed her hands over her face. "OK, OK," she repeated and loosened herself from him. She turned in the hallway as if searching for an escape. "OK."

"Margit and Andreas. Can you?"

"Yes. When? And where should I send them?"

Edgar's face fell. Like her, he was struggling to hold himself together. He hadn't thought that far, yet. Kitty touched his hand.

"What can I do?"

"Watch the newspapers. You'll know, Kitty. You'll know whether we've succeeded or not. In a few weeks, a month at most. If we don't, you'll know. And then I need you to please have an escape plan for them."

Kitty nodded. "I know someone in Graz. I'll at least get them that far."

His face crumpled again. "West would be better."

Kitty closed her eyes. "I'm not that far, yet. What about Salzburg?"

He nodded then shook his head. "I'm running out of time. Graz it is."

"All right."

"What about you?" Edgar asked gently. "Are you managing?"

Kitty looked up at the ceiling, keeping the tears from spilling. "No." She paused. "Yes? Maybe?"

"Is there something *I* can help you with?"

She put her hands on her waist, leaned forward, and groaned softly. "It's one reason I came. It's one reason..." She straightened and bit her lip. "I've learned some very important news, Edgar. And I've got a whole list of things I need to deal with. And I should go. To deal with them."

"I can help." He took a step toward her. "Let me help."

They worked alone. They were supposed to work alone. But they never really had, had they? Never. Not really.

Kitty finally relented and began with her most immediate need. She had to greenlight Operation Dupont. She looked meaningfully at him. "I need to communicate a message. It's time for me, as well."

Edgar snatched her hand. "I can help you with that. I have the means... What time?"

"I should be with my crew at eight. We send out at twenty after."

"We'll do it. We'll do it together. Kitty. Stay tonight."

She stepped to him, searched his face, the lines, the dimples, the aqua sea of his eyes. She stroked the patches of gray hair above his ears. He allowed her to familiarize herself with him again.

Finally, she kissed him, the ache for him so great that it burst. Relief followed. Relief at having him here, now.

"Does this mean you'll accept my help?" he asked before withdrawing from her.

She pulled him back to her, put her arms around his neck. This had to be what a last meal before one's sentence felt like.

Into his ear, she whispered, "I'll stay for supper. And dessert."

21

JUNE 7TH–JUNE 8TH, 1944

After dinner, Edgar took Kitty down into the cellar of the apartment building and showed her a room that she had never known about. In it, was a trove of pilfered espionage tools, police taps, and bugs, and all sorts of equipment locked behind a heavy, steel door. He also had a radio. Not an OSS model, but a clunkier British one that would have been too difficult to transport and hide for her.

Kitty tapped out the message on her own, not exposing Edgar to her codes. Bern came back with questions as to where she was and why she was sending the message herself.

"What should I tell them?" she asked Edgar.

"Tell them you're with Rover. They should let your people know you're safe if your messages cross."

She'd widened her eyes but he shrugged.

"Shoot first, ask questions later," she muttered under her breath. She also let the OSS know that another Cassia member had been detained and that she was waiting for information about the Becks. Bern came back with no further news but message received.

When she was finished, she helped Edgar dismantle the

radio and hide the antenna, then decided to ask him for one more thing.

"There is a woman. Frau Dr. Stella Beck. R&D at Semperit Vienna. She's a pretty big fan of the Führer. Deutsche Mädels, certificates and medals, kids, and supposedly a husband on the front. She was also recommended directly from someone at the Ministry of War and Armaments."

Edgar's eyebrows shot up his forehead. "And? You think she's been planted."

Kitty nodded. "When Dr. Messner and I were in Budapest, we ran into her in the train station on the way back to Vienna. She was coming. We were going."

She motioned with her hand as if carrying a case and looked pointedly at him.

Edgar's expression went dark. "She saw it?"

"More like she appeared to be looking for it," Kitty said.

"If you suspect her in any way, then..." Her husband drew a finger across his throat.

Kitty recoiled. "Without orders?"

"What did you whisper back there?" Edgar pointed to the hidden room. "Shoot first...?"

He took her shoulders. "Or you can wait. But I don't think the result is going to be much different. This is a war, Kitty. It's either her or you. And if you don't think you can do it, find someone who can."

"Have you?" she asked. "Have you ever killed someone with the slightest suspicion they might be on to you?"

He took in a breath and looked away. "I never gave them the time to suspect me."

Kitty stepped into his view and searched his face. She'd known. There was no way that her husband had gotten this far without having had to kill someone.

She had expected she would get an executive order, a kill

order for Dr. Stella Beck. He'd only confirmed for her what she already knew. Yet, what if everyone was wrong?

The next morning, when Kitty stirred next to Edgar—in her old bed, in his arms, pressed up against his nakedness—she squeezed her eyes with pleasure. And then she shot up, filled with panic.

Edgar stirred, looked at her.

"I'm not prepared."

"For what?"

But her heart was racing. What she meant was, she was not prepared to career off the metaphorical cliff. She wanted off the bus. But how should either of them escape when neither was in the driver's seat?

"Kitty?"

She got out of bed and Edgar watched her. Neither reached for the other, yet once again, she was welded to her husband. It was not just their deeds, it was their thoughts, their *way* of thinking. And she realized the massive loss she faced if he did not succeed.

She would not be able to bear it if he didn't make it.

"I have to go," she said.

"Don't say anything," Edgar said. "Save it for when we meet again."

She looked up at the ceiling and took in a shaky breath.

No goodbye then. Not this time. It was too final.

Corpus Christi was the day of processions and celebrations. Church bells usually rang all through the city, but as Kitty made her way to Nussdorf, the atmosphere was subdued.

Edgar had pulled her old bicycle out of the cellar the night before, and she was grateful for the mobility. She would explain nothing to the boys. She would simply say that she had been delayed. Her aim now was to make sure the first OSS agents landed safely, got integrated and were operating. Then she would ask for her extraction orders and wait for news about Edgar.

A light rain had fallen in the night and the air was cool. In Nussdorf, Kitty climbed the steep road leading to the church. In the case of her not showing up as planned, she was normally to go to Gustav's, who would then inform Giovanni that she had arrived. But today, the entire town was likely involved in the Corpus Christi services and procession. She would try her chances there.

She pushed past the brewery, then the pink baroque villa where, Giovanni had told her, he and Rachel had performed their last concert together. Branches with green and red ribbons adorned the doorways she passed.

Kitty leaned her bicycle on the cemetery wall just before the churchyard and peeked around the gate. There was a large rectangular square where four altars had been set up. Riflemen from the local veterans' guard were already milling about, waiting for the procession to stream outdoors.

Kitty lingered outside. Two rows of altar boys appeared in the doorway. They were dressed in white surplices and red capes, the priest between them, wearing red and gold. The riflemen lined up in a straight row. The parishioners began appearing, and it was Gustav Kitty spotted first, and he her.

As the priest headed for the first altar, Gustav hurried over to her. "Giovanni and Stefan are inside, but they're coming."

"I can't stay," she whispered.

"Go to Stefan's. We'll meet you there."

Kitty nodded and slid away back to her bicycle.

In the cellar, Kitty lit the oil lamp and turned the knob for it to burn brighter. Everything was in order. She knew where Stefan hid the chemicals for the photos, knew where they stored the provisions and their radio, but she did not touch anything. This was Stefan's territory.

It took the boys nearly an hour, but when Stefan lifted the cellar door Kitty blinked up at the sudden sunlight. Stefan came down the steep stairs first, followed by Gustav. Giovanni landed on the dirt floor last, and grasped her upper arm.

"What happened to you last night?" he asked angrily.

"Everything is fine." Kitty pulled away from him.

She faced the other two. She had to lie or there would be questions about how she'd gotten access to another radio.

"I was able to cable one of my assets with the green light. The operation is under way. We'll get word when the first agents are to land."

Gustav was testy. "So you got the message out. Good to hear."

"It's the least I could do," Kitty said. "Start with the good news, that is."

Stefan folded his arms and leaned against a wooden shelving unit. It wobbled behind him, but he reached out and steadied it. "So what's the bad news?"

Giovanni narrowed his eyes.

Kitty gave it to them. "Our friend from the convalescent home has been taken in for questioning."

Giovanni dropped his head. "Damn it. That's two then, isn't it?"

Gustav kicked the dirt.

"That we know of," Stefan said.

Giovanni linked his hands behind his head. "Do we know why?"

She shook her head. "And I don't know anyone who can tell me. Nobody who is on the inside." She looked at Stefan. "What about you? Do you know someone in the Wehrmacht? Someone who might have access to the police? We need information."

Stefan sighed. "Let me think about it. I might."

Kitty turned to Giovanni. "Where were you on Tuesday?"

Giovanni blinked rapidly. "Tuesday? This Tuesday? I was... I was running errands."

She put her hands on her hips.

"For the restaurant." He shrugged. "And Stefan needed medication for his father. I had to go to the pharmacy."

Stefan scratched his neck. "That was Tuesday?"

Giovanni nodded. "But, Katrin? What does this mean for us? What's going on?"

Kitty took in a deep breath. "I don't know. Did you transmit or receive anything from here. You were here last night, right?"

"Yes." Giovanni went to a shelf in the cellar, unscrewed a jar of dried barley, stuck his hand in and gave her a slip.

Kitty brought it closer to the lamp. She began transcribing the code and goosebumps rose on her arms.

No on the First Panzer Division. Norway, yes. But not Eastern Front. Found a GB from Braunschweig, killed in an air raid in 1942. Awaiting further intel. Caution!

"*Scheiße*," she hissed. She swore again and again as she crumpled the paper and paced the cellar.

The men shifted out of her way except Giovanni, who stepped in front of her, hands out to stop her.

"When did you get this?" she demanded.

"Last night."

"What time?" She had radioed Bern last night as well, but there had been no response to her inquiry.

Giovanni shrugged. "I don't know. The regular time?"

She grabbed his collar. "What time, Giovanni? Exactly?"

Stefan frowned and stepped forward. "Hey. Hey, what's going on here?"

"Eight twenty-four," Giovanni cried. He wrenched himself from her. "What is wrong with you?"

Kitty paced in circles in the cramped space. Eight twenty-four. She and Edgar had transmitted some minutes later. Had they crossed wires? Had Bern not responded because they had already sent the message to Giovanni? Because they didn't *have* the "further intel" yet?

She looked over Giovanni's shoulder. Gustav and Stefan were nervous and rightfully so. "Gustav, I know you have a farm, but you need to initiate the escape line. Stefan, your father. Is there any way you can take him somewhere else?"

Stefan shook his head. "No. I'll take my chances."

Kitty stamped her foot, and sighed. "Do you have enough L-pills?"

"For both of us," Stefan said gravely. "Katrin." He was now trying the soothing approach. "Can you please tell us what is happening?"

But she snatched Giovanni and dragged him to the far corner of the cellar.

"Katrin?" He was scared.

She was trying to think clearly, gripping his arm. He tensed beneath her hold, but he was not fighting her.

She decided. "There's something I have to take care of. I need you to stay here, in Nussdorf. Keep your eyes, peeled, though. Promise me. I'm going to need your help."

She had to find Dr. Messner. She had to tell him about Stella, the extreme danger they might be in. But Messner and Franka were in Budapest. She could try to reach him at the Semperit offices, or she would have to wait until Sunday and intercept him somehow. She had no idea whether Stella knew about them in Nussdorf, but that did not matter right now. Even if she did, Kitty was going to make sure the Gestapo found nothing.

"Gustav, pack up the radio," she ordered. "Take all the parts with you and find a new hiding spot."

"*All* of them?"

"Yes," she said. "Put them somewhere where none of us knows about it."

Now all three were unnerved, but Stefan was already pulling out the receiver from its hiding spot.

"The power pack is with me," Giovanni said. "But why?"

She turned to Stefan. "Take everything that could be considered evidence of clandestine work. Move it. Don't tell any of us where it is, until I say so. As of now, you are all operating on your own. The only person you answer to is me. And if Giovanni needs the radio, give him the radio."

She looked at Giovanni, whose arms were wrapped tightly around his midriff. She couldn't use him without telling him what she had in mind.

"You're coming with me," she said and started the climb to the top of the cellar.

"Katrin!" Giovanni called behind her. "Wait! Would you —*verdammt nochmal!*—tell me what is going on?"

"I suspect a mole," Kitty said when she was above ground. She whirled to him.

"Here? One of us? Is that why—"

Kitty grimaced, and squeezed her head. The pressure was causing searing pain.

"Anything is possible," she snapped. "But I am pretty certain I know who it is."

She looked up at him, still in pain.

He took a few steps away from her. "You suspect one of us?" he asked tonelessly.

"Right now, I suspect everyone!"

"Is it possible you're overreacting?" he hissed.

"Yes," she said honestly. But she wasn't. Not about Stella.

Relief flooded his face. He reached for her waist, but she placed her hands on his chest.

"What are you planning to do?" he said.

"I need some time. When I'm ready, I need you to drive. I need you to.... I need you to be an accomplice."

His eyes widened. He covered her hands with his. "All right. Yes. I can drive you anywhere you need. I'll help you."

He took her by the wrist and kissed the heel of her palm. But that initial attraction, those initial sparks, that was over. With Edgar, she knew who she was. Giovanni was in love with Katrin Handel, and that was not her. She was Kitty Larsson Ragatz, and that was the person she would have to face when this was all over.

Kitty stepped away. "Giovanni, you and I..."

His chest expanded as if to defend himself from the blow she was about to deliver.

"You don't know me," she said softly.

He looked at the sky, a slow, sad smile growing. When he looked back at her, he was hurt. "Do we ever know anyone?"

"Yes," she said. She touched a hand to his face, then left him.

It was time to get to the bottom of Stella Beck's story. First, Kitty had to find a way to warn Messner. Stella had lied not only about her husband but why she'd been in Budapest on the day they'd picked up the OSS radio.

22

JUNE 8TH, 1944

Kitty's hope was that Messner had changed his plans and was at home. She biked to the villa in Hasenauerstrasse, but at first glance at the empty street, she knew. The Messners were not at home, their vehicle was not there, which meant they had probably driven to Budapest.

She could try to reach the Semperit offices, but it was a public holiday. The post offices were closed, the office in Budapest as well. Either way, she had to pack her things. If the situation was going to take the turn she anticipated, then she would have to go into hiding.

It was late afternoon by the time she returned to her apartment, exhausted and hungry. She needed to get her wits about her and pack everything she would need if she had to run. She reviewed her list for the possible first safe houses, and she needed a plan. A clear route. No checkpoints.

Kitty went into the washroom, bathed, re-dressed, ate what little was left in the ice box, then packed a change of clothing, her hairbrush, a toothbrush, and the sliver of soap. Next, she pulled out a coil of rope she'd found in the cellar, and a kitchen towel to use as a gag. She was not going to "shoot first."

In the lining of her rucksack, she had the OSS 9mm, the L-pills, the pen that could stab someone, the money she had left. All of it. She packed her canteen and provisions, with no idea whether she would have to hide somewhere where she had no access to basic needs.

In the small bathroom mirror, she studied herself. Her eyes were bloodshot. The morning with Edgar seemed ages ago. She went to the bed, shut the curtains, and curled up beneath the blanket.

I never gave them the time to suspect me.

If she was to kill Stella Beck, Kitty would have to draw the woman away somewhere where she could dispose of the body and buy herself enough time to escape. After today, she would be on the run.

Lives were depending on her to get this right. Including her own.

Excited and angry voices outside the window awoke her. Kitty sat up, checked her watch. It was nearly half past six in the evening. She'd been asleep for two hours. She pulled back one of the curtains. Below, in the park, she recognized some of her neighbors speaking animatedly. Willi was on the bench but it was not he who was causing the fuss.

She peeked out into the hallway and padded past Giovanni's empty apartment. A small crowd was gathered at the front of the building. Kitty listened as two women were heatedly discussing with the others. She recognized them from the parish.

"Yes, this morning!" the nearest woman cried. "They dragged him away, right in front of us."

"Four Gestapo," the second woman confirmed. "I saw them come in and ask Hanni where the monsignor was."

Kitty pushed into the crowd, stood next to a man who was listening. "What happened?"

He looked her up and down. "Father Maier," he finally said.

"Hans Steam," a second man said to her.

Kitty's hand flew to her throat. "What about him?"

The woman called Hanni stuck her hands to her hips as she turned to Kitty. "The Gestapo," she said. "Took Hans Steam right out in the middle of procession."

Kitty began to shake.

"Something about a radio," the second woman volunteered. She had a small girl by the hand. "I overheard the Gestapo asking questions about it."

A *radio*? Kitty's chest constricted. Father Maier got reports from the BBC, probably on a normal radio. Had it been detected? Had someone reported him? Did they seize it? Or were they looking for it still?

Head reeling, Kitty thanked them and hurried back to her apartment. Dr. Caldonazzi. Dr. Wyhnal. And now Father Maier, the core of the entire spy ring? Were they talking, these doctors? Had Dr. Wyhnal given up Maier in return for a lesser charge?

Or had the spy ring been infiltrated by a V-man, just as Peter had warned her? Because she could not connect Stella to this group now detained by the Gestapo.

Back in her apartment, Kitty shut her door and leaned against it, panting.

"Wait!" she hissed to herself. What if the Gestapo was looking for a *different* radio? Not one that Father Maier would get the BBC on, but an OSS radio?

Stella!

But how did Stella know anything about Father Maier?

Kitty yanked at her hair. "Think! Think!"

Stella did not know Dr. Caldonazzi, did she? How would

she know Dr. Wyhnal? So who was the common denominator? Or were the two detained doctors really talking under torture?

She had to reach Messner. Now. And she was not even sure whether she was safe. *The noose is tightening*, she thought. Just like it had in France. She was in a trap, had felt and heard the warning of the coil spring.

One wrong move and she would be caught in it.

23

JUNE 9TH, 1944

Early Friday morning, Kitty locked her apartment door, likely for the last time. She wheeled the bicycle out onto the street, slung her rucksack onto her shoulders and pedaled to the first post office.

She asked the operator to connect her to the Semperit offices in Budapest.

"The lines are down," the woman said.

"Pardon me?"

"The lines are down. I cannot connect you to that call."

Ears ringing, Kitty shakily hung up the receiver. She looked around before picking up the phone again but she was not registering much of anything except for the black pins before her eyes. She managed to ask the operator to connect her to the restaurant in Nussdorf.

To her relief, Giovanni picked it up on the third ring.

"Now," Kitty said. "The cafe. Two o'clock. If I'm not there..."

He knew where. And he had to understand that if she was not there, they all had to run.

"Give me half an hour," he said.

Kitty nodded into the phone and hung up then fled to her bicycle. Stella had told her that she would be working that Friday, despite the extended weekend, but if she was going to go through with an executive order, she needed a route that would avoid checkpoints. She needed a place to take Stella to. A place where a dead body would not be found for a long while.

At noon, Kitty mustered up the courage to take the side entrance of the Semperit building. The security guard recognized her immediately.

"You're working as well, today?" he asked in a friendly tone.

Kitty feigned not to know what he might mean. "As well? Who else is here?"

"Frau Dr. Beck. Everyone else took the company's offer, but she is always here. Most Saturdays, too."

Kitty's heart thumped hard. "Is she here now?"

"Got in eight o'clock sharp," he said.

"I'll just be in and out," Kitty said. "Something I need to do for Dr. Messner before his board meeting on Monday."

With goosebumps running over her limbs, Kitty headed up the stairs, unlocked her office and withdrew the pistol from the rucksack. She had purposefully chosen a pair of loose slacks, and put the weapon into the deep pocket. She inhaled, pressed her hand to her ribs, and stared at her reflection in the window facing the road.

When her heart was beating regularly, Kitty turned away and left her office. At the door of the R&D department, she reminded herself that she had the advantage over the German woman.

Stella Beck was not expecting Kitty.

. . .

The door to Stella's office was closed, as usual, but when Kitty tried the doorknob, it gave way. The chemist's office was empty.

Kitty stepped in and glanced at the University of Leipzig diploma as she went to the door of the adjacent laboratory. It stood open, and her heart flipped at the sight of Stella hovering over a whirring machine. She wore safety goggles and a lab coat. The air was thick with the smell of chemicals and rubber.

"Good afternoon," Kitty called, her hand next to her thigh.

Stella jumped. She pulled the goggles over her head.

"Fräulein Handel," she murmured with annoyance. She looked up at the clock. "What are you doing here? Surely you're not here to take me out to lunch!"

Kitty was filled with such relief at the scene that she smiled briefly. "Frau Doktor, you made a joke!"

Stella frowned and turned off the whirring machine, then moved away from her stool.

"I had to come in and prepare something for Dr. Messner's board meeting on Monday."

Stella crossed her arms and tilted her head. "Surely, Dr. Messner let you know that the board meeting has been canceled."

"Pardon?"

"Yes. He won't return from Budapest until Tuesday."

Kitty drew up. "Tuesday?"

Stella arched an eyebrow and reached over the table where she produced two small paint pots. Kitty recognized the glue pots from the Hungarian office. "He's having Budapest do a full analysis on the glue they are using there."

The glue that the factory is making is defective.

Kitty took in a breath. "I did not know."

"No," Stella said acidly. "You wouldn't have known. You were already gone for the long weekend when I *finally* managed to speak to him about it."

Kitty remembered Stella's request to see Messner on the

day he'd told Kitty about his meeting with the industrialists. About August Eigruber, and the SS, and Gusen. But this wasn't about that. This was about the glue.

The weapon was close. She had the upper hand. "Then, I suppose I can return home. How long will you be here?"

Stella sighed, made an impatient flick to the clock. "Until I am done. Would you mind closing the door on your way out?"

Kitty was only too glad to. She backed out, shut the door on the laboratory and retreated. Just before she was to leave however, she looked over her shoulder. The machine was whirring in the laboratory again, but on Stella Beck's desk were the photos of her family, the one with her two children and the mysterious Günter Beck.

Kitty strode over and picked it up. Stella's arm was linked with the man's, his arm pressed up against his middle. Kitty nearly dropped the photo.

On his ring finger, a thick band with a raised dark stone, like onyx. It was identical to the ring Gedeon wore!

24

JUNE 9TH, 1944

Inside the Volkswagen, Kitty and Giovanni were parked opposite the green and across from the Semperit building. They were waiting for Stella Beck. It was after four o'clock, and Kitty had checked the windows. The laboratory lights were burning. Stella was still inside.

"You said she has two children?" Giovanni asked quietly.

Kitty peered through the windshield. "She also said she had a husband on the Eastern Front." In her lap, she was coding a message to Khan in Istanbul.

At the same time as she wrote, she said, "When it's time, I need you to get a cable out with this message."

His brows knitted. "All right."

Stella was a spy, but Kitty was not convinced she was the only one giving up Cassia members. What Kitty did not understand, however, was why hadn't anyone come for *her* yet? It had been weeks since she'd picked up the radio. Surely, if the two of them were working together, then one of the first people Gedeon would give up was *her*.

What were the Gestapo waiting for?

Kitty finished formulating the message and checked it. It

reported that Cassia was compromised, and named Gedeon as a suspected V-man.

She switched to another sheet. "This is for Sunday," she muttered to Giovanni. "Organize the radio with Gustav." In her message to Bern, Kitty called off Operation Dupont and summarized the situation with Dr. Beck and Istanbul.

She was just about to hand it over when Giovanni nudged her and pointed out the window. "Someone's coming."

Kitty groaned softly, blood rushing to her head. "That's her."

Wide-eyed and pale, Giovanni started the motor and steered out into the road.

"Just drive slowly behind her for a moment," Kitty instructed. Her eyes were glued to the no-nonsense gait. Stella was taller, but she was also slighter than Kitty. Before Stella could reach the corner, Kitty threw open her door and jumped onto the curb. She charged for the woman and grabbed her elbow. Stella whirled around.

"Fräulein Handel?" she exclaimed. "What are you—"

But Kitty jabbed the barrel of the 9mm into the woman's ribs and held on tight. "Move, and I'll tell you what I am!"

Kitty caught sight of Giovanni's frightened expression as he watched her shove Stella into the back of the vehicle. He turned around, his eyebrows raised, as he pointed his own weapon at the woman until Kitty got in next to her. She held the gun to the woman's temple and slammed the door shut. Giovanni whipped back around to the steering wheel and pulled out onto the street.

Stella remained still, her face drawn.

He followed the route Kitty had gone over with him to get them to Floridsdorf and avoiding checkpoints.

Rigid, Stella asked, "You're making a big mistake. Where are you taking me?"

"Am I?" Kitty asked. "Where is Günter Beck?"

The woman's eyes narrowed. "Ah."

"Ah," Kitty retorted. "I know who you are. I know what you did."

"You don't know anything," the woman said icily. She glanced to her left.

Giovanni suddenly veered around the corner. "Checkpoint!"

It happened fast. Stella slammed against Kitty, and her elbow came up, smashing into Kitty's nose, but Kitty was faster. She raised her hand and pistol-whipped Stella with the barrel of the gun.

Stella grunted, then slumped over and into Kitty's lap. She was out cold.

Giovanni looked over his shoulder. "*Scheiße!* Did you kill her?"

She checked where the skin on Stella's head had split. There was a trickle of blood, but Stella had a pulse. Groaning from the throbbing pain in her face, Kitty propped Stella up and fumbled for her rucksack.

Giovanni's gaze darted between the road and Kitty in the rearview mirror. She got her bearings.

"Turn right at the end of the road. Immediately after is an abandoned lot. Pull over." She finally found the kitchen towel.

She pressed the towel against her nose. No blood. She pressed it to the woman's head then leaned Stella back towards the window. Kitty had the rope ready when Giovanni pulled into the lot.

The stench of the Danube canal tunnel flooded Kitty's head with awful memories. Of her time with Khan, of finding Artur dead. Her ears were ringing from the pressure in her head as she and Giovanni dragged Stella Beck's body—gagged and tied —to the mouth of the tunnel.

They were both sweating, and covered with dust by the time they'd propped the woman against the cement wall. Panting, Kitty took a drink from her canteen, handed it to Giovanni, who tipped it to his lips, then wiped his mouth with the back of his hand. Kitty went to Stella and slapped her cheeks, then sprinkled some water over her.

Stella groaned but did not come to.

"Are you sure she's the right person?" Giovanni lamented.

"Shut up," Kitty hissed.

"If it is," he cried, "You should shoot her right now."

Kitty reached into the lining of her purse and withdrew the L-pills, shaking the bottle. "I've got a better way. Less blood."

"What are you waiting for?" he asked.

"I'm going to talk to her first."

"She tried to attack you," Giovanni argued. He rubbed his forehead as he paced before Stella's feet.

But Kitty was going to wait. Killing someone was going to complicate her entire mission. She was running through all the things she would need to do. She'd need new identity papers, a new look. She also had to make good on her promise to Edgar and deliver new papers to Margit and Andreas. She looked at Giovanni.

Giovanni halted, his eyes wild. "I can help. It's what you trained us to do. If you don't want to do it."

"If what you say is true, the Gestapo is already looking for you boys," Kitty said flatly. She pointed at Stella. "I don't know if she is the one who is giving everyone away, I'm not connecting it all. But if she is—"

"We'll dump her body into the canal," Giovanni said. "The police won't find her for days. Maybe weeks, if we're lucky."

She looked curiously at him. "Have you done this before, or what?"

He scoffed. "No. You?"

Kitty turned back to the tunnel. "If she is an informer, then yes, we'll have to get rid of her. If she's not..." She glared at him. "If it's not her then it's someone else, and she's innocent."

Giovanni stared at her. "Someone else? Like..." He shook his head. "Not Gustav. Not Stefan. They—"

"You?"

Giovanni took a step back. "*Me?*"

Stella's eyes were opening, but they had stuffed a rag into her mouth. She moaned, her eyes blinking rapidly as she realized where she was. And with whom.

Kitty hurried back to her and squatted down before her. "I'm going to remove the gag, and then I want you to answer some questions."

But Stella was unable to focus.

"Maybe you hit her too hard?" Giovanni suggested, panic in his voice.

Kitty looked up at him, the hard realization dawning on her. Even if Stella Beck was innocent, was not giving them away, Kitty could no longer just let her go. She had backed herself up against the wall.

Slowly, she rose to her feet. She thrust the canteen at Giovanni.

"Give her some water. Make sure she's comfortable. If she tries to run..." She handed him the pistol next.

Giovanni stared at it, then snatched it, the rims of his lips white.

Kitty paced to the mouth of the tunnel and squinted up at the sunlight. Her head felt woozy. She threw her hands over her head, groaned up at the sky. On the horizon were the twisted and blasted ruins of the oil refinery, then the low buildings of several factories. Some with bomb damage to their roofs. They'd had to maneuver around a crater in the road. Nobody came out here. Not really.

Kitty faced the tunnel again. Suddenly there was screaming, a painful cry.

"Giovanni," Kitty cried.

Stella was on her feet! How?

Kitty had to slam herself up against the wall as Giovanni charged toward her. Kitty spun away, and threw herself on Stella behind him. Stella released an *Oof!* as she met the ground. Giovanni rolled over and came up on his knees. Stella screamed and Kitty scrambled up, then pinned her to the ground. Kitty reached beneath her and clamped a hand over the struggling woman's mouth.

"She tried to kill me!" Giovanni shouted.

Stella struggled, kicking her feet out and gnawing at Kitty's hand. With an angry cry, Kitty snatched her hand away and repositioned herself so that she knelt on the back of Stella's neck.

"What the devil is going on!" Kitty shouted at Giovanni.

He was scrambling on all fours, collecting the dusty rag and the rope on his way. "She wanted to talk, so I took the rag out of her mouth!" he cried.

"That is not your job! Why did you untie her?"

"She must've done it!"

Stella was fighting but with Giovanni's help, Kitty got her tied up and gagged again before dragging her up onto her feet and back into the tunnel. Kitty's pistol was lying in the dirt.

"You could have gotten yourself killed, you idiot!" Kitty cried. "Bring the gun here."

Stella had tears streaming down her face, her eyes rolling with panic as Kitty shoved her back onto the ground.

"What the hell is wrong with you?" Kitty shouted at her. She tried to catch her breath. "I just want to talk to you, Stella. Just *talk*."

Stella kicked her feet out, muffled cries behind the rag. Her look turned defiant now.

"I'm going to take the rag out—"

"Don't do it," a shaky Giovanni said. "I did, and she bit me. Hard."

Kitty looked up at him. There was a bite mark on his forearm. Stella was again wriggling and trying to scream through the rag.

Giovanni cocked the pistol. "Don't you *dare...*" he warned.

Kitty gulped for air, her chest exploding. "Stella! Calm down! I'm going to take this rag out of your mouth, and then I want to know only one thing, Stella. Who the hell are you?"

Stella's eyes were wide, snot was blocking her passageways. Kitty gazed at her and nodded. "All right? On the count of three. One. Two. Three." Kitty yanked the rag out of the woman's mouth. At that very moment, the thunder of a motor and shifting gears sounded above them.

Stella's eyes rolled toward the tunnel entrance. She twisted and got onto her knees but lost her balance and fell, face forward. The truck was just over their heads, crossing over the tunnel.

Stella wrenched herself onto her back, her eyes wild, blood streaming from her forehead. *"You traitors! You traitors!"*

Kitty stood up. She rushed to throw herself on top of Stella again, to keep her quiet.

Bam!

Kitty halted. The truck. It had backfired. But her ears were ringing.

Bam!

Kitty flung herself up against the wall at the vibration. Giovanni's silhouette was against the entrance of the tunnel. Stella lay at her feet.

"Oh, my God," Kitty hissed. "Oh, my God!"

She cocked her head toward the road, the sound of the truck fading.

"What in God's name," Kitty cried hoarsely. She stumbled to Stella's body. The back of her head was blown open.

"She was going to kill you," Giovanni's voice was far off. "She would've tried to kill both of us."

He came toward her, and Kitty stared up at him in disbelief.

"Katrin... Katrin, she was going to get us killed. She as much as admitted it. You heard her."

Panting, he was still holding her gun.

"Give me the pistol." Kitty was measured, calm.

Giovanni's chest heaved. He looked at her, shook his head.

"Give me the gun, Giovanni," she said more urgently.

"She was the one, wasn't she?" he said.

Kitty took a cautious step toward him. "Yeah, she was the one."

Slowly, with a shaking hand, he stretched his arm over Stella's body. Kitty grasped the gun. She put it into her pocket.

"Help me get her into the canal." She was clear about what they had done. What they had to do next.

They grunted and strained but finally managed to get Stella's body over the rim and into the canal. The water splashed. Kitty backpedaled away, then slowly reached into her pocket and cocked the weapon at Giovanni.

"Why did you shoot?"

Giovanni's eyes were wide, his face a mask of hard, dark fear.

"Katrin... She attacked us. She was going to run."

A sharp pain stabbed her temple and Kitty gasped, then blinked, dizzy from the pain.

"Katrin? Are you all right?"

He was at her side. She kept the gun pointed at him but she couldn't see straight. The stabbing pain again. She groaned. What was wrong with her? The canteen at her feet came into focus.

Giovanni's arms came around her, his face came into focus, his eyes filled with concern and renewed panic. He held the canteen to her lips. "Here, drink something."

She pushed the canteen away, her head muddled.

As if in an echo chamber, she heard Giovanni's voice. "Katrin, let me get you to where you need to go."

"I need a safe house," she murmured. She fell against him, her legs weak.

She met the back seat of the Volkswagen, her hand still clutching the pistol. It was the last thing she remembered.

She had no idea how, but Kitty found herself in a bed. Giovanni was gone. She was with a woman she did not know. The woman pressed something cold to her head and said, "You're safe here."

The next day, Kitty found her pistol inside the lining of the rucksack. She blinked up at the woman. "Who are you?"

"A friend. And I am to tell you that Dr. Messner was arrested in Budapest."

PART FIVE

JULY–OCTOBER 1944

Vienna, Austria

25

JULY–SEPTEMBER 1944

A summer in hiding. That was how Kitty told herself she would remember it.

What she most certainly congratulated herself on—and wryly—was the escape line. The vast array of safe houses she had managed to curate gave her the ability to move from one to the next with couriers preparing the next location for her well in advance. She never used the same courier more than once.

Kitty took up residence in cramped rooms, attics, a cubby-hole under a stairwell, and even—quite imaginatively—in a wardrobe, the back of which led to an unused closet.

Besides the constant worries that burdened her, Kitty was haunted. Haunted by Stella's death. By the uncertainty whether she had really taken care of a mole or been responsible for killing an innocent woman—even if she was a Nazi.

Was Gedeon still alive? What if the ring in the photo had also been a coincidence? What if she'd orphaned two children? Or had Stella lied about the children like she had about Günter Beck? This reminded her of Andreas, and of Margit, and the promise she'd made to Edgar to take care of them. She did not know how to help them when she was this reliant on others herself. So far, there had been nothing—not a clue—about whether Edgar had executed some sort of mission, and whether he had succeeded, or failed. He'd predicted that she would know, but she had limited access to the outside world and information.

Kitty never stayed longer than a few days in any one place, but even so, the strain and the anxiety were back. She had too much time to think, and it was taking its toll on her health.

Her headaches came often. Her muscles cramped from tension. She had fevers that seemed to come from nowhere. When she was well, Kitty forced herself to think of how she could transform herself once more. She angrily pulled herself together and risked dyeing her hair, this time a reddish brown. Her name—according to her new documents, and not very good ones at that—was Angelika Hofer, but her head was muddled, and when she tested herself, she knew she was not ready to convince anyone. Least of all herself.

In mid-July, she was enjoying better health, had more energy and was beginning to believe she might have gotten through the worst of it. She was sunning her legs in the window of an attic after several days of rain. The heat was welcome. She was in the home of a music professor and his sympathetic and generous wife. In her lap were clippings from articles written by Otto Bauer, Bertolt Brecht and even Dorothy Day. The wife had given them to her.

"All banned," she'd said, and pressed the album into Kitty's hands.

The boys in Nussdorf, in the meantime, reported separately to her. She communicated with them via dead letter boxes; unable to leave her safe house, she used her assets as couriers. Twice, they told her that some Gestapo men had come around asking questions, but nothing came of it. In return, she told them to stick to their normal routine. As soon as she felt safe, she would give them the green light to radio Bern and tell them they were back in business. But for now, the OSS and their teams for Vienna would have to wait.

July was also the month the skies rumbled with RAF bombers. The air raid sirens shrieked at regular intervals and any time Kitty had to go outdoors, she had to fight through the ash that coated the city, the stench of burning oil, smoke and fire. The Austrian locals lamented about the end of days. The Allies were getting closer.

Two days after Kitty learned that the Heinkel-Süd factory in Floridsdorf had lost all its airplane prototypes and frames, Kitty's hosts invited her downstairs and handed her their *Volksempfänger* with cautious smiles.

"Maybe you can... You know?" The woman made turning motions with her hand.

The music professor nodded at Kitty. "The BBC," he whispered. "There are rumors."

It was never an easy feat, and always dangerous, but after Kitty turned the dials, they caught the static of a signal, and the BBC announcer's crisp British accent came through. Kitty smiled from ear to ear. Hearing his voice was like tasting the first, crisp apples of the season.

All three of them were bent over the radio and when they heard that the Americans had landed in Sicily, they beamed at one another, clasped hands and released muted cheers.

The woman brought out a bottle of *Kir*, and three thimbles. They drank and toasted one another with broad grins but did not say a word.

It was hours later, when she was lying on her makeshift bed in the attic, that Kitty wondered where Sam might be now. The fact that she could even think of her family proved that she was hopeful for the first time in what felt like years, though it had only been months since her arrival in Vienna.

A few days later, it was time to move again. Warning him to tell no one else about it, Kitty asked Gustav to meet her at the zoo in Schönbrunn; there he stuffed her into the back of his truck, using up precious petrol to drive her to the home of his sister-in-law, Elfriede. Kitty was the first to hide on the farm in Neustadt.

Gustav embraced her, ready to return to Nussdorf.

"How is everyone?" Kitty asked him softly.

"Everyone is doing fine."

"Do you have any news whatsoever about any of the other members? What about those Gestapo? Did they ever return?"

"Nothing more on arrests, but Giovanni is really keeping a low profile. He doesn't dare to even return to the Cottage District."

"Good," Kitty muttered. "That's good."

"And no sign of any Gestapo. Just the usual patrols. A lot more Wehrmacht, but the German army is scraping the barrel for conscripts. Young kids from the Hitler Youth, and old men."

Kitty nodded. "This is a good sign. A very good sign. But stay alert."

It was a hay loft for her this time, with an easy escape route if need be, out onto the slope at the back. The refuge of the woods was just a few seconds' sprint away.

Kitty had liked Elfriede from the first moment she'd met her back in the spring. She was a middle-aged woman, plain and kind, a devout Catholic, a mother of three, and a widow. Her husband—Gustav's brother—was supposed to have taken over his parents' farm in Nussdorf, but had been killed in a machinery accident six years earlier. Elfriede returned to the childhood home in Neustadt after her mother passed away, dug up potato fields, chopped wood, kept her children in school, and kept four goats which supplied her with milk, cheese, and—eventually—meat.

Kitty ventured out at night to swim in the pond, luxuriating in the cool water and the ability to do something good for her battered body and mind. Afterwards, Elfriede and she would sit together in the house after the children were deep asleep and enjoyed each other's quiet company. It was to Elfriede that Kitty admitted she had been responsible for a woman's death. It was Elfriede who then gave Kitty a rosary and urged her to pray for her soul and that of the woman.

One day, after Elfriede returned from church, Kitty heard her sending the children off to play in the garden. Soon after, the barn door creaked open. The top rungs of the ladder appeared and Kitty crept over to the edge of the loft, wondering what brought Elfriede to her at this time of day.

The woman's eyes were wide with excitement. "Someone tried to murder the Führer," she whispered.

"What?" Kitty cried hoarsely. "When? How?"

"A bomb. It was planted during a meeting, but it did not injure him."

Kitty rolled her eyes heavenward. "How? How does that man escape each time? Who plans these—?" Kitty clamped a hand over her mouth.

"What's is it?" Elfriede asked.

Kitty finally croaked out a request "A newspaper? Can you bring one later?"

Elfriede said she would.

Kitty did not know whether she needed the paper to search for clues, to search for hints. Of course Edgar would not leave her a message in one of those papers. But she was positive— there was no question about it—that her husband had been involved in that attempt on Hitler's life. And in that failure.

She had to get to Margit.

The geraniums were on the balcony exactly where Edgar had left them. All three of them. It could mean nothing, however.

Kitty might be too late. She had no idea whether Margit and Andreas were at the Rennweg penthouse any longer, or whether they were suspected. Whether Edgar was even alive, on the run, or dead.

So when the front entrance to the apartment building opened, and Margit stepped out onto the street with Andreas in tow, Kitty remained hidden in the park kitty-corner. Margit led her son to the corner, waited for a fiacre and a tram to pass by, and crossed the street, heading to Landstrasse.

Kitty tailed them, frowning when they crossed the main road and continued on toward the edges of the Rabenhof settlement. It was the same area that Kitty had lived in with Millie when she'd first arrived in Vienna.

Margit spoke in low tones to Andreas, who then wrenched himself free of her hand and skipped ahead, occasionally waiting for her to catch up before moving along.

A few blocks further and Margit stopped before an iron gate, and let herself in. Children were running around on a playground. It was the kindergarten. She was bringing Andreas to kindergarten.

A few moments later, Margit reappeared, and spoke with one of the other mothers before adjusting her shopping basket and heading back to where she'd come from. Kitty followed again, sometimes having to jog a bit to make sure she kept enough distance between them. When she cut through a green, Kitty kept her eyes peeled for anything suspicious.

But Edgar's sister continued past the theater, and after stopping at a pharmacy, she came out, and went into the post office.

This time, Kitty decided to approach her. As Margit waited to cross Landstrasse again, Kitty stood behind her.

"Don't turn around."

Margit's shoulders jerked but she did not look over her shoulder.

"Rover?" Kitty asked.

Margit shook her head a little. "Nothing!"

Kitty drew abreast and looked both ways. "Wait for this bus to pass."

Margit tensed and turned her face to Kitty's. Behind the sunglasses, her eyes were wide. Kitty nudged her to cross the street and they did so.

"I have to disappear—"

"You, too?" Margit asked in hushed despair.

"The cellar. Do you know the room?"

"Yes," Margit said.

"You'll find what you need in there," Kitty whispered. They'd reached the corner and were in front of a vegetable stand. "Look at the tomatoes."

Margit hesitated, but then moved to the display of tomatoes.

Kitty examined a small watermelon, her voice low. "There's a farm in Graz. But if the Soviets break across before the others, you must head west."

"And go where?" Margit whispered. "I'm not like you. I'm not brave."

Kitty glanced over. Their gazes locked. Margit looked defeated.

"I'll take my chances," Margit whispered. "That you will come for us."

Kitty sighed and walked away, glancing only once behind her. Margit cut a lonely and abandoned figure.

When she returned to Elfriede's farm, she threw herself into the hay and ran her fingers through her hair. It was the first time she had returned to the city like that, and as Angelika Hofer. She would try it again, to build up her confidence. And soon. It was time to get those OSS agents here, and herself out.

. . .

The last night she spent in Elfriede's hayloft, Kitty fell asleep before it was dark out. She could feel the weight of the night pressing in on her. And shadows. Men in uniform. Fedoras and leather coats. Gestapo. Abwehr. She was surrounded. Kitty tried to claw her way out of the nightmare, could hear her breathing rapid and panicked, but the dream pressed down on her, strangled her.

And then, from nowhere, Edgar's voice. *It's almost over.* His touch. A reassuring caress.

Just as she leaned into it, a shadow darted from above, like a bat. Edgar slumped against her and faded away.

Kitty awoke screaming, finally tearing her eyes open. It was pitch black, and she was coated in sweat. The fear still clutched her tight, and she whimpered.

The only response was the orchestra of crickets, and the rustle of the startled goats below.

By August, Kitty had stopped counting how many places she had stayed in. She was numb. There was no word about Edgar. No word about him from Bern, who was also maintaining radio silence according to her instructions. No word about how Margit and Andreas were faring.

She met Giovanni at the cafe they always met at. He nearly passed by her, then halted, turned slowly around and tipped his head. Kitty looked up from the newspaper and rose to greet him.

"You look..." he started, then leaned in to kiss her cheek. In her ear, he whispered, "Blue eyes."

"If you want something to drink," Kitty said, "You'll have to go get it yourself."

Giovanni nodded. "Ersatz for you?"

"Beer."

He cocked an eyebrow, but nodded.

Angelika Hofer liked beer.

He returned a few minutes later with two glasses of beer. He toasted with her and she tipped her head to the sun after taking a sip.

"I'm ready," she said. "Within the next week. Organize it?"

He cleared his throat. "It's the harvest right now."

Kitty rolled her eyes. "Let me know when you're *all* ready."

A few days later, Kitty's malady returned. She came down with fever, the cramping, the chills. Her scalp felt as if it were splitting from her skull. She had just gotten back on her feet when the news of Paris's liberation reached her.

She immediately couriered a message to Peter, who agreed to meet her at Türkenschanz. He brought the news she had been hoping for about Messner and Franka. Franka had been questioned, but released, then questioned again, the following time about Katrin Handel. By some miracle, Messner's wife had convinced the Gestapo that Katrin had fled back to Paris, frightened by the prospect that her boss had been arrested. Then they asked Franka about Stella Beck. Franka truly knew nothing about her, she'd told Peter. The Gestapo showed her photos and once, the interrogator slipped up and said, "Maybe she ran away, too?"

Peter smirked when he told Kitty that part.

"Which means they are still looking for Frau Dr. Beck," Kitty said.

Peter deduced the same. "And if she was working for the Gestapo, it also explains why they are looking for her."

Kitty decided on the spot that it *had* been Stella who had betrayed Messner, but then Peter said, "There were four more arrests this past week. And a trial date. It's set for October. All ten from the spy ring will face the judges at the same time."

Kitty bit her trembling lip. The news did not bode well. Somebody was either still giving spy members away, or those incarcerated were succumbing to the Gestapo's brutal interrogations.

Next, she sent for Giovanni and they met at the Belvedere Park this time, Kitty's steps grinding the gravel walks past perfectly sculpted cypress and hedges. Giovanni was at the fountain, and she sat down on the corner, her back to him.

"We have to move onwards," she said. She heard him shift behind her. "You look terrible."

"*You* look terrible," he said.

She nodded and hugged her purse to herself. "Thank you. Any trouble in Nussdorf?"

"No."

"Nobody has searched for you? None of you have been taken in for questioning?"

His intake of breath was ragged, and when she glanced at him over her shoulder, he was shaking his head.

"Is that a no?" she asked, irritated.

"It's a no. But the Gestapo was snooping around about two weeks ago. They were gone within two days. It could have been anything."

Kitty mulled this information over. This was the third time. This time, however, there'd been arrests. Not her Nussdorf boys, but others.

"I need money. I have to get out. And I need information. I need my *people*." She glanced over at him again. "I want to meet with Gustav and Stefan."

"When?"

"As soon as you can make it possible. If I'm satisfied, I'll green light the operation again."

That night, she once again turned her thoughts to Edgar. Where he might be. How he might be faring. The rumors she'd heard about Hitler's furious response to the assassination attempt were horrifying. He'd had his men hunt down perpetrators, implicating anyone remotely responsible in the plot. Over seven thousand arrests followed, and more than four thousand executions or death sentences were then handed down.

In Vienna, troops who had been waiting for this turn of events, had been wrongfully informed that the assassination attempt had succeeded. They had stormed Nazi Party offices and arrested Gauleiters and SS officers, only to discover that Hitler was far from finished. The mutiny had turned them into walking dead men. It was this greater net that the Führer cast that worried Kitty most.

The only thing that gave Kitty any peace was that Edgar's name was nowhere in these reports. The not knowing was weighing down her own morale. It took all of her strength to focus on the task she had at hand. She had to finish her job, and get her OSS agents into Austria.

In a dank cellar of her current safe house, Kitty looked at her reflection in a cracked mirror. Giovanni had been right. She looked terrible. Her eyes were bloodshot, her skin haggard. Her left eye had been twitching on and off uncontrollably, and sagged. She curled up on the cot, pulled the blankets over her and forced herself to fall asleep. *Soon*, she thought. *Soon, I'll be fit enough to finish this.*

On a balmy night in mid-September, she arrived in Nussdorf, her hair long and dark, her eyes blue, no glasses this time. Angelika Hofer descended into Stefan's outdoor cellar and met with her reception team.

"Are you men ready?"

They nodded, Giovanni was staring at her, as if trying to come to terms with her new persona.

"Tell Bern Operation Dupont is a go."

The response from Bern came moments later. She read the decoded message aloud. "By the last quarter of the next moon." Kitty frowned and looked at Gustav for answers.

"Last quarter of the next moon?" He scratched his hair until it stood on end. "That will be beginning to mid-October. Three to four weeks."

Kitty nodded. "Stand by. Go about your business, but stand by."

Operation Dupont was a go. There was no turning back now.

26

OCTOBER 1944

The darkness was a comfort, even if the cold fall air was not. A stiff breeze rattled the dead leaves on the branches where Kitty crouched in the woods. They were on the outskirts of Wiener Neustadt. Suddenly, the air exploded with the pop of anti-aircraft guns, small balls of fire arcing across the sky. Kitty hunkered down although the flak towers were quite a distance away.

She waited breathlessly. It seemed an eternity until the wind finally delivered another sound—that low and steady buzz of an approaching airplane.

Kitty was awash in a moment of serenity. This was going to happen. The first three-man team of OSS agents was about to land.

One of the boys shifted behind her. She looked over her shoulder and gave the three silhouettes—Gustav, Stefan, Giovanni—a thumbs up. This was it. They were all looking up, searching the clear sky above. Moments later, the first whisper of silk, then the descent of white jellyfish-like chutes. Three airborne agents drifted down toward the field, one after the other. The pilot had nailed the landing zone.

At the first thump, Kitty and the three boys scrambled out of the woods.

"Sparrow," Kitty hissed into the dark.

"Phoenix," came a male voice back. American. He unsnapped the harness and started pulling the strings of the chutes in.

Kitty hurried to him and offered her hand. "I'm Dahlia. Welcome to Austria."

"Taylor," he answered.

Giovanni greeted the second man, who whispered, "Mascot," before also shaking Kitty's hand. The third one was further away, but when he reached them, he introduced himself as Fredericksen.

Kitty was surprised by the accented English. "Austrian?"

"This is Corporal Fredericksen," Mascot said. "He's friendly. Found Jesus in a POW camp, made his vows to Uncle Sam, and volunteered to be our native."

Kitty had no time to respond. Two more chutes appeared in the sky above. She squinted up at them. Packages!

Stefan and Gustav were already hurrying down the field after them. Those canisters would contain radio, gear, supplies, and likely weapons and ammunition. Reichsmarks. Food. Maybe even chocolates and cigarettes.

"There should be three of those following us," Taylor said to Kitty.

She whistled softly and waved for the boys to go looking for the third canister.

"We'll find it," she said.

Just like she had in France, Kitty helped Taylor and his team bury the chutes in a hole she and the boys had dug up earlier. Gustav and Stefan returned, their eyes bright with excitement in the moonlight as they carried a "C" canister and one "H" canister. The former had compartments stuffed with various supplies, the latter would contain longer items like machine guns and rifles.

The agents were fitting their gear when Giovanni returned to say that he could not find the last package.

"We don't have time to keep looking," he warned.

Kitty disagreed. She went searching for it herself but had to admit it was useless. As bitter as it was, it was not uncommon to lose material in airdrops. She just hoped it stayed hidden wherever it was.

Taylor and Mascot were examining the two canisters that had landed, and Taylor swore under his breath.

Fredericksen turned to Kitty. "The radio was in the third package."

Kitty repeated Taylor's curse. "Patrols will come searching around here soon. Follow us."

The men jockeyed up to carry the supplies, and Kitty took the lead. They trekked through the woods for about two miles, then veered off to follow the stream that led to Elfriede's farm. Gustav's sister-in-law let them all slip inside the house, checking behind them before shutting the door and lighting a lamp. Kitty pressed the black boards into place to make sure they were secure then turned around to examine her new team.

Taylor was tallest and Fredericksen was the slightest of them all. Mascot had the square, compact figure of a boxer and wore a beard and mustache. His balding head gleamed in the lamplight. Fredericksen fished out a pair of glasses from his kit and now put them on. He looked a little bit like Kafka, with a head of thick dark hair, large eyes, and elfin-shaped ears.

Kitty beamed at them. "We're very glad you're here."

"Glad to be here," Taylor replied.

"We're going to get you packed up," she said, "and then we move on. Elfriede here will help you to hide the materials you want distributed to our local operatives."

Taylor, studying the canisters, replied distractedly, "Sounds good."

Gustav helped Elfriede set out some food and ersatz for the two men. Giovanni then offered them all schnapps from a flask.

"Austria has a schnapps for everything," Kitty teased as all three men drank. "Stomach aches, headaches, for digestion and now for successful landings."

"Semi-successful, anyway," Taylor grumbled. "We really need that radio."

Kitty glanced at Giovanni. "We have one. But that won't help you when you need to be on the move."

"In an emergency, it will do," Mascot suggested.

"And Dahlia has a very good circuit to help courier messages," Giovanni said of her eagerly.

Taylor mulled it over. "We'll figure it out."

Gustav and Stefan excused themselves and headed out to keep an eye out for patrols. Somewhere, the Wehrmacht were scrambling around the countryside looking for enemy parachutists.

Fredericksen had already popped open the H canister and was showing Giovanni the rifles inside. Kitty was distracted, delighted by the weapons, and found that she could not stop smiling.

"What's the situation for patrols, anyway?" Mascot asked Kitty.

"They're mostly old men," she said. "Sleepy."

"*Sleepy*?" Mascot asked.

She turned her attention to him. "Yeah, lazy, unfit, unmotivated, and not very vigilant. It's in the city that you need to be careful. Gestapo is quite the opposite. They are coming down harder than ever."

Fredericksen turned to her and acknowledged her.

As Giovanni and Elfriede handed the agents their clothing

—including Dutch caps, Fedoras, gold watches, wallets and other accessories that would make them look "normal"—Kitty got a better look at all three agents.

In the light, Taylor had receding dark blond hair and a general All-American look, almost movie-star quality.

"You are going to have challenges getting by any patrols," Kitty said, pulling him aside. "You're too fit. Too young. So, do you have a plan?"

"He won't be able to speak," Fredericksen interjected. "Shot in the mouth."

She looked at him in disbelief. "Who's going to believe that story?"

"I'm his spokesperson. And I'm very convincing," the Austrian said with finality.

Surrendering, she asked the men to provide her with their individual headshots. Giovanni collected them and he and Stefan would affix them onto the men's forged identity cards. Then, they would be able to move more freely and do what they had to in order to integrate themselves behind enemy lines.

She jerked her head at Giovanni. "All right, I think we're ready. Let Stefan and Gustav know we're on the move."

Giovanni bent toward her. "I know that you want to take precautions, but I think you're making it more difficult for everyone. Gustav and I could use the vehicles to transport them."

Kitty rubbed her temples and sighed. She had worked hard to keep their final location secret and to get them there safely.

"I'm making it difficult," she said, "because convenience most often compromises security. Ten people, Giovanni. Ten Cassia members are going to trial later this month and I don't see it turning into a happy end."

She said goodbye to him, then to Elfriede, and slipped out the door with the three men. They hurried to the back of the farm. Soon enough, all four were under cover of the forest again.

Some twenty minutes later, Kitty herded them into a small shepherd's hut far from the main house, and they each picked a spot in the fragrant hay for the night. Kitty lit the lamp she'd taken from the house, and retrieved the blankets she'd hidden, the sack of bread and apples, some cheese, and walnuts. Elfriede had also slipped in dried goat sausages.

As they settled in, Taylor told her they would be reporting on troop positions, fortifications, and other related military intel. "British and Soviet agents are already on the ground, too. We'll need to know what kind of defenses are planned."

"Giovanni will wire Bern as soon as I tell him to. Until I know that nobody is looking for you, you will all be split up," she said to Mascot. Nobody from her group, except she, would know where they were located. Not Giovanni, not any of the boys. Nobody, except their safe house hosts. From now on, everything was on a need-to-know basis.

She turned to the taller American. "Are you aware that I've had to go underground?"

Taylor nodded gravely. He was packing the rest of his food into a sack. "We were worried about that. What's the news on Cassia?"

Kitty sighed. "Of the ten, two were the ring leaders, including the man who signed with the OSS. Their trial is in two weeks."

"Any chance you can pay someone off? Get someone to vouch their innocence?" Mascot asked. He rested his head on the back of his hands.

Kitty scoffed. She had finally managed to meet with Franka about a week earlier and had gotten as many details as possible. "Fat chance. But one of them is a naturalized Brazilian citizen, and the government is trying to negotiate for him."

"Where is he being held?" Taylor asked.

"At Morzinplatz—the Hotel Metropole."

"Gestapo headquarters," Fredericksen confirmed.

"And the other, a priest, is at the Liesl, the prison. The Brazilian citizen has a lawyer, so he's often transferred to the Vienna Regional Court for negotiations."

"Interesting," Taylor said. "How many guards are there when they transport him between the two?"

She squinted at him. She had two O5 members and a policeman—one of Maier's spies she connected to—watching and reporting on developments. "Four."

"Where's the nearest Brazilian embassy?" he asked.

"Hütteldorf," Kitty said quickly. "The western outskirts of Vienna."

Taylor glanced at Fredericksen and Mascot. "What's the Metropole like?"

Kitty shuddered at the thought. "It's a hotel, converted into a torture center." She cocked an eyebrow. "Why are you asking all of this? Sounds like you're planning to break him out."

"Me?" Taylor asked. "Aren't *you?*"

Kitty blinked. Now that he'd said it, she wondered why she *hadn't* thought of it. There was one very good reason, though. "Any attempt, especially if we fail," she said slowly, "would put those prisoners' lives on the line."

Taylor's expression was expectant. "Or save them."

She studied him. What kind of military training did he have? He looked to be made of serious stuff. He most certainly exuded the kind of audacity the OSS loved to have in their ranks and files. Both of the Americans. Mascot's eyes flashed. He was also keen. Fredericksen, on the other hand, had the edginess of someone who'd been put through the wringer and had learned his lesson, which was no bad thing. The two Americans needed someone who could keep their feet on the ground.

"Will you help me plan it?" she asked Taylor finally.

He grinned. "Absolutely."

Mascot grunted. "I'm in."

Kitty looked at Fredericksen.

"Do you have the resources to pull this off?" he asked in English.

"I could." She had Peter. She also had Franka, who had provided quite some insight into Messner's routines, situation, and condition.

"You'll need Wehrmacht," Fredericksen said. "At least one on active duty, and access to a truck."

Taylor agreed.

"All right," Kitty said. "Before we get ahead of ourselves, my first priority is to make sure you three are all set up. Identity cards, your quarters, the whole kit and caboodle."

The men agreed and settled into their spots in the hay. Kitty took the furthest corner. Taylor suddenly stood up, put his kit aside and moved to her. He squatted in front of her and rubbed his face with a hand. "I'm supposed to relay a private message to you."

Kitty tensed. "From whom?"

"You heard about the attempt on Hitler's life in July."

Kitty could not breathe, so she just nodded. Here it was, her worst nightmare realized.

"Bern wanted to let you know that Rover was involved."

"*Was* involved. And now?" she whispered.

"He's in hiding."

She dropped her head between her knees for a moment. "So he's alive?"

"When I got the message to pass on to you, he was."

Kitty looked up. She understood what he was implying. "How is he to get out?"

"They're attempting to courier documents to him. Documents and a cover. But it's hairy. Bern wanted me to tell you that. They are doing everything they can, but it is hairy."

She swiped at the escaped tear. "Thank you. Thank you for letting me know."

"They didn't want to send it on the airwaves in any way."

"I understand." She grasped his lower arm and squeezed, thanking him once more.

Taylor returned to his place and lay down in the hay. He pulled the blanket over him, glanced at her then stretched his hands behind his head. "Let's go get these sons of bitches, shall we? The Nazis won't know what hit them!"

But Kitty wished these men were the ones who were going to rescue Edgar. Wherever he was.

In the morning, Kitty stood against the door with her arms folded as the men gathered their things together. Taylor and Mascot were too young, too fit; even if their clothing and their looks passed casual scrutiny, their youth and obvious good health would not. They'd be questioned, and likely detained. Kitty considered submitting and taking up Giovanni and Gustav on their offers to help transport the men. But she'd learned her lesson. The hardest way imaginable.

Instead she huddled with the three agents over a road map. "On the way out of Neustadt, there is this bridge, and when I scouted it out, I found that there are four reservists stationed on each end." Kitty fished out the packet of Austrian-brand cigarettes from Taylor's shirt pocket.

"I'm going to need these to create a distraction. While I do that, you men are going to cross the bridge *beneath*."

Taylor's smile crept slowly as he glanced at Mascot. Mascot scratched his head and nodded, grinning like a kid. Fredericksen was the only one who looked critical.

It was time to move. It was drizzling outside, which Kitty found to be splendid. There would not be much foot traffic. Again, they navigated through woods, over fields, and crossed a small stream running parallel to the road. About a hundred yards from the bridge, she stepped out of the brush and walked on in the open. Kitty saw two guards speaking and smoking with one another. On the other side, she also saw only two guards. They'd been reduced. With a bemused look on her face —she wouldn't need Taylor's cigarettes after all—she approached them.

At the sight of her, the guards straightened and repositioned themselves near the barricade. Even at a distance, she could tell they were assessing her, and had already decided she was interesting enough.

"Good evening," she said silkily, and shook the rain off her dark hair after handing over her papers. She watched them for a moment. "I hate to be a bother, but you wouldn't happen to have a cigarette for me, would you?"

The guard on her left fished one out just a little faster than the one on her right. She smiled gratefully and leaned toward him as he lit it for her.

"*Danke*," she said.

"You're not Austrian, are you?" the one on the right said.

Kitty smiled apologetically. "My father was Austrian, but I grew up in Paris."

"And what are you doing here now? In Wiener Neustadt?" the other one asked.

"My cousin lives here. I have to return home, though. Before curfew," she said and winked. "Did you boys see the posters for the dance at the town hall next week? My cousin is helping to plan it. Will you be going?"

The one on her left told her they didn't know about it, but yes, they would go if they were not on duty.

"You shouldn't be walking out in the open like this," the other one warned her. "The RAF bombers are sudden and unpredictable."

"But that's why we have you here, no?" she asked coyly.

He wiggled his eyebrows and chuckled. Neither man looked fit to fight.

She exhaled and flicked the cigarette over the landing of the bridge, and looked at the river. Not a thing in sight except the bank and the water.

"I have to go," Kitty said, calculating that she'd had enough time. "I hope to see you next week," she added.

They good-naturedly promised to do everything they could to make that possible.

Kitty crossed the bridge, reached the opposite end, and began the whole spiel from the beginning again. A few moments later, she heard a soft splash, laughed loudly and shared a joke. After leaving the next two guards entertained, and with promises of a dance the following week, Kitty hurried down the road again, certain that her three agents had had enough time. If they were safe, they'd successfully pulled themselves across the river over the steel girders beneath the bridge. She would soon find out.

As soon as she made it around the bend, she heard a bird call. She called back and waited. Taylor, Mascot and Fredericksen materialized out of the brush. They were wet, but they had made it.

"How did it go?" Mascot asked.

Kitty rolled her eyes, stuffing Taylor's cigarettes back into his shirt pocket. "Men are so easily distracted."

Fredericksen flashed her a grim smile.

Taylor clapped her on the shoulder. "Good going, boss."

The men moved on up the road, but Kitty stood frozen to her spot, remembering how Marie had called her "boss", back in France. Kitty had gotten them to Spain, but then Marie was murdered.

Taylor looked over his shoulder and turned around. "Are you coming?"

For a split second, Kitty wanted to run. But where to? All

she could do was hope that misfortune would not befall this group.

But with a mission like the one Taylor had in mind—springing Messner out of jail—she was walking straight into the fire. If getting Edgar out of wherever he was hiding was a hairy business, as Taylor had put it, she would really complicate things for Bern if she failed.

27

OCTOBER 28TH–NOVEMBER 9TH, 1944

Dr. Walter Caldonazzi. Dr. Josef Wyhnal. Police officer Michael Hofer. Franz Messner. Father Heinrich Maier. The People's Tribunal found them all guilty of conspiracy to commit high treason, and the judges ordered sentencing to take place in early November.

Kitty waited near the driveway to the Palace of Justice. Huddled against the cold wind, her scarf pulled up high, hat tilted over her face, she wondered what the small groups of people were waiting for. To jeer? To attack? Very likely. To commiserate or grieve? Certainly not in public...

The tension was thick. This was one of the biggest Nazi trials Vienna had seen and it had shaken the community. Father Maier was a beloved parish priest. Franz Messner was a valued member of the business community. The others who had been captured from the spy ring included a famous pianist, a chief of police, a former mayor. Everyone standing in the dock knew that their sentences would be death by guillotine. The Reich would make sure to send a powerful signal to the population that treachery would not be tolerated.

Franka suddenly appeared at the top of the courthouse

stairs with the attorney who'd represented Messner. He hurriedly ushered her down the steps while she dabbed at tears. Before Franka could get around the corner, Kitty stepped out in front of her.

The attorney put a protective arm out in front of Messner's wife. Franka's expression was a mixture of surprise and hostility but when she locked eyes with Kitty, the woman's face betrayed recognition.

"Just a moment," she said to her companion.

Franka moved closer to the building with Kitty.

"I'm not going to ask how you are," Kitty muttered. "I just need to know. Is Brazil going to help negotiate your husband's sentence?"

"They'll try for a prison sentence. But high treason is a death sentence."

"What about you?" Kitty asked.

"The Reich is confiscating our home," Franka wailed quietly. "They've given me until Friday to leave."

Kitty took in a shaky breath. "Where will you go?"

"To Tyrol. To my family."

"If we could get your husband to the Brazilian embassy, he might be able to sit out the war in exile. Are you prepared to do that?"

Franka grabbed her wrist. "What are you planning?"

"I just need to know whether you would be prepared to do that."

Franka released her grip. Her voice was shaky. "If that is the plan, I would be."

"Pack your things, send what you need to Tyrol, and go to the Brazilian embassy."

Kitty turned away and walked across the plaza and back to the street. She signaled the black Volkswagen at the crossing. It flashed its lights twice. Signal received.

With her heart in her throat, Kitty walked a few blocks

more before Giovanni's vehicle pulled up alongside the pavement. With a single sidestep, Kitty yanked open the door and was inside.

"It's on," she said. "Drive."

Giovanni did as she said, gripping the steering wheel. "When is the meeting?"

Kitty looked out the window. "Everyone will know what they have to do when it's time for them to know." She looked at his profile.

He jerked his head back and slowed down. Swallowed. "As you wish."

Kitty turned back to the window. That moment of disquiet over Stella Beck's body between them had been enough for her. There was no room for mistakes. None.

Planning Messner's escape meant bringing all three OSS agents under one roof again to hammer out the final plan. This was going to be the last thing she did, and then the OSS would extract her.

The idea was to overwhelm the four guards in the Green Henry—the green vans used to transfer prisoners to and from the various facilities—and whisk Messner away to the safety of the Brazilian embassy.

Kitty learned that Taylor was a Navy SEAL—the first of his kind—and his expertise was to plan exactly these kinds of high-risk missions. Taylor, Mascot and Fredericksen came up with the details. Kitty patrolled the area and drew a map of the courthouse, the surrounding streets and where the best view would be to observe the back gate, where the vans came and went. Taylor and Kitty would observe and act as rear guard. Kitty was to inform Franka in case the mission failed, a job she really hoped she would not have to do.

They needed four people to overwhelm and take over the

Abwehr guards. First, they recruited Stefan's friend, Bruno Schmitz. Bruno was an active soldier who had become greatly disenchanted with the Nazis. It was he who had informed Stefan about how the Wehrmacht detected radios.

To spring Messner from jail, Bruno would be responsible for finding out who was on detail, get the documents required for the three non-Wehrmacht assets: Gustav, Stefan and—the OSS agents and Kitty decided—Fredericksen, who would be the third.

Bruno had already procured Wehrmacht uniforms for Stefan, Gustav and Fredericksen. They unnerved Kitty, but not in the way they had at the beginning. Stefan could make fake documents for them, and a skeleton key for the Green Henry's back door.

It was only on that day—when they were all together in an abandoned warehouse along the Danube—that Gustav pulled Kitty aside.

"What about Giovanni?" he asked.

Kitty cocked her head. "Did he say something to you?"

"*Nah.*" Gustav scuffed the floor with his shoe. "But I can tell he feels left out."

"History, Gustav. It's about a history together."

His brows knitted. "I didn't know that. I mean, I suspected that he... you know, has feelings for you, but..."

She let him think that. The less said, the better.

"It's just that he has thrown himself into this with such... He's worked hard. For a little recognition. His father doesn't give it to him, you know? And I know he's eager."

"I've got something else for him," she said.

Gustav looked up. "Something else?"

"Yeah. When you get back to Nussdorf, tell him I'm going to pass the radio to the agents. We'll be done here. Taylor and I will pick it up that same afternoon."

"At the shed?"

"Is that where it is?"

"All three parts."

Kitty nodded and patted his shoulder. "Good. Then have him be ready there."

Gustav grinned. "I'll tell him."

"You'll need a decoy," Taylor addressed the group now. "Something that will detract the four authentic soldiers, so that our guys here can overwhelm them, and get their hands on the Green Henry. They'll need to be tied up and gagged in the back."

"The best method for this," Kitty volunteered, "is to drug them. Knock them unconscious right inside of the van if possible, or immediately outside of it."

Mascot nodded at her with narrowed eyes. "Yes, that's the way."

"Get Messner to the Brazilian embassy, and the rest of you scatter," Taylor said. "Dump the Green Henry where it can't be found. Wipe it down."

Bruno said he had an idea of where they could dump the vehicle, went to the map, and showed Taylor and the others.

It was agreed upon that the men would need syringes with an incapacitating agent that they could quickly inject into their victims. Kitty had an idea of where she might get her hands on some. In her work at the convalescent home, she had become acquainted with at least three other people there who had assisted Dr. Wyhnal, including the cold, frizzy red-headed nurse, Frau Jovanovic. None of them had been discovered. Yet.

Fredericksen was frowning, and examining the diagram. "You all should know that no loitering is allowed around any of the Nazi's government buildings. We need to look natural."

"Timing will be everything," Mascot added.

The men began to assemble the items they would need. They would meet back here on the day, as soon as Franka sent word about the negotiations taking place between the Brazilians and the court authorities.

When everyone was clear about what they had to do, Kitty stepped before the four "Wehrmacht" soldiers. "These are your L-pills. Just in case." She handed each of them a small tube containing one of the poison pills.

Stefan looked gravely at her as he took his. Who would take care of his father? That was what she read in his eyes. Gustav hardly looked at it as he took his, sticking it into his pocket, but he jutted his lower lip and scuffed the floor with his shoe. Bruno handled his pill for a moment, then hid it on him.

Fredericksen did the same with a flicker of defiance in his gaze. "Right," he said. "Let's hope we don't have to use them."

Rain splattered onto Kitty's umbrella in big, fat drops, collected and rolled down in thick rivulets off the edges. Kitty was glad for it, for something that hid her, made her more nondescript as she watched for the men from the bus stop.

Messner's attorney was inside with Dr. Messner and the Brazilians, in negotiations about his sentence. The Wehrmacht patrols had been transferring him back and forth between the Gestapo headquarters and the courthouse for days.

Suddenly, Kitty's attention was drawn to the neighboring park. Four men in long army overcoats appeared and hurried across the road to the Palace of Justice. Kitty was alert. Fredericksen and Gustav were the first she made out. Then Bruno and Stefan. Kitty was relieved to see their easy strides, how they turned to one another and talked—Fredericksen even seemed to be joking with Gustav. It all appeared very natural.

She checked the clock tower. It was ten minutes to four. Parallel to the men, she headed for the northeast corner of the courthouse. She positioned herself in the plaza and could quickly cross over to another vantage point in case police patrols showed up. She spotted Taylor in a trilby and raincoat hovering near a food vendor.

The Green Henry would come out of the gates to her right. The boys would stop it, Bruno with news about something or other, official papers in hand. The guards would be alert, but would relax at the sight of the four uniformed soldiers. Their own. With news. About something Bruno could easily explain. Bruno carried the OSS cigarette case that exploded. He would offer the driver one. The flash was enough to cause harm but not loud enough to draw attention if nobody was very close. It would shock and awe the other guards, though. That would be when the others would make their move. Gustav, Fredericksen and Stefan would attack with the syringes filled with an incapacitating agent. In case of trouble, Fredericksen—who would take the rear guards, had her pen which, if pressed to the neck or chest, injected a lethal bullet. Gustav carried the skeleton key.

Bruno and Stefan paused on the right-hand side of the gate. Fredericksen and Gustav hung to the left. Bruno took something out of his pocket, cupped his hands to his mouth, and blew out smoke. A cigarette. He offered one to Stefan. Stefan apparently declined.

"You're soldiers," Kitty muttered. "You all smoke. *All* of you. Come on. Take the damned cigarette."

Bruno must have said something similar, because Stefan suddenly put one to his mouth. She relaxed after he blew smoke. Gustav did the same. Fredericksen did not. Kitty clicked her tongue, and took a few steps behind a bench, checking her watch.

Two minutes to four. The Green Henry had to appear soon. Every time someone came around the corner of the building, the men made as if they were leaving.

Two minutes *past* four now. Five. Six.

Kitty crossed over to the plaza, looked back. The men were

also getting nervous. They were huddled together against the rain. They were beginning to look suspicious.

Ten minutes after four. They gathered together away from the gate. Now even Fredericksen was smoking. They were not the picture of relaxation.

"*Komm schon!*" she muttered. *Come on!*

Suddenly, a policeman appeared from around the opposite corner. The men all shuffled away from one another. Everyone moved, except Bruno. Fredericksen took some awkward steps in the opposite direction, paused and turned around.

Gustav looked to follow him, then also halted and faced the gate. Kitty hissed with irritation again. Bruno turned to the policeman as he neared him. Stefan moved behind Bruno. The policeman's steps faltered. He was talking to Bruno now. His attention was then on the other three. Now he beckoned to Fredericksen and Gustav to come closer. They were reaching into their coats.

"*Scheiße!*" Kitty muttered. "*Verdammte Scheiße!*"

She looked for Taylor and spotted him near another monument.

He gave her the signal to wait. Kitty's arms tingled and she switched the umbrella into her other hand.

The policeman now had them gather around. Documents. He was asking for documents.

Fredericksen turned toward the gate once more. Kitty's eyes darted to the vehicle entrance, too. No sign of the Green Henry. The policeman snapped his fingers at Fredericksen, moved closer to him. Fredericksen shook his head and shrugged.

"*Scheiße!*" she hissed again. She hurried to the other side of a monument, craned her neck, but tipped the umbrella so nobody would really know what she was looking at.

Bruno was doing the talking. Stefan had his hand behind his back. The policeman was not returning the papers. Now he gestured to the corner where he'd come from. The boys all shifted on their feet. Gustav shook his head. Stefan's shoulders dropped. The policeman now stepped off to the side of the group, like a shepherd. He was rounding them up, asking them to follow him.

Kitty shivered in her coat. From the other side of the court-house, two men suddenly appeared. Black leather coats. The Fedoras. Supposedly under cover but everyone in Vienna knew what Gestapo looked like. That, too, was on purpose.

With her panic rising, Kitty searched for Taylor. He was now giving her a different signal. *Go!*

With her heart in her throat, she pushed off. The Gestapo agents were crossing the road, heading for the corner from where she'd been watching them.

Kitty took one last look. The boys were two streets across from her. Going around the corner with the policeman. Stefan, Bruno and Gustav, hunched into their coats at the front. Fredericksen trailing behind.

The two Gestapo men took up the rear.

28

NOVEMBER 9TH, 1944

Kitty arrived, breathless, at the warehouse where Mascot was waiting for news. Taylor appeared moments later. He strode over to her and grasped her shoulders.

"Hey. It was a long shot."

"You don't say!" Kitty cried. "What will happen to Fredericksen! They've got my guys being questioned right now. Stefan has a lot to lose. His father, for one, is ill. If they slip up in any way, in *any way*, the Gestapo will be in Nussdorf in minutes."

"The radio," Mascot said. "We need to get that radio."

But Kitty was pacing, hot on the trail in her mind. "The guards left the courthouse on time, like clockwork, every day for a *week*! And today? Why today?"

"It could have just been a routine police patrol," Taylor said.

"Maybe the negotiations are going on longer because the Brazilians have broken through?" Mascot offered.

"Or someone told them," Kitty cried impatiently.

Taylor and Mascot both stiffened. She was angry. Angry with herself for not having taken care of this earlier. She'd known and she'd blinded herself.

"Giovanni," Taylor said.

"He's the only one," she confirmed.

"Or it could have been a routine patrol," Mascot repeated.

But Taylor's brows knitted. "If you suspect, why aren't they after us? Here? At this warehouse?"

"Because," Kitty snapped. "I never told Giovanni about this location." But now it made sense. The headaches. The sudden fevers. Since the day of Stella's death, she'd had sudden attacks. Her canteen. The beer, Giovanni had brought. But why? If he'd been poisoning her—crippling her—why? Why hadn't he just turned *her* into the Gestapo.

Her heart stopped.

"He's waiting for us," Kitty said slowly, "to come pick up the radio."

Taylor stopped in front of her. "That son of a—"

"But why? And why wait so long?" Mascot asked. He moved between the two of them.

"We need that radio," Taylor said, his gaze still locked on Kitty's. "Or we have no reason to be here."

Kitty nodded. "Someone needs to tell Franka that we failed. And you two are not going anywhere near Nussdorf."

It took them a long time to convince Kitty that neither of the OSS agents was going to let her go alone. Only when Taylor came up with a plan, did Kitty relent. It was evening when they arrived in the woods and disembarked from Gustav's old truck. Kitty led them through the woods and to the edge of Gustav's field.

Shivering from cold and tension, she crouched down, Taylor and Mascot on either side of her. Taylor held the binoculars to his eyes, pointed at the shed across from them.

"There's a little light."

Kitty nodded. She saw it, too.

"But no vehicles," Mascot said, also from behind binoculars.

The Gestapo never came on foot. Always in black vehicles.

There was no movement but the darkness around them was growing steadily deeper and it began to rain again.

"I'm going in," Kitty said.

Taylor reached out and grasped her arm. "You don't have to. We can wait."

"We don't have time," Kitty said. "We have no idea what's going on in that police interrogation room. If the sluice gates fall, we'll all be trapped."

He let go of her and Kitty—with a surge of determined energy—made a dash for the back of the shed. She peeked through the cracks. Lamplight. She saw a shadow beneath the uneven slats of the floor and heard the footsteps. Pacing. One set of footsteps. No voices.

Crouching, she ran to the front entrance. The woods were quiet. She stepped out of hiding and into the shed.

Giovanni spun to her, startled. An expression of surprise bloomed across his face. He was alone.

"Katrin, what are you doing here?"

She looked around. Nothing was amiss, but her skin tingled. Her pulse was jumping. Her gut was screaming danger.

"I'm here for the radio." She looked to the spot where the straw and earthen floor hid the three radio parts.

"What about Messner?"

She studied him. "It failed. But you know that."

Giovanni swallowed. His forehead glistened beneath the lamp hanging from the rafters.

Kitty did not wait. "Give me the radio, Giovanni."

"Where are the agents?" he asked measuredly. "I've been waiting all this time to deliver the agents. Not you. All this time, just not you."

Her blood froze. That's why it had taken so long.

"Why?"

Giovanni rubbed a hand over his head. "Because they were going to give me Rachel."

Kitty gaped at him. "Rachel? *Your* Rachel?"

Giovanni crossed the space between them in a flash and snatched her upper arms. Kitty tried to wrench herself free, but he was surprisingly much stronger. He shook her violently.

"They showed me her identification photo. She's in Auschwitz. They told me they would release her if I just gave up Cassia. I did that. I gave up Cassia. Now they want your agents."

Kitty cried as he bruised her, then released her violently. "Giovanni! They're not going to give her to you! How could you believe them?"

He whirled around to her, stepped up again but this time he was sorrowful. "That's right. They didn't. But I believed them. If you had the chance to save someone you loved, wouldn't you do the same?"

He turned around and went to the radio hiding spot, digging up the straw, digging up the radio.

"No," he said through gritted teeth. "They didn't. They got Cassia." He looked up. "That's where I was that Tuesday. *That's* where I was. Negotiating their terms. But I wanted to keep you out of it. So, I kept you sick. But then, they found out about you."

He turned away from the hole in the ground. "So, they took my father. Took him and are holding him at the Metropole. A nice suite at the Metropole. I told them you're working for the Americans. That I'd give them the agents. So, they waited. We all waited. And now..."

He produced the three radio parts wrapped in cloth and tied with string. "Now, *you're* here, instead of them."

He went to her, reached for her face. Cold terror was coursing over her. She flinched away. His hand hovered in the air.

"I wanted to spare you this, Katrin. Angelika. Whatever your name is. I wanted to spare you this."

That was it. Like a cue. The sound of motors revving outside in the field. Those black cars.

Kitty snatched the radio from him, her voice cracking. "I'm not letting you get away with this. I'm not letting you."

As she had told Taylor and Mascot she would, she rushed to the back of the shed and flipped the loose slat open that Gustav had once shown to her in private. They were there. Both of the OSS agents were there. She tossed the package to them.

"Run!" she cried. The space between the slats, however, was not large enough for her.

When Kitty turned around, Giovanni was facing her, his back to the shed's entrance. The whites of his eyes were large in the lamplight. He shook his head slowly.

"I'm sorry," he said. "I'm so sorry but you shouldn't have done that."

He spun around, opened the door to the shed wide open, as if to welcome guests. Headlights cut through the dark, sharp and bright. He turned back to her, reached behind him and drew a gun.

There was no escape. None. Kitty raised her hands, but Giovanni turned then, walked out into that light.

Shots rang out. She took cover.

The Gestapo's sedan headed to Salztorgasse, and pulled up to the back entrance. In the back, Kitty was mute. At the sight of Hotel Metropole, Kitty's thoughts turned to ice. Even if she'd wanted to say something, she knew she would not be able to talk. They tugged her out of the back seat, these men in black, and dragged her through the back entrance and directly into a holding cell.

Six other people were in there. Nobody spoke. Kitty fell

against the wall and slid down to the floor. She dropped her head between her knees, hiding in the darkness.

She heard that entrance open and close several times. The Gestapo were bringing in people like corn from the field. On occasion, the cell would open. A man called a name. Someone would go. Someone else would come in. Only once did she look up and it was at the sound of Stefan's voice.

"*Dieser verdammte Arsch!*" he cried. That fucking ass!

Kitty stared as the men were shoved into her cell. Bruno. Stefan. Gustav. Fredericksen. They stopped at the sight of her, Gustav's face falling. He was about to say something, to come to her, but she gave the slightest shake of her head.

Fredericksen stared at her and he pulled Gustav back by the shoulder. He then pressed Bruno up against the wall and muttered something. Nobody looked in her direction again.

They only had a chance if they did not implicate one another. Stefan and Gustav did not have to know yet how their friend had betrayed them. They needed their energy.

Inconsolable, she dropped her head between her knees. This time, her grief turned to guilt. What if Stella had not been an informant? What if she had just been a fervent Nazi?

Kitty rose, groaning. She turned to the wall, her palms pressed up against it and bent in half just before she vomited.

They asked her name. She said nothing. Her *real* name. She did not answer. They asked where she lived. She remained silent. She stared over the man's head, aware that at any moment the blows would come.

"Giovanni Ricci said you are the one who coordinates the group," the interrogator said. He was speaking to her in a very conversational tone. As if she'd just walked in the door and he'd offered her coffee.

They were sitting in a cement room. It was very cold. Kitty

shivered, even though she had her overcoat on. They had cleaned out her pockets and taken her bag at the shed.

The man that sat before her was named Steffel. The table was metal. She was not handcuffed, but there were two more goons in the room with her, one on either side of her.

"How did you know Giovanni Ricci?"

She looked at him. *Get it together. Get it together!*

"Stefan Zotter?" Steffel asked her. "Gustav Melk? Bruno Schmitz? Do you know them as well?"

She shook her head. But said nothing.

He half-smiled, nodded, and pushed himself out of his chair. He was big. Barrel-chested. Bald.

"Giovanni Ricci signed a confession."

"A lot of good it's going to do you now," she said, her throat tight with rage.

Steffel grunted satisfactorily. "He delivered the spies. We have them. Father Heinrich Maier will be guillotined. Dr. Messner, sentenced to life in prison. The pianist, guillotined. The former mayor, guillotined."

She could not mask the despair.

"That's right, one after the other. Slowly but surely. I think the most clever was when he got rid of Dr. Beck."

Kitty's chair squeaked on the floor and she locked eyes with Steffel.

He made a regretful noise. "She was one of our finest."

Kitty's insides cinched together and she doubled over before catching herself on the edge of the table. Stella *had* been working for the Gestapo. Then so had Gedeon.

"Now," Steffel drawled. "*Fräulein Handel,* we got nearly everyone we wanted. But where are the American agents? We've been waiting a long time for them. I'm very upset that they got away that easily. I think we'll make you pay for that, either way."

Kitty's chest was constricting. She kneaded the heels of her palms beneath her ribs. She was shivering uncontrollably. Her teeth chattered.

Steffel leaned in, dangerous. "Let's begin with who *you* are? What is your *real name*? Because it's not Angelika Hofer either."

Kitty's knees began to bounce. She dropped her hands onto them, willing her body to give nothing more away.

"How many more Americans are coming?"

At this she flashed Steffel a derisive smile, and laughed. "A lot. A whole hell of lot. And they will bring you to your knees, you *Hurensohn*."

Steffel was fast as lightning. He grabbed her by the collar and slammed her back into her chair. It fell over backwards, and Kitty hit her head against the floor, then lay sprawled on the ground.

The two goons picked her up. One jerked her upwards, the other righted the chair and both of them shoved her into the seat. She could feel blood trickling from her scalp.

"We want the agents," Steffel said. "Give us the three agents and we will only send you to a concentration camp. Otherwise, Fräulein *Handel*, or Frau *Hofer*, it will be *Nacht und Nebel* for you. As a spy in the Reich, we are not in the least bit obliged to inform your country of your whereabouts. Or of your demise."

"*Du verdammter, blöder Arsch*," Kitty hissed.

Steffel pulled out his chair and slowly sat down, folded his hands and transformed himself into that more conversational character. "Let's start at the beginning, shall we?" He spoke in English. "Who are you? And what are you doing here?"

She stared back at him. To hell if she was going to talk. Just like Judith had, she was going to die here, at Hotel Metropole.

PART SIX

DECEMBER 1944–APRIL 1945

Vienna, Austria

29

DECEMBER 1944–FEBRUARY 1945

The lowest price for remaining mute was to be restrained in a contorted position in an extremely cold room. Naked, face down, Kitty lay on the concrete floor, hog-tied. She was gagged. Breathing was excruciating. It was so cold. So cold that her muscles cramped and protested. But that was the least of the pain.

The darkness threatened to envelop her. If she passed out they would come with water hoses. And batons. They would wrestle her awake, only to send her right back to the brink again.

Her body begged for relief. From the cold. The lack of air, her screaming lungs. From fear. She could just pass out for relief. But then they would come for her.

At some point, she heard music. Before the hotel had become the chamber of horrors, guests had smoked, eaten, lounged all year long under a glass dome. Now she heard music. And laughter. Right above her head. Mocking her.

It was a party. And then, she recognized the music. *"Alle Jahre wieder!"* Every year again. A popular Christmas carol.

She had been trying to keep track of time. Trying to be

conscious of how many days had passed. But it had been difficult, because often she was unconscious for hours, maybe days.
But the carol made it clear. She had been here at least six weeks.

She sobbed and laughed through the gag at the same time.

The Hotel Metropole's grandeur had been sucked dry. The
mezzanine was now used for twelve isolation rooms. Six rooms
on one side, six on the other. The windows were cemented
nearly to the top, where bars covered the rest of the window.
When Kitty was moved to one of those rooms, the lights were
never turned off. Cold, harsh lights. Not a drop of warmth came
from them. There was no toilet. Kitty was taken out three times
a day for the sole purpose of relieving herself. Each time they
came, the terror was such that she nearly soiled herself anyway.

They never left her in peace for long. They not only wanted
the agents, they now wanted every member involved and the
addresses of safe houses.

They had switched over to torturing her with water. Her
hands and legs tied, lying at the bottom of a tub, they would fill
it with ice-cold water to just below her nose. Just when Kitty
was certain she would drown, they would pull her up. As she
gasped for breath, they poured buckets of water over her face,
until she was certain she would drown again.

This went on—so it seemed—for forever. At one point, she
ducked her head in on purpose, sucking the water into her lungs
through her nose. *Let it be over. It's almost over. It's—*

They yanked her out. Turned her on her side. She threw up
water before they dragged her back to her cell, promising to
continue tomorrow. Unless she talked.

She only had to talk.

. . .

Dance music. Cheering. *Ein gutes neues! Sieg heil!* Had she been here that long? Could it be the new year? What was it? 1945? Or 1946?

On New Year's Day, they flogged her, and when she rolled off the floor, she saw blood and strips of her skin left behind. She had talked. Had she? No. *You never moved your mouth. No. You're hallucinating.*

When a knife suddenly appeared in her hand one day, she tried to cut out her tongue to make sure she wouldn't talk. Blood pooled on the floor. Lots of it. Rivers of blood from her mouth. But when she dropped the knife it made no noise when it hit the concrete floor. Blood and knife disappeared.

The fever got worse. They took her to the infirmary. They left her alone. For a day. Maybe two. Maybe a month by the carnival streamers on the floor.

"Who are you?"

She did not open her mouth. Everything tasted of iron. She was feeding off her own blood.

"Who are you?"

They grabbed her by the hair. Examined her eyes.

They had her glasses. The several pairs of contact lenses.

They realized the birthmarks were tattoos.

They shaved her head. She cried quietly.

"It's only hair," they mocked. "You spoke English yesterday."

"What did I say?" she asked through thick lips.

"You told us to go to hell."

At least she had not given names.

Three photos. Her face. Young. Whole. Wearing the wedding dress Judith had designed for her. A photo of her at a cocktail party with John Cooper Wiley and his wife, Irene. Then one of her and Edgar. On horses. At the Vienna Woods cottage.

The Gestapo had been to the penthouse.

"We know who you are."

She had to hold the photos very close to make them out, and Steffel was blurry. Her eyes were nearly swollen shut.

"You are Gertrude Larsson Ragatz. You are the wife of Dr. Edgar Ragatz."

Kitty giggled. It was involuntary. Insane.

"We know he was involved in the assassination attempt on our Führer."

Double bonus! Jackpot! They had her now. It would soon be over.

More photos. Elizabeth Hennessy at the Pera Palace with Edgar. An extract from a wanted list out of France. *Gesucht! Recherché!* Followed by a description of Yvette Archambeau.

"You were in France. You were working for the British. You returned for the Americans."

Go to hell.

Then, very seriously, they wanted to negotiate with her.

"We've arrested Dr. Ragatz in Berlin. Give us your agents and we'll let you see your husband. He is your husband, isn't he? You're not really divorced, are you?"

She smirked, her split lip cracking open again. *The way you gave Giovanni his Rachel back. You betcha.*

They strung her up by her hands after that. A large man— she could only make out the shape of him—removed his belt as if in slow motion. The large metal buckle glinted through the fog between them. Kitty groaned. She whimpered at the clang of metal. Flinched as he snapped the leather together.

But the beating began from the back. There was someone else there in the room with her. She screamed. Only then did the first figure raise the belt and whip her, the buckle landing on her face. On her head. On her shoulders. She gave in to the darkness.

Cold water. She gasped. He stood over her. She was on the floor. Flat. No longer tied by her hands. Everything was burning. Hurting. Everything. Her entire body was in flames. Every bone felt as though it had been crushed.

He was panting above her. Exhausted. She opened her mouth. A grin was too much of an effort.

In slow motion herself now, she curled up into a ball on the floor, pulling all her parts together again.

They sent her to the infirmary.

"Fix her up," they said. So that they could have at her again.

The whip.

"Give us the agents and we will give you your husband. We have Dr. Ragatz. He's here in Vienna. We'll give you your husband, if you give us the agents."

Wouldn't you do it, too, if it meant saving the person you loved?

"No." Her voice was not her own. She tried again. "No."

That one word took all her strength.

At some point, my body has to give up. Doesn't it? So that I can finally rest?

They made sure she saw Jack Taylor. He lifted his head. He stared at her.

"Who is she?"

She had said nothing.

She had said positively nothing.

Not a word. Not about them.

Had she?

They led him out in chains. They led her to the horror chamber. Now the assets.

She saw the tub of water.

She wept.

Music again. The faint smell of oil from shimmering genie lamps attached to fake stone archways. A mosaic floor.

Kitty is in Khan's arms. They are at Achmed Beh's, the night-club in Vienna. Laughter all around. Smoke from cigarettes. The floor slick beneath her high-heeled shoes.

Khan spins her around and she sees Oskar at the edge of the stage, wearing coattails and a top hat, a red rose in his buttonhole. He sticks a cigarette between his lips and claps in the direction of the stage. Khan spins her toward it. Agnes! In the red dress! Moving to the microphone, bending to it, and singing "Leben ohne Liebe kannst Du nicht". You cannot live without love.

Khan stops dancing and steers Kitty in a new direction. Judith and Macke are illuminated at their usual table and, out of the shadows, Big Charlie—his coat buttons straining beneath the muscles and girth—leans into the light, watching. Waiting.

The stage lights suddenly swish over to the back of the table. From behind the fog of dust motes, Kitty sees Millie holding playing cards in her hand. She laughs before setting them down. A royal flush.

The lights move again, now to the opposite side of the club. At a roulette table, Wild Bill Donovan and Allen Dulles peer down at the wheel with Nils. Donovan lays poker chips on red. Dulles spins the wheel. Nils looks up at her and from behind him, the Senator materializes.

"Come back home, Kit," they say in unison.

Khan turns Kitty to the entrance. Claudette, on Sam's arm, strides in.

"Cherie! What have you gotten yourself into now?" her

mother exclaims. She hurries over to clasp Kitty's face in her hands. Kitty wants to reach for those hands, to tell her mother she is sorry, but Sam barges in.

He is in uniform. He grasps her shoulders. "Go on, chum. Get outta here."

Kitty wants to go to him but the music suddenly stops. The lights dim. Claudette, Sam, the Senator, Nils, the roulette table— they vanish. She spins back to the stage. It is empty. The whole club is empty. Even Khan is gone.

"Kitty."

She whirls to him. Edgar is standing in his tuxedo, jacket open, a small red dot on his left shirt pocket.

She finally finds her voice. "You're here?"

"Kitty."

"What?" The red dot grows bigger.

"It's almost over."

"I can't."

The red spreads and grows over his heart.

"You can," he says. "You will."

In horror, she watches a red rose bloom straight out of his chest.

30

FEBRUARY 1945

Soup. Ninety-nine bowls of soup. And silence. Her fingernails were growing. Her hair was coming back in tufts, but if she pulled at it, it fell out. Her skin was yellow. From bruises or disease, she did not know.

Again, soup.

She poured it down her throat, then something hit her mouth.

Kitty lowered the bowl and searched. A small metal tube. Tiny. She stared at it. Blinked. It hurt even to blink.

She snatched it, to break the mirage, to make it disappear. But it was in her hand. It was solid. It was real.

She examined it. Unscrewed the two parts, hoping it contained an L-Pill. But it was paper. She unrolled it and put it close to her eyes, squinting. The words would not stop moving. They were tiny, and they would not stop moving, like ants. Finally, they lined up.

Create an emergency. Get yourself to the hospital.

She examined the tube. There were no sharp edges.

That day, they came back for her. This time, they took her to the interrogation room.

"You will be charged and your trial date set by the People's Tribunal. This is your last chance. Edgar Ragatz will be guillotined tomorrow. Is there anything you want to say?"

What if they're not lying?

"Go to hell."

"Your arraignment is tomorrow."

The rooms were soundproofed. They wouldn't hear her screaming. They had to find her.

What had she learned about appendicitis? Sam's face swam before her. He was on the floor, she on the bed, on her stomach, leaning over the mattress, her legs swinging in the air above her, carefree. The medical tome was in his lap. Her hair long enough that she could lay it over his head and laugh about it.

Focus, Kitty. Focus. Appendicitis. Left or right side?

Right.

Acute would put her at fever stage. That wasn't difficult. She was almost always feverish. Nausea. Vomiting. Also not difficult.

She stuck her finger down her mouth right after eating. Then lay herself in her own vomit, so that they would find her like that.

The door to the cell opened. Three guards came in.

One tapped her with his toe. Kitty groaned.

"What's wrong with you? Get up."

"Get her out of there," Steffel ordered. "And get her cleaned up."

Steffel, Steffel, Steffel. I'm going to get you, Steffel.

They dragged her onto her feet, but Kitty doubled over, screaming in pain, her hand grasping her right side.

They tried to straighten her up again. She gagged and dropped onto all fours.

"Get the orderlies in here."

All of her symptoms pointed to appendicitis.

The doctor ordered transport to the city hospital.

They shut the door on the Green Henry.

Now I'm here. What next?

31

FEBRUARY–MARCH 1945

The pain woke her. The inability to move without feeling pain. When she opened her eyes, Kitty could not take in her surroundings. She blinked several times, groaned, and tried to sit up.

"*Nein!*"

Kitty turned her head to the woman's voice. A nurse.

The woman finally came into focus, and Kitty peered at her. She was not hallucinating. It was the same woman from Dr. Wyhnal's office. The same frizzy, red hair, thin as a rail. Not a very attractive woman, and very strict.

"I know you!" Kitty's tongue was thick. "You're—"

The woman then frowned down at her. "Shhhh... It's time for sleep. You are not getting up. You've just had surgery." Then, softer, "Erika. You can call me Erika. I'll give you some morphine again, so that you can be more comfortable."

Kitty lay back, the pain fading, as if water was lapping at her body. She let the tide of relief carry her away.

.   .   .

The next time she awoke, she realized she was in a private room, and not a very nice one. Just as in her jail cell, there were no windows. She tried to lift her arms, to prop herself up. One hand was handcuffed to the bedstead behind her head. She groaned, yanked, jerked. But she was weak. Very weak.

"Nurse?" she called, her voice parched. "Nurse?"

Nobody came.

The third time Kitty awoke, Erika was poking around her. She looked down at Kitty. A syringe was in her hand.

"You're going to be OK. You survived it."

"The surgery?" Kitty croaked.

"Your appendix had already burst."

Kitty blinked at her, then jerked her head back. She had only faked it.

Erika, that scowl always there, nodded at her. "You're going to be fine," she repeated before inserting the syringe.

Kitty tried to move, but couldn't. She lifted the blanket, her leg was in a cast, bandages were wrapped tight around her middle.

Erika pointed to Kitty's hands. "You're free of those at any rate."

The handcuff had been removed.

Kitty whimpered, but this time, when she faded off to sleep, it was with something she had not felt in a long time.

Hope.

The next time she saw the nurse, Kitty was able to get a full sentence out, but did not dare. She was more awake than she had been in what felt like years.

The nurse was adjusting her IV and bent close. "Messner is in Mauthausen. Your American, too. Jack Taylor? You know him?"

Kitty groaned and nodded. "What about the others?"

"Father Maier will be executed in the coming days. They're keeping it quiet because they're afraid of riots."

Kitty's sight blurred behind the tears. Why was this woman telling her all this?

"What about Dr. Ragatz?" she asked.

The woman frowned. "I don't know anything about a Dr. Ragatz. Dr. Caldonazzi was the first to go. Then..." She paused, her hands in midair. "Dr. Wyhnal."

Kitty turned her face into the pillow.

"Your arraignment has been postponed until you get better. We're going to get you better. And then..." She grabbed Kitty's chin in her hands and looked at her sternly. "Then you will die. There are plenty of ways to make that happen."

The nurse finished then bustled out. Kitty craned her neck after her. She was alert enough to understand.

Someone was seeing to it that she would get out of here.

It was the beginning of March when Kitty began to walk again. She was gaining strength. The Gestapo sent someone to check on her on occasion. Each time they came, each time the report was the same: Kitty was not well enough. And she was not faking that. They had done enough to her, that the very sight of a black leather coat sent terror through her. Those visitors returned to the Hotel Metropole with the same report: Gertrude Larsson Ragatz needed more time.

But when Kitty began walking, Nurse Erika led her through the halls. In low, soothing tones, she directed Kitty.

"Now, there you go. See? Take a look at the hallway. Do you see? No barricades. We can have you try on your own. Nobody else is here. What? Are all the guards sleeping? No, no. They're likely flirting with the nurses. A bunch of dirty old men, that's what they are. They prefer to doze on their shifts, or take their cigarette breaks than stand guard over us."

Kitty looked at her pointedly, and Erika—who never smiled —smiled now.

When Kitty returned to her room, Erika once again fixed the IV to her.

"Tonight, it's a new moon. The Americans, the Brits, the French. They are coming. The Red Army is said to be at our door. The last of the reserves are organizing evacuations for civilians. There are buses heading to Graz tomorrow."

Grasping the woman's hand, Kitty asked, "What does this mean for me?"

"Tonight, young woman. You leave tonight. Get to the central train station and wait for the buses in the morning."

Kitty's heart raced.

"Bus number 3342," Erika whispered. "Go to the driver. You'll have a seat. You'll find clothing and what you need in a laundry bin at the back door for you. It is your only chance." The nurse straightened. "Now that you're able to move about, it's time to get a good meal into you. Tomorrow morning, the Gestapo will get a call. A woman your age, your size, died today. She'll be you for a number of hours, and then all we can hope is that they are too busy burning documents and fleeing themselves that they forget about you."

Erika held a key up between her fingers, dropped her hand over Kitty's and slipped it into her palm. "The back exit is always locked."

After she left, the door clicked softly behind her.

That night, Kitty set her feet gingerly on the ground. She clutched the bed frame and rose, wincing at the old pains. She opened the door. She was facing the nursing station. A woman was bent over, a pool of light shining on the desk. Kitty had walked the hallways, to the back entrance and stairs with Erika many times by then. Kitty was on the third floor and Erika had taught her the escape route.

The nurse looked up.

"I need the toilet..."

The woman asked whether she needed help, and Kitty told her she did not. She shuffled slowly to the toilet and as soon as she reached it, she turned to see whether the woman was watching. She was not. Kitty switched to the gait she was now capable of, hurried down the hall, slipped through the double doors, and followed the route to the downstairs. She heard footsteps, and then keys. A guard appeared at the end of the hall, and Kitty ducked behind a medical trolley. She peeked around the corner. A large man, in his fifties, Kitty guessed, took off his cap and wiped his brow. He looked up and down the hall, then moved on and away. Kitty rose and tiptoed to the doors. She heard him heading into one of the other departments.

She got to the back entrance, to the stairwell. The laundry bin was parked next to the elevator. Kitty lifted the dirty sheets and towels, and found a sack. Shoes. A winter coat. She threw on the shoes, the winter coat, and was about to throw the sack over her shoulder when she halted. A cardboard card was attached to the string through a hole. She flipped it and read the familiar call letters.

O5.

She tested the last door in her way. It was locked. Holding her breath, Kitty inserted the key Erika had given her.

Kitty slipped out into the night. O5. Peter. And Khan. She knew that, somehow, he'd helped to facilitate her escape. And her freedom.

32

MARCH 1945

Beneath a shallow pool of light in an empty lot, Kitty rummaged through the O5 sack. When she'd arrived in Vienna, it was with a fairly professional kit for her clandestine work. It had included gear and gadgets, a pistol, and other weapons, clothing and all the other accessories she needed for her "mask." She was leaving the city with a little bit of food, someone's ill-fitting clothing, a pair of too-tight shoes, and a scarf over her head that hid the tufts of blond hair that had grown back in patches. In addition to some Reichsmarks, whoever had arranged for her escape, had also managed to get her an official document stating that she had filed for a replacement identity card. With civilians vacating the city, losing one's documents was not unheard of.

Her name was now Frau Gertrude Waldmann. *Gertrude*. She was Gertrude again. Now *that* made her laugh into her hand.

What was remarkable was how few guards were left. Security was light, and that was a telling sign.

Kitty found a way into the rail yard where several carriages from a goods train had been abandoned. Usually, these wagons were tightly locked up and fully guarded, but the train had taken direct hits from enemy fire, either from Allied bombers or from shelling and mortar fire. Some of the doors had imploded. The roof of one wagon yawned open, its top peeled back like the lid off a metal can.

Kitty decided to explore. Who knew what kinds of wares were in those cars?

She got into the first one. The boxes she opened up were filled with bandages and medical instruments, meant to go to the front. She took a few and stuffed them into the bag, but it was food she was looking for. Food was now the currency she'd need on the black market.

The second train carriage reeked of burned flesh, and Kitty backed away. Whatever was in there, she did not want to find it. The third carriage's lock had been broken, either from the barrage the train had taken or by someone else who'd found the goods before her.

She slid the door open a crack. Boxes had tumbled all over. Kitty jumped up and reached for the nearest one, pulling it to the edge of the car where she could see inside. She tore it open, sniffed.

"What on earth?" She took out a pouch, and ripped that open, too. She sniffed again. Put a finger in, and tasted the powder. "Ha! Eggs!"

She was definitely taking that with her. She pulled out the packets, realizing these were also meant for the soldiers on the front. The poor bastards!

A second box contained some kind of dark chocolate powder. It was bitter, but Kitty took several pouches of that, too. It would be a nice reprieve from Ersatz. A third box contained tins of stew, some sticky from the coagulated streams of gravy that had leaked out. She found a few that were a bit banged up but still whole.

She was deep in the wagon by now, and rummaging. Her bag was getting heavier by the minute. Suddenly, Kitty nearly tripped over something large lying in her way. She bent down in the dark and her fingers first felt heavy wool. Then a leather glove.

"Damn it!" She sprang up. How had she missed him before?

Kitty jumped out of the car, shuddering at the thought of how the German must look. He was dead, at any rate.

"Be happy with what you've got," she muttered.

She entered the main train station, held her bag close, and waited for the buses to Graz to arrive.

"The Germans and Austrians have so much to answer for," a middle-aged woman shouted on the seat next to Kitty. It was a sudden outburst. She was speaking to nobody. Or maybe everyone on that bus. The bus rolled down the country road, the Semmering mountains on either side of them as they headed toward Graz.

"The Allies *have* to win this war!"

Kitty scooted closer to the window, and put a hand to her face to cover it. Another woman behind Kitty told her seat partner to shut up.

"Mark my words," the first woman said quietly instead. "We will *pay* for this."

They would pay, Kitty thought. Yes. As had she. It was the first time she was truly alone with her thoughts, thoughts that were much too clear. She looked out of the window, suddenly realizing she had traveled this very road before with Khan in a truck filled with crates of vegetables and an idea to forge documents for the Jewish families who wanted to get out of Austria. They had been scared then, and so naïve, Kitty thought. So idealistic. Back then, she had thought they were nearly invincible.

But now? She had been beaten. Literally and figuratively. And she had no idea whether Edgar was alive. With tears threatening to spill, she pulled the edges of her scarf over her battered face, hugged the heavy bag on her lap to herself, unable to veer away from her thoughts about Edgar. If the Gestapo had not lied to her, he was dead. The Gestapo had only tried to get her to talk. Otherwise, like they had with Jack Taylor, they would have shown him to her. Dragged her to the scaffold and forced her to watch them slice his head off.

Maier had gone like that. Caldonazzi. Wyhnal. Messner, according to Erika, was in Mauthausen. Jack Taylor as well. Kitty's job was now to get out of the country, back to American-occupied territories, and to Herrengasse 23. She would report on Cassia's victims. Then she would search for Edgar. But first she had a promise to keep.

If they had made it, Margit and Andreas were taking shelter in a small town east of Graz called Eggersdorf. It took her another half day riding the bus to reach the town. It was going on evening by the time she found someone who could take her by horse and cart to the farm where Margit and Andreas were living and working.

The Graber farm was high on the plateaus of the mountains, with wide panoramic views of mountains and valley. The evening sun cut through steely-blue rain clouds. In early March, there were patches of snow on the ground. The house was a rustic, two-story building with an attached stable. As Kitty walked down the drive, she spotted a woman in a red headscarf plucking laundry off a washing line, the wind whipping the ends of the white sheets and the edges of her open coat. Kitty paused and watched her for a moment. It was her sister-in-law. And Kitty suddenly realized how Margit would see her.

She was about to turn away when another woman stepped out of the house and gestured to Kitty. Margit turned around, put her hands on both hips, then dropped them. She started toward Kitty, her first few steps faltering, and then she was jogging to her.

Kitty dropped the bag laden with medical supplies and food and, when Margit reached her, fell into her embrace.

"*Gott sei Dank!*" Margit muttered. "Where have you been?" She palmed Kitty's face, pulled the scarf back a little and gasped. "*Um Himmels willen!* What happened to you?"

"Morzinplatz. Gestapo."

Margit shook her head, her eyes wide. "How did you... Are they after you?"

"They think I am dead. They think I died from my injuries." Kitty hung her head, and took deep breaths, but her body shook with her sobs. "I should have," she wailed. "I should have died!"

For a long time they stood in one another's arms. Kitty noticed the other woman vaguely, Andreas's hand in hers.

When she had quieted down, Margit cupped Kitty's face. "Come inside. Come."

She lifted the bag but Kitty snatched her hand.

"Have you heard?" she pleaded. "Have you heard from your brother?"

Margit's face fell. "No. And you?"

"I might have killed him." Fresh tears came. "Forgive me, but I might have killed him."

Margit reached for the bag again and took a deep breath, as if the bag weighed ten times more than it did. "Come," she coaxed again. "What should I call you?"

Kitty laughed abruptly. "My papers say *Gertrude*. Gertrude Waldmann."

Margit frowned and led Kitty to the house. When they reached the second woman, Margit introduced Kitty to Frau Graber. The woman told Kitty that several farmhands—mostly older men—were also lodging at the farm, as they began planting potatoes and early vegetables, but would see to it that Kitty at least got a cot in Margit's room.

"The men are in danger of being found by warrant officers. There is total martial law. Anyone who can fight, women included, must fight."

This sent new despair through Kitty. That meant getting over the border would be impossible. Not with Austrian papers in hand.

"I need to speak with Andreas." Margit pulled Kitty off to the side. "I need to speak to him about *you*. Though I don't know if he would recognize you the way you are right now." She stroked Kitty's face, her eyes shining.

"Dear God," she whispered. "What did they do to you?"

Frau Graber was brusque and showed Kitty to a storage room then promised to draw Kitty a bath. As Kitty unfolded the cot in Margit's bedroom, she saw Margit outside speaking with Andreas. He'd gotten taller since Kitty had last seen him, and his face had lost the round baby fat.

"There's word that the Soviets are headed to Vienna," Frau Graber said as they pulled the sheets over the mattress. "And if they break through, we'll be next. There have been a lot of air raids in Graz these past weeks."

"In Vienna as well," Kitty said.

The woman sighed and put her hands on her hips. "It will all be over soon. The only thing we can hope is that the Wehrmacht will begin evacuating the areas here, as well."

"And go where?"

"That is the question, isn't it? I would rather be where the Americans and Italians are, but I don't believe that is our choice any longer."

"I need to get over the border," Kitty said. "I was thinking of Yugoslavia and then Italy. Finding those Americans."

"*Nah*." Frau Graber crossed her arms and looked around the room. "I don't think you can run, Frau Waldmann. There are partisans just across the border, more than happy to get their hands on a German woman, if you understand what I mean. You don't do something like that as two women with a small child."

"Thank you," Kitty said, and meant it. Though she was disheartened.

"If the city officials are smart," Frau Graber continued. "They'll smooth the way for the Red Army's occupation and spare us any unnecessary damage and casualties. But there are plenty of fanatics left who would rather put their children and their grandfathers out there on the streets as human shields than give up the dream. If I were you, I would stay put until the worst is over. If you have ties to the Americans... use them."

She left the room and Kitty sighed. Everywhere she looked, there were greater hurdles to overcome. She had no idea what to do next. Chaos was headed her way, again.

The spring air was filled with wafts of smoke, and the valley's horizon was black and red from fires. The city of Graz, like Vienna, was experiencing hard hits to its infrastructure. The skies in the distance buzzed with RAF planes by day, American bombers at night, or vice versa. Regardless who was flying which shift, the goal was the same: to incinerate the Nazis' morale.

From the east came the rumbles of a different storm. The Soviet Front was inching its way closer. Newspapers lauded a civilian defense in Vienna where street-to-street fighting was taking place. The articles glorified the Hitler Jugend and Deutsche Mädels. A leather-glove-clad major was showing a group of children how to use machine guns in a photo. Kitty stared at it. There was no background—no buildings, no woods, nothing. Just a vast white space. Had they shot this in a studio? Advertisements called for all able-bodied men, women, and children to take up arms and stand against the Soviet enemy. To underscore the fact that this was a duty and not a suggestion, the paper also published a photo of several Nazi officers strung up by their necks and left hanging in the streets of Vienna.

I conspired with the Bolsheviks!
I was a coward and refused to fight!

As Kitty and Margit dug up potatoes in a field one early April morning, four other men were with them, ranging from their thirties to their seventies. They were all Socialists. None of them had any intention of putting up a fight when the Soviets came.

When Vienna fell to the Soviets, it was as clear as that bright morning that the Red Army was headed to Graz.

33

MARCH–APRIL 1945

Kitty and Margit were lounging before the tiled oven late one night. Both women were exhausted, but neither wanted to go to bed. Everyone else in the house had turned in, used to the shelling by now, even as the mortars crept closer to Eggersdorf. Beyond the multi-paned window, flashes of light illuminated the dark sky. Shelling and mortar fire reverberated in the distance like a violent thunderstorm.

For the past few nights, Kitty had revealed little about her time in Hotel Metropole. She did not have to share the details. To Margit's credit, her sister-in-law did not ask for them. Everyone could see it in the scars on Kitty's face. The circles under her eyes. How her hair was growing unevenly.

They had instead wept over Edgar then took turns reminding one another that there might still be hope.

"What do you remember about yourself?" Margit asked suddenly. "What I mean is, what were you like before the war? I'm having a hard time remembering everything before this."

Kitty looked curiously at her. "I don't know how I was. Happier? I used to laugh a lot. I went to a lot of parties."

"Oh, yes," Margit said. "We were rather spoiled, weren't we?"

Kitty drew in a breath, immediately remembering how, the first night she and Edgar had talked into the morning, he had referred to his sister as a spoiled brat. As always, tears sprung into her eyes, but she tried to keep her tone light. "You weren't."

Margit lifted her chin, her smile thin.

"All right," Kitty admitted. "Maybe we both were. I do know that I loved winning at cards and surprising people who underestimated me."

Margit's smile turned wry. "My *parents* certainly underestimated you."

Kitty laughed abruptly.

"You *were* funny then," Margit insisted. "A breath of fresh air. I wished I was more like you. Still do," she muttered. "You have a diplomatic way of telling people to go to hell."

Kitty appreciated this and laughed while swiping at the stray tears.

"See?" Margit wagged an index finger. "You can still laugh. But it is a different kind of laugh."

"Mmm. What about you? What has changed about you?"

"This war set me free."

This was surprising. "How?"

"All of my mother's attention and *intentions* were diverted away from me. Hitler gave her new purpose. Even if it was in the Sudetenland."

"Do you have contact with them?" Kitty asked guardedly.

"No! Not since they left. I'm not interested. I don't..." Margit trailed off, looked down at her hands.

"And now?"

Margit shrugged. "And now? I'm farming."

"I picked up gardening around the end of the Great Depression. My brother Sam, you remember him, right? He took me to a camp in Iowa, to help with those who'd lost everything."

"Then you should get your hands back into the dirt. Frau Graber swears it's a miraculous cure for melancholy."

A deep, violent rumble made them both look to the window. The Red Army. The last of the Wehrmacht.

"Are you afraid?" Kitty asked quietly.

"Yes. You?"

"Yes."

"Of what exactly?"

"Everything," Kitty sighed. "You?"

Margit was staring out the window. Her shoulders were shaking. Was she laughing? But when she turned to Kitty again, tears were streaming down her face. "I'm afraid that the only good German is a dead German."

"That's not true," Kitty said gently. She swallowed the lump in her throat.

Margit wiped her face. They were quiet again before she said, "I don't want Andreas to have any memory of this."

"I promised to get you both out. We can go to the U.S. I'll do everything—"

But Margit pointed to herself. "The U.S.? Me? Kitty, I know what they do to your own citizens in America. The South? The Native Americans? Oh, yes, the Americans will win this war and revel in hero status, but your head is in the sand if you believe that the Nazis were unique. What is it they say? History is written by the victors, right?" Margit leaned forward, her brows knitted together. "Imagine what they'll do to me!"

Kitty shook her head. "You've got it wrong."

"Do I?" Margit challenged. "Because I'm blond? Blue-eyed? Rich?"

It could be you, next time! Kitty had said that to Edgar on the roof of the penthouse—the night of Kristallnacht— *Next time, it could be you!*

Kitty leaned into Margit. "I know how frightening that future must look from where you sit."

Margit stared at her. "After years of calling him my *cousin*, how is Andreas to reconcile himself with the fact that I am his mother? That his father was murdered by Nazis? I don't want Andreas to ever know that I was his mother. A *Ragatz*!"

"Margit, then you're discrediting Edgar and everything he's done. He's a Ragatz, too."

"No," Margit cried. "He always stood up for himself. I did not! I'm not like you. I'm not like Edgar. Take Andreas. Take him with you. Tell him he was a Polish orphan. Tell him about his father. But never..." she sobbed. "He will never grow up proud of anything if I have to raise him here."

Kitty reached across the gap and grasped Margit's clenched hand. "Think about this. No irrational decisions."

Margit smiled thinly through the tears. "That's what Edgar would say."

"That's what Edgar *did* say to me." Kitty squeezed her hand again. "Andreas is young, Margit..."

"He's almost five. And he's not stupid. If that child is anything —Austrian, Polish, illegitimate, whatever—he is *not* stupid."

"Every child loves his mother."

Margit recoiled. "Is that so? Then tell me why I revile mine so much that I would rather see her hang than face her at a dinner table again!"

Kitty stared at her.

Margit dropped her head. "How am I supposed to live with myself knowing that? How?"

The following morning, it was the cuckoo, not the shelling that awoke Kitty. It was quiet in Eggersdorf. Which could only mean one thing: the Red Army had broken through the line.

Andreas was kneeling on the bed, looking out the window. Margit was asleep.

"What is it?" Kitty whispered.

The boy glanced over his shoulder then turned back to the window. "Soldiers. Trucks."

Kitty flipped the covers off of her and went to the window. Margit stirred as well. Four vehicles and one tank were slowly coming to a stop. The figures of soldiers on the turret were too far away, but the gun was aimed at the house.

"Are those ours or theirs?" Margit asked ominously.

Kitty shook her head. "From all the bombardment yesterday, I'm going to guess theirs."

Eyes widened with panic, Margit kneaded the nightshirt over her heart and took deep, shaky breaths.

"We'd better get downstairs," Kitty said.

They met Frau Graber at the top of the landing. The other bedroom doors opened, and four farmhands spilled out in various stages of dress. The engines revved up and, through the window on the landing, Kitty saw the convoy turning into the drive.

"It's the Red Army," one of the men warned. "They're going to be hungry for blood."

"Go," Frau Graber said to the men. "All of you, go. Take to the woods, just as we said. You hide until I know we don't have any trouble."

The men did not wait to propel themselves down the stairs, except for one. He fished a pistol from his trousers and held it out.

"Who here can shoot?"

Kitty was about to take it, but Frau Graber put an arm out to stop her.

"We will not provoke them," she said. He nodded and followed the others out the door. She then turned to Andreas.

"Be a good boy and go into the cellar. You can now go break all those bottles just as I taught you."

Kitty asked her what she meant, but Andreas was already scampering down the stairwell.

"No alcohol," Frau Graber said.

"What are we going to do?" Margit asked. She was trembling. Kitty put an arm around her shoulder.

"We welcome them," Frau Graber said. "Let them bivouac here if they need to. They won't have any liquor, but they will have food. And we do not provoke."

Margit slipped from beneath Kitty's arm and faced her. "If anything happens—anything, Gertrude—will you look after Andreas?"

"Of course but, Margit, we're family. You can count on me. I'm an American. They will have to at least listen to me. And I won't leave you behind. Not you, not Andreas. Not Frau Graber. I made a promise I intend to keep. All right?"

Through the narrow window in the stairwell, all three women peered out as the tank rolled to a stop a few feet away from the house. Gear and kit rattled as the soldiers scurried about and surrounded the yard. Two officers stepped out of a truck and approached the house, the soldiers behind them training their rifles on the front entrance. Kitty volunteered to go first.

At the door, she raised her hands above her head. In Russian, she called, "We are friends. We have no weapons."

The two officers beckoned for them to come nearer. Margit and Frau Graber, clutching one another, stepped out. A sudden crash sounded from inside the house. Kitty flinched, everyone in the yard tensed.

"Who else is inside?" the first officer called to Kitty.

Another shatter followed by a joyous cry from Andreas, then the sound of breaking glass once more. The officer began waving his men to head indoors. Kitty was struggling to remember the words. Another explosion from the basement, and an order from the officer.

"*Spasiba!*" Kitty cried. "*Mal'chik! Prosto mal'chik!*" Please! A boy! Just a boy!

"How old?" the second officer demanded.

"Four."

"Where? What's that noise?" The first one raised a hand and stilled the charge into the house.

"In the..." She didn't know the word. She pointed to the floor. "Down. He's breaking the bottles. Beer. Wine."

The officers looked at one another, confusion on the first man's face. His companion rolled his head and groaned.

"So we don't drink," he lamented.

The first officer grinned broadly and laughed.

His companion scratched his forehead. "Come down here, all of you." He then waved the two waiting soldiers in. "If it's just a boy, don't scare him. But hurry, damn it! Save the beer!"

Commander Lys and Commander Vovk informed them that the Ukrainian First and Third Panzer Division of the Soviet Army would bivouac on the farm. When Andreas reappeared with one of the soldiers, he was wide-eyed but curious. He ran to Margit and excitedly told her that he had broken nearly all the bottles, but not all. Commander Lys found it humorous. Commander Vovk, not so much.

The soldiers were told to search the women, then the house. Commander Lys asked where the men were, and didn't seem all too bothered when Kitty admitted that the farmhands had fled. That was when she told them that she was an American.

Everything shifted. First, Commander Lys did not believe her. Then, she gave him the information he would need to corroborate her story. She switched to English and convinced both commanders enough that they began to relax. With her, anyway. With Margit and Frau Graber, they were not so persuaded.

Frau Graber was instructed to bring food. Margit, however, remained sullen and quiet, her arms around Andreas on the front stoop. All of the women agreed that the Soviets were being polite, but they would not let down their guard.

That night passed with remarkable quiet, but at sunrise, another vehicle arrived and a Soviet major stepped out and marched up to the house. He asked to speak to Kitty, introduced himself, and after questioning her, he gave her two options.

"You can either wait here until our rearguard arrives and we will have someone drive you over the border and to the Americans. Or you try on your own by crossing the River Mur and finding the Yugoslavians. Make your own way to Italy."

Kitty was most certainly not prepared for another adventure on the run. He then promised to send word to the Americans and arrange for safe transportation for her.

"For us," she said.

"For you and the boy," he replied.

"For my sister-in-law, too."

"She and the farmer woman, they stay."

"No," Kitty insisted. "I'm taking my sister-in-law and my nephew, and Frau Graber."

"Not a chance," he suddenly said in English. "The boy, yes. The women, until we know who they are and how they are involved, they stay."

"Major!" Kitty put her hands flat on the table and rose. "You will guarantee their safety until you have cleared that then, will you not?"

He raised his eyebrows, and stood up as well, eye to eye with Kitty. "We'll see to that transport as soon as possible. For you. And the boy."

．　．　．

Three days later, Commander Vovk, his face tight with anger, shot a pistol into the air and demanded that Margit and Frau Graber get into a truck. Kitty would not allow them to go alone. An argument ensued and Kitty won. All of them went, including Andreas.

Two other vehicles followed them and the driver stopped in the center of Eggersdorf. Women and children were gathered in the square. They were loaded into the other trucks. Kitty asked again and again what was happening, but the officer only waved a dismissive hand at her.

She grasped the women's hands—Margit's and Frau Graber's. "It's going to be OK. I promise."

But she was not so sure.

They drove approximately forty minutes through the mountains and down to Graz, Kitty craning her head and trying to guess what the Soviets were up to.

From the back of the truck and through the pulled-back canvas, they watched the scene in reverse as they rolled through a city of destruction. Cavernous holes in warehouses. Smoke rising from the crumbled ruins of bombed-out buildings. The air was a cocktail of leaked wreckage, gases and rot.

The truck veered suddenly, and Kitty put out an arm to hold them in place. As the driver straightened, they saw what obstacle he'd had to get around. Oddly, a single wooden chair, beautifully carved, stood straight up in the middle of the road. Around it were the spilled-out guts of a furniture store. They passed by a sign that marked the end of Liebenau, which meant they were heading into the Graz township.

Margit faced her on the opposite bench. "If anything happens to me, please take Andreas. Take care of him."

"I promise," Kitty said. "Nothing is going to happen. I'm going to make sure you come with me."

"When they find out who I am," Margit said, her voice

strange. "Who my father is. We will all hang. My parents. Me. And it will be well deserved."

Kitty grasped her arm, violent. Refusing. "I'm taking you with me."

Margit stared out, and Kitty could not get her to speak to her again. Suddenly, the vehicle slowed and they turned left, followed by the high cement walls of a compound. Barbed wire was stretched across the top. Beyond the wall, birds sang and trees had begun to unfurl bright green leaves. Kitty had to pinch her nose shut.

Slowly, they drove in, passing by a large group of Soviet soldiers milling about. But they were not the source of the stench. At least she did not think so. Then a Red Cross ambulance. A second one. A third. Kitty gasped. Margit turned her head to her, her expression filled with horror.

The vehicle braked to a halt. The women and children were shoved out and they spilled onto the dusty ground, a crowd of reluctant tourists. The Ukrainian division made them walk through the internment camp. Commander Lys's face was dark. Commander Vovk's a mask of contempt as he pushed his group of women to move faster.

"These men!" one Soviet soldier shouted in German, "were headed to Mauthausen! These men were going to march all the way to Mauthausen! Look at them! This is what you people are responsible for!"

Wide-eyed and numb with shock, Kitty stopped and waited for Commander Lys. She could hardly get the words out. "Who are they?"

"Hungarian Jews," he said.

But they were not. The dozens and dozens and dozens of men were skeletons. Men with skin stretched over their bones. The striped pajamas like bars over their souls. Their eyes, accusing. Accusing each of the women. Every child that was paraded before them. Accusing Kitty.

Kitty stopped before one man who spat in front of her. She dissolved into tears. *We knew! We* knew *about this!* Frantically, she began searching those faces for Big Charlie.

She did not find him.

Kitty threw her head back and screamed to the sky. "We knew about this! We told you! You sons of bitches! We *told all* of you!" She was not addressing the Germans. Not the Austrians. She whipped her head to Commander Lys. "We told the Allies *years* ago!"

Grave, he walked away from her.

Kitty turned around in that spot in the compound, releasing sob after sob at the scene of misery, at the face of each suffering man. At the living, walking hell before her.

Across the way, the Austrian women and children were rigid and stone-faced at the spectacle Kitty was making. Only Margit was different. She was clutching her middle. Her shoulders were hunched as if carrying a heavy load. Her face was awash with tears.

That evening, nobody spoke to one another. Even Andreas was subdued. Frau Graber led him to the bedroom. Kitty was also going to turn in, but Margit passed by her in a nightshirt and headed for the basement. Kitty stopped on the stairs and watched her disappear. Then her sister-in-law returned with six bottles of beer in her hands, and headed for the front door.

"Where are you going?" Kitty asked.

She followed her out, descended into the camp where the men were sitting around bonfires, eating, cleaning their weapons. Margit approached the first group. They stopped speaking, wary as she began handing out the beer.

"It's the last of it," she said.

The men reacted differently. One grinned, another smiled

warmly, another sneered but took the beer. The last one muttered a thank you without looking at her.

"Margit?" Kitty nodded at the men, their expressions and movements paused, uncertain. "Good evening," she said to them. Then to Margit, "What are you doing here?"

Margit shrugged. The firelight revealed her figure beneath the nightshirt.

Kitty did not want to create a commotion. No misunderstandings. She looked around to see whether one of the commanders was around. Margit, her eyes locked on Kitty, then lowered herself next to a soldier on a log. They all shifted. Like the fire, the air crackled. The first *pop*! of a beer bottle. A second. Kitty's nerves twitched.

Margit then said, "You know Russian. Tell them that I am very sorry."

Cautiously, Kitty translated.

The men's faces turned to stone. They looked down at the bottles of beer. One held it out as if he wanted to return it.

"Tell them," Margit continued, her voice shaking a little. "That I hope all Nazis are brought to justice."

Kitty did not want to. She did not want to start that discussion. Not with this group.

"Tell them, that if Austria is taken over by the Soviets, however, it will only make things worse."

Kitty stared at her. She was definitely not going to translate that. But the men were watching them, curious, wary, and now gazing at her with anticipation.

"I'm not going to translate that," Kitty told her.

"Tell them!" Margit cried.

The soldier next to Margit shifted. "What is going on?"

Margit grabbed his arm. He shook her off. Vehement, she cried again, "Tell them!"

Kitty's heart tripped in her chest and she faced the group.

"My sister-in-law is not well. Please forgive her. She is filled with grief."

But Kitty realized her mistake. The men had sensed the ticking time bomb as well.

Margit suddenly grabbed the collar of the soldier next to her. He sprang up, his gun in his hand. A Glock. He pressed it to her head. Time slowed down. As if they were underwater. Kitty watched in horror as Margit moved, stepped directly in front of him and faced him. He moved the gun with her, the barrel pressed against her forehead.

"Please," Margit whispered. "Please do it."

Kitty took a cautious step toward them. The men were all rising to their feet now. Everyone was talking. Everyone. Behind them, someone called from another campfire. So much noise, and all Kitty could manage to get in between all the words was, "Margit. Margit. Margit."

"*Mach es!*" Margit cried. Tears were rolling down her cheeks.

"Margit. Margit."

"*Schiess mich! Schiess!*"

The soldier was shaking his head and spoke a language Kitty did not understand.

"Margit!" Kitty pleaded. "Please!"

The soldier looked at Kitty. His eyes told her. He did not believe there was any real danger. This was grief, his eyes said. Crazy grief. And Kitty knew that Margit would be all right. That they would all calm down and be rational.

It was one swift motion. Margit and the soldier.

The shot went off. Margit took a step back. Stood for a moment. Then, as if someone had let go of a marionette's strings, she crumpled to the ground.

. . .

When the cuckoo called from the field, Kitty was still wrapped in a blanket on the front stoop. For the second time in just under a week, the major arrived with the sunrise and strode to the house. He stood before Kitty.

"We have a driver for you. As soon as you are ready."

Kitty did not look at him. She could only nod.

"I imagine you will want to leave after the funeral. I'll need you to answer some questions."

"It was not their fault. It was not your men's fault." More than that he would not need to know from her.

They did not tell the priest about how Margit had intended the accident. If Kitty could not keep her promise to Edgar, she would at least bury her sister-in-law on consecrated ground.

The following day, with Andreas packed with what little he had, Kitty waited for the Soviet driver who would bring them as close to the American envoys as he could.

PART SEVEN

APRIL–MAY 1945

Bern, Switzerland

34

APRIL 1945

From the moment Kitty left Frau Graber's, Andreas stopped talking. He responded to her when she said it was time to go, to get into the truck, to get into the next vehicle, to get on a train. He ate a little bit. Drank a little bit. But he did not say a word. If she did not ask a yes or no question, there was no response at all.

On the second day, it was the same. He did everything she said. He dressed, tied his shoes, pulled up his knee socks, and swung the rucksack over his shoulders—much too big for his skinny legs and small frame—and followed her wherever she went, like a stray puppy: cautious but desperate not to be left alone.

On the third day, they were on a bus through Italy. To avoid the areas with the fiercest fighting, it took the bus four times longer to reach Kitty's destination. Andreas still did not let her touch him, did not respond to her offer to take him into her arms. Instead, he kept his distance on the ragged seat between them. But when he finally fell asleep, he tumbled into her lap, so exhausted he did not wake. She shifted him into a more comfortable position, and put a protective arm around him.

She stroked his light brown hair. Covered his ears to protect him from the noise of the engine backfiring as they climbed mountains. The bus descended into a valley and the landscape flattened out. Later, Andreas twitched and muttered something, and Kitty bent over him and pressed her lips to his ears, just to let him know that someone was there for him.

Another checkpoint. The Swiss border was not much further ahead. Kitty rose, nudging Andreas awake.

"*Schatz*, we're here. It's the Americans."

He blinked and rubbed his eyes, then looked around, startled. Again, he moved only mechanically.

"Come," Kitty said. She rose and the patrol, a sergeant, told her to sit down in German and in Italian.

"I'm an American," Kitty said. "I need to get a message to your headquarters."

The sergeant eyed her suspiciously, and Kitty tried again. "I'm sorry. I'm Senator Arne Larsson's daughter, of Minnesota. My brother, Nils Larsson is a U.S. diplomat in London. My brother Sam Larsson is a medic with the Fiftieth Armored Division. I need to get to Bern, Switzerland. Is there any way you can help us?"

Apparently her English convinced him.

"Come with me. Do you have any papers? Who's the boy?"

"My nephew."

"Nephew? What is he doing *here*?"

She tried to explain and his suspicion returned, saying without documents she could expect to stay put for a long while. Defeated, Kitty nodded and said she understood. The sergeant then reached into his kit, and produced a flat bar wrapped in brown paper. Silver foil. White lettering. A Hershey's chocolate bar.

When Kitty unwrapped it and broke off a piece, Andreas's eyes lit up.

"*Danke!*" he said.

. . .

Kitty arrived at Herrengasse 23 by taxi. She had to peel Andreas out of the back seat. She had no money left, but she had not been able to bear walking another step. They had fled nearly a week earlier, and all she wanted to do was drop onto the ground and kiss it. But Andreas was dead asleep. She lifted him out of the taxi and the two bags she had, and carried him to the door.

Jacques answered, and Kitty whimpered at the sight of him. His eyes widened with horror. "Madame! Madame!"

"Is Mr. Dulles here?"

He moved to take Andreas but she shook her head. He bustled her inside, exclaiming, "We were expecting you days ago."

"There's a war still going on," she said tiredly. "In case nobody here knows." With a pleading expression, she jerked her shoulder toward the taxi driver. "Please. I have nothing left on me."

The butler hailed the driver, and told him to wait before turning back into the house and leading her to Dulles's study.

She smelled the pipe smoke first. Then saw the two men bending over the round oak table. Dulles had his profile to her. But it was the back of the second man that made Kitty burst into tears.

Jacques caught Andreas in his arms as Kitty sank against the wall.

"Edgar!"

He spun around. His eyes flicked from her to Andreas. "My dear God! Kitty! Finally!"

She clasped her hands over her face, keening in pain, flooded with relief and swamped by grief. She shook her head; even as Edgar tried to pry her hands away, she clamped them harder to her face. He would never recognize her. Never.

He murmured her name. She gasped for air. Great tidal waves of sobs wracked her body. She wailed afresh when his arms came around her. When he caressed her head and tugged at the scarf, she pleaded with him not to.

"Margit," she wailed. "Margit...!"

He pressed her to him and she let her legs finally give out. Edgar half-steered, half-carried her into the room, and lowered her onto the sofa. When she finally lifted her face, Edgar—his face dissolved beneath his emotions—spoke soothingly.

Clutching his pipe in one hand, Dulles handed her a handkerchief, but even she caught the look of horror on his face.

Vaguely, she understood that Jacques was asking to take Andreas to the suite. She covered her face with the handkerchief, and wiped her face.

"Thank you," she said behind it. "Thank you."

It was all she could say, over and over.

Nobody slept well that night. Andreas awoke crying, disoriented in the second bedroom. Kitty brought him to her and placed him between herself and Edgar. She had nightmares again. Loud and vivid dreams of being beaten that made her flinch and scream out.

In between waking and sleeping, Edgar and Kitty unraveled their stories in whispers over the sleeping boy. The order of those stories was random. She first told him about the labor camp in Graz, he told her about the news of liberated concentration camps discovered by the Allies as they closed in on Berlin. She told him about Messner's last days, about Stella Beck's death. He told her about how he'd been involved in the planning of Hitler's assassination attempt—a large-scale and intricate operation. She told him about Giovanni Ricci. That he'd betrayed Cassia for a girl named Rachel. She grieved over Big Charlie, whom—after seeing the Hungarian Jews in Graz, she no longer believed to be alive. Edgar told her that the Soviets were in Berlin and the rest of the Allies were rushing in, too. She voiced her rage about all the betrayals in Cassia's demise, and blamed the OSS for not protecting them better.

Edgar told her that Khan, after learning of how Cassia had been infiltrated, had fled to Cairo. She gave Khan credit for helping her escape Vienna.

Edgar then described how he had hidden in a Berlin apartment for over six months. Someone brought him food. He never left. He didn't have any exercise. No fresh air. He did not dare go out. He nearly lost his mind and had held a gun on himself several times. Then one day, the documents came. An asset delivered the papers he needed to get out of the country. He put on a Wehrmacht uniform again, and headed out. He was certain he was going to die of a heart attack along the way. Some of his closest assets, involved in planning Hitler's assassination at the Wolf's Lair, had been guillotined. He was certain he would meet the same fate.

He got to Switzerland in late January. Like Kitty, he was so relieved, he could barely talk, and had not functioned for weeks. That was when Dulles told him that two of the OSS agents Kitty had gotten into Austria had been arrested. The third was now working with the Soviets that occupied Vienna. Dulles had known of her demise.

"I had nearly lost hope," he said. "I wished I had just blown my head off in Berlin. But then, a week ago, we got the call that you were on your way."

He grasped her hand, entwined his fingers in hers.

"Margit..." Kitty then said. Tears choked her.

Edgar nodded into his pillow.

"Margit," she tried again. "Could not go on. I failed you."

He hissed. Grasped her face. Leaned close and kissed her cheeks. Andreas stirred.

The room was lighter. They'd forgotten to close the curtains. The first birds were beginning that careless song to call in a new day. Edgar's gaze caressed her. He pulled her in, hugged her. She knew what he was seeing. She was feeling it all over her body again—the torture, the beatings, the pain and suffering under the Gestapo interrogations.

She sobbed again in great heaves, trying not to wake Andreas.

"You survived," Edgar whispered into her ear. "You survived! You survived, Kitty. You're alive."

When she was calm again, the first dawn light was creeping across the comforters. Andreas sighed between them.

"We're nearly finished," Edgar whispered.

She clenched her eyes closed. "Do you know how many lives I have lived since the last time you said that to me? Do you know how many worlds of suffering I went through, waiting for this end?"

"I know. I see it on your face."

She heard him weep then. He slipped his hand from hers. He covered his mouth but Andreas awoke anyway.

The boy turned his head to her. Then to him. He took her hand in his, and Edgar's hand in the other one, then closed his eyes and went back to sleep.

35

MAY 1ST, 1945

Millie lay the brush to the side, and rubbed Kitty's aching neck. Birds sang through the window and the scent of lilacs from the back garden wafted in. An urgent knock on the suite's door made Kitty straighten in her seat.

"Edgar?" Kitty called. "Andreas?"

She heard Edgar's voice. Then Dulles', followed by a rap on her door. Both men stepped in, Edgar looking grave. Dulles was beaming.

"Kitty," Edgar started.

"Hitler has killed himself!" Dulles announced. "The Germans are preparing to capitulate!"

Millie's mouth dropped open and she stared at Kitty and the men through the mirror for a moment. Kitty averted her eyes.

"We have to celebrate," Millie gushed. She turned away and rushed to Dulles, throwing her arms around his neck. "Allen, the Belvedere. I'll book us a table."

Dulles snapped his fingers. "Let's!"

Edgar protested first. Kitty turned to him in her seat, as grave as he was.

"I can't," Kitty finally managed.

"Something quiet," Millie said. "For four. Just the four of us. A quiet table."

"I can't go out like this."

"Nonsense," Millie chided. "I'll bring you something."

It wasn't about that, Kitty thought.

"I'll be back this afternoon," she said. "We *have* to celebrate!"

"Why?" Kitty snapped.

Millie frowned. "Well, for one, your head is still on your neck!"

Dulles' grin faded, and he reached for Millie's hand, kissed it for all to see. "Give them some time. Make the reservations, but we can always cancel."

Kitty paid no attention as they left, she was just relieved when they finally vacated the suite. As Edgar reappeared, she was studying the specter in the mirror, the stranger reflected before her. It wasn't only this broken person that she could not face. She could not face the new world. The sunlight. The happy birds. The earth that shifted beneath her now. The joy of a victory. Whose *victory*?

Edgar moved behind her. He put his hands on her shoulders, leaned in and kissed the nape of her neck as she pulled the scarf back over her head.

"They will never understand," he said. "Never. And we have to forgive them for that. Or we will never go on."

By the afternoon, the celebrations had spilled out into the streets of Herrengasse and along the Aare River. Americans, Brits, Swiss, French. When Millie returned, she even claimed that the Germans had vanished from the city.

Sheepish, Kitty apologized and relented. With gentle ceremony, Millie placed a hat box on the vanity table. Kitty was about to protest.

"This is not a hat," Millie interrupted. "So, no. You don't need to worry. If I'm to talk you into having dinner with us tonight, it might be a help if you... feel like yourself?"

She removed the lid. Inside, the head of a dummy and a blond wig. It was nearly Kitty's real color, even had waves. Kitty fingered the curls.

"You hate it," Millie lamented.

Kitty shook her head.

Millie groaned. "You really hate it. I'm so sorry. I don't know what I was thinking."

Before Millie could close the hat box again, Kitty put her hand on her arm. "I think it's so... kind. So thoughtful. Thank you. Thank you very much."

"Do you want me to help you?" Millie asked.

"Would you?"

Millie had brought a dress, too. A red one that wrapped around Kitty's waist and tied off to one side. The neckline plunged low. Millie produced a chain of rhinestones in ruby and diamond.

"They're not real. But they'll do the trick," she explained.

Next, a pair of heels, and then Millie insisted on doing Kitty's make-up.

By the time she was finished, Kitty gazed at the transformation. She was still scarred. Still battered. But she looked whole. The phrase was "put together".

"As good as new," Millie said softly.

"As good as new," Kitty repeated, just so Millie could enjoy a feeling of accomplishment.

A single knock and Millie straightened. Edgar walked into the room.

"Are you ready?" He pulled up as Kitty slowly turned around.

"*Liebling*," he said with emotion. "My darling. You look wonderful. You look—"

"I need a coat," Kitty said.

He went to the wardrobe, took out a fur stole—also not hers —and covered her shoulders. Millie came back from the sitting room with a hat, and held it coyly out to her.

"This *was* in the box."

Kitty allowed her to adjust it on her head.

"Gorgeous," Millie said. "Now, you two go on. We'll meet you in a jiffy. I need to get ready."

Kitty grasped her friend's hand. "Thank you. For everything."

Millie pecked her cheeks and bustled out, her own coat slung over her shoulder.

"Are you ready?" Edgar asked her again.

"It's early," Kitty said. "What about Andreas?"

"Dulles said the neighbor lady is keeping him very well occupied. He'll be fine."

"Will he?"

"We could enjoy a cocktail at the bar."

Kitty did not have the strength to argue. She waited for Edgar to escort her out of the suite then followed him to the front entrance.

"You do look marvelous, Kitty," he said. He took her into an embrace and turned her to the mirror. Together they gazed at one another.

"I promised you something," he murmured into her ear. "I promised you that I would want nothing more in this world than to start my life again with you. To share it with you. Marry me, Kitty. Marry me, again."

Kitty bit her bottom lip to keep it from trembling, her eyes never leaving his face. This was the one person—the *only* person—who saw straight into her soul. Who knew her better than anyone. Who knew how to put together all the parts of them again.

And this was their story: this war, their work, these bits and pieces of them that—when they were *put together*—made them whole. And they were surprisingly so—they *were* whole.

"Yes," she whispered.

He turned her to him and kissed her. First her mouth, then her neck, then peppering kisses along her jawline, over her brow, her nose, her mouth again.

He stopped suddenly. "There's something I've been meaning to tell you."

She waited. He smiled, gave her a meaningful look. It took her another moment but when it dawned on her, tears sprang to her eyes. Their private joke.

"I love you," she said quietly.

"Yes." His lips were soft, tender. "I love you, too."

He opened the door and ushered her up the street toward the American consulate, toward the city center. Kitty linked her arm through his elbow. Edgar beamed down at her.

That smile! That light! Her heart lifted. She had arrived!

The hope was a luscious indulgence. Maybe. Maybe everything *could* turn out for the better. Maybe they *had* changed something. Maybe the world would *never* let something like this happen again. Maybe it had been worth it and everything *would* be all right!

To her left, a shadow. A trench coat. Beige. A dark hat. The gleam of black shoes. The man sprang out from between two parked automobiles and onto the pavement.

"Edgar Ragatz?" Indistinct voice. Indistinct accent.

"Yes?"

Flash! Puff!

The man lowered his arm. He nearly knocked Kitty off her feet as he shoved past her. She whirled around. Loose belt flying behind him, he veered right. Then disappeared.

Kitty spun back to Edgar. Her surprise mirrored the expression on his face. That spark. That puff of air...

Edgar slipped from her arm, and bent in half. He lost his balance. He grasped the wrought-iron fence post. With a deep groan, he crumpled to his knees and toppled sideways.

"Edgar!" Kitty was over him. His legs slid out from beneath him. Left. Right. The whites of his eyes rolled upwards. Kitty dropped to him. She grasped the hand that was clutching at his heart. Blood bloomed beneath his fingers, beneath *her* fingers. Bloomed, and bloomed.

Kitty opened her mouth to tell him no. Not to go. To hang on. She tried to scream. Scream for help. She covered him with her body. It was all she could do.

She had no voice.

36

MAY 1945

One shot. It had been one, clean shot with a silencer. One clean, professional shot. That's what Kitty knew she'd remember for as long as she lived. It was what convinced her that, whoever the assassin had been, he'd been waiting for a very long time.

For days, the Swiss officials came by and questioned her about the perpetrator. Dulles sent for an American detective to come as well. It was fruitless.

"Who were his enemies?" everyone asked.

Anyone. Everyone.

I never gave them the time to suspect me. That was what Edgar had told her that night in the penthouse in Vienna.

Nobody knew. Everyone had a theory. British MI6. German Abwehr. A personal vendetta. Even OSS.

We all work alone. But they never truly had, had they?

Kitty did not exclude any of them.

She was taking refuge in the guest suite at Herrengasse 23 when Nils flew in from London. Her Viking-sized brother's grief was stretched across his entire face.

Kitty embraced him but felt worlds away from him. He'd been Edgar's friend, but she had been Edgar's wife. Nils had worked as a diplomat, facilitated intelligence, but she and Edgar had been on the front, operating behind enemy lines. She allowed her brother to try and comfort her because she knew it brought *him* comfort.

"I'm disturbing you," he said after she'd put Andreas to bed.

"No," she claimed. "Tell me about Sam. He's returning to St. Paul?"

"Soon. He's in Salzburg with Patton's Army right now," Nils said. "Figuring out the mess. He said it's sheer chaos. So many displaced people. He's never seen anything like it. He said there are Soviet refugees throwing themselves in front of our tanks, begging the Brits and the Americans not to send them back."

Kitty huffed softly. "It's a long way from over, isn't it, Nils?"

"Kitty?"

"What?"

"I've got a friend at the United Nations. You know, the Relief and Rehabilitation Administration? UNRRA for short. You should meet her."

Kitty shook her head. "I'm not ready for another job, Nils."

"Sure. I know that. But..."

She covered her face and sighed. "Thanks."

"A lot of people need help."

"I'm one of them," she snapped. "I'm so angry, Nils. I'm so *furious!*"

"Yeah, Kit. I get it. I know."

"Do you?" she challenged.

He did not flinch.

"I have a boy to take care of. I have to figure that out first."

Nils folded his hands over his paunch. "Any ideas? Take him to St. Paul?"

She was about to tell him she'd put in a call to the family, but someone rapped on the door. A big booming voice sounded from behind them, above Jacques' more genteel protests.

Nils frowned and rose. "Is that...?"

Eyes wide, Kitty snapped at the hem of his blazer. "For God's sake, don't let him in. I'm not ready for him!"

But Wild Bill Donovan burst in and filled the room. White hair, bright blue eyes, the man was on a mission. The head of the OSS was coming to smooth things over. It was all about politics.

"Kitty!" Donovan cried. "Kitty!"

But when Kitty sprang off the sofa, her gaze was locked on the man behind Donovan. He was in a Navy uniform, the cap under his arm but she recognized the face, the receding hairline. The All-American good looks. Like her, however, he was weathered by grief. Stamped by ghosts.

"Taylor?" she whispered. "Jack Taylor?"

The OSS agent she'd received in Vienna had aged much more than the nearly six months since she'd last seen him; before the Gestapo had dragged him away. To Mauthausen.

"You're alive?" She took a wobbly step. "I didn't want to..." She faltered. "I didn't want to give names. I didn't want to tell them—"

Taylor moved to her. "You didn't."

"I didn't?"

"You didn't. The Abwehr captured me. The Gestapo was trying to break you."

Kitty covered her mouth. "I didn't give them your location?"

He took her hand, grasped it. "Mrs. Ragatz, I'm Lieutenant Jack Taylor. Very glad to meet you... again."

"Kitty," she murmured. "Just call me Kitty."

"You saved our lives, Kitty."

"You were at Mauthausen... How did you...?"

He nodded, a dark shadow passing over his face. "It's why I'm here. Major Donovan here asked me to meet you in person."

Kitty's face crumpled and she covered it with her hands, but just then Donovan stepped around Taylor, opened his arms, and swallowed her into a placating embrace.

"Kitty," he murmured, more gently this time. His eyes shifted over her and he swallowed hard. "I placed all my bets on you. I knew you'd make it but... Dear God. I'm so very sorry about Dr. Ragatz. So very sorry."

She pulled away from Donovan, her focus on Taylor. The lieutenant pointed to the seating area with his hat.

"We know it's late. But if you have a moment. Do you mind?"

"Lieutenant Taylor flew in from Austria especially for you, Kitty," Donovan announced. He was still talking in that soothing voice, as if he could make everything better with that soothing voice.

Kitty turned to him where he sat next to her. "No B.S. from you, Major."

Donovan pulled back. "What do you mean?"

"It means, I want no *bullshit* from you. I have things to say to you. I didn't think I'd have the energy to do it now, but I might never have another chance." Her voice shook. "You failed Cassia. You failed my husband. You failed Lieutenant Taylor here. And you failed me."

Donovan frowned, folded his arms over his large chest. "How so?"

"You placed all your bets on me? You and Mr. Dulles forced me to place all my bets on Leonard. He was the man who invited the foxes into the henhouse. I warned the office but you allowed inexperienced agents to jerk off in your institution. And I know you, Major. I know that you reward creativity. Audacity. The crazier, the better!"

"That's not fair, Kitty," Donovan warned. "We were *all* new to this. Nothing like the OSS had ever been done before. Hell! You sound like Truman now. Focusing on everything that went badly. What about what we *did* accomplish."

"Kitty?" Nils rose. "Do you want them to leave? Maybe now is not a—"

"Stay," she snapped. "All of you stay. You owe me that. To hear me out."

Donovan's face fell. Her brother lowered himself to the sofa again. Taylor nodded once, his gaze encouraging. *He* understood her.

Kitty turned her attention back to Donovan. "Cassia *trusted* us. They were a bona fide, altruistic group of people, who laid their lives on the line for *us*. For *us*!"

Donovan dropped his hand, opened his mouth, but then a look of resignation passed over his face.

"You are the director of America's first intelligence agency," Kitty said. "I know that this was all new. Even I was green behind the ears!"

"You got through *France*, Kitty," he argued. "You were one of the first agents we had who'd worked for the Brits beforehand."

She scoffed. "And that's the other thing! I brought someone who'd been in Auschwitz! In *Auschwitz*! I brought him to the Brits alive, with all the information the Allies needed to stop what was happening in those concentration camps."

"We're still getting to the bottom of that," Donovan said and looked at Taylor.

"Still?" she cried. "You mean finally, right?"

Her neck was on fire. But it was Taylor's expression that made her pause her rage.

His head was bent over the cap resting on his thighs, his eyebrows raised. When he looked up at her, it was with assent. "I shouldn't have talked you into trying to help Messner escape.

He would have been at the Liesl if it hadn't been for us. I met him."

Kitty gasped softly, her hand flew to her throat.

"I was there, with Dr. Messner. In Mauthausen." Taylor worried the brim of his cap. "I should have died with him, Kitty. I should have died four times in that camp. Every time the guards called my name, one of the other inmates stepped in for me. Dr. Messner included." He brushed his face, blinked back tears. "He stepped in for me because he wanted me to live. The American. The American who could tell the world about it, so that people would believe."

Kitty dropped her face in her hands and sobbed. She didn't care who saw her. After a moment, someone grasped her lower arm. Nils had reached over the coffee table and held out a hand-kerchief for her. The room remained still for a long time as she took hold of herself.

Donovan then shifted toward her. "Lieutenant Taylor is collecting documents, witnesses."

She stared at him in disbelief. *Too little, too late!*

"There are going to be tribunals," he added.

Kitty wiped her face furiously and held her breath until she was composed.

"I have lists of people I want to find. A whole list of people," she said flatly, "that need to be honored. And another list of those to be brought to justice."

Taylor put his hands over his heart. "I'd really appreciate your help."

She shook her head. "I'm not offering my services. I have a boy to take care of."

Donovan cleared his throat. He nodded at Taylor, and the lieutenant rose. Quietly, Taylor asked whether Nils could show him the restroom. Nils looked baffled, but Kitty sensed the shift.

"Please," Donovan said. "I need to speak to Kitty in private."

Now she was alert.

Nils led Taylor to the adjacent bedroom, and when they shut the door, Kitty waited for Donovan to explain.

"I take your disappointment to heart, Kitty. Your anger. I really do. You always said you had no interest in politics. Unfortunately, there's very little room for altruism in intelligence either."

Kitty folded her arms. Nothing he said was going to make her feel better now. On the contrary, he was making things worse.

"Anyway, President Truman and I don't see eye to eye on what will happen to the OSS in the future. He's going to turn it into a debating society by the time he's done with it. So, before we start figuring out which documents to lock up for the next decades, I..." He reached into his breast pocket. "I thought I'd get my hands on this for you." He put a finger to his lips. "I trust your discretion."

Kitty peered at the folded sheets he held out to her. "What is it?"

"You'll see." Donovan's face was filled with anticipation. "I know you said, no politics, but..."

She took the thick wad of papers and unfolded it. Typed pages. A memorandum. From Rover. She pressed the papers to her chest. "From Edgar? What is it?"

"His recommendations. For a self-determining and democratic administration in Austria. But Kitty, the Russians have already installed their own picks in Vienna. There are going to be a lot of painful negotiations ahead. Your husband, however, outlined a full list of people we can trust, a full list of those we should not, and... Well, the rest you can read for yourself."

Her eyes skimmed over the pages. Edgar's plans. Edgar's hopes. His future was laid out in these pages. *Their* future.

It was too much. Much too much. She pressed the pages against her once more. "Major Donovan," she started. "What happened to me... What they did to me... to my family. I'm so sorry, but there is nothing I can do for you."

He frowned. "Kitty, it's a chance to honor him. I put this into your hands because I thought that would be what you would want."

"I'm not going back to Vienna. Ever. I'm never going back there again."

"What about the boy?" Nils asked quietly behind her.

Kitty whirled around on the sofa. Her face crumpled. "I can't," she pleaded. "I just can't."

Nils took in a breath. "Gentlemen, I think my sister has made her decision. It's time to go."

Donovan stood. Kitty got slowly to her feet.

Jack Taylor moved to the door first and opened it, letting Donovan step out after goodbyes. But the lieutenant moved before her and grasped her hand.

"Mrs. Ragatz. Kitty. I know you have been through a lot. Have lost much."

"So have you," she said.

He bent his head and swallowed. "Yes. Give it some time. We survived. We're alive. For a reason. May I be in touch with you, later?"

Kitty pulled away and covered her mouth, shaking her head.

"These lists," Taylor added. "If there's anything I can do. Anyone I could..."

Kitty's back straightened. "Steffel," she whispered.

Taylor looked curiously at her.

"At Hotel Metropole. His name was Steffel."

Kitty slowly removed the wig from her head, all the scars there for them to see. She heard Donovan groan deep in his throat, and he dropped his head.

Taylor gazed steadily at her. "Steffel. Yes."

He squeezed her hand, turned and left. Kitty closed the door, alone with Nils.

Before either of them could say a word, the telephone rang. Kitty remembered the call she'd requested. Nils and she looked at one another, and he nodded at her before she went to the console and picked up the receiver.

You survived. You survived, Kitty. You're alive!

"Dad?" The tears were in her voice.

"Kit! Your mother and I—"

"I'm coming home, Dad. I'm coming home."

EPILOGUE

SPRING 1946

The scent of Folger's coffee wafted up the mahogany stairwell as Kitty, in a coral rose dress, stepped out of her bedroom and shut the door. She reached the hanging Japanese tapestry at the top of the landing just as Claudette's voice drifted in from the garden below.

"*Mon cher, enfant!* Andreas, you are very clever. Come to your *Grand-mère!*"

Kitty reached the bottom step and Sam appeared from the sitting room as if he'd been waiting to pounce on her. He had a book in his hand. But it was not a medical one. It looked like a photo album.

"There you are," he greeted her. "Sleep well?"

She never slept well and he knew it—was treating her for it and a slew of other ailments she still had—but she kissed her brother's cheek then drew the book toward her.

"It's from the boys," Sam said. "I just received it. It's from our tour in Africa. Then Sicily... You can see the progression of..."

She looked up at him and he dropped his gaze to the cover.

"Anything I say right now will just sound trivial," he said.

Her father called from the kitchen. "Coffee's ready! Kit? You up?"

"I'm here," she called back.

Sam placed the photo album on the coffee table and Kitty paused at the portrait of her parents hanging above the mantel. Like her parents, the Larsson mansion had changed very little in appearance, but the air was lighter, perfumed not only by the vase of lilacs on the side table, or the banana pancakes, or the maple syrup her father warmed up. Her family, happy to have at least two of their kids back home, had things to look forward to. And there was also Andreas. She had to give him credit for the happy distractions her nephew provided.

Kitty followed Sam to the back of the house, to the glass-domed terrace and seated herself nearest to the red maple. Her father stepped out, carrying the tray with a silver pot of coffee. Especially for her, he had whipped up a pot of cream. She'd never found the heart to tell him that she preferred to drink her coffee black now.

Claudette lured Andreas to the breakfast table with the promise of hot chocolate. The boy abandoned the blanket and their game, and brought Kitty a small bouquet of red and white tulips from the beds she had planted many years before.

"Look at that." She smiled. Even if she could not take them with her, she was delighted.

Kitty patted the seat to her right, and offered up her cheek to her mother. Claudette gave her a kiss, then sat down and encircled Andreas's waist before pulling him into her lap. She pointed to the scattered Memory cards behind her.

"We were practicing English," Claudette declared. "And he's doing so well. Making remarkable headway!"

Andreas shied away from her kiss but grinned.

"That's quite an accomplishment, Maman," Sam jested

with her. "Because from where I sit, you speak more French with him than *anglais*."

Claudette pressed her lips together and turned to Kitty. "Is that so bad?"

Kitty patted her hand. "*Tout va bien.*"

The Senator handed Kitty a mug of coffee, and she spooned a dollop of cream into it, because her father had made the effort.

"Your Aunt Julia," Claudette said to her and Sam, "has written to say that she is adjusting in Boston."

"That's good," Sam said, and licked his spoon. He checked his watch. "You ready to go, Kit? They'll be here any minute."

She paused, her nose in the mug. Where she was going, the Folgers fetched a steep price on the black market. She met his eyes. "They can wait."

"Airplanes don't wait," Sam teased. "I don't care who you are."

"Let her drink her coffee," the Senator chided.

The doorbell rang, muffled and distant from where they were sitting, but everyone heard it. Everyone paused.

"That must be him." The Senator rose and pointed to Kitty's mug. "Drink your coffee."

Kitty had the best view—from the patio doors, past the family room, down the dark hallway and, where through the beveled glass, she saw the shadow of a man in a cap. She fought the rising panic. Shadows. Hats. Leather coats. They still had an immediate effect on her.

Claudette's smile was pinched as she patted Kitty's hand. "Do that," she murmured. "At least drink your coffee. At least that."

Andreas must have registered everyone's pensiveness because he crawled out of Claudette's lap and into Kitty's, wrapped his arms around her neck and pressed into her as if to keep her in that chair forever.

"I don't want you to go," he whined in German.

Sam shared a sympathetic look with Kitty. "You want me to take over?"

She shook her head. Soon enough, Sam was going to have to, anyway.

Kitty kissed the top of the boy's head and spoke in German, as well. "My taxi is here."

"But I want you to stay," he said.

"I know you do," she told the boy.

"Why do you have to go then?" He twisted the pearl necklace she wore around her neck as if it were a collar and might be used to keep her from leaving.

She stroked his head, peppered kisses on that soft brown hair. "I told you, Jack Taylor and I have a very important hearing we need to attend. He and I have to talk to a large room of people in a court. And then, I need a little time in Vienna. Your grandparents are going to be here with you. Your new friends from kindergarten will be here. And Uncle Sam, he's going to do so many fun things with you. You'll see. Time is going to fly."

Andreas nodded but he did not let go of the pearls. "When will you be back?"

Kitty looked at Sam again. When would she be back? When she and Jack Taylor had chased down all the bad guys? When the Russians had left Austria? When Kitty had found all the answers she was looking for? None of that was realistic. Andreas would be all grown up before she'd made a dent. She was going to find the right people with whom to share Edgar's visions. Lay the first cornerstones. Only that, because her true purpose, in the end, was here, with this boy.

She tipped Andreas's face to hers and stroked each of his dimples with her fingertip. The Ragatz trait.

"Hey," she said in English now. "There's something I've been meaning to tell you."

Something they'd been practicing; her and Edgar's private joke.

"I love you," Andreas said.

"Yes."

A LETTER FROM CHRYSTYNA

Dear reader,

Thank you for reading *The American Wife's Secret*. If you enjoyed it, please consider recommending it to other readers and leaving a review. If you'd like to keep up to date with all my latest releases, just sign up at the following link. Your email address will never be shared and you can unsubscribe at any time.

www.bookouture.com/chrystyna-lucyk-berger

Part of the fun of writing historical fiction is hunting for inspiration among real accounts. I love learning which parts of a novel were historically accurate, and which were fiction. For this reason, I write a blog that details the background stories that inspire my plotlines. You can read all about this series in my blog on www.inktreks.com or sign up to receive bi-monthly highlights by subscribing to my newsletter at www.inktreks.com/#newsletter.

Is there another Kitty Larsson book? I have ideas for one, but let's see if there is a call for it. Either way, I hope to meet you on my next storytelling journey!

All my best,

Chrystyna Lucyk-Berger

KEEP IN TOUCH WITH CHRYSTYNA

www.inktreks.com

facebook.com/inktreks

twitter.com/ckalyna

instagram.com/ckalyna

goodreads.com/ckalyna

bookbub.com/profile/chrystyna-lucyk-berger

AUTHOR'S NOTE

In any book I write, I have to make a lot of choices about how to build and tell my story on a frame of historical facts or the historical records (they are not always one and the same). This particular series has been an eye-opening journey, filled with discoveries and tragedies I'd never known about before. Cassia was a spy ring in Vienna. A Semperit secretary did try to break Dr. Messner out of the Palace of Justice by using three German deserters and an active Wehrmacht soldier. The Allies *did* know what was happening in the concentration camps because several inmates had escaped, were brought to safety, and urgently reported on the conditions and atrocities being committed by the Nazis and their henchmen. Over Cassia's intelligence reports, Franz Josef Messner reported on the gas chambers in Auschwitz and the mass murders taking place. OSS agents did land in Vienna, and lose their radio. Lieutenant Jack Taylor was the first U.S. Navy SEAL and the first OSS agent to land in Austria. He was sentenced to Mauthausen after drawing attention from the Gestapo. He was unable to reach the OSS about his precarious situation, because no Kitty Larsson existed who could provide him with the means to make contact. And Helene Sokal, a member of the Cassia spy ring, did escape the Hotel Metropole by faking a serious illness, and then fled from the lightly-guarded hospital. She was hidden by a network of safe houses until the war's end.

Edgar's story is a compilation of several German dissenters who worked for the OSS and provided intelligence. Some of those agents involved Allen Dulles and the Americans in the plot to assassinate Hitler. Operation Valkyrie failed and thousands of Nazi officials and officers were purged. As I write this, the same thing is now happening in Russia under Vladimir Putin.

Cassia *was* betrayed by an egoistic OSS chief in Istanbul, codenamed Dogwood. He had a Czech friend named Alfred Schwarz, who eventually—perhaps inadvertently, perhaps for money—led the Gestapo to Messner when Messner retrieved the OSS radio in Budapest.

For the purposes of my story, I fictionalized the timeline, and the events of those arrests. Father Heinrich Maier of the Gersthof parish was the spymaster curate who, with Franz Josef Messner, formed the cornerstone of the clandestine operations in Vienna's Cottage District. He was guillotined. Messner was gassed and cremated in Mauthausen weeks before it was liberated. Jack Taylor's life was spared several times by volunteers who wanted the American to live and tell about the camp.

Kitty and Edgar are fictitious composites of the many brave and committed people who fought the Nazi regime and inspired the deeds and dilemmas throughout this series.

If you are one of those readers who enjoys learning about all that was true and not true in a story, I invite you to visit my website at www.inktreks.com/guide-diplomats-wife/. You'll learn all about the anecdotes, the tidbits and history that went into this series; about what was based on reality and where I took fictional license. In other words, I'll take you back on my own journey!

ACKNOWLEDGMENTS

I am tremendously grateful to all of my friends, family and my editorial team—Jess Whitlum-Cooper and the Bookouture team, Jessica Vander Stoep, Theresa König, Lesya Lucyk, Olga Pundyk, Chip Brink, Angelina Berger, Ursula Hechenberger-Schwärzler, and my superstar linguist, Christine Boos. I bow to my two best guys, Fredy and the Little Guy, for giving me the time, space, and the extra nerves (e.g., wine!) to get through the writing.

Last but certainly not least, my amazing Book Launch Team has my everlasting gratitude. These people are my cheerleading section made up of die-hard fans and early reviewers. I am grateful for all they do to shout out about my work. Thank you for joining me on this journey: Malgorzata B., Valerie, B., Brenda C., Trina D., Darlene G., Rennette G., Vivian G., Kristie H., Annmarie P., Tania Rina P., Jill M., and Martha S. (who's been with me since the beginning!). For those who prefer to remain anonymous, you know who you are. You are all true champions!

Printed in the USA
CPSIA information can be obtained
at www.ICGtesting.com
LVHW040951231023
761872LV00004B/41